SECRETS WE KEEP

LOST AND FOUND TRILOGY

DARCI ANN BAKER

PEAR LAKE PRESS

AUTHOR NOTE

Content Warning: This book contains material which may not be suitable for sensitive readers, including domestic abuse/violence, drug and alcohol use/abuse, cancer, suicide, grief, on-page sex scenes, swearing.

Real novel guarantee: This author does not uses AI at any stage in her writing process. Thank you for supporting human authors!

CHAPTER ONE

LYRIC

*W*ho knew there were so many tequilas on the market? I certainly didn't. Gold tequila, silver tequila, premium. And holy hell, the prices. Who would pay over a hundred bucks for alcohol? I mean, seriously? That's like a month's worth of groceries.

Scanning the different bottles, I wait for one to jump out at me. Not even a wiggle. And Zoe's text didn't specify her preference. But I'm sure her plan for Grace's birthday didn't involve bankrupting me.

Why did I say yes to her invite? I could be home in my PJs. Instead, I'm standing here in the liquor section of an unfamiliar grocery store, staring at the too-large selection of tequila.

Just pick something!

The guy snoozing under a sombrero on the vibrant label of a large and moderately-priced bottle seems like a good indicator of quality tequila—at least in my mind. I snag the hefty bottle off the shelf and read the back. You'd think it'd say *Perfect for Margaritas!* or have a recipe, or something, but no.

I roll my eyes and glance around for help, but come up short. A liquor store would have been a better option, but this huge grocery store is closer to Grace's. Plus I'd have missed out on the dated mix of background music. But I sure could use someone to tell me whether Old Oaxaca tequila would make rocking margaritas or strip the enamel off our teeth.

The smooth voice of Paul Davis assures me that *it's gonna be a cool night*, while some middle-aged woman in a business suit grabs a bottle of mudslides a few feet down from me. Chocolate and alcohol? A way better idea than margaritas in my opinion—but it's not my opinion that counts here.

Some guy passes by at a steady clip, probably headed toward the beer section. No help at all. But for the moment I'm distracted by the way his ass fills out his dark jeans.

No men! a loud voice in my head scolds.

Doesn't hurt to look, a quieter one retorts.

As if he hears my internal argument, beer dude's head turns. There's eye contact, along with a slight flutter in my stomach the wiser side of me tamps down without mercy. The same side that's kept me celibate and safe these past three years. I should listen to her, but when grocery-store guy stops dead and turns, then gives me a slow smile that says the beer run has been put on hold, it's a struggle to remember why.

I turn away, closing my eyes tight, but the soft tap-tap of footsteps tells me he's approaching. *Stay strong, Lyric.* I let out a slow, measured breath and turn, ready to brush him off, but my mind goes blank. Almost on cue, Pat Benatar starts belting out "Heartbreaker" like it's this guy's theme song.

Words vanish as I stare up into the most stunning pair of blue eyes—almost black around the outside, they fade to a pale blue toward the center. My insides do a free fall straight into the land of giddy excitement at the way Mr. Gorgeous is gazing at me like a starving man contemplating a steak dinner. *Someone get this man a napkin.*

No, no, no. No men!

"Pretty sure you're going to regret that," he says in a sexy rumble that blocks out the annoying voice of reason screaming inside my head.

"Oh? Oh, the tequila." I frown down at the forgotten bottle in my hand, then let out a little laugh. *Focus.* "It's not for me. I mean, I'm not going to drink it by myself. I have friends. We're making margaritas..."

Oh, for God's sake. Shut up.

His warm chuckle has me pressing my lips together to silence my nervous ramble.

"I didn't think you planned on polishing off a bottle of tequila yourself. But, if I could suggest an alternative? Maybe something that won't have you swearing off margaritas for the rest of your life?"

"S-sure." Great, now I'm stuttering. Good thing I'm not trying to impress this guy.

I watch as he pulls down another bottle, taking a moment to appreciate my grocery-store hero. The combination of his warm, woodsy cologne and the rugged scent of his worn leather jacket waft around me. His chiseled cheekbones and unshaven jaw are a killer combination, even without those pretty blue eyes. And the way his dark jeans mold around his thighs—not that I'm gawking or anything—but seriously? Could this guy be any more attractive?

No!

I smother my sigh of regret and force myself to focus on the bottle in his hand. Three years ago I swore off men for good reasons, reasons even his pretty face can't make me forget.

"Try this one."

The sleeve of his jacket shifts, revealing scrolls of ink that disappear under the leather. This time my sigh is harder to hold back, and so is my curiosity to discover how much art lies under this man's clothes. Why must I have a weakness for tattoos?

"Thank you." I pull the bottle from his hand after a second of hesitation. No matter how sexy this man is, no matter how much

I'd love to get to know him a whole lot better, there's no place for a man in my life.

He runs a hand through his dark, perfectly messy hair, shoving it back from his forehead. A wayward lock immediately falls back in place, giving him a boyish quality even the dark scruff on his jaw can't tarnish. Combined with those eyes and that sweet smile, he's hard to resist.

I take both a physical and mental step back. There's nothing Mr. Gorgeous can offer that my vibrator can't supply with a whole lot less drama.

"I'm Zane, by the way." He gives me another dazzling smile, his eyebrows disappearing under that fringe of dark hair for a second.

I flash him a brief, polite smile in return. "Thank you for the help with the tequila."

Setting his bottle in my hand basket, already filled with the makings for some serious nachos, I turn and walk away.

"Wait. Aren't you going to tell me your name?"

Halfway down the store aisle he's at my side, his interest obvious. This time I offer him no polite smile with my answer, just a withering glance that says *go away*, along with a stern "No."

He stumbles to a stop, confusion clouding his expression. I pause for only a moment, then head toward the front of the store. The sooner I'm out of here the better.

"But... but I told you mine." He catches up, my stupidly high heels no match for his long legs.

I stop and turn, avoiding direct eye contact with those ombre-blue eyes and sexy smile that make this brush-off a hundred times harder to pull off. "Wasn't aware reciprocation was mandatory."

Why are pretty men so hard to resist? Whatever. It's time to set Mr. Gorgeous—*Zane*—straight and send him on his way.

"Look, I appreciate the tip on the tequila, but that's all I came here for. You're wasting your time here."

He sighs again. "You're forcing me to be that guy."

"What guy?" I ask, giving in to my curiosity. *Stop encouraging him!*

"You know, the one who calls women obnoxious nicknames, *sugar*."

My nose scrunches up on reflex.

"No, definitely not sugar. She's more spicy than sweet," he says to himself. At least, I think he's talking to himself. "Babe, baby, sweetheart... Ahh, you're torturing me here, honey buns."

"Call me honey buns again and you *will* be in pain." I attempt to deliver the threat with an equally menacing stare but fail epically.

He laughs. "Whoa. Violent. I'll make a note."

"Maybe not violent, but..." I offer him an apologetic smile to soften the truth. As charming as Zane is, there's no way I can let this go any further than innocent banter. "You know, there's probably some hot babe in produce that would appreciate your attention much more. You're definitely wasting your time here."

"See, that's where you're wrong. Even if this is the only conversation I ever have with you, it wouldn't be a waste of time. Every encounter, every connection with another human being makes our lives richer."

Great, I've found a philosopher.

A lone grocery-store employee wields a mop in aisle twelve. Poor kid probably wishes he was anywhere else on a Friday night. I slow my pace as my four-inch heels hit the damp floor, because, lets face it, I've impressed Mr. Gorgeous enough with my verbal skills tonight. Don't need to land on my ass as well.

The pimply faced kid looks up at the two of us with a grin, his eyes shifting from me to my escort. "Happy Friday, Mr. Brody."

"Kyle..." he replies, giving the kid a fist bump.

"Do you know everyone here?" I ask once we pass. "Wait, is this your entertainment on Friday nights? Hanging out in the grocery store, making awkward conversation with strange women?"

"I get it, really. You're leery. Stranger danger and all that. Knowing what I do, you know from my perspective, if I were a woman, I'd probably be leery too. Some guys… they're douches." He blows out a dramatic breath, running his hand through his dark, tousled hair again. "But that's not me. I promise."

My eye catches a sales display strategically placed near the checkout. I toss a package of Ho-Hos in my basket. *Yes*, I'm the kind of impulse buyer those displays are designed to catch. I don't care.

"You know that shit'll kill you?" His voice is all surgeon-general warning, like I'm about to shovel pesticides into my mouth. For the first time since he invaded my life, his lips curve into a frown.

I give him a challenging stare while tossing another package into my basket *just because I can*. Then ignore the laugh that comes from behind me.

Of course the line's a mile long at the registers, leaving me stuck with the healthy version of Prince Charming.

"Don't you have shopping to do?"

"Plenty of time to shop, Angel." He leans against a large sales display of bagged charcoal. It's barely sixty degrees outside, but this is Minneapolis and the people here have no common sense when it comes to the weather.

And there's grocery-store guy's smile again. It really is a nice smile, and so is the slight dimple in his chin that his scruff is trying to hide. I've never considered chin dimples cute, but this one is. Or maybe it's just this guy.

"Angel?" I question. Not that I hate it. At least not as much as *honey buns*.

He pauses, pointing a finger into the air. For a second I'm confused, until I recognize the unmistakable voice of Steven Tyler singing "Angel." "It's our song."

I barely restrain my eye roll as I stare into this guy's handsome face. "*We* do not have a song."

"If you say so." He's right by my side, singing along with the chorus. The guy has a decent voice. *Okay*, more than decent. "So, this party…"

I can see where he's going a mile away, so I cut him off. "Girlfriends only."

"Well, I'm sure your girlfriends will appreciate the Patrón." His eyes lock onto mine for a beat as his teeth worry his bottom lip. "You gonna need a ride home later? I don't want to be responsible for your bad choices tonight."

"I don't plan on getting drunk. It's a birthday celebration. One margarita with dinner, then off to see some band." I shake my head. Why am I smiling? And talking so much? "I've no idea why I'm telling you this."

"Because you like me." His left hand rests against the end of the counter as I move forward. It's a nice hand, large and strong and tattooed with symbols I can't make out from where I'm standing. No ring, not that it matters.

"I like you?" *The audacity.* I don't even know him.

Mudslide lady gives me a look of amusement from her spot in front of me at the register. Given the jumbo pack of diapers, Grape Nuts cereal, and super plus tampons, this conversation is probably the most excitement she's gonna get tonight. *Good choice on the mudslide, sister.*

"This band… they any good?" Zane asks, pulling my attention back to him.

"I don't know. They could suck for all I know, but my friend's boyfriend is the drummer, so…"

"So you're a good friend," he finishes. "Tell you what, give me the name of this place, I'll meet you there, and we'll find out together. If they're as bad as you fear, we can punch out and find something better to do."

I bark out a short laugh as I set my basket on the counter.

Okay, his tenaciousness is a little admirable in its consistency. "I honestly don't know where we're going. Bars are not my thing, but for my friend…" His face splits into a grin as I explain how Grace has been talking about tonight for ages. How her boyfriend wrote a song for her birthday. A romantic gesture I can't even begin to fathom, but for some reason it sends Zane into hysterics. *Typical guy.*

"Hey, it's not funny. It's sweet. And once again, I'm not sure why I'm telling you this."

He chuckles again, and I tell myself I don't like the way it vibrates under my skin—like a shiver, but more… intense. In two minutes I'll be out the door, forgetting the way his eyes rake over me making my skin heat. Or the way his laugh feels like an invitation to something more. *Beautiful things can turn ugly really fast.*

"People like to talk to me. I have one of those faces." If he means unsettlingly gorgeous, yeah, he has one of those faces. He nibbles on his bottom lip again and then gives me a goofy smile, forcing an unwanted laugh from my lungs. "You might regret not taking me up on my offer."

I sober up, because allowing myself to laugh with this guy is a slippery slope to nowhere good. "We'll never know, will we?"

He throws his hands up and lets out a slow breath. "I accept defeat for now. But promise me if we ever meet again you'll give me your name… and your number."

I laugh. His persistence really is admirable, even if it's directed at the wrong person.

"I can easily promise you that." I plan on never stepping foot in this store again.

He turns and waves a hand. "Bye, Angel."

"I HOPE this is the right tequila, Zoe." I hand her the paper bag, hoping the stud in the grocery store didn't steer me wrong.

Zane, my brain corrects. *His name was Zane.*

"As long as it says tequila, it works." She twists the cap open and pours a generous slug into the blender. The whirl and crunch of the machine's blades pulverizing ice halts conversation.

Birthday girl, Grace Nichols, mans the steak and veggies sizzling on the grill. My stomach growls, reminding me I skipped lunch. The adventures in the grocery store are forgotten for the moment with the smell of meat and spices filling the backyard, along with the talk of the principal's sudden retirement on this balmy spring evening—balmy by Minnesota standards, that is. Having little grilling or bartending skills, I head inside to assemble the nachos, grab the plates and silverware, and warm up before hauling it all outside along with the dips and spreads.

Silence blankets the backyard as we're busy inhaling the yummy food and potent drinks that have me forgetting the near fifty-degree air around me. I'm not the only one starving, having skipped lunch for our emergency staff meeting.

This is my second year at Grove Elementary. Grace and I make up two of the three kindergarten teachers. We've bonded over bloody noses, bathroom accidents, and the occasional lice outbreak.

Zoe teaches fourth grade, which is on the other end of the building, so I don't see her all that often except on the occasional times she decides to eat lunch in the teacher's lounge. Grace and I are closer to thirty than twenty, with all the bills and responsibility of living on our own. Zoe is a young, energetic twenty-four-year-old, with the financial freedom that comes with living with her parents.

I'm not sure why, but I find myself spilling the general story of my grocery-store adventures earlier this evening.

"Did he look rich?" Zoe asks. It's no secret that her goal in life is to find a handsome, wealthy doctor or lawyer or, well, she's not really fussy with what he does as long as it keeps her in designer purses and weekly manicures. "What was he wearing?"

"Jeans, T-shirt, worn leather jacket," I answer as the memory of Zane invades my brain once again. "Probably not rich."

Zoe pouts. *Oh girl, rich guys are so not worth it.*

"Mm huh," Grace adds, mouth full. She swallows and continues, "More important, was he good-looking?"

I raise my shoulders in a nonchalant shrug. "Average," I lie.

Zoe looks at Grace, her lips pursed as she folds her arms over her chest. It's like she can sense the inaccuracy in that one word. "What's your definition of average?"

I shrug again. "I don't know. He didn't stand out, you know?"

Liar, Liar. Better grab a fire extinguisher, 'cause your pants are on fire, the specter of Zane whispers in my ear, his pretty blue eyes dancing with humor.

"Dark hair? Blond? Tall? Short?" Grace lets out a laugh. "Why are you blushing, Lyric?"

"I'm not blushing. It's the margaritas." I raise my glass in defense, even though the heat spreading across my face has nothing to do with its contents. "Alcohol always makes me flush. And these are strong."

Grace and Zoe share another look, then Grace says, "Fine. But someday you're going to give a guy a chance."

If only she knew.

Besides the fact I'm divorced, almost no one at Grove Elementary knows the details of my marriage, or how horrible my ex was. And believe it or not, I have moved on. Two years ago I never would have imagined this life. It's a dream come true. Just me and my dog. No excitement, no man. Just peace and quiet. It's exactly what I want, whatever Zoe or Grace or even sexy Zane thinks.

I wave a hand in dismissal, hoping to derail Zoe's line of questioning. "Who needs a guy? Guy's are only trouble."

Zoe snorts.

"Unless you find the *right* guy," Grace adds, clearly not ready to give up.

"Well, you're lucky. Your right guy is also a good guy." I down the last sip of my margarita, licking the residual salt off the rim.

"His friends are good guys." Grace pauses for a second, then her face lights up as if a light bulb just went off over her head. "In fact—"

"We're celebrating your birthday, Grace." I give my friend a narrow look, squashing whatever brilliant idea has just popped into her head. "Not setting me up with one of Aaron's bandmates tonight."

She blinks at me with mock innocence. "Of course not."

CHAPTER TWO

ZANE

I glance toward the bar's entrance for the tenth time in as many minutes, attempting to stay busy. Checking the equipment on the stage, the instruments. Basically fidgeting, because... shit. *Will Lyric show or won't she?*

I mean, it's Grace's birthday. We have cake and Aaron's stupid song and everything. Well, Grace only knows about the song because some dumb blond bass player can't keep his mouth shut without the help of duct tape. But according to Aaron, she's Grace's best friend. She has to show.

Unless Grace tells her about me. If she pieces together that I'm her grocery-store guy... Well, shit. Maybe she won't come.

Okay, I might have fucked up. Come on a little strong. I don't know. I was going on instinct. How was I to know my grocery-store angel was the same woman Grace mentioned last week? At least, I didn't know who she was when I first walked up to Lyric.

Yeah, her name is Lyric. I just about fell over when Aaron told me. I'm a musician. I write songs—notes and lyrics. If that isn't fate, I don't know what is.

But when I told Aaron what had happened earlier, the look on his face said it all. I fucked up. Turns out this girl is shy. Somewhat an introvert, according to Aaron. *Bars aren't my thing.* Those were her exact words, not that I had taken them for more than a blow-off at the time. But now?

If ever there was a red flag, a Caution, Do Not Enter sign, it would be staring me in the face right now. My life is complicated enough. I don't have time for women, and I definitely don't have time to coddle an emotionally fragile one. I've enough of those already. Why add one more?

But there was nothing fragile about the woman I met just a few hours ago. Nothing introverted about the way her forest-green eyes stared into mine while she so eloquently shut me down. And there was nothing shy about those sky-high heels that made her sexy-as-fuck legs look like they went on forever. There was something about her, something bold and different from any other woman I've met. She knocked me on my ass in every possible way, and the more we talked the more I was certain. I have to have her in my life.

Now I have to figure out a way of convincing her of that fact.

And that's why I haven't sat down since I got here. Anticipation gnaws away at my gut while I try to figure out how to show Lyric the awesome guy I am and make her forget the cocky asshole I might have been earlier.

Aaron bolts toward the door and I follow his course easily from my vantage point on the stage. Even kneeling next to the amps I'm supposed to be checking, I'm heads taller than everyone on the floor. Grace enters and her face splits into a grin the minute she spots Aaron. They're cute to watch, and everyone is doing that as he gives her a Hollywood-worthy greeting. Well, everyone's watching but me.

My attention shifts to the woman that just slipped in the door behind her, and I forget to breathe. She's arm in arm with a raven-haired woman that Grace has brought a time or two. Zoe's pretty in her own right, but my eyes are only for Lyric.

Excitement fizzes in my veins and I have to remind myself to take it easy, dial back the enthusiasm. I force myself to stay where I am, when all I want to do is sprint across the room and pull her into my arms the way Aaron just did to Grace. *Probably get a knee to the stones for trying, dude.*

She's here and even more goddamn gorgeous than I remember. Golden hair and emerald eyes, and when she slips her knee-length coat off... damn. I just about fall to my knees as I take in her feminine curves that are impossible to miss in a delicate pink dress that's the perfect balance of revealing and concealing—and definitely not shy.

And those skyscraper heels... sexy as hell. How she walks in those damn things without breaking an ankle is a mystery. The memory of her striding away from me has my dick pressing hard against my zipper. *Fuck me.* There's something about the chase that's a definite turn on.

Dave and Dillon, my bandmates and twin trouble, spring up from our table, eager to greet Grace's friends. Dave gives Zoe a hug that says the two might know each other better than I'm aware of, while Dillon turns an interested smile toward Lyric. *Hell no, brother.*

Long strides take me to the opposite side of the platform. I jump off, tackling Aaron, and in the process distract the brothers from their fatal mistake.

Aaron laughs and glances at me. "There you are, jackass." Slapping a hand on my shoulder, he turns back to the women. "This idiot is Zane. Lead singer and rumored musical genius."

Lyric's expression is priceless. Her lips part and her eyes widen.

"Thanks, Aaron," I say, not breaking eye contact with the woman of my dreams as I walk toward her. "Hi, Angel, or should I say Lyric. Love the name, by the way."

She breathes out the cutest little growl. Her eyes make a slow trip from the top of my head down to my boots then back, narrowing, as if inspecting every inch of me. It's bold and sexy as fuck. My skin heats and my already too-tight jeans constrict even more. Tonight's performance will be interesting if she doesn't stop looking at me this way.

A blush creeps up her cheeks as if she realizes she's been caught staring. It's a nice blush. A pretty contrast to her pale winter skin tone. I'd love to take her somewhere private, strip off that dress, and find out where else her skin turns that lovely shade, and all the ways I can make it happen. Unfortunately, I've a job to do. A job that, until this moment, I love. But standing here staring into Lyric's mesmerizing emerald eyes, it's the last thing I want to do.

"Zane. Brody." Her lips twist into something unpleasant, pulling me out of my fantasy. She gives me her back, her attention shifting to Grace. "Is this a joke? Some kind of setup?"

"What?" Grace frowns, her eyes darting between us.

"He's tequila guy." She points a finger at me, her glare hot enough to melt me to the floor.

"What?" Grace lets out a quick, sharp laugh that morphs into a cough, shooting me an accusing scowl. Aaron shakes his head in a silent *I told you so.* Dave and Dillon send each other an amused grin.

I ignore everyone, choosing to follow Lyric around the table like a desperate puppy dog. I'm bordering on obnoxious asshole again, but this reunion is going a lot worse than I expected. And I have to fix things.

"Hey, I saved her from making the biggest tequila mistake of her life. You ladies should be thanking me," I defend.

Grace and Zoe share a look that says I'm not making this situation better.

Turning away from the group, I focus my attention on the one woman who matters. In five short minutes Wally's gonna call us on stage. I'm not wasting another breath on anyone else.

Lyric takes a seat at the far side of the table from the stage in her attempt to escape me. I want to laugh, but I don't. Grabbing the chair next to her, I turn it around and sit, resting my arms across the back. My chin drops to my forearms, and I flash her my most charming smile. My mom used to say it was irresistible. *Better hope it still is.*

"I'm sorry, but you can't blame a guy," I whisper, leaning toward her and getting a whiff of vanilla and coconut in the process. I linger in her intoxicating scent, enjoying it much more than the stale odors of the bar.

"You set me up. You h-had inside information. You... you... you knew," she sputters. Tiny gold flecks sparkle in the green of her eyes. I want to count each and every one of them. Instead, I back off, recognizing the all-too-familiar signs of a woman about to commit violence.

"Well now, there's where you're wrong. You never told me Grace's name, or *your* name. You didn't give me the name of the bar you were going to. I may have fantasized over the remote possibility I'd see you later, but... do you have any idea how many bars are in this city?"

She leans back in her chair, crossing her arms. Her eyebrow arches with such adorable skepticism, I want to kiss it.

"That's the slipperiest defense I've ever heard, Zane Brody." Her eyes narrow, but her lips strain to hold back the smile that threatens.

"You remember my name."

"That's what you're focusing on?"

I can't help but laugh. I told her my full name hours ago. I must have made enough of an impression that she didn't forget me.

"You know, studies show couples who meet in grocery stores have a better chance of staying together than those who meet in bars." I pause, giving this place a critical glance. Not that I need to. I've been playing here for almost a year. Enough time to know I'm not going to find someone like Lyric inside these dingy walls. I return my focus to this rare woman and give her my best smile.

"Listen. I'm sure you're great and all, but like I said earlier, you're wasting your time. I'm taking a really long break from dating."

I lean back and sigh. My Aunt Mary once told me the best things in life are worth the effort, but shit. "Really long, huh?" I'm about to dive into the specifics of this really long break, but the music from the jukebox stops. My time is up.

"Ladies and gents, welcome Heartattack," Wally yells from the stage, and Lyric jumps at the sudden noise from the crowd. I stand, severing our moment with reluctance.

Pulling my phone from my pocket, I unlock it and set it in front of her. "You promised me... and no fake number."

Walking away, I spot Jacki, the middle-aged waitress who has hit on me more times than I want to remember. I motion to her and she walks over. Her smile is all hungry shark spotting a juicy sea lion.

"Drinks for the ladies are on my tab," I instruct, and her smile fades.

Turning back, I wink at Lyric, then jump onto the stage. Even more cheers erupt as I sling the strap of my trusty black Stratocaster over my shoulder and do one last check on the tuning. The notes blast through the amp, reminding me to check the equipment again.

"Ready?" Dave asks, bending down to inspect the plugs one last time.

"Yeah." I kneel down and nod, then freeze as Dillon says something to Lyric that makes her laugh. *Dammit.* "Shouldn't your brother get his ass up here?"

"Relax." Dave punctuates his words with a shrieking slide on his B string. The group of girls that always huddle in front of the amps cover their ears and giggle as my guitarist gives them a playful wink. "Your pretty blue eyes are turning green, bro."

"Cute, Dave. Just let your brother know Lyric's off limits." I stand back up. My eyes go to her, and a satisfying warmth spreads through me when our eyes meet. She looks away after a second, but I know she's watching me when I catch her gaze a minute later.

Time flies in the last-second prep. I make a last-minute change to our setlist of original songs and covers that has Dave bristling.

"'Angel?'" he asks, frowning.

"You know, Aerosmith," I elaborate. Not that I should have to. The guy knows every damn song ever written. But, just in case, I sing a few bars of the chorus. Quiet, so a certain someone doesn't hear me.

Adrenaline pumps into my veins as I look out at all the faces, pushing away the thread of doubt. This cover isn't on our regular rotation of songs, but besides Dave, everyone's on board. Well, Aaron's expression shows his own bit of doubt—not on his drumming but my motivation.

Eventually Dave caves, once I assure him I can make my guitar synth work for the piano accompaniment that comes in with the second verse.

"Welcome everyone," I say, and the crowd cheers. A thick wall of women line the front of the stage, gazing up at me like I'm some kind of god, but I only have eyes for the one sitting at our table. "Thanks for making it tonight, and to Wally and the staff here at Mill City for having us. For all you first-timers here tonight, welcome." I'm talking to the crowd, but my eyes are on Lyric. This time she doesn't look away, and the connection is the kind of magic I feel everywhere. "And for our regulars… are you ready to rock?"

The crowd screams out an incoherent answer, making me laugh at their enthusiasm.

"I'll take that as a yes," I yell over the shrieks and whistles. "This one's for Lyric. Hit it, Aaron!"

I grin and point at the girl I'm slowly losing my mind to, watching as she buries her face in her hands. Yeah, I'm a cocky asshole with a mic. But hey, if you've got it, use it.

Aaron taps out the rhythm and then Dave and I join in, our guitars screaming in on the next beat. The crowd recognizes the song in an instant and goes nuts.

Lyric gives me a shake of her head, but she's smiling. I'm counting it as a win, as I watch her explain this song to her friends. At least, that's what I think she's doing, because Grace turns and gives me a thumbs-up.

I'm riding high, but a moment later, my molars grind together as I watch some dumb shit talking to Lyric. Is the guy's head up his ass? Did he not hear me dedicate this song to her? Did he not see me point her out?

She shakes her head and, to my relief, he takes Zoe's hand and leads her onto the dance floor. The next second, Grace drags Lyric out as well. Hell knows if I'm getting the words to this song right at this point. All I can focus on is Lyric dancing to my music. She's stiff and self-conscious at first, but before long she's getting into it. Her eyes crinkle with laughter as Grace pulls her into a half-assed swing, their skirts flaring out as they alternately spin each other. And damn, once she loosens up, this girl can dance.

We get to the bridge and Lyric's attention is solely on me. It's like we're the only two people in this room. It's just my voice, my words to her. When I sing the part about breaking down and crying, I trace an imaginary tear down my cheek. She rolls her eyes, but I'm pretty sure at some point this woman will own every inch of me, even my tears.

Thank god I'm singing someone else's words, because right now I'm not sure I'd be able to express my thoughts. Whatever this thing is between me and Lyric, it goes way beyond lust. Which is sorta crazy since we've barely met. But I can't help but feel there's something special about her, something that's about to turn my life upside down and inside out.

Grace keeps her dancing for the next song, and the next. And then another. No one's saying anything, so we must be doing okay. More than okay by the big smile on Wally's face when we play one of our new songs. The crowd is enthusiastic, and I'm fucking high on adrenaline.

Of course, there's always an asshole that has to screw things up.

Halfway through the fifth song, some fucker isn't willing to take no when he cuts in between Lyric and Grace, giving my girl a slick grin I'd be more than happy to wipe off his pretty-boy face. Her polite smile and gentle brush-off isn't discouraging him one bit. A moment later he's back trying out a more aggressive form of charm. My blood boils, and I know my next note falls flat as he puts his hands on her. She swivels away, but he's persistent. Grace cuts in, eyes narrowed, raising her hands in frustration, but the bastard turns his back on her. His focus is all on Lyric. When fear washes over her face, I've had enough.

Fuck this guy.

Holding up my hand, I stop the music.

"Sorry, folks. We have a small problem on the dance floor," I breathe into the mic, trying to find my calm. I'm seconds from hopping into the crowd and pummeling this asshole. I point him out instead. "Hey *buddy*, when a lady says no, she means no."

"What are you, my chaperone?" he spits out. "Just play your fucking music."

"Not when you have your hands where they don't belong." I shake my head in disgust and look toward the bar. "Wally, I think it's time this guy calls it a night."

"You bet, Zane," Wally yells, and seconds later Lewis, his bouncer, escorts the jerk and his friends from the bar. Grace and Lyric walk back to the table. I'd give anything to follow them, make sure she's okay, but I need to wrap up the set with one more song.

"Thanks for your patience, folks. We've got one more before the break. Let's bring it down with 'Summer Rain,'" I announce, and watch the couples pair up as we start into the slow song.

TOO MANY MINUTES later I towel off and hop down from the stage. Jacki hands me a much-needed ice-cold beer. I find my seat next to Lyric, ignoring the fans that are vying for my attention.

I lean toward her. "You okay?"

Her fierce frown has me pulling back. "Thank you for what you did, but I've handled bigger assholes than that guy. You shouldn't have made a big deal about it."

I shake my head and spit out a bitter laugh. So much for being her hero. "I'm sure you can handle bigger assholes, but I'm not gonna sit by and watch them grab you like he did."

"I appreciate it, but I'm still not interested."

Her glare is deadly and I hold up my hands. "I know. Really long break. Maybe you need a break buddy."

"A what?" She rolls her eyes and scoffs. It's fucking adorable. I want to take a picture, write a song about her spunky attitude. "What the hell is a break buddy?"

I give her a confident grin, as if I know what the hell I'm talking about. "A break buddy. You know, a guy who'll cover for you when you don't want to be bothered. Guys are gonna hit on you if they know you're single. With just a few words, I made sure the entire bar would respect you. It's a talent not every guy has. I'll listen to your complaints. I've been told I have great shoulders for crying on. The perks of having a break buddy are endless."

Like never having to watch her walk out of here with another guy.

The tinkle of her laughter dances across my skin. "You're a smooth talker, Zane Brody, but I have friends for most of those things." She pauses for a second before sobering up, looking straight into my eyes. "I'm not going to sleep with you."

I gasp in mock horror. "Of course not." Not that the thought isn't there. It's there all right.

She lifts her long blonde hair from her neck and fans herself with her hand. Her face is dewy from her exertions on the dance floor. A bead of sweat trickles down her neck, and I imagine the salty taste on my tongue.

Instead of acting on the impulse, I hand her my beer, then watch her lips cover the glass on the same place mine were seconds ago. She thanks me and hands it back. I take another sip and slide it back to her. It's as close as I'm going to get to kissing this girl, or anything else tonight, but I'll take it.

"A break buddy is more than a friend. He's there to make sure you don't weaken and sleep with anyone else." I glance across the table. Aaron, Grace, and Zoe have their heads together like Shakespeare's witches. The girls look up and burst out laughing. Aaron wiggles his eyebrows at me, driving home the fact they've been talking about us. "Seriously. Do you think any one of them would stop you if you left here with me tonight? I don't think so. Probably send us off with a pat on the back and a box of condoms."

Lyric makes a cute little noise, her shoulders slumping.

"My point exactly." I nod, then pick up my phone from the table. I check, but as expected, Lyric's number isn't in there. "You forgot something."

That eyebrow arches again. It seems to be her go-to expression when all else fails. It's cute, but it's not distracting me from my goal.

I set the phone in front of her again. "Listen, I'd rather you give it to me, but I can easily get it from Grace."

She snorts, as if ready to breathe fire, folding her arms over her chest. "Awfully dishonorable, sneaking around to get my number."

"Is not. I'm telling you right out what I'll do." I nudge my phone an inch farther in her direction. "Not honoring your promises… now that's dishonorable."

She rolls her eyes but picks up the phone. I want to do a victory dance but settle for leaning back and finishing my beer.

"Don't make me sorry," she warns, handing my phone back to me.

"Never." I send off a short text to the number she entered. Her phone pings a second later. While she's distracted with my message I take a covert picture to save with her contact.

Her eyes shift over my shoulder. "You're neglecting your fans."

I turn and acknowledge the group of women that seem to hover like flies wherever I perform with a quick wave, then turn back to Lyric.

"Not interested," I explain. "They're there every week. They don't want me. They want him." I point at the stage with my empty beer bottle.

"And that's not you?" Both of her eyebrows rise, in surprise or disbelief. Either way I'm about to make this crystal clear.

"It's just a small part of my life. I enjoy being up there, but that doesn't define me."

"What does define you?"

I can't help but grin. She's curious, which is one step away from letting her guard down. "Go out to dinner with me tomorrow and find out, break buddy."

Lyric sighs.

"Back on," Jacki announces, collecting the empties from the table with brisk efficiency.

"We'll discuss this later." I stand and point to the dance floor. "Go back and dance. It gives me something to think about while I'm up there."

Grace and Zoe laugh as I pass on my way back to the stage.

We're halfway through the first song when Lyric walks out of the bar. I want to run after her, pull her back. We haven't even celebrated Grace's birthday yet. She didn't even wave goodbye. *Well, fuck.*

CHAPTER THREE

LYRIC

$\mathscr{I}$ exhale in relief once I get home. Sacha's more than happy to see me after the long day away. Her stubby tail wags a fast tempo as I grab her leash.

"Just a short one tonight. It's dark and it looks like rain." She stretches out her front legs, letting out a loud doggy yawn, expressing her opinion. Short walks stink, but I haven't worn heels in years, and after dancing with Grace the past hour I'll be lucky to make it around the block before my aching feet call mutiny. "Mommy's tired. It was a long day for her."

She tilts her head, her sad eyes questioning.

"I know. I should get out more." Snapping on her leash, I slip my feet out of their four-inch torture devices and into something more appropriate for Sacha's mad pace before we head down the porch steps. She bounces on happy feet once we hit the sidewalk.

"You're right, girl. I had fun. And I survived." Sort of. One of Zane's songs plays on repeat in my head, his whiskey smooth voice telling me to *hold on to love*.

Did I actually suggest to him that his band might suck? Not that I'd known the guy I'd met at the grocery store would be the lead singer of the band we'd be seeing later. But still. If Grace finds that little embarrassment out she'll never let me live it down.

I pull my head out of my thoughts and turn my focus onto every shadow that dances in the whistling wind. I don't have the luxury to contemplate a sexy musician, not when my ex-husband could be waiting to strike.

My phone vibrates with a text as we round the next corner.

UNKNOWN: You missed cake :(

Zane Brody.

I let out an exhausted breath and shove my phone back into my jacket pocket. Maybe if I ignore him…

A handful of seconds later that hope dims when my phone chimes again. And again. And again. Sacha halts her pursuit of furry wildlife and gives my pocket a curious sniff.

UNKNOWN: You also left without saying goodbye. Going to cry in my beer and write a very sad song now.

UNKNOWN: Sweet dreams, Lyric.

UNKNOWN: Talk soon.

Thunder rumbles a warning in the distance. The wind dies down and the smell of ozone thickens in the still air.

"What have I gotten us into, girl?" I pick up my pace, and Sacha's happy to follow along. The next flash of lightning raises the hairs on my arms. Or maybe it's the sudden silence. It's as if every creature is holding their breath. Watching and waiting to see how bad the storm will be.

My fingers grip the edges of my prepaid phone until they ache. I'm watching and waiting as well. Tonight was supposed to be a simple night out. A one off from my boring routine. But every action has a consequence, and only time will tell how bad this one will be.

Fat raindrops pelt against my head as I rush under the front porch. Unlocking the door, I let Sacha in and lock back up. A brilliant flash of lightning gives me a second's warning before the loud crash of thunder shakes the house and the rain comes down in earnest. If only Zane Brody had come with a similar warning. Would I have been able to avoid him?

A WEEK later my phone is loaded down with texts. Of course I haven't answered a single one, and my guilty heart thumps a sad beat as I read the last message.

UNKNOWN: You're passing up something good. Fear should never control your future.

Fear governs every minute of my life. It's how I've survived. However, Zane's words chafe at the core of my beliefs, but encouraging him would be a slippery slope to nowhere good.

"Earth to Lyric, you reading me?"

I blink back to the present, Zoe's and Grace's giggles rising above the din of the crowded teacher's lounge.

"Gosh, you're out of it again." Grace nudges my foot with hers under the table. "Hot musician on your mind?"

"No," I huff, rolling my eyes.

All I've heard from her is Zane, Zane, Zane. You'd think the guy was running for president the way she's been talking up his credentials all week. I get that the guy is generous and grounded, willing to give his last dime to his friends. I appreciate that he's not a womanizer like he could easily be, given his profession. And I certainly don't need Grace to point out his looks. His face is etched inside my eyelids every night when I close my eyes. Probably because my best friend won't shut up about the guy. Is it any surprise I've taken to tuning her out?

"Have you talked to him at all since Friday?" Zoe asks while digging into the last bits of the salad in front of her.

I groan to myself. *And now it's interrogation time.*

"I've been busy with projects all week, getting a jump on the end-of-the-year crazies, you know. Figured maybe it would be better to wait to make plans until school is out." Or maybe he'll give up by then.

Zoe scoffs, she and Grace giving each other looks of wide-eyed astonishment. "That's almost five weeks away."

"Did you let Zane know that?" Grace asks, frown on her face.

"Um, not really." Glancing down, I drag artistic trails through my chocolate pudding with my spoon, ignoring their disapproving looks.

"Lyric," Grace gasps. "Please call him. He was so disappointed when you left Friday night. At least text him."

"I will." Maybe. Not. I stand, cleaning up my lunch. "You know how crazy things are about to get. I've a half dozen IEP meetings, then one with the moms to discuss the end-of-the-year picnic, then grades have to be completed, and—"

"Hello? Same boat here." Zoe wags her finger between her and Grace. "Do you see either of us putting our life on hold until the end of the school year?"

Grace nods. "Please. For me."

"Sure, Grace. I will," I say, and the wide-eyed panicked look on her face relaxes. I've no clue why she's invested in my social life, but I don't plan on dating this guy just to make her happy. I give her a reassuring smile and step back. "Have to check with the nurse on Bobby Miller's allergy medicine. See you later."

The bell rings as I make my way down the hall to the office. Students rush in the opposite direction, shouting and laughing. Allison Reynolds, a first grade teacher, gives me a weary smile that says the next four and a half weeks of school can't be over fast enough.

All the children are antsy. Excited. Looking forward to family vacations, beach days, and no homework. Hours of uninterrupted time with nothing to do. Last year I had taken on a summer class, but this year none are available. A little over a month and I'll have all the time in the world to imagine the possibility of my ex-husband making good on his threats.

I attempt a deep calming breath once I'm behind the nurse's office door.

"Hounds of hell chasing ya?" she asks, glancing up from the paperwork on her desk. "You look frazzled. Sit."

I blow out a stress-filled exhale and fold myself into the tiny chair reserved for her patients. "You could say that."

Kelly Moore, school nurse and confidant, grasps my wrist, taking my pulse. "A bit fast."

"End-of-the-year anticipation. You know..." I give her a significant look. "Also went out this weekend. Sorta met a man."

"That's fantastic. Isn't it?" She cocks an eyebrow.

"He's pushy and... and... I don't know. Way too confident." The words rush out and I let out a quiet groan, dropping my head onto my one free hand.

"Damn those confident men. I much prefer the weak ones who have no backbone until they find it in their fists." She twists her lips, significant look returned.

"I prefer none at all, but he's wormed his way into my life in one night. Now Grace and Zoe won't let it go."

"Maybe they're onto something. You need to enjoy life. One bad experience shouldn't ruin your entire future."

"Bit of an understatement, don't you think?" I let out a shaky breath. Kelly is the only one here who knows my whole story. Her sister runs a women's shelter in the city—the third shelter I stayed at on my long journey to freedom. I owe everything I have to them. My job, my home, my life. "I'd rather be left alone. Grayson's been out of jail for two weeks. I'm scared to death."

"Isolation isn't the answer." She shakes her head. "Besides, he's on probation. Crossing state lines would mean an immediate return to prison."

I'm skeptical that would stop him. The man thought he was above the law, until he wasn't. And another man isn't the answer to my problems.

"I'm not isolated. I don't want a man. No matter how nice Grace says he is, I just—"

"Who's in jail now, Lyric?" Kelly gives me a sympathetic smile.

"You sound like a therapist," I snap to hide how much her words affect me, then soften my harsh words with a smile. My situation isn't her fault.

Her lips purse anyway. "Speaking of... when was the last time you talked with yours?"

"Dr. Harmon?" *Call me Margie*, she insists every time I step into her office, like we're friends or something. I've never had to pay my friends to listen to my problems or offer advice. "We cut back to once a month; it's been a few weeks. But it's always the same thing. *A busy mind is a healthy mind.* Last time she suggested I learn a craft, like maybe knitting. So be forewarned. I've never been crafty, but with a whole summer ahead of me everyone might be getting my sad attempts for Christmas gifts this year."

"You should come work at the shelter. Not that I don't appreciate handmade woolen accessories, but the residents could use a strong role model. You certainly fit that mold."

I bark out a bitter laugh. "I'm not fitting anything, Kelly. I'm just surviving."

"Come anyway. It'll keep your mind busy and you'll see how far you've progressed." She pats my wrist where she's been monitoring my pulse. "Back to normal."

Normal? I don't think so. Normal isn't looking over your shoulder all the time. Normal isn't jumping at every little sound. I'm like a turtle, sticking my head out for brief periods when I've no choice. Will I ever feel safe enough to come out of my shell?

The piercing sound of the bell signals the end of our quiet moment. I stand to leave. "I'll consider it. If nothing else comes up in the district, I'll do it."

"And consider the man, too. I think your therapist would approve even if he doesn't like fiber crafts. There's nothing like a summer fling to keep you busy. If Grace likes him, he can't be all bad. Right?"

Million-dollar question. Bigger question though, am I brave enough to discover the answer?

THE REST of the day goes by in a flash. Before I know it, another week is over. Summer break is coming too soon. I'm going to miss my students. Last year my heart broke a little as I watched my kids walk out the door for the last time. A little over a month and this troop will be gone as well.

I wave to the moms at dismissal time, making sure my students connect with their rides safely. A tall man stands in the shadows by the gate, leaning against the old maple, watching me. My heart lurches in my chest. He moves forward and the sun shines down on his dark head. *Not blond.* Then my pulse races for a completely different reason when Zane holds up his phone.

"This didn't work out so well. Grace suggested I try a different tactic," he calls out, strolling in my direction, confident grin in place.

Dammit, Grace.

The security monitor glances at me and I nod. *No need to bring in the cavalry.* Grace says he's harmless—maybe.

"Zane..." I meet him halfway, ignoring the way his name slips breathlessly from my lips like I've been running a damned marathon. It's completely unfair the way his crisp blue dress shirt stretches across his broad shoulders, or the way his hair is combed back off his forehead. It's a really nice forehead that leads straight to that ombre-blue smolder.

"Grace tell you where to find me, too?"

"Pointed me to your door, but I've been here all day." His eyes light up and his smile—shit that smile. It's the kind that says he has a secret he might share, if I'm lucky.

"Huh?"

"See. If you had gone out to dinner with me Saturday, you'd be privy to all this inside information. Now you're at my mercy to show pity on your poor oblivious soul."

"I can't do this. Just... please go." I sigh and turn away with a heavy heart.

Zane bounces around me, blocking my path. I jump out of my skin. My heart springs into my throat, choking me. He reaches out to touch my shoulder, but I jerk back.

"Jesus. I'm sorry." He holds up his hands in the universal sign of surrender. "You okay? You're white as a ghost."

I nod, swallowing the bile that flavors the back of my throat. "Hair-trigger reflexes. I hate loud noises, too. Fireworks, popping balloons, those darn biscuits in a tube."

"I'll keep that in mind." He scans my face, his eyebrows lowering. "Please, just give me five minutes."

Five minutes for what? For me to freak out some more? For me to show this guy how unprepared I am for normal social interactions with the opposite sex? For me to fight this goddamned attraction I don't want? But then Kelly's words come back, echoing loud in my head.

Who's in jail now?

I give Zane a hesitant nod and turn toward the sidewalk. With his hair disciplined by comb and gel and his dress shirt covering the murals on his arms, I'm willing to pretend he's as safe as Grace promises. At least for now. "Five minutes. My dog's waiting at home, legs crossed."

He beams a smile like he's won the lottery.

"You were telling me you spent the day at school. Brushing up on multiplication tables?" I joke in an attempt to lighten the mood.

"Exactly." He returns my laugh. "Never really got those sevens down the first time. Think I'm golden now. So, I thought I'd take my break buddy out to dinner to celebrate."

"Your break buddy says it's only three thirty. And you're not on a break, I am."

"Sure I am. You women are a cruel bunch. My heart's a roadmap of scars, and my ego's torn to shit." He cringes while scanning the quiet, tree-lined neighborhood that surrounds the school. We're alone though, just us and an angry crow squawking in the tree above. "Sorry. It's been hell remembering not to swear all day."

"Yeah. Don't want those f-bombs going off prematurely." I give him a tentative smile that makes his widen.

"Then I'll follow you home, and we can go from there?"

I stop and turn to face him. "What? Why?"

"Dinner. Remember, we're celebrating."

I fit my fist into the dip of my waist. "You haven't even answered my question. Why were you at school today? Are you stalking me?"

He laughs, loud enough to offend the pesky crow, sending the noisy bird flying off to a new perch on the opposite side of the block. "A stalker? You have a vivid imagination, Miss James."

A quiet snort escapes me. *If he only knew.* "You've deprived me of the truth before, remember, Mr. Brody? My imagination only supplies what information you choose to withhold."

"Then have dinner with me, Miss James. I promise all the information your imagination desires."

Silence descends for a moment as we put distance between us and the school. Just the steady rhythm of our shoes on the sidewalk and the slightly less steady rhythm of my hammering heart. Grace better be right about this guy. I haven't been alone with a man in over three years. And the last time... I force the next breath into my cold lungs and shove that unpleasant memory back into the deep hole where it belongs.

My step falters and I look up at him. "You're serious?"

"As a heart attack." He laughs, as if he's said the funniest thing. "Get it?"

"Funny." I roll my eyes but smile despite myself. Zane Brody may have the worst sense of humor ever. This talented, gorgeous, perfect man has a flaw. Probably an annoying one, but at the moment it's endearing. "Come back Monday morning. My kindergarten class tells jokes to start the week off right."

"Really? That's brilliant."

"Zane…" My eyes focus on the light traffic at the intersection, trying not to look at him. Because endearing or not, I need to stop encouraging him. "I really don't think dinner is a good idea."

"Seriously? Are you on a starvation diet or something? Protesting world hunger?" He bends his knees to look directly into my eyes. "It's. Just. Dinner. You know, food, conversation. You tell me your sob story, I'll tell you mine." He pauses for a moment, then sighs. "I'm not a serial killer or anything. Please, give me a chance."

I give my head a slow shake as we cross the street. "You said five minutes, now you want dinner. What's next, Zane?"

He turns toward me, his hands raised, palms up, as we stop on the other side of the intersection. "It's Friday night. You have plans?"

I look down at the darkened circle of gum that's embedded in the sidewalk between my feet and shake my head. I can't lie.

"You'd rather stay at home. Friday night TV sucks. Rather binge-watch Netflix than have free pizza?"

My mouth actually waters. He's speaking to my weakness. When was the last time I had restaurant pizza? In a restaurant. I don't remember that far back.

He gives me a small, sad smile. I shake my head and it fades.

"Dessert. I can buy you something way better than those Ho Hos you picked up last week. Whatever you want. Cannoli, tiramisu. The place I have in mind makes a kick-ass chocolate cake."

"Cake?" I groan as my resolve fades with one word. *Chocolate.* This would be a lot easier if he wasn't so damn good-looking.

Maybe. I don't know. I don't trust any man, good-looking or not. But I trust Grace.

He chuckles like he knows he's won. "You missed Grace's birthday cake. You *need* cake."

Over the last ten months Aaron's dragged Grace to the bars for their performances, I'm sure she's seen every side of Zane. She says he's a good guy, and she'd never lie to me.

And who's in jail now?

Fuck you, Grayson Thorpe.

I rub the knot of tension that's formed between my eyes and look around. If my ex-husband has someone watching me I've signed a death sentence for both me and Zane.

Stop with the paranoia. You'll be checking behind the bushes soon.

My ex is probably lounging in a pool somewhere, surrounded by silicone-enhanced bleached blondes, and I'm about to pass up free pizza and cake. *Kick-ass* chocolate cake.

"Fine. One dinner. No sob story, though."

Zane's smile is off the charts, and my stomach takes a dive at the pretty sight. "You won't regret it. I'm an awesome date."

"And humble. Don't forget humble." I breathe out a thin laugh. What exactly have I agreed to? It doesn't escape me that he's now calling it a date.

"Humble doesn't get you anywhere in life. You gotta grab the brass ring with both hands."

We wander down the next block while Zane offers me more of his philosophies. He's confident—way more than I am—and smart. There's definitely a brain behind that pretty face.

Halfway down the street, he stops next to a vintage Mustang Fastback, black and sexy. Now that school's out for the day the streets are empty; it's the only car around. But even if every parking spot had been taken, I'd know it's his. Zane just isn't a Honda guy.

"Where's your car?" he asks, looking around.

"Um… I actually walk."

"Oh, so you live close." He steps back onto the sidewalk where I stand.

Is an hour-long walk close? Somehow I don't think Zane would agree.

"Not really." I look down, scraping tracks in the dust on the sidewalk with the toe of my comfortably worn shoe. "I'm off Minnehaha, south of Lake Street."

Zane's eyes widen. "You're shitting me. Your car in the shop? How long have you been walking to school?"

"Two years."

"Every day?" His voice rises an octave. He unlocks the passenger door and then waves me in with a frown. "Geez. Hop in."

His frown deepens as I direct him to the tiny two bedroom bungalow that sits a couple miles from school—maybe more than a couple. At almost every turn he shakes his head and gives me a pained "Lyric…"

I should have left him in the school yard. By the time he pulls into my driveway his hair's back to the same disarrayed mess he'd had on Friday from raking his fingers through it. He engages the brake lever on the center console, then taps his finger on one of the shiny rimmed dials in front of him.

I give a critical eye to the house I've been renting for the past two years. *Am I making a mistake?*

"Four and three-tenths miles. Lyric… I can't believe you walk four and three-tenths miles, twice, every day." He exits the car and stalks around the front to my side, closing his eyes and pausing as if to take a breath before opening my door.

Restraining my eye roll, I hop out of his car. "You're being dramatic."

He shoves the hair off his forehead, his brows rising. "I'm being dramatic? You're a beautiful woman, walking by yourself, on busy streets with God-knows-who passing by? And in all kinds of shitty weather—rain, snow, sub-zero temperatures?"

"And you say I have a vivid imagination?" I press a finger against my chest. "I have an umbrella and snow boots. And if the weather gets too bad, there's public transportation."

"And if someone harasses you?" He turns his attention back to me on the short walk to my front porch. "How did you get home from the bar the other night, or do I even want to know?"

I sling my purse over my shoulder and cross my arms over my chest. "You always this bossy with women you just met? You're gonna be single a long time, Mr. Brody."

"I'm not bossy, I'm concerned." He narrows his eyes for a second, then he blows out a slow breath I'm interpreting as a sigh of surrender. "Fine. This conversation is on hold, for now, Miss James."

Before he can proceed up the porch stairs, I press my hand against his chest, blocking him at the bottom. "You can't come in."

"Reason?" He glances over my shoulder at the house.

"Sacha doesn't like strangers."

He tips his head, giving me the full impact of those damn eyes. "Sacha? That your dog? I love dogs."

"Sacha may not love you. You're a man. And a stranger." I pull my hands back from the solid curve of his pectorals. "Th-that's two strikes against you."

"I can't help the man part, but introduce me. We won't be strangers. Or..." He pauses for a moment as if deciding something, then bends down and dusts off the first step of the porch with his palm. "If you prefer, I can wait out here. Although, I promise not to judge if you didn't put your breakfast dishes away. It's not like you were expecting company."

"I put my dishes away," I say a little more sharply than necessary. I'm what some would call a neat freak, but with good reasons.

Before I can analyze my motives, I pull my keys from my purse and start to unlock the front door. Serves Zane right if Sacha pins him down on the living room floor. *Questioning my housekeeping skills?* "Just don't blame me if you walk out missing parts."

"Bad neighborhood?"

I turn and frown at him before opening the door. "No. Why?"

He shrugs. "Everyone has three deadbolts. No reason."

I've gone insane. In the past two years no one has entered my home, except my landlord. Once. Mr. Dunkelstein installed my deadbolts while keeping one eye on Sacha the whole time. After that we'd come to an understanding. Sort of a "don't call unless the roof is falling in" agreement that I'd been more than happy to make. Now I'm letting a complete stranger into my private world, my safe harbor. It could be a step toward normal or a grave mistake.

Sacha greets me, her happy tail vibrating with excitement until she sniffs out the man behind me. Her body stills and her eyes meet mine in question.

I hang my coat on the hook by the door. "Sacha, be nice."

I give her a scratch on her head, and she visibly relaxes. Her tail twitches slowly, not the eggbeater it was, but in wary acceptance. I step aside for Zane to come in.

"Slowly. No fast moves. She's trained for protection."

"Holy shit. A Doberman. Hey, Sacha. Don't eat me." He finishes in a voice a few octaves higher than his normal baritone.

Zane extends his hand for Sacha to sniff while my mind reviews the steps to making a tourniquet. Not that I've experience in such things.

My dog's tongue darts out at the offered hand—probably judging it for palatability—then she drops down on her front legs and lets out a bark. The next second she goes nuts, bouncing around Zane, her tail as out of control as the rest of her.

Well, shit.

"Take it easy, girl." I snap my fingers and she follows me into the living room with obvious reluctance.

"Can I move?" Zane smirks as my dog brings him her favorite toy. "Unless she's going to chew off my face."

He waves her faceless duck at me, then tosses it across the room.

"I think she's good," I snap back, watching Sacha bound after her toy.

"You think?" He strides over to the sofa and sits. "Am I the first person to meet your dog? She really needs to work on her aggression."

"Just shut up, okay? She actually hates my landlord."

"Maybe it's your landlord that's the problem." He tosses Sacha's duck again. "Wow, you have a K-52? Damn. Do you play?"

The awe in Zane's voice is apparent. Less than five minutes in my house and the man's cataloguing my possessions.

"No." I let out a heavy sigh and give Sacha an exasperated look before turning toward the hall. "Give me a minute to change. Then we can take my *watchdog* for a walk."

"I could teach you," he calls out as I shut my bedroom door.

The sound of very off-tune scales drifts through the house for a brief second, then Zane's curse. Ignoring him, I strip out of my school clothes liberally covered in splotches of Elmer's glue and God knows what else. I pull on a sunshine-yellow sundress from my closet, then slip on a cardigan because it's May in Minnesota.

"You know, neglecting a Steinway piano is a mortal sin. We should discuss tuning the poor thing." He glances at the piano, eyes soft with sympathy, then turns toward me and smiles. "You look beautiful."

"Thanks." I brush my hands down the front of my dress. For only one dinner we're amassing a lot of *later* conversations. "For the compliment. Not the tuning. It's not in the budget."

"Whatever." He stands. "Now let's see your scary neighborhood that requires three deadbolts and Sacha the attack dog."

Sacha leans against his leg, her tongue lolling as she stares up at him.

39

He stares back at my dog, his eyes wide, his lips pulling into a mock grimace. "I'll bring cookies or maybe steak next time. You know, for my safety."

"Let's go." I snap Sacha's leash onto her collar, ignoring his remark.

Zane opens the door and scans the block from the top stairs. "Neighborhood looks fine to me."

"I've had no complaints. Why were you at school?" No need to talk about my security obsessions, or the reasons behind them.

"Oh, right, school," he says slowly, his lips twitching. "It was music appreciation day for the fifth graders. I help out every year."

"Music appreciation day... Why you?" Sacha stops to sniff. I look up at Zane.

"Me and the middle school orchestra teacher, Bill Santos, bring in a bunch of instruments for the kids to play with. If they're interested, they can sign up for the school orchestra next year. Guy should be deaf from listening to all those kids torturing strings, but I appreciate it. Once he whips them into shape, I get the finished product. The ones that stick with it, and hopefully *practice* every day." His eyebrows rise on that dreaded word, and his long pause after seems filled with expectation of more information. *You're in for a long wait, mister.*

Sacha stops to study a squirrel that's prancing across the street. The moment stretches on toward uncomfortable. How much of my past is even safe to share with Zane?

I blow out a weighted breath. "When you choose something, you're probably more likely to commit."

I can almost see the wheels turning in his mind as he digests the information I've given him. He's quiet for a couple of minutes, but I can tell by his furrowed brow the interrogation isn't over yet.

"So, you didn't choose that beautiful instrument in there? Quite an expensive room ornament."

"It was my father's," I answer, my voice weary, exhausted by the conversation potholes I'm dodging. "'Finished product.' What does that mean? What do you do?"

"See. If you had stayed the other night, if you had given us time to really talk, you'd know all about me now." He turns and sticks out his hand. "Hi. Zane Brody, high school music teacher, orchestra director, and rock god of the Twin Cities."

"Impressive. And definitely not humble." I shake his hand, doing my best to ignore the tingles that run up my arm. "Lyric James, queen of kindergarten room two."

"And not a pianist?"

I shake my head once with finality. "Definitely not."

"Hmm. So, the piano is your father's, huh? Nice of him to give it to you."

I'm silent for a moment, but Zane's eyes are on me, waiting for an answer. "You might say he didn't have a choice. My parents were killed in a car accident a half dozen years ago."

His smile vanishes. "Shit. I'm so sorry."

I shrug. "Not your fault."

"No, but I should have realized. A guy doesn't give up his piano. Not—"

"Zane, it's okay," I interrupt, placing a hand on his chest for the second time today. Under his thin dress shirt is a really nice chest, all hard muscles and warm flesh. And tattoos? *Someone help me.*

"No. Losing a parent isn't okay. I know this shit. My dad died when I was little. I don't remember him much, but I've always felt something was missing. You know?"

I nod, recognizing the pain in his eyes. He looks away, and I sense there's more he wants to say, but he doesn't. When he looks back the crease between his brows has vanished and his smile is back.

"Your dog's tongue is dragging the ground. I think she wants to go home," he says instead of whatever had been on his mind. I don't push it, respecting his privacy.

"Two blocks around the next corner and we'll be back. She needs a long walk or she's, like, crazy all night." I scratch her head and she looks up at me with innocent eyes. "Aren't you, girl?"

"How long have you had her?"

"Since I moved here. Two years in June." Damn, another pothole.

"And before that. Where did you live?"

"Bounced around. Nothing felt right until I landed here." I give him as honest an answer as I can.

We walk in silence for a few minutes, and I relax with the break in the questions.

"So far I know you teach kindergarten, you have an expensive piano wasting away in your living room that your father played, and you moved here two years ago." He ticks off his knowledge of me on his fingers. "Oh, and you're obsessed with walking and security, and you don't know shit about tequila. You're pretty miserly with the information, Miss James."

"You know my dog, Sacha, too," I remind him. He frowns.

"Keeps me interesting. Don't want you bored on our..." I pause, not wanting to call this a date. *We're not dating.* "Whatever break buddies do when they go out."

"Oh, you're interesting all right." He stops at the bottom of the stairs and motions me up with that sexy smirk. "So, you're accepting my dinner offer."

"Do I have a choice?"

CHAPTER FOUR

LYRIC

*Z*ane takes me to this tiny Italian place—Sarapelli's, the vintage neon sign affixed to the front of the old brick building proclaims in cherry red, white, and green. Inside, the space is long and narrow with booths on the perimeter and a few small tables running down the center. Black and white linoleum floor tiles, rustic wood tables and red upholstered chairs, chianti bottles complete with candles flickering, local landmarks set in dark frames on stark white walls. Soft music plays in the background. My skin tightens with discomfort. The place is cozy and a touch too romantic for a friendly dinner.

The fragrance of garlic, tomato, and oregano permeate the air along with an undercurrent of the yeasty bread smells of a bakery. My stomach growls loudly, not seeming to care that it's early and we're the only ones in here.

"Zane!" calls a busty older woman, with jet-black hair shot with silver, rushing forward from a doorway in the back of the place. Her piercing blue eyes are a dead giveaway that they're related. "How's my favorite nephew?"

"Good, Aunt Mary." He gives her a quick hug, then turns toward me. "This is Lyric."

"Hi, Lyric." Her eager smile and appraising glance make me think the whole Brody clan will soon be speculating over Zane's current love interest. "Sit wherever you like."

Zane pulls me into a cozy booth by the window overlooking the busy street out front. I stare at my hands twisting in my lap. My face warms. I agreed to dinner, not a romantic dinner with family surveillance. *Is that even a thing?*

And now Zane's eyes are on me. Without even looking up, my stomach can tell. It's those damn ombre-blues. The way he watches me, it's like a fifty-foot-drop thrill ride. I need to get off to catch my breath.

Outside, the sidewalk teems with the Friday night crowd, everyone getting together after a long week to let loose. An every-week experience for them, but for me... I'm out of my comfort zone here.

"Aunt Mary is my dad's sister. This place has been in her husband's family forever. Best pizza in the city, but I might be prejudiced." Zane pulls my attention away from the window. "I hope it's okay I brought you here."

"As long as you don't read more into this than it is. We're just having dinner," I snap, then squeeze my eyes shut. This man is buying me dinner, and I'm repaying him by being a bitch. My mother would kill me.

"I'm sorry. That didn't come out right. It's been a long week and... well, that's no excuse for bad manners." I straighten the napkin-bundled silverware in front of me, then let my gaze wander up to Zane's. "You're lucky to have close family, and I appreciate you bringing me here."

"Mary and Joe are like a second set of parents for me." He points to the back of the restaurant, toward the door his aunt disappeared behind. "Did a shitload of homework at that small table back there. My uncle makes amazing red sauce, and his calc skills are pretty good too."

"That's an impressive resume." My fingers smooth over the

wide window trim. Up close, I see the white painted wood has been covered in writing. Initial-filled hearts win out on popularity, followed by random thoughts, drawings of pizzas, people eating pizzas... a moose eating pizza? Someone named Sonya wrote a poem about garlic breath—take note, guys—and Randy proclaimed *She said yes!*

Zane grabs a black sharpie off the sill and uncaps it, releasing the acrid smell. "This is a tradition. You have to write something before you leave."

"Have to?" My nose twitches with the scent, and I frown. "Is that a rule?"

"Yep." He stares off for a second, then starts to write. "No profanity, though. This is a family place."

"What are you writing?"

He lifts a shoulder. "You'll see."

A moment later he hands me the marker. "Your turn."

"What did you write?"

"Can't tell you." Zane covers his writing with his hand. "Not until you write something."

"Like fortune cookies." I shield the spot on the window sill from Zane's prying eyes while I scribble what would look like an innocent message to anyone else.

His brows draw together in a frown. "Fortune cookies?"

"Nothing." I shake my head and wave a dismissive hand, but the look on Zane's face tells me he won't let it go. "When I was younger, it was a rule in our house. You couldn't say your fortune aloud until everyone had theirs. My mom thought they wouldn't come true, or at least that's what she said. Weird, I know."

"Not really." He lifts his chin toward the window, reminding me of my task. "It must have been difficult losing your parents. You have anyone else? Aunts, uncles, close friends?"

"I'm an only child in a long line of only children. I had friends, and..." I trail off, lifting a shoulder, feinting casualness, then shifting the conversation back on him as I doodle something silly

45

onto this windowsill. "So it's your mom and you. Any other brothers or sisters?"

His eyes narrow a fraction and he lets my question hang for a long second, letting me know my nimble change of subjects wasn't quite so slick.

"My sister Tess is eighteen. She's still at home until fall. She's actually my half sister. My mom remarried, then divorced when I was a kid. And there's Laura, my older sister. She's married with two kids. They live in St. Paul." He pauses, looking out the window. "This is a hard place to leave."

I set the marker back on the sill. "Is that a good thing or bad?"

Mary interrupts, dropping off water and menus at our booth. "How's your mom?"

Zane's smile is forced, at least it's nothing like the ones I've witnessed. It doesn't reach his eyes and it's just... off. *Huh.*

"She's good."

"Say hi for me." Her lips quirk up in a similar smile. Odd, but before I can contemplate its meaning, she shifts back into waitress mode. "What can I bring you to drink?"

Zane turns to me. I say, "Iced tea, please."

"Furious IPA," Zane adds, winking at Mary.

"Of course." She laughs, walking away. "Need I ask."

"You obviously eat a lot of pizza. I'm envious." I smile, watching his aunt stop and chat with a couple of teens who just walked through the door for a second before heading back into what I assume is the kitchen.

"Not really. Order pickup every now and then when my sister begs, but this is the first time dining in quite a while." He grabs one of the menus and slaps it down between us. "What do you like on your pizza? Need to tell you first, I don't do meat, but if it's an issue we can get two."

My eyebrows rise a fraction. *Interesting.* He doesn't look like a vegetarian, but then what does one look like?

I lift a shoulder in a nonchalant shrug. I've known more than a few vegetarians over the years. And a real pizza, even without meat, is heads above all the frozen disks I've suffered with. Barely giving the menu a glance, I answer, "I'll eat anything, really. I'm not fussy."

He shakes his head. "Can't be that easy. Pizza is the perfect first-date food. It's a negotiation. If we can work this out, the future is hopeful."

"Does this follow with your supermarket philosophy on meeting your soulmate?" Once again I ignore his reference to our dinner as a date. He's pushing it, though.

"Maybe. What can't you possibly allow on a pizza?" He points to the list of ingredients on the page with a long finger decorated with a treble clef. *Is there anything this man hasn't tattooed?*

"Nothing weird. Never been a fan of pineapple or anchovies." I wrinkle my nose. "Peppers aren't really my thing, but I can pick those off."

"I can work with that. Spinach and mushrooms sound good?"

"Add olives and you got a deal," I say just to add something to the negotiations.

"Great. Next hurdle, picking baby names. I'm partial to Jane for a girl and Olaf for a boy."

"Olaf is a no-go." I scoff, crossing my arms over my chest. He's joking, right? "I have nightmares about men in metal hats with horns."

"Damn. So close." He looks around the almost-empty restaurant. Right now it's just us and the teenage couple who are clearly on a date. "You do know you moved to Viking country?"

"Oversight on my part. The blizzards drew me in." I nod, glancing out the window on this warm evening. Winter's about as far away as it can get at the moment, thank God.

He leans forward, a serious look on his face. "No kidding. We need to fix that car problem before next winter."

"Public transportation has worked so far. And I thought you said we'd discuss that later."

He opens his mouth, probably to argue, but Mary interrupts with our drinks and takes our pizza order. It's the perfect break to take a step back from where our conversation is heading. In one afternoon he's overstepped so many boundaries. He means well, which is why I'm not walking out of here, but he's a bit too... confident? Approachable? Handsome? Whatever, I don't know what to do with that.

Grayson was all that.

I don't need another Grayson.

"So, high schoolers? From my perspective that looks a bit scary. Raging hormones, attitudes, bitchy girls, and horny guys. Recipe for disaster?" I raise an eyebrow at the thought of dealing with that on a daily basis instead of my babies, while peeling the paper from my straw.

Zane laughs, carefully pouring his beer into his precisely tipped pint glass. If the whole teaching and musician thing doesn't work for him, he could probably get a job at a bar with his skills.

"From my perspective, kindergarten looks a little scary. Talk about disaster. They don't really have the whole control-of-bodily-fluids down, right?"

"I don't buy a lot of dry-clean-only clothes. But most of the time they're sweet and innocent." I scrunch up my face, picturing what his day must be like. Teenagers. Chaos. *No thank you.* I look up at Zane and smile. "I feel like I'm molding clay into something amazing."

"You wield a lot of power, Miss James. Kindergarten teachers leave a lasting impression on little minds. Good or bad. A kid's first teacher is the mold the rest of us need to fill or break to be successful."

"A responsibility I don't take lightly."

He bites his lip for a second, his gaze locking onto mine. My stomach flutters in response. Those damned eyes of his are dangerous. Like staring into the sun.

He takes a slow sip of beer, then sets his glass down. "Tell me about your first love." He pauses, grinning. "Tell me about the poor sap that probably still pines for you."

"Oh…" I breathe out the word while stirring the ice in my drink around, pushing the lemon slice down into the dark contents of my glass. Zane offers me a packet of sugar, but I shake my head. "There's nothing to tell, really."

He sets the packet on the table in front of him and blows out a slow breath. "No boyfriend? No weird dating story? No embarrassing crushes?" I shake my head and he continues, "I highly doubt that. You're killing me here with the lack of information. At least tell me your favorite color, for God's sake."

"Purple." My smile wilts as I take in the disappointment in Zane's eyes. I've spent the last three years keeping secrets. My secrets keep me safe.

"So, what are you doing the rest of the weekend?" he asks, knocking me off guard with his sudden change of topic.

Of course I've no plans. I haven't had plans for the last two years. If Grace hadn't begged me to go out last Friday I wouldn't be here right now, having what's supposed to be a one time dinner with this man. But now he's asking me for more. Again.

"Don't know." I motion to the window. "You never did tell me what you wrote."

His lips tip up into that half-smile, half smirk that says he's enjoying this little game of evasion. "What did you write?"

"Zane Brody is the most infuriating man ever."

He leans forward to look, but I cover my words with my hand.

"Pretty sure that's written on a few windows here. Is that actually what you wrote?" He chuckles.

"No, but if I tell you what I did write, you'll take it the wrong way, and maybe your ego will explode. Your fans wouldn't like that."

He laughs harder. "Now I might explode from curiosity. You're a cruel woman, Lyric James. But two can play this game."

"What if I'm not the least bit curious, Zane Brody?"

"I think you're very curious. But I think you're a master at hiding your feelings." He runs a finger around the edge of his half-empty glass and bites that lip again, which is a total distraction. "Want to come to my class concert in a few weeks? It's the last of the year. You can silently satisfy your curiosity about my teaching abilities. And I can show off my students. I'm really proud of their talents."

I blink for a second as his proposal sinks in. It's a bad idea. A few weeks is way more than a one-time dinner. But I've never been good at saying no. And the naked hope in those ombre-blues? *Shit*, I can't squash that.

A short time later Mary brings the pizza and dishes it out, ending the one moment of silence. It's not uncomfortable, though. Zane hums something pleasant while I watch a couple corral their small kids toward the entrance of our restaurant. At one time that had been my future. Or so I had thought. Me and Grayson and a big house filled with kids. It had been our dream. But dreams turn to nightmares when you least expect it.

We dig into the hot pizza, cheese strands stretching between our plates and the pan. Kind of like me and Zane. The more I try to distance myself, the more resilient whatever this is between us becomes.

This is the best thing I've tasted in forever—the pizza, not this man. *Although...*

I squash that thought down while inhaling the slice in my hand. Zane chuckles when I reach for seconds—okay, maybe thirds. But this isn't a date. I'm not here to impress him with my ladylike table manners and dainty eating habits. Those are reserved for dates, and this isn't a date.

"I guess an early dinner wasn't such a bad idea, huh?" He grins before biting into the last slice I graciously let him have. "I forgot

I was going to the grade school today until I ran into the sub walking into my classroom this morning. Thankfully I wasn't expected until nine, or Santos would have had my ass. But I also forgot how inedible your lunches are. How do you survive?"

"Vending machine." My answer earns me a small scowl I sort of expect. "Don't knock the Ho Hos. The guy stocks them in the machine in the teachers lounge just for me." I suck the spicy sauce off my fingers, giving him a slow grin. After his reaction to my purchases at the grocery store last week, his look of disappointment is no surprise. "I'm joking. There's this thing called lunch meat? You put it between bread? Quite edible." I pause to sip my tea. "Not quite as edible as this pizza, but... who knew there was good pizza in this town?"

"Where have guys been taking you?" Zane looks at me like I have two heads, his eyes wide with disbelief. "I may be partial to this place, but there's plenty of good pizza spots in the Twin Cities."

"Um, well, I haven't really gone anywhere." I wave off his shock. Locking myself in my house for the last two years isn't normal. My eccentricities stand out like the neon sign hanging above this restaurant's door. "This is my first time out. I guess I've been busy."

"First time out? Are you telling me this is your first date since moving here?" I start to correct Zane, reminding him that this is technically not a date, but he shakes his head slowly. "The single men in Minneapolis must have their heads up their asses. A woman as beautiful as you should not have been sitting home alone for the past two years. But I shall take full advantage of their incompetence."

I swallow down a frisson of anxiety with a sip of tea. "I'm not alone. I have Sacha."

He laughs. "You're crazy. And smart and feisty and gorgeous. And you can eat. You kept pace with me, and that's saying something."

DARCI ANN BAKER

I've had enough of your fuckin' feisty attitude. Grayson's voice echoes inside my skull and my earlier confidence vanishes in a wave of sick panic. My apology comes out automatically.

"Hey. Don't be sorry." Zane shakes his head, his eyes locking onto mine, making my stomach drop. It should be pleasant, but it's not. I barely hear whatever he says next over the hum inside my head.

I swallow with difficulty, my heart racing out of control. "I need to go."

His voice softens along with his eyes. "Whoa. I'm sorry. I didn't mean to upset you. I'm just being honest."

I bite my lip, hard, and close my eyes while concentrating on the painful throb. My feet pressing into the floor. The familiar. Anything but the handsome stranger across from me.

He reaches for my hand, but I pull it back, wiping a tear from my cheek. "Bad idea. Stupid," I mumble to myself as my breath freezes in my lungs and my skin prickles. Kelly was wrong. I'm not strong. Not enough to flirt and accept compliments and stoke the desire of another man. Not at all. I'll always be the weak little girl under Grayson's control. Trapped in his prison. *Too fuckin' feisty for your own good.*

I suck in a painful breath as the tightness in my chest increases. *Not here, please.*

"Can't be dating yet. Probably never," I tell myself as my airways constrict and oxygen trickles into my lungs.

"Shit." Zane slips onto the bench next to me, wrapping his arms around my shoulders and pressing me into his chest. In the past, any contact at times like this sent me spiraling further, but for some reason Zane's presence has the opposite effect. "Relax, Lyric. Take slow, deep breaths. You're okay. I've got you."

I take a deep shuddering breath, relieved by the accomplishment, but his words set me off and my tears drench his shirt in seconds. Zane hands me a stack of paper napkins and wraps my coat around my shoulders.

"Shhh. Let's go. Let's get out of here," he whispers, his lips in my hair.

He lifts me out of the booth, throwing a wad of cash on the table. I don't recall the trip down the sidewalk, but by the time he tucks me into the passenger side of his car, I've regained some control.

"I'm sorry. That was embarrassing." I sniff, wiping my eyes on the soaked and shredded napkins.

"Nah. It's the Zane effect. It's not a successful date unless one of us is crying." His lips twist in a grimace. He tucks a few strands of hair that have fallen in my face behind my ear. "Aw, Lyric. You got a lot of shit bottled up in there. I can feel your pain from here. Please, let me help you."

I huff out a bitter laugh. "I doubt that's possible."

"Buckle up. I owe you dessert, and it just so happens break buddies have an endless supply of ice cream for these situations."

"I think you've stretched the boundaries of this break-buddy thing a bit far."

He swipes a finger across my cheek, removing a soggy bit of napkin, then starts the car. "Fine. Let's call it friends who support each other no matter the situation."

...no matter the situation. That takes care of any of those pesky boundaries nicely. The guy would have made a great lawyer, or used car salesman. *Pay no attention to that loophole clause there, little lady.*

"BACK TO THE scene of the crime?" I ask when a few minutes later we pull into the same supermarket where Zane crashed into my world a week ago.

He offers me his hand out of the car. Not that I need it. But I take it just the same. Tonight the parking lot is just as full as a week ago. Shadows settle between the cars, but unlike the other night, I pay less attention to the dangers that lurk in the dark. It's the first time I've allowed myself to let my guard down.

"We need a cart for ice cream?" I ask, frowning, as he pulls one from the entrance.

"Need a few things, if you don't mind." He winks. "Nothing more relaxing than shopping for food."

"If you say so." I'd rather do anything than grocery shop, but I follow him anyway, wincing at the nasty fluorescent lighting that's probably washing out my pale skin tone to that of a corpse.

At least the view is enjoyable. I trail a few steps behind Zane while The Weather Girls advise me that it's raining men. *Hallelujah!* Zane's dark hair glistens in the harsh lights. I take in the impossibly broad span of his shoulders, the way his dress shirt narrows down, tucking into the slim waist of his dress slacks. Does the man have any fat on him?

And speaking of those dress slacks—

He turns around with his signature smirk and motions me forward with a curl of his finger. My face warms with the heat of a thousand suns, betraying my thoughts. Zane tsks, pulling me alongside him.

I try not to notice the way he rests a possessive hand on my waist, or the aching way I'm responding to his touch. It's only a moment, but the heat from his fingers lingers, leaving my traitorous body wanting more. All signs of my earlier panic attack have vanished, leaving me dazed, subdued, vulnerable to Zane's charms, even with the giant pile of produce he's amassing in the shopping cart. *Yuck.*

I head toward the next aisle, assuming he has enough, but Zane stops me with a finger to his lips and a motion of his eyes.

"Adorable toddler on your four o'clock. Watch." He leans back against a stack of bagged potatoes, arms crossed.

"Is this what you do when you're not accosting women?" I whisper, watching the mother of a toddler negotiate over a box of cookies the tiny boy brought over from the bakery.

He shoots me a scowl at my accusation. "Socializing, not accosting. Grocery stores are the perfect microcosm of life. I find inspiration in watching people."

The mom lifts the little boy and lets him set the cookies into the cart.

I can't stop smiling. At the scene in front of us, and that Zane would be interested in such things. This man has way more layers than I first suspected. "Okay, that was adorable."

He sighs heavily. "My mother would have made me put it back."

My smile vanishes. "Seriously? Don't tell my students, but I'm a sucker for sad eyes and tiny voices. I never would have been able to say no to you."

Zane grins. "I can do the sad eyes, but I'm afraid my tiny voice disappeared around my twelfth birthday."

"And you're not a toddler anymore."

"That too." He nods. "In my mother's defense, she was a young widow with a shitty job and two mouths to feed. It wasn't easy, from what I remember."

A whisper of guilt settles over me. I had the fairy-tale childhood. An only child with two loving parents, there was nothing I wanted for. *Coddled* would be an accurate description. My mom wouldn't have thought twice about buying me a box of cookies.

I shiver as other colder memories slither down my spine. My fairy tale ended five years ago. And a million boxes of cookies couldn't make up for everything that happened after.

In between throwing stuff in his cart, Zane's hand finds its way back to my waist. I should say something—set him straight—but I don't. There's comfort in his touch. A domestic simplicity I never had with my ex-husband. We're just a happy couple walking the grocery aisles. A perfect illusion.

Grayson found me right after my parents died. Alone in the world, except for a few college friends. He easily isolated me from any support I desperately needed. At the time, I had clung to a different illusion. One where Grayson was all I needed. One where he'd take care of me. One that vanished the minute I said *I do.*

I've learned my lesson. And even if the warmth of Zane's hand on my waist feels right, I can't let it sink in. Even if the comfort is addicting. In the past three years I've learned to stand on my own. To trust my judgment. To never let another person become my world.

At some point I find my hand resting on the waistband of his slacks. How it got there, I don't know. *Bad hand.* I should remove it. Not give in to this weird domestic vibe we've got going here. And pretending… well, that's stupid. The guy's a produce freak, his choice of bread makes me gag, and he already let me know he has an aversion to Ho Hos. Even without all my baggage, we'd never work out.

My eyes widen in shock when a box of cocoa crisps lands on top of his whole-wheat pasta.

"Yes! I knew you had a dark side." Pulling away, I point at him, laughing, while Quarterflash warns me to harden my heart.

His brows lower in confusion. "Dark side?"

"This healthy stuff you're throwing in your cart. It was driving me crazy. Finally, something nutritionally barren." I point to the cereal. "I knew you couldn't be that perfect."

"That's Tess's. I tried to get her to eat a healthy breakfast, but it's a war not worth fighting in the end."

My smile melts off my face as disappointment replaces my short-lived triumph.

"Bravo to your sister. Never get between a girl and her vices." I nod, giving him my personal advice and a warning. A happy day requires a happy breakfast. There's no way a bowl of whole-grain nastiness counts as a happy breakfast. But the challenging look in Zane's eyes has me keeping that thought to myself.

He shrugs. "You are what you eat."

"You don't want to know what I am, then." I toss the words

over my shoulder while walking away. The cocky bastard better not try to control my grocery list. "Chocolate is the foundation of my food pyramid. It is the hill I'm willing to die upon. my friend."

Behind my back, I flash him my middle finger.

"Saw that. And this is a family store. Keep your gestures PG, ma'am."

A minute later we stand in front of the freezer case.

"Pick what you want." Zane waves a hand, presenting the ice cream with a Vanna White flourish.

"Ice cream?" I raise both my eyebrows. "Not exactly *healthy*."

He leans against the freezer door, arms crossed. "Psychology of ice cream. Flavors tell a lot about a person."

"O-kay." I clear my throat and turn away, suppressing my laughter. "I'm guessing you'd be Half Baked?"

"Is that a dig?"

"Observation." I turn my attention back to the wall of ice cream, scanning for something worthy of this crazy day. "Think I need some Chocolate Therapy."

"Hmm. Interesting, but not surprising. Everything But The… for me, Cherry Garcia, and Chunky Monkey. Let's go." He tosses the ice cream in the cart and walks away.

"You're eating three pints of ice cream? No wonder you need all that healthy crap," I say as I catch up. His long legs have me practically running to keep up.

"Not crap, and only one is mine. The others are for my mom and sister. There'd be hell to pay if I forgot them."

"Aw, a sweet guy." I pat his arm and then help him unload the cart.

"Yep. That's me."

SOMEHOW I DIDN'T REALIZE when he said *home* he wasn't referring to mine, until we pull into the drive of a fairly large colonial surrounded by other fairly large homes. It's an older neighborhood, but nice. Much nicer than mine, that's for sure. Teaching high school must pay really well.

"Um... Zane?"

"Yes, Lyric?" He shuts off the car and faces me.

"This is your house?"

"I know. Learned the address when *I* was in kindergarten." He grins. Cocky bastard.

"What exactly are you expecting?" My heart hammers in my chest. "I'm not the kind of girl—"

"Lyric, relax. *I'm* not the kind of guy who screws women in front of my mom. I want to show you who I am so maybe you can relax and show me who you really are."

His mom?

I'm filled with apprehension as I follow Zane up the walk to his nice, normal house. To meet his mom. After meeting his aunt. So not a first-date activity. Not that this is even a date.

"Mom, I'm home," Zane calls as he walks through the unlocked, leaded-glass door.

Inside, I pause to take in the elegant staircase that sweeps up to the second floor. Zane takes my hand with his free one—the one that doesn't have six bags looped around it—pulling me through a wide arched doorway that leads into a cozy living room thick with the stagnant smell of illness.

"You're home early." His mom sits on the sofa, a book on her lap. In the warm room, she wears a thick robe that would have left me sweating. *Thin.* She's too thin. Dark eyes dominate a gaunt face. The wrists that stick out of her sleeve are that of a skeleton. Her cheekbones could cut glass. Her skin's paler than mine, almost translucent with a hint of unhealthy gray. A scarf decorated with roses covers her head. *Shit.*

"Mom, this is Lyric. Lyric, my mom, Janet Cox."

Her fingers are bones covered with skin when I shake her hand. "Nice to meet you."

"We brought ice cream. Your favorite, Cherry Garcia." Zane's voice is soft. Gentle. As if his voice could break her if not careful. "And groceries. Lots of fruit."

"Thank you, baby. You two enjoy. I'm heading off to bed. I'll eat later." She smiles. It's Zane's smile.

"Where's Tess?" Zane asks, looking around, his jaw hardening.

"A date," his mom replies.

"Seriously? She was supposed to stay home. What if you needed something?"

"Zane, I told her to go. I'm not an invalid. I can take care of myself." Janet gives him a derisive snort. "Stop acting like I'm going to die any minute."

I look away, trying not to wince, but gosh that's a blunt thing to say. My skin tightens with discomfort. I'm a stranger in their midst, witnessing the poor woman's vulnerability.

"Did you have dinner?" Zane asks, his voice strained, his brows pinched with concern.

"I nibbled." His mom's tone holds an undercurrent of frustration beneath the exhaustion that's evident in her every move. It's like every action she makes is done in slow motion.

Zane shutters his eyes. He takes a deep breath, then flashes the same fake smile I witnessed at the restaurant. "Fine. But Tess will hear about this. It was her night to make dinner."

Janet waves her frail hand as she climbs the first stair with obvious difficulty. "Whatever. Go enjoy your ice cream with your pretty girl. Stop worrying for tonight."

The kitchen's large but in need of an update. Zane sets our ice cream on the chipped island counter, putting the others in the freezer, then quickly puts the rest of the groceries away. Coming back, he hands me a spoon.

The gulf between us widens with my knowledge of his mother's illness. Cancer, I'm guessing. How do you move beyond that into a pleasant conversation? A heaviness lingers, a roadblock that can't be skirted around without awkwardness.

"Zane... I'm so sorry." I look down at the worn Formica, forcing words from my mouth before the air's so poisoned with discomfort we won't know how to move forward. "I don't know what to say."

I glance up, gauging his response.

"Nothing to say. Life sucks sometimes." He scrubs his face with his hand. The smile he gives me is the forced one from earlier. "Then you eat ice cream."

"Share my Therapy?" I offer him a spoonful of chocolate goodness. He accepts, his hand closing over mine to take the bridge to our combined pain.

We share ice cream in silence for a while. Both alone with our thoughts. His hand covers mine on the counter, and I don't have the heart to break the connection. The tension is loosened but not completely gone. Like a specter in the corner, waiting out of sight.

"I came back for her," Zane says, breaking the silence. I look up into eyes filled with so much pain I can feel. "She was diagnosed with breast cancer when I was in high school, but she beat it. Remission for over five years. *Supposedly cured.*" His voice holds a hint of bitterness. "I was working in New York when Tess called me. Mom kept everything quiet. Started chemo and radiation with no help. She's to start another round soon. Not really beating it as quickly this time."

"Your sister's eighteen?" I ignore his last comment. He's got to be in denial. I doubt his mom's beating this at all.

"She's a senior. I guess I can't blame her for wanting to go out. This should be a memorable year for happy things." He exhales a heavy breath, then scoops a spoonful of ice cream into his mouth. "Is it true women eat a ton of this shit when a guy breaks their heart?"

"Tons." I give him a sad laugh, leaning my head on his arm. "You're killing me Zane. I thought my life was bad, but you're making me feel self-indulgent."

He squeezes my fingers. "So, tell me your story."

"You really don't want to know." I look up into his oh-so-curious eyes. "It's not a contest of who has it worse. Let's say there's many shades of misfortune."

He turns my stool to face him, pulling my legs between his. The warmth of his thighs is both comforting and unnerving.

"You owe me this." His smile is small and sad, and breaks my heart even more. "I've bared my soul to a woman I've known for hours. But I feel something here. If you feel it too, trust me."

I blow out a breath and drop my head down. The tension slithers out of the corners of the room, wrapping itself around my chest. "That's the problem; I don't trust anyone."

"So, you lock yourself up in your house with your dog. I can see why a simple night at a restaurant would give you a panic attack. How long have you been having them?"

"Long time. How did you know?"

"Had a few myself. Not in a while, but you don't forget them, that's for damn sure." His eyes are full of sympathy as he runs a finger along my jaw. "Now why don't you trust anyone?"

I lean back in the chair, breaking his contact. I can't confess my past with his hands on me. I shouldn't do this at all. He has issues, I have issues, together we're the perfect disaster. But for some reason I can't resist those damn blue eyes, so sad, as if I hold the key to his happiness in my next words. I don't—far from it—but the words spill out anyway.

"*Ugh.* Because I trusted my ex-husband and he destroyed me."

The pain in his eyes is replaced with wide-eyed shock, and silence. "You were married?" His question is barely a whisper. "When? How long?"

"Sixteen months, eleven days, and three hours too long." I look away. I know what he'll see in my eyes. "Divorced two years. Well, a little over. Could have been longer, but he fought—"

His hand's back on my jaw, turning me to face him. His eyes sharpen, and I can't hide the truth. His reaction is instantaneous.

Shock. Anger. "Jesus. He hurt you?"

I nod, my voice taking a leave of absence.

Zane explodes from his stool and paces across the room, then back. Across and back.

"Fuck," he whispers, raking both hands through his hair as if one isn't sufficient to relieve his emotional turmoil, the anguish clearly marked on his face as he stalks back toward me. The tiny hairs on my arms rise. A small voice in my head assures me he won't hurt me, but I've heard that voice before.

He touches my face and I flinch, my heart hammering loud enough for the entire neighborhood to hear. Zane presses his lips in my hair, and his arms surround me. After a minute I relax into his embrace, into his warmth, accepting his comfort.

"You know when we first met. Last Friday." He pulls back a fraction and smiles down at me. "I couldn't even breathe. You scared the hell out of me. The way you stared me down, challenging me to prove my worth. You look so small and fragile, but inside…" He shakes his head. "You're tough and brave and… shit. I'd never hurt you. That's a promise."

"Gr-Gray had a twisted perception of love." I stumble over my ex-husband's name. Even shortened it's like bitter ash on my tongue. Grayson, Gray—does it even matter? Am I sharing too much? "Unfortunately, I found out too late."

Zane pulls away, and I have to restrain myself from reaching out for more of his embrace. It's addicting, his warmth and his scent and just… him.

He caps up our ice cream while I pull myself together.

"For next time?" He raises his eyebrows in question. I nod. The guy's growing on me for some reason I can't explain. He stashes the ice cream in the freezer, then sits back down.

"So, you moved here after the divorce?"

"In a roundabout way. Gray has money and influence. The restraining order wasn't worth the paper it was printed on. Twenty-four hours after the judge signed it, he was at my door. It took the cops almost a half hour to get there. He had broken the door by then and a few other things as well. It was all a blur by the time the police arrived. I don't remember much."

I rub my eyes, trying to rid myself of the memories I *do* have of that day. I'm sugar coating my past for Zane. From his expression, the brutal truth would be more than he could stomach.

"I spent a week in a women's shelter in LA, then moved to another one a few states away. Then another when Gray's threatening letters started showing up. Sold my car, changed my name, moved again. And then again. The last shelter's director is my school nurse's sister. She helped me move, got me the job. I always questioned why Gray insisted I finish college, but my degree's been my saving grace."

"You're strength is awe-inspiring. They say men are strong, but I think women are much stronger." His thumb rubs unconscious circles on my knee, sending warmth to unexpected places.

A bubbly teen girl comes in moments later, breaking the new kind of tension building inside me. One that's been dormant for many years.

Brown eyes, not blue, give me an appraising look similar to the one his aunt gave me earlier. Her hair's a shade or two lighter than Zane's dark hair, but the knife-straight nose and slight cleft in her chin tell me the two are related.

"Lyric, this is my sister Tess."

"And also his favorite violin player," she singsongs, giggling.

"Maybe," he growls out. "You were supposed to make dinner for Mom. Maybe I'll change my mind on your solo."

"Nooo. You can't. Mom made me go out. You know how she gets." She pouts. "Please, Zane. I need that solo. Caroline is green with envy. Everyone loves it."

"Don't be catty. It's not attractive or mature."

Her "Yes, Dad," is accompanied by an eye roll.

He pulls me off the stool. "I'm taking Lyric home. I'll be back later."

CHAPTER FIVE

LYRIC

*Z*ane shades his eyes as we pull into my well-lit driveway. "More of your security, I see. Blind unsuspecting intruders?"

"It... helps—"

He squeezes my hand, turning in his seat to face me. My mouth dries and my skin prickles with awareness. Without even looking, I can feel the weight of his gaze, and the expectation building as the seconds tick by. *Shit, he's going to kiss me.* It's been a long time since I've been on a date—there's no use denying this is a date— but I remember enough to know this is definitely the part where the kissing happens.

"You changed your name?"

I stifle a groan. I'd have preferred a kiss to all these questions. The man is too nosy. But then I did let him in. Told him just enough to pique his curiosity. Gave him an inch. Should've known he'd want the whole mile. I've no one but myself to blame now.

Sacha's face appears in the front window, then half her body as she jumps on the sill. She's barking to raise the dead at the unknown car in her driveway. There'll be complaints from the neighbors, and the landlord won't be happy with the scratches on his millwork.

Zane's face is half light, half shadow in the glare of the flood lights. Two sides of the moon. Dark and light. Is it a warning?

"Sacha's about to go through the window wondering who's out here." I tip my head toward the house and swallow down my reservations. "Come in. I'll tell you."

He comes around to open my car door, smug smile firmly in place. I shove my finger in his face. "But there will be no sex."

I march past him, ignoring his unhinged laugh as if what I said is somehow funny. Inside, Sacha gives him a thorough sniffing while vibrating with excitement. He scratches behind her ears—her favorite spot. I may as well not even be in the room.

I walk past the love fest and head into my small kitchen. Zane's breaking down my walls faster than a SWAT team. My instincts say to trust him, but my instincts have proven to be flawed. Maybe Sacha's are better? My well trained guard dog is laid out flat at his feet, enjoying the thorough belly rub Zane is providing.

"Want a soda?" I call, staring into the fridge. I turn and yelp. Zane stands less than a foot away, making my heart leap into my throat. *How did he move so fast?*

"Don't do that!"

"Do what?"

"Sneak up on me. You scared me to death. You're too close."

He tips his head, frowning, as if he's trying to figure me out. *Good luck, buddy.*

"Would you rather I leave?"

Would I?

"Yes. No. I—I don't know."

His small, sexy smile triggers the buzz of attraction that's been vibrating under my skin most of the night. A magnetic pull that's way too dangerous inside this tiny eight-hundred-square-foot house.

65

"You don't trust me." His smile fades and his expression turns serious. "I get it. But I'd like to change that. And I can't if we don't spend time together. But that's your decision… Stay or go, I'll do whatever you tell me."

The easy thing would be to send Zane home. Never see him again. Never challenge my fears, never face the possibility of getting hurt again. But Kelly's words ring loud in my ears, making too damn much sense. My ex-husband's been in jail for the last three years, but so have I. Without even realizing it, I've turned this house into my self-imposed isolation cell. But sixteen days ago Grayson Thorpe, former darling of the NHL, was released on parole. And I'm still here. Stuck in this prison. This is my chance at freedom.

I blow out a slow breath and force a smile. The ice-cold sodas have nothing on the frigid ball rolling around in my stomach.

I shove one of the cans toward him like a peace offering. "Just… just give me space, okay?"

"You got it." He drops down on the far side of the sofa, his lips quirking up at the corners. "Is this enough space, or should we move the dog?"

Sacha's curled up on her favorite chair, long legs extended up in the air, doing her best impersonation of a dead bug. A *snoring* dead bug. So much for my guard dog.

I sink down on the edge of the too-squishy sofa, opposite Zane, and pop open my soda. "Leave her."

He sets his can on the table. "You look like you're about to shatter. Relax. I promise not to move."

I give him a slight nod and let out a long, slow exhale, forcing my tense muscles to loosen as I lean back against the sofa.

My attention shifts to his unopened can, and I latch on, desperate to change the subject. "Let me guess, you don't drink soda." I'd rather talk about anything than my anxieties, even his eating habits.

He scrunches his nose. "Not really. Too sweet. Guess I'm one of those weird people who don't like sugar."

I blink slowly, trying to process the concept. A half hour ago we had ice cream. I fed him some of mine. Did he hate it?

"You from New York?"

"No. Why?" *New York?* Where did he come up with that? I certainly don't have a New York accent.

"Soda. They say *soda* in New York. We say *pop* here in the Midwest." He settles back, turning slightly to face me, relaxed, arm draped across the back of the sofa as if he owns the place.

I sip my soda. *Relax.* I can do this. It's not like Zane's going to attack me, for God sake. He's not my ex-husband, nothing like him. But at one time I thought Grayson was nothing like Grayson. And we'd had that crazy attraction, me and him. Just like Zane. At the store. Then the bar. And now? With Sacha snoring on her chair this feels dangerous. Even with his assurances.

Get a grip.

"Pop," I say, pushing my ex-husband out of my head. He's always there. Fucking with me. But no more. "No, I'm not from New York."

"Okay..." Zane raises an eyebrow. Like he's waiting. "So... where are you from?"

Why the questions? I've known this guy all of like two seconds, which is to say not at all. And maybe he's curious. Maybe this is normal dating get-to-know-you questions. And maybe I'm paranoid. Maybe five years ago I'd have spilled every last detail about myself by now, but I'm not that girl anymore. I've too much to lose.

"Lincoln. Nebraska." I force the question out of my voice. Or attempt to. It's not technically a lie. I spent a few months in a women's shelter there.

He tips his head a fraction and his eyes narrow, making my stomach dip. It's an expression of his I'm starting to recognize.

Every time I skirt one of his invasive questions or try to pacify him with some vague answer, I get that squinty-eyed look. It's like his bullshit detector is going off.

"Lincoln?" He crosses his arms over his chest. "Funny, I helped run a music camp in Lincoln one summer on Branched Oak Lake—Acorn Arpeggios. Maybe you heard about it? What with your dad being a musician and all."

I pause a second as if thinking about his question. "'Fraid not."

"Hot as hell. And the food. Don't get me started there. I remember there was this bakery in town, though, the one in Haymarket. Best bagels this side of New York. What was its name?"

I open my mouth to answer, but I've got nothing. I barely stepped foot outside the shelter, much less frequented trendy bakeries. *Dammit.*

I let out a guilty exhale and drop my head. "Zane…"

"Lyric?"

"Okay, I'm not actually from Nebraska."

"Okay… I mean, it's not okay. I don't want you to feel like you have to lie. If you don't want to tell me where you're from, that's okay. Although I'd really like to get to know you somehow."

I let out an anxious breath, taking in my home. The last two years have been nice. Comfortable. Am I ready to give this up? Because trusting Zane could be risking it all. Even my life.

"I don't know you. I don't know if I can trust you. I don't know if you work for Gray. The chances are—"

His mouth drops open and those blue eyes go wide with shock. "You think I work for your ex-husband?"

His words make me realize how crazy I sound. But he doesn't know Grayson. And crazy is always a possibility with my ex-husband. "I don't know. And I can't take the risk."

He leans forward, pulls his wallet out of his back pocket, then hands me his license. "Unless you lied about New York, that's where I've been the last nine years. Until last summer when my sister Laura called about my mom. I dropped everything to come back here. I swear on my mother's health I don't know this guy, Gray, you said?"

I nod and hand him back his New York license with some Brooklyn address and a really crappy picture. If it's a fake, it's a really good fake. But my conscience tells me it's not. I'm overreacting and paranoid, and it's time I stopped letting Grayson ruin my life. "California. I'm from LA."

Zane barks out a laugh, his eyebrows vanishing under the lock of hair that's fallen across his brow. "And you decided to move here? Were you serious about the blizzard thing?"

His shocked expression and his tone has me laughing.

"Maybe. Yeah." Zane's look is skeptical. His eyes narrow as I explain the connection between Nebraska and here. "Where else would you hide a SoCal girl?"

"SoCal?"

"Southern California. I grew up in WeHo, West Hollywood, if you want specifics."

Zane whistles, his eyebrows rising again. "You're out of my league, growing up with movie stars."

I snort, an unladylike sound my mother would have scolded me for if she ever heard it. But in the past few years there've been many things she would've scolded me for. If only...

Shoving those memories back where they belong, I sweep my hand to the side with a flourish, indicating my humble surroundings. Humble is being generous, to be honest. From the dull beige walls and scarred oak floors to the equally dull thrift-store furniture I've filled the place with, nothing about this home is remarkable, or lavish.

"Look around you, Zane. Do I look like I rubbed elbows with the Hollywood elite? My parents were regular folks." I let out a quiet laugh. "You don't believe me?"

He shrugs, his face blank, giving nothing away. "Do you miss it?"

My lips twist into a grimace before I can stop them. But I deserve his skepticism. Why should I be believed? "Yeah. I miss the sun and the heat. I miss Leo's tacos and In-N-Out Burgers. I even miss the Santa Anas, the May Grays, and the June Glooms. But I can't risk it. I have to make it as hard as possible for Gray to find me. I've a new life and I'm making the best of it."

"You lost your tan and your name, Cali girl," he whispers.

I restrain the cringe that threatens at that label, but by the way Zane's eyes sharpen, obviously not enough.

"What?"

"Nobody says *Cali* in California. It's annoying."

He laughs.

I set my soda on the table and stare. "What?"

"Well, just my opinion, but, if you're trying to slip under the radar, you shouldn't be annoyed by something only a *Cali girl* would be annoyed with."

"Well—"

His smirk is back as he pulls me off the sofa. "Say it."

"What? No." I shake my head, trying to pull away, laughing. *God, he's nuts.* But at least he believes me. For some reason I can't put my finger on why it's important that he believes me.

"Come on…" He grins and starts to sing NoClue's "Cali Girl."

I let out a quiet groan. "Don't. Really, dude."

Zane laughs again, then continues on with the song to spite me. He's not bad, but his ego doesn't need me to tell him that. He dances over to me, putting his hands on my shoulders. "We're getting off track. Say it."

"No."

"Cali girl. I'm gonna keep saying it until you do, Cali girl."

I bite my lips to hide my smile, because… Jesus, this guy.

"You're my Cali girl," he sings, pulling me against him as his hips move to the beat in his head. I close my eyes. *I'm not enjoying this.*

I laugh, unable to fight it any longer. It's been so long I almost don't recognize the light sensation in my chest for what it is. Joy. Happiness.

He spins me out and back, leaving me breathless and dizzy, clinging to him for balance. I'm a shitty dancer—the worst—but I don't care. And by Zane's wide smile, he doesn't either. There must be some kind of magic in the circle of his arms 'cause I haven't stumbled once. His hands, his hips. Those eyes. *Serious magic.* And I'm molten, following his every move to the beat of the song he's singing. Just for me.

"Be mine, Cali girl," he whispers in my ear, his hands pulling me against the unmistakable hardness of his desire. "Sing with me."

Something shifts and the magic vanishes. In its place panic slithers up my spine like icy fingers. My mouth dries.

"I'm not yours," I whisper on paper dry lips, taking a step back. Then another.

"Lyric." He reaches out, his smile collapsing.

I clear my throat and take a further step back, wrapping my arms around my waist. All the air's been sucked from the room and my heart's hammering its way through my ribs. It's been too long since I've been touched in a way I've enjoyed, and my stomach twists with painful memories.

"I can't, Zane."

"Shh. It's okay. Trust me, please."

Turning me, he pulls me back down on the sofa next to him. Close. The heat of his body radiates into mine across the inch of upholstery separating us. So much for that vast arm's length of personal space.

I slide away a fraction. "Zane, I can't do this."

Calloused fingers brush against mine as he folds my hand in his much larger one, causing sparks to travel up my arm. Or maybe it's his proximity. Everything about Zane seemed more manageable—safer—a few minutes ago. Before he touched me.

"Can't do what? Sit here and talk with a friend? That's all I'm asking for."

"Friends? Be honest, Zane. No more of this break-buddy bullshit."

"I'll be honest if you will."

I swallow down my anxiety. There's only so much honesty I can give him, but I nod anyway.

"I get that your ex was an asshole and he hurt you. But I'm not him, Lyric. It kills me to even think..." He squeezes his eyes shut and shakes his head. "I might fuck up—say stupid things, do stupid shit—but I've never hit a woman. Never will. And I know you don't know that yet. And I know it's going to take time for you to trust me. But if you give me a chance. I'm so damn attracted to you... and I think you're just as attracted to me. Tell me if I'm wrong, but I don't think this boring, old-lady-hermit lifestyle makes you happy."

He gestures around the room and I shake my head unable to say the words that gut me. *No, I'm not happy.* Happy is a luxury I can't afford. I'll exchange happiness for safety any day.

"Honestly, it's been so long I don't even remember what happy feels like." Until now.

"Let me help you remember. I promise we'll take this slow—as slow as you need—just give us a chance, okay?"

Grayson would gut me if he could see the two of us on the couch, my hand in Zane's, our bodies almost touching. Somehow that thought spurs me on, and I nod. He presses his soft lips against my knuckles, then shifts over, giving me space.

"Tell me more about California. I can't imagine growing up without snow or brutally cold winters. Have you been tempted to go back?"

"Zane..." I shake my head. The man is too nosy for his own good. "My secrets keep both of us safe."

"Secrets keep no one safe, Lyric. It's an illusion." He drapes his arm over the back cushion, as if settling in for the night, stretching his long legs off the couch at an angle in front of him. "But right now we're getting to know one another. You tell me about yourself, and I tell you about me. If you don't want to talk about your home state, tell me something else. Right now I got..." He waves his hand in front of him. "Nothing."

"Nothing..." I repeat, narrowing my eyes at him. I've told him plenty today. Tons more than I've told Grace. But I'm being paranoid. Crazy. The only thing I have to fear from Zane is his charm. "Whatever you say. I've been back once. To get my license renewed. That's it."

"Why don't you get a Minnesota license?"

"Can't risk it. No public records. Gray can afford the best private detectives if he chooses. They could be searching for m-me." My voice breaks with the thought.

"You're safe here."

I shake my head hard. "I have to keep up the illusion that I'm still in California. My lawyer set everything up. The tiny SRO address in San Francisco. A bank account in my real name that pays the rent and utilities. My license with the same address. If Gray looks too hard it probably won't fool him, but... And now I've told you way too much."

"You think he'd torture me for this information?" Zane's voice is all skeptical, but my expression isn't. "Or do you think he'd beat the shit out of me for just being here?"

He inches closer, his thigh brushing against mine, his hand sliding down from the back of the sofa, resting lightly against my shoulder. The man is smooth, I'll give him that much. I should pull away, fight this, but his warm comfort is addictive even if his suggestion sends a chill through my bones.

"He'd kill us." I choke on the three little words that can't possibly describe the living nightmare that is my ex-husband, or what he's capable of.

He presses his lips into my hair. "You underestimate me. I won't let anything happen to you. That's a promise, you hear?"

Zane Brody, seducer and protector. And complete idiot. He should run now. I should push him away. Save him from what's coming. Because I know in my heart Grayson will eventually come. And both me and Zane will be dead. It would be selfish not to at least warn him. To tell him everything. Let him make his own choice. But a part of me doesn't want to face Grayson alone. And maybe I have time—at least a little—to remember what normal life is like. To drop my defenses and be happy, if only for a little while.

"You were gonna tell me about your name. Is your first name really Lyric?"

I breathe out a quiet laugh. I'm a lousy person to play twenty questions with. At some point Zane will give up. At least I hope so. "You really don't want to know. Honestly, I don't even know all the details. I got to the third women's shelter and there was a package from my lawyer waiting for me. I was Lyric James from that point on."

"Sounds shady."

"I trust my lawyer. She's kept me alive so far."

He strokes my arm with his fingers, raising goosebumps on my skin. "I'm really happy about that. And your real name? I guess I don't get that."

"Sorry. That person is long gone." Zane has broken down more of my defenses in one day than I thought possible, but this wall holds firm. Nothing on Earth would get me to say that name again.

"Someday I hope you can trust me enough to introduce me to that person. I bet she was pretty amazing." He pauses for a second. "What are your plans this summer?"

I fold pleats into the fabric of my skirt while remembering the crazy girl who used to occupy this body. The one who never turned down a dare and trusted everyone. She's the ghost that I grieve every now and then.

I bring up Kelly's suggestion about working at the battered

women's shelter this summer. It's not ideal. Lyric James is a cash-strapped kindergarten teacher who could use a summer job. But volunteering at the shelter where I spent my last month will give me something to fill my time, if not my wallet.

"I could probably find something for you to do."

I roll my eyes and let out a quiet snort. "I'll bet."

"Of course I'd expect you to shield me from my groupies. What is a girlfriend for if not to protect her man's virtue?"

I suck in a quick breath and shoot him a sharp look. Did I miss something? When did I become the girlfriend? I don't remember agreeing to that.

"Relax, Lyric. I was thinking piano lessons. Your Steinway will appreciate it."

His fingers dance a soft glissando across my shoulders.

"Piano lessons? Have you forgotten you decided I need to save money for a car?"

"Free lessons, right here." He squeezes my shoulder.

"What else can you play?" I ask, sidestepping the issue of piano lessons.

"Let's see… started with piano when I was five. The violin at seven. By twelve I wanted to be cool, so I begged for a guitar for Christmas. After that, the rest came easy. Pretty much anything with strings I can play."

"Impressive. Just string instruments, though?" I ask, and before I can think clearly, I add, "You could probably pull off the tuba and still look sexy."

Zane's laugh vibrates through my bones. "I'll pass. I'm not into horns or woodwinds. I prefer to use my mouth for better things."

My pulse accelerates, my skin tingles with awareness. Zane's words are like a match to a flame. Warmth pools in long-forgotten places as my imagination offers a detailed list of the many uses of his mouth.

His low chuckle tickles the shell of my ear. "Lyric, Lyric,

Lyric. Such a dirty mind. Did you forget my amazing vocal talents so quickly?"

"Of course not. O humble mistral." I reel in my hair-trigger libido.

His fingers thread with mine, and my focus shifts to the swirls of color running up his arm. There's a few other designs, some faded, some crisp, as if each one was added over time.

"Do these have meanings?"

"Not really. Some were just for the hell of it. Woke up after an interesting night, not sure how it got there." He chuckles. "My college roommate, Evan, and I got in all sorts of trouble."

"His influence or yours?" I turn his arm, inspecting the swarm of ravens that travel from just above his wrist to the back of his hand. A nice hand otherwise. Large, but not out of proportion, with long, tapered fingers and neat square nails.

I rub my finger over the faint white scar that bisects a knuckle. There's similar marks on his other knuckles, but before I get a chance to ask about them he pulls his arm back, then offers me his left one for my perusal.

"Both, I suppose." His chuckle hints at dark secrets and a life before me. One filled with loose women and violent fistfights?

"I can only imagine…" My thumb rubs over a broken and bleeding heart. "And you inked your exploits on your body? From the looks of it, you two lived on the dark side of campus. Or are the happier times chronicled where I can't see them?"

"That was a long time ago."

"Where is he now? This wild roommate of yours."

"Brussels, I think. Last I heard he'd landed an assistant director position in the symphony there."

My hand stills over his warm skin. Woven in among the dark images is a lot of music. Crammed in and hidden at times, the most prominent is a large grand staff of piano music that spirals around his arm like ivy. I trace it back to the beginning where a bold treble clef intertwines artfully with the bass clef, exploding into droplets of blood—the only color on his body. At least, from what I've seen.

It's a complicated piece, and nothing I recognize. C-sharp, in five-four time. Too late I realize I said the last bit out loud.

His head tips in contemplation. "Maybe I need to reassess your lesson plan."

I bolt to my feet, my eyes widening a fraction as *I* reassess my opinion of Zane Brody as well. His music the other night was good—better than I had expected for a local bar band. But the music inked on his skin hints at so much more. *Who is this guy?*

"I told you, I haven't played in years," I call out from the kitchen, then rest my spinning head on the solid counter.

"No, you said you didn't play."

I pull a fresh soda from the fridge and grab a glass of ice for Zane, then one for myself. Then snag the small and slightly dusty bottle of spiced rum from the back of my cabinet, peeling the *For Emergencies Only* post-it, written in Kelly's bold script off the label. Whether she'd consider this an emergency is debatable. But I certainly do.

Zane chuckles when I drop the glass of ice and bottle of rum in front of him. "Nice. I knew I liked you."

He pours a generous slug of rum in his glass, then tops it with a splash of cola. *Shouldn't it be the other way around?*

"Yeah, whatever. Take it easy." I snag the bottle of rum out of his hands. "Remember you do have to drive home."

He gives me a small smile and a wink. "Not to worry. I'm a professional."

Driver or drinker? I keep that thought to myself as I throw a splash of rum in my glass and return the bottle to the kitchen before my impulsive decision bites me in the ass.

His lips curve into that signature smirk as I sink down on the opposite side of the sofa, once again putting a healthy distance between us. "You obviously know your rum better than your tequilas."

"Not really. It was a housewarming gift. You'll have to thank the school nurse if it's any good." I take a sip from my glass and wince.

Zane laughs. "Not much of a drinker, are you?"

I take another eye-watering swallow from my glass and shake my head. "Not really. I like wine on occasion, but more than one glass and I'm out."

Zane stares into his half-empty glass for a second, then sets it on the table. "Probably best. This stuff will kill you. Eventually."

I drop my glass next to his. "For once, something we can agree on."

Our eyes connect, sending a dangerous thrill swirling around my stomach for the hundredth time tonight. There's something about Zane Brody. Something I can't put my finger on. Something more than his sharp good looks. More than those piercing blue eyes, chiseled jaw, and perfect knife-edge nose. Or maybe not so perfect.

He shifts closer and I see it. The soft glow of the table lamp reveals the tiny imperfection. More of a shadow than a bump. Invisible unless...

My fingers skate over the flaw. "How did you break your nose?"

He pulls my hand away, kissing my fingers before dropping them. His eyes darken and his laugh is sharp and brittle.

"Line drive, center field. And the final straw of my tortured relationship with sports in general." His long, slow exhale hints at more secrets better left uncovered. At what point will our combined secrets bury us?

The room falls quiet for a bit, save the occasional passing car out front and Sacha's quiet whimpers as she chases rabbits in her sleep. Normally I hate the quiet. The odd creaks and groans of this old house make me jumpy. But not tonight. Not with Zane here.

"Don't you normally play on Fridays?"

"Usually," Zane breathes out the word on a slow exhale. "Dillon canceled and we couldn't find another bass at such short notice. If he wasn't Dave's brother…" He pauses a second, taking a slow inhale. "Wally's not happy. I think even Dave's patience is starting to wear thin. Dil's taken the whole sex, drugs, and rock-and-roll shit too far."

"And you have your priorities straight? No sex, drugs, and rock and roll for Zane Brody?" I stifle a yawn that threatens to dislocate my jaw.

"I moved back home last July to take care of my mom, Tess, and Laura. They're my priorities. I'm so far down on the list I barely register. So no on the sex. A definite no on the drugs. And as for music, it makes me money. Teaching music, playing music. But Heartattack is a high school garage band that's gone on far past its expiration date. It was never meant to be my career, but don't tell Dave that. Break his heart."

Record straight, I scoot closer, nestling into the warmth of Zane's side. Blame it on the rum or two years of solitude or even the wind rattling the drafty windows, but maybe for tonight I can let my guard down a little.

CHAPTER SIX

LYRIC

*B*rilliant sun filters in through a wide gap in my bedroom's curtains, hitting me dead across my eyes. Sacha must have nosed the damn things open again in her need to watch the squirrels in the backyard. Normally I remember to close them at night but... *Ugh.*

Head pounding, vision fuzzy, I fight off the mummified wrappings of my cotton sheets and heavy blanket. Damp fabric clings to my chest. My legs are tangled in the equally moist cotton of my... skirt? I slept in my dress? And by the nasty film coating my tongue I'm guessing I didn't brush my teeth before going to bed either. *Gross.*

All because I let Zane Brody waltz into my house. And why did I bring out that damn rum? Not one of my more brilliant ideas, that's for sure. The second drink had been an epic mistake, along with letting Zane pour. At least I'm still in my clothes—thank God. What time did he leave last night? Way past my boring, old-lady-hermit bedtime, my tired body tells me. My throbbing head and unhappy stomach agree. No more rum. *Ever.*

Sacha licks my hand, then rolls over and is snoring in seconds. The clock says it's too damn early on a Saturday to be awake. I'd give anything to go back to sleep, but once I wrestle with my restricting clothes I'm wide awake.

Shower. My skin crawls with sweat, and I sigh in relief as the moisture evaporates off my body once I shuck my clothes. I crack open the tiny window in the bathroom and turn on the water to full blast. The scorching hot water clears my head some, but a morning person I am not.

My stomach rumbles its discontent and my brain begs for coffee. I give my hair a quick towel dry, then finger comb the semi-damp strands into order. My silky robe slides deliciously over my still moist skin while I debate breakfast options. Cocoa crisp cereal or toast slathered with a thick layer of Nutella? Milk with my carbs or just straight carbs?

My still queasy stomach suggests holding the milk.

I stop short at the half-naked figure fumbling around my dim kitchen. Dark hair, broad shoulders, and tattoos. The smell of coffee hits me and the missing pieces of my night start clicking together. Unless intruders make coffee before they take off with your valuables, Zane never left.

Sacha's nails click on the tile floor as she strolls past me into the kitchen, nudging her head between Zane and the counter.

He chuckles, giving her a scratch behind the ears, then turns. "Hey."

I flip on the light and his eyes dart from my bare feet to my makeup-free face, widening a fraction somewhere below my shoulders. I look down and cross my arms over my chest. My damp robe leaves little to the imagination. Go back and put clothes on, or pretend my nipples aren't flashing the man in front of me? They approve most heartily of shirtless Zane. From the thick ridge in his day-old dress slacks, I can tell he's approving of my approval. *To hell with it.* I stand my ground, ignoring the burning attraction that's pulling me in his direction.

"Funny. Somehow I don't remember you *not* leaving." I busy myself with feeding Sacha—the traitor. Could she have warned me in some way? Even Lassie let Timmy know when trouble was brewing. My Lassie is leaning against Zane's leg, looking up at him with the adoration usually reserved for me.

"You really are gone when you sleep." Zane scratches her head while doctoring up his coffee with the milk from the fridge. He turns away and I give my loyal friend a scathing look. "I didn't have the heart to wake you, and I wasn't about to leave without locking up."

"Next time, wake me," I snap, opening the back door to let Sacha out, ending their love fest.

"Next time... maybe we should get your dog her own bed. She doesn't appreciate me tucking you in."

I suck in a quick lungfull of crisp morning air along with his cocky attitude. Only a guy could pull off sleeping on a sofa that's a good eight inches too short for him, bedhead, and morning breath, and still be sexy. I can't blame Sacha, it's those goddamn eyes.

I grab the doorframe to steady myself. "Maybe you should take a shower?"

"That an invitation?" And there's that smirk. Can't forget that.

"For one." I point toward my bedroom. "Go. I'll make breakfast. That is, if you eat eggs."

"I'll eat anything you offer me." He licks his bottom lip and raises an eyebrow, making me wish for clothes, underwear, a blindfold? Minutes in his presence and my thighs are slick.

"Go!" I turn away to preserve my sanity.

I let Sacha in and search for ingredients the vegetarian health nut would want in his omelet, trying not to think too hard on his parting words.

Clothes. While he showers, I can slip into my closet and dress. Two naked people in this house spell danger. Sacha bolts past me into the bedroom, jumping on the bed.

"Don't worry, baby, he won't be kicking you off. Buying you a bed, so cocky, right?" I mutter to Sacha while pulling underthings out of my drawer.

Sacha jumps down and, before I can stop her, noses open the bathroom door and wanders in. The volume of the water splashing against the shower walls increases without the barrier of the door.

"Shit!" I whisper yell, my eyes going wide as I take in the steam-filled room where Zane is showering. Naked and wet. Goddamn me for not fixing that latch. "No, Sacha. Come here, baby."

I creep to the edge of the door and kneel, peeking around the corner.

"Sacha, come," I whisper, keeping my eyes glued to my dog. "Please."

She tips her head, blinks twice, circles the bathroom rug, then lies down with a groan.

"No, no, no." I squeeze my eyes shut for a second then, look up, you know, just to make sure Zane hasn't noticed me kneeling in the doorway like some creeper.

My eyes widen and my mouth gapes open. *Holy hell*, he's gorgeous. If I didn't look like a creeper before, I'm pretty sure I do now. Not that he's looking. Thank God.

I should stop. I most definitely should. Crawl away right now. But I'm frozen to the floor. Trying to take all of him in, but it's impossible.

His profile reveals the music that spirals around his muscular arms, drapes over his broad shoulders, and continues along his back like a mantle. There's something large beneath, centered on his back. With the way he's standing and the water droplets on the clear glass enclosure, it's impossible to tell what it is.

"Fuck," he groans, turning my way. I jerk back, but his eyes are closed tight. The whole scene comes into focus and—*oh my God*. My breath catches and my pulse rockets. I scoot back behind the doorway, self-consciousness warring with curiosity. Out of his line of sight, I peek around the corner.

Because, holy shit. I. Can't. Stop.

He stretches his left arm above his head, bracing himself against the tile while his right hand is gripped tight around what looks to be an intimidatingly large cock.

"Holy hell..." I squint in an attempt to focus between the water droplets on the glass. Flashes of hard flesh appear between the rhythm of his strokes. Is that... color? *No way.*

I slip back behind the doorway for a second to catch my breath. Who the hell gets a tattoo there? And why? And did it hurt? *Of course it hurt.*

His tricep bulges and flexes as he pumps. My heart thunders loud in my ears, and my skin heats, tingling with desire, while my brain wrestles with the logistics.

What would make someone consider a tattoo there? And what kind of artist would do it?

The questions keep flooding my brain. Each one more demanding than the next. I mean, besides the logistics, why would you get a tattoo there? And how many women has he shown it to?

His glutes tense and the dimple in his hip pulses with the rhythm of his thrusts. I should walk away, give him the privacy he deserves. But he's in my bathroom. It's like my own personal porn channel.

You should help him.

Whoa. No thank you.

I shove that ridiculous thought aside, ignoring the almost painful throb in my core. Sure, I'm slick with desire. Who wouldn't be? Zane Brody is sexy as hell. But just the thought of joining him sends my heart into palpitations. The man is a spectator sport, not an interactive two-player game. At least not for me.

A hoarse cry breaks me out of my inner argument. He comes, spilling himself onto the tile floor.

A quiet moan slips from my lips. Three years without sex has taken its toll. My body's wound so tight, one touch and I'll follow him. But I'm jolted back to the reality of where I am. A slight turn of his head and he'll spot me. I scoot back behind the doorway, then stand and run out into the hall.

"Good luck looking him in the eye now," I whisper to myself, glancing down at my semi-sheer robe. So much for getting dressed. No way I'm going back in there.

I head back to the kitchen, slowly slice an onion so as not to remove a finger. Could lose a lot more than my digits if I'm not careful around Zane Brody.

"Lyric!" Zane shouts, making me jump. "Can you grab your dog?"

I squeeze my eyes shut and mumble a curse. Sacha. My little troublemaker. Totally forgot about her.

I rush through the bedroom doorway as Sacha's barks get louder and more excited. Palms moist and heart racing, I contemplate the half-open bathroom door. Like iron filings to a magnet, I'm helplessly drawn to the man on the other side. The hold on my dangerous attraction to Zane is tenuous at best. Even that first day in the grocery store, there was something. Like a high-tension wire running between us. I should have run out of the bar the minute I saw him, but now it's too late. This crazy train has left the station. There's no turning back.

"Sacha, you bad girl." My voice rises above the noise. "Sorry the latch is broken. I keep meaning to fix it, but with just me…"

"Yeah, well. Little Miss Sunshine wants to help me dry off and—"

"Are you decent?" My hand trembles on the doorknob, waiting for an answer. But all I hear is Sacha.

I push the door all the way open and gasp, my face warming. "Holy hell. Out Sacha. Now."

Zane leans casually against the tile on the other side of the shower door, not at all in danger. His one large hand is doing a piss-poor job of covering what needs to be covered while the other scratches at his chin.

Shielding my eyes with my hand, I pull Sacha up by her collar and guide her away from her spot in front of the shower. "So much for decent."

"Towel was on the other side of her," he explains with a laugh. "And let's just say she's inquisitive and assertive."

I toss a towel over the shower door and nudge Sacha the rest of the way out of the room with both hands before she changes her mind.

"Great. Your important bits are safe now, could you please cover them?"

The irony of the situation isn't lost on me. Not five minutes ago I had been more than happy to watch those important bits in action, but now that Zane's aware of my presence I'm not so bold.

"As a divorced woman, I'd assume I've got nothing you've never seen before," he says, close behind me.

I've never seen a penis tattoo. I choke back the words that would send this conversation beyond my comfort zone. Not that we haven't raced past there already.

"Get dressed." I turn to face him. Which is a mistake. Even with a towel wrapped around his hips, there's a lot of skin on display. And a fair amount of ink. Which reminds me...

My face goes from warm to molten hot. Etched behind my eyelids, a vision of his face contorted in pleasure plays on a reel, his voice rasping out my name.

"I'm not going to touch you. Unless you want me to." When I open my eyes, his hands are raised in the universal language of surrender. "That frightened look you give me just about kills me."

I nod, looking down at the floor between us. Even his damn feet are sexy. "I'm sorry."

"Don't be. It's not your fault."

"You barely know me, Zane." Even from a couple of feet away, the heat of his damp skin is distracting. His words, comforting. I could easily fall under his spell. But I've been here before, and I'm all too familiar with the dangers of a sweet-tongued stranger.

"I want to, though."

I give him a sad smile while shaking my head. "That makes two of us."

When I first moved here, I thought it would be easy to slip into a new name and a new life. But it's not. I'm like an incomplete puzzle, and someone's mixed up the rest of my pieces with another puzzle. No matter how hard I try, I can't seemed to make a complete picture.

"Maybe we can figure that out together. One small step at a time. Pizza and faith?"

"Huh?"

"What you wrote on Sarapelli's windowsill. Pizza and faith. Not a bad start."

"Oh." My brows pinch together as I try to figure Zane Brody out. The man has women lining up to catch his attention. "Why me? You could have your pick of any one of those women at the bar, and they'd probably be a lot less work."

"I've never been afraid of hard work. Something tells me you'd be worth it."

He captures my hand and places it against his chest. The steady thump-thump of his heart beats against my fingertips. "Feel that? It's saying Ly-ric, Ly-ric."

The absurdity of his words makes me laugh until I'm almost breathless.

His lips curve into a smile. "What?"

"You're certifiable."

"Probably. I'm also hungry. How about I go back into the bathroom and get dressed, and you're gonna do the same. 'Cause if I have to watch you running around in this…" He rubs the lapel of my thin robe between his thumb and fingers. His breath rushes out and his eyes meet mine, a sliver of blue swallowed in a sea of black. "I promised not to touch you, but Jesus, Lyric, I'm no saint."

I nod, breathing in his sweet, mint-infused breath. The poor man is probably choking on my disgusting morning breath.

My eyes widen and I take another sniff of his clean, minty breath. "Did you use my toothbrush?"

He gives me a cheesy grin showing all his perfectly white, perfectly straight teeth, then turns and closes the bathroom door behind him.

"Asshole," I yell, then quickly close the bedroom door on Sacha's inquisitive face. *Little troublemaker.* I grab my bra and panties out of my drawer and close myself in the closet, knees still shaking, skin tingling, my stupid, senseless vagina aching for so much more of the cocky asshole that's invaded my quiet life.

I'm in so fucking deep. *Too deep. Or maybe not deep enough?* I don't know.

My mind is a whirl of thoughts and questions all fighting for attention, but one stupid crazy question stands out above the rest.

What kind of man gets a tattoo on his dick?

ZANE'S BACK SUNDAY AFTERNOON. We made a deal Saturday morning. I would go with him to Mill City, if he helps me with the school project I would have been doing last night.

It's not a date. I'm not wearing date clothes. In fact, I'm dressed to un-impress today. A top stained from a dry-erase marker accident I had a couple of months ago and a pair of ratty jeans that might be sporting an extra tear from Sacha's exuberance during her bath today. My hair's pulled up, and the only thing on my face is moisturizer.

"I'm ready to help," Zane says as I open the door. "Miss James. Sacha…" Once again, his voice pitches up an octave, sending my dog into an excited frenzy. She takes off, but a second later she's back showing Zane her favorite toy.

"Is that for me?" He tries to grab it, but she spins around at the last second. Zane lunges. She spins again, giving him a playful bark. Classic keep-away game. Which is about to get out of hand.

"Okay, you two." I clap my hands. "Work now. Play later."

"You heard Mom." Zane offers Sacha a pout, tosses her her toy, then turns his attention toward me, rubbing his hands together. "So what are we doing? Coloring? Stringing beads? Painting?"

I laugh because he's a tiny bit ridiculous in a cute way. "Nothing that creative. We're cutting paper."

"Okay." There's a notable lack of excitement in his voice. Not that I blame him. Ninety percent of my project prep involves scissors. "Don't your kids know how to do that?"

"Of course. But if I want to teach them something besides scissor skills, I have to do some of it at home," I explain while heading into my kitchen.

On my little table I've set out two sky-high stacks of white construction paper, along with scissors and baggies.

"We're doing a unit on color next week. Mother's Day's coming up, so I thought they could make cards with rainbows and flowers." I hand him my sample card. "The flowers they can color whatever they want, but the bands of the rainbow are marked with the correct color."

"Cute."

"Say that when we're done cutting everything out. Six petals for each flower, three flowers on each card. Then six bands for each rainbow. Times fifty-two kids, plus a few extra for emergencies."

"I haven't mastered double-digit multiplication yet," Zane says.

"Neither have I. Let's just say a lot of cutting." I grimace. "Want something to drink?"

"Water's fine."

I grab two glasses from the cabinet, fill them with ice and tap water, and head back to the table. Zane's started cutting already, but I see an immediate problem.

"Hang on. I think I have a bigger pair of scissors in the kitchen."

"You don't think I can work with these?" He holds up the pair of kindergarten-child-sized scissors in his man-sized hands.

"Can you?"

"I may have to." He opens and closes the scissors a few times. "I think they're stuck."

"Nooo. Seriously?"

We both laugh as he shakes his hand and makes an *Edward Scissorhands* joke. A minute later his index finger's free, but his thumb is another story.

"Zane, you're not supposed to put your whole thumb in there."

"I hadn't intended to. It just sorta slipped. This might be a problem tomorrow." He grins. "Think the kids would mind if I conducted with these things dangling off my hand?"

I laugh again. "I think you might have other things to worry about besides conducting."

He tugs at the scissors, wincing. "Probably."

"Hang on. Stop before you hurt yourself." Last thing I need is to maim Heartattack's rhythm guitarist. His female fans were glaring at me enough last night for just walking in with him.

I run into the kitchen and grab the dish soap. "My mother got stung by a bee on her ring finger once," I call out, trying not to let him hear the panic in my voice. "Swelled up and her wedding band wouldn't come off. I remember she slicked up her finger with dish soap."

"Sounds reasonable."

I drizzle a fair amount of soap on his knobby knuckle that seems to be the sticking point and then wrap my hand around the digit, smearing the goop up and down.

"I—I think I can handle that," Zane says, his voice hoarse, his eyes squeezed tight. For one stupid, naïve moment I fear I'm hurting him. Then it dawns on me what the hell I'm doing, and...

Oh my God...

I step back, my face burning. The reel of him in my shower yesterday runs though the back of my mind. "I'll... um... get you a towel. To clean up. The soap, that is."

Then I'm going to find the nearest hole, crawl in, and die.

CHAPTER SEVEN

LYRIC

Grace sends me a brilliant smile as she approaches me on the playground Monday morning. I send her back a hard stare that says this isn't the place to discuss my personal life—at least in my opinion.

Undeterred, she reaches me, giving me a big hug. "I'm so happy for you."

"Why?" I shove my chilled fingers into my coat pockets, ignoring my friend's smug look. Our breaths fog the crisp morning air that seems to sink right through the layers of my clothes. It's the beginning of May, but it feels more like March. It's days like this I miss California.

"Well, first of all... Zane." She almost squeals his name. "I've never seen him smile so much."

I turn my attention to the children swarming the playground —like I'm supposed to, like I'm getting paid to do—and not my best friend's minute description of my return to Mill City Saturday night, this time at Zane's side.

"You two are so cute together."

"We're not together. We're just friends," I correct. Grace is one of those happy people that thinks it's her job to make everyone else just as happy. Which is great and all, but at the moment she's got her sights set on making me and Zane happy *together*.

"If you say so." She pauses to call out to one of her students who is going way too high on the swings. We've got one month until the end of school, and besides a few skinned knees and bruises, our track record for playground injuries is perfect. "It was nice to have you there Saturday night. I mean, don't get me wrong, I enjoy watching the band, but it gets a little awkward sitting at the big table by myself."

I sling an arm around her shoulder—a bit of a feat considering I'm five-three and she's five-eight. "Don't worry. As long as Zane wants me there, I'll be there."

Grace's grin is back. "I think you're going to be there a lot."

I turn away and roll my eyes. Then shout out a warning as I watch Kira Darvitz dart in front of the swings, missing the gauntlet of flying feet by inches.

"Kira," I call out, then meet her halfway in order to give her a lecture on being aware of her surroundings for the hundredth time this year.

"Can they just wait until school's out to do the daredevil stuff?" I mutter when I finally return to my spot next to Grace. Of course the third kindergarten teacher, Mrs. McMurray, is on her phone.

"Zane wants me to go to his students' concert." The grin on Grace's face makes me wish I could take my words back. "Calm yourself. I'll be sitting in the audience with his mother and his older sister and her family."

"Nice."

Not so nice. There's something about his mother that, I don't know. Maybe it's all in my head. Or maybe it's her illness. She just seems cold.

"I haven't decided."

"What's there to decide? Go, have fun."

"I don't want to give the wrong impression. I mean, this is—"

My phone bings a text. The screen shows a selfie Zane attached to his number at some point over the weekend. It's me and him and Sacha in the middle, all of us crammed together on the couch. Just as he took the photo, Sacha licked Zane's face. His goofy, wide-eyed expression is priceless.

When he added this picture to my phone is a mystery—as much a mystery as my attraction to him. The guy I met in the grocery store a week ago had been such a cocky asshole, but the more I get to know him the more I see the silly, shameless yet vulnerable guy underneath all that bluster. And I like that Zane Brody. Maybe too much.

ZANE: *I'm so fucking bored. It can't be only 10:40. I may die. Seriously.*

Another text appears under the first, dinging its arrival.

ZANE: *Send me a picture, a joke, something. I may not make it through the next 4 hours. My life is in your hands, Angel.*

"Speak of the devil." I flash my screen at my curious friend.

She grins. "Aww, you guys are adorable. *Angel?*"

I scoff, ignoring the nickname Zane gave me that first night coming out of my friend's mouth. "He's not adorable. He's bossy. He showed up this morning as I'm about to leave for school, insisting on driving me." Well, maybe not insisting. But what was I going to do, walk past him?

"So?" She frowns like she doesn't understand.

"So, I like the exercise," I offer as a lame excuse. The only reason I don't drive is because I can't afford a car, and the risk of creating a record Grayson could use to find me.

"There's safer ways to get your exercise than walking on busy streets for miles."

Why did I think she'd take my side on this subject? It's not like she hasn't gone all worried-mother on me for the past two years.

"Yes, Mom." I shake my head in resignation.

"So you figure out your summer plans yet?" This has been an ongoing discussion between us. Up until a few weeks ago, we'd thought we'd both be teaching summer school, just like we did last year. But due to our principal's surprise retirement, the summer program was transferred to Summerset this year, and they've graciously allowed only one teacher per grade here at Grove to teach.

I glance over at Linda McMurray and scowl at the unfairness. Grace and I put way more effort into our classes. But Linda has seniority, so she'll be the kindergarten teacher this summer.

"I'm thinking of volunteering," I say.

"You are? Where?"

"Kelly's sister runs a women's shelter. She mentioned that they needed help."

"You're so good. I haven't decided what to do yet. The receptionist in Aaron's office is going on maternity leave, but, God, I don't want to spent the entire summer cooped up in an office. Answering telephones, taking messages. I'll die of boredom. Volunteering sounds nice, though." She pauses for a second and my mouth goes dry. Do I really want Grace knowing about this side of my life? Would she treat me differently if she did? Before I can contemplate those questions, mayhem breaks out on the playground in the form of a fifth-grade class. At least, I think they're fifth graders. They're huge.

"Hey, hey. Stop," I yell, rushing forward, stifling a curse that would likely get me fired, pointing at the spinning wheel of death that should be on no playground ever. "Why are there big kids out here?"

My eyes widen and my heart races, reflecting the fear in my student's tearful eyes as his tiny fingers grip the metal contraption while some older boy pushes him faster and faster. "Blue shirt, whatever your name is. Stop pushing him."

"Jack..." one of the fifth-grade teachers yells in a lazy voice. "Stop before he throws up. Now."

She walks toward the miscreant, finger wagging at the freckled, blond boy who doesn't show the least bit of remorse in his wide blue eyes, while I comfort Sam.

A minute later Grace and I discuss the surprise addition to our recess with the three fifth-grade teachers while keeping a watch on our tiny students. Of course no one is at fault, just one of those crazy end-of-the-year scheduling mistakes.

"We should go in before someone gets hurt."

Grace looks at her watch and shrugs. "It's only six minutes early."

Linda grumbles when we tell her we've decided to end recess early. The three of us yell for the kids to line up, ending another recess without an injury.

Inside my classroom, the secretary has left me a note that I have a delivery. I scratch my head in confusion. It's the end of the year. I haven't ordered any supplies.

Once my morning class leaves, I head to the office. Karen, the secretary, sports a funny grin when I walk through the door.

"You dating a dentist?" she asks.

I give her a confused frown, until I see the flowers. Flowers and toothbrushes. Pretty tulips, a rainbow of colors, interspersed with a dozen plastic-wrapped toothbrushes like they hand out at the dentist.

I slip the card from the tiny envelope tucked between the blooms.

It was my greatest error
To steal your toothbrush
Before stealing your heart.
Zane.

I open my mouth to explain. I got nothing. The chances of Karen buying my story of having a completely innocent co-ed sleepover is about as likely as a balmy Minnesota winter.

"Yeah. He's a dentist," I say. "But I don't think it's gonna work. Too obsessed with my teeth."

CHAPTER EIGHT

LYRIC

*Z*ane Brody waits on the sidewalk at the end of the day, just like he has been doing every day for the past week. His arms rest on the top of the fence that borders the playground; a small smile curves the corners of his lips. My gaze lands on him the minute I walk my class out the door. Not like I can miss him. He's a hot fudge sundae melting on the counter, impossible to ignore. I'm not the only one who thinks so if the rubbernecking moms are anything to go by. Mrs. Halligan nearly runs smack-dab into the big maple as she passes him, clearly distracted.

Kneeling down to hug my students goodbye, I wince as another woman stumbles on a crack in the sidewalk, arms pinwheeling to catch her balance. Zane's completely oblivious to the added chaos around him as the children connect with their preoccupied caregivers. You'd think these women never saw a good-looking man before. I need to post warning signs, mark all the obstacles, have 911 on speed dial. It's a miracle no one has gotten hurt so far. But we might not be so lucky if Zane continues to bless the kindergarten exit of Grove Elementary with his presence until the end of the school year.

"I appreciate your concern, but you don't have to do this, you know." I glance back at the cluster of women who should be supervising their children on the playground. Instead their eyes follow me and Zane as we make the short walk to his car. The gossip train is full speed ahead. It's probably all over school how the sweet kindergarten teacher with her boring cardigans and modest below-the-knee-length dresses might not be as innocent as previously thought. Not with a man like that waiting for her after school.

I don't need gossip, and Zane Brody with his sexy swagger is a magnet for gossip. My back muscles tighten uncomfortably with the thought of the attention this talk will create.

But I'm wasting my breath. He already knows I'm more than capable of finding my way home safe. I've been doing it for two years.

Zane opens my door with a patient smile which is so different from how Grayson would have reacted if I disagreed with him. I'm still frustrated with the man standing next to me, but that thought has me sliding onto the warm leather seat without another word.

He leans into the car, his lips twitching. "Thank you for allowing me to see you home safe."

He closes my door and walks around the front of the car, sending me an ombre-blue smolder that has my mouth drying up and my stomach doing that roller coaster drop. *Why can't I control myself around this man?* I look away and fumble with the window handle. Two years ago I'd never have set foot in his car. Two years ago I never would have gone out to dinner with him either. But then two years ago I never would have accepted Grace's birthday invitation. Never would have known Zane Brody existed.

"It's a beautiful day," I point out once he's in the car. "It's a sin not to be walking."

He turns the ignition and the car roars to life. "If it's nice tomorrow, we can walk."

The sound of his turn signal fills the moment of silence. I slip my shoes off and tuck my feet under me, then settle back against the door to study the man next to me.

When I was little my grandmother had collected cameos. Pendants, brooches, rings, each with a regal profile raised above a dusky background. Zane Brody has the perfect profile for a cameo. His smooth, broad forehead, and that long, straight nose. On anyone else his nose might be considered overly long, but with those high cheekbones and sharp jaw, it fits perfectly. And in the harsh afternoon sun slanting through the window, the shadow of that childhood break stands out. A minor imperfection that somehow makes Zane even more attractive.

My insides do that flip again, but this time it's not only my stomach.

"I thought you said you started your mornings later than me." I straighten in my seat and force my eyes forward, my stupid, traitorous organ thumping hard inside my chest. Staring at Zane Brody is a dangerous occupation. Watching the strong fingers of his left hand curl around the steering wheel, the muscles of his right forearm flexing as he shifts gears. "Shouldn't you be in school still?"

He gives me a long stare while we wait for the light at Lake to change. "Worried I'm cutting class?" His laugh fills the car for a moment. "God, you're precious. Don't fret, Angel. I don't have an eighth period class scheduled this semester."

"That sucks."

He jerks his shoulder. "Not really. As long as they extend my contract to next year. Getting out early has been… helpful."

Silence fills the car as we speed down Lake, Zane's attention focusing on the heavier traffic of the four-lane road. He's a good driver. A safe driver, despite the muscle car surrounding us. I can't say I'd show as much restraint if I were behind the wheel.

Zane makes the turn onto Thirty-Fourth, and a minute later another turn down my street. No hesitation. He pulls into my driveway like he's done it every day for the past week. Which he has. "Even if I wasn't free, I'd have found a way to drive you home."

"Okay." I shake my head and hop out of the car, saving him from further discussion.

My eyes narrow as he walks around the back of the Mustang instead of leaving like he should.

"Thanks. I guess I'll see you tomorrow, then." I wave, then take a step toward the house. If I turn my back on him maybe he'll get the hint and leave?

No such luck. Peeking back, I notice he's popped open the trunk and my curiosity gets the better of me.

"What are you doing? What's that?"

"I promised to tune your piano," he explains while pulling a duffle bag from the depths of his car.

"What?" I give him a critical look. "No. Do you even know how?"

He gives the bag a little shake that has its contents clanking together and then heads toward the house. "About to find out, aren't we?"

"Whoa, whoa, whoa." I catch up and stop in front of him, arms spread wide. "No, we aren't. You're not touching my piano. No way."

He flashes another one of his killer smiles. "Relax. I'm kidding. Do you think I'd mess with an expensive piano if I didn't know what I was doing?"

I give him a long appraisal. My worst nightmare is coming true—well, maybe not my worst, but allowing this man one evening of my time has obviously been a mistake. He's becoming a bad habit.

"Look I appreciate the offer, but I can't afford this." Shortly after I moved here I'd checked into tuning the piano and quickly dismissed the idea. I'd have had to eat peanut butter sandwiches for months to afford it.

"Your dog will raise the dead in there. Maybe we should continue this conversation inside?" Of course Sacha's in the front window barking her fool head off.

"Fine." I wave my hand carelessly, gesturing him forward. "But there's nothing to discuss."

Once inside, Zane opens that bag of his and pulls out a package of dog treats. Fancy organic ones you can only get at those boutique dog shops downtown. The kind of places I pass by. Somehow Sacha knows these are more special than the economy treats I get at the grocery store. She turns to complete putty in Zane's hands, rolling on her back begging for those treats and the overenthusiastic belly rubs he's more than happy to supply.

"Easy," I say after the third fish-shaped nugget goes into my dog's mouth. "She's got a sensitive tummy. If she gets sick at two a.m. I'll be calling you."

One more vigorous scrub behind the ears, then he stands and hands me the package. Sacha gives me an accusing look, like I've ruined her day.

"Call me anytime. Now let's see what we got here."

"Wait, okay?" I head into the kitchen and let Sacha out the back door—her afternoon walk is on hold for now. I'm not about to leave Zane alone to do God knows what with my father's beloved piano.

When I return he's got the top up and the dark walnut panel below the keyboard off. So much for waiting or talking. My heart lodges in my throat, because the way he's groaning, something must be seriously wrong.

"Zane, stop. I thought... I can't afford..." My words stumble out, all incoherent. I'm down on my knees next to him in a flash, staring at—I don't know what—a mess. Layers of dust cover everything, clinging to the strings like moss on trees.

"Make me dinner. We'll call it even." He offers me a small reassuring smile. I return it with a you-got-to-be-kidding glare, not much different from Sacha when I forced her out the back door. There's no way the contents of my fridge will produce something equal in value to his labor.

"When exactly was the last time this piano was tuned?"

I pull my thoughts from possible dinner options and give his question a moment to sink in. "I have no idea. My parents died six years ago. I was a junior in college and living in a dorm at the time. The neighbors kept it until graduation when I moved in with Gray. They might have had it tuned, but I'm not sure." Memories of my short but unpleasant marriage surface, but I shove them aside. Maintenance on a piano had been the last thing on my mind back then. Not that I'm going to get into that time of my life with Zane again. "I hope you like grilled cheese and tomato soup."

"Love it." Zane shakes his head while digging into his bag. "You realize a piano should be tuned every six months, maybe a year if it isn't played often. Steinways hold a tune longer than most pianos, but they still need attention."

"Sorry," I snap, my defenses rising. We had other pianos, but this was the one in my dad's studio, the one he used every day, for decades, to create the music that paid the bills. The keys bear wear marks from his fingers. The guilt I feel from neglecting his baby is real, not that I've had much choice.

"It was a nightmare bringing it here, and a risk. My lawyer wanted me to get rid of it, but—"

Zane gives me a gentle pat on the shoulder. "Don't worry. I don't see any serious problems, just a lot of dust." He pulls an aerosol can from the bag. "You got a vacuum? If I blow it out, it'll end up everywhere."

I shudder at the thought. "Hang on a second."

I SETTLE the perfectly browned sandwiches on plates, giving myself a mental pat on the back for not burning them as usual. Shut off the burner, turn down the heat on the soup, then take the plates to the table. My stomach growls at the scent of melted cheese and hot butter drifting up from the sandwiches.

I dart a glance through the doorway into the living room as I set the plates on the table. Zane finished up with my piano a while ago, even polished the exterior until the dark wood gleamed. He said something about a sound check, and since then he's been playing a mix of music. A little jazz, some old rock classic, a Mozart piece.

I still in the doorway, watching his sure hands drift over the keys, his back curved and his brow creased in concentration. He switches over to something unfamiliar that has every hair on my body stirring along with my heart.

The music is classical in structure, but with a slight modern edge to the light and airy notes, and somehow I know this soft and beautiful masterpiece is his. Not the notes inked on his skin but another piece.

The melody awakens something deep inside me. The love of music I buried in a grave in Southern California alongside my parents.

Damn him. I could have fought his overconfident attempts at bulldozing his way into my life, but this kind and thoughtful side? Does he know he's playing to my weakness? Literally.

My heart squeezes and a tsunami of nostalgia and longing washes over me strong enough to suck the air from my lungs. I press against the wall as my knees threaten to buckle.

How many times had my father sat at the big grand piano that took up half the living room, entertaining us with his latest creation while my mother made dinner? I can almost smell my mother's soft perfume, hear my father singing some crazy lyrics he created just to make us laugh, or something so painfully beautiful it left us with tears in our eyes.

I had been sure Grayson could fill the void left when my parents died—well, not the music part. My ex-husband couldn't carry a tune if it came with handles, not that it mattered by then. Six months living in the hole left by my parents' death, I'd been desperate for anything resembling love.

My mother probably would have seen right through Grayson's bullshit charm, but she'd never warned me against smooth-talking older hockey players with more money than God. Only velvet-voiced musicians, like the ones that had hung around our house since I was little.

Would she have made an exception for Zane? I let out a sigh and cross my arms over my chest as if to protect the organ inside, but it's probably too late.

Zane would've fit in perfectly with Daddy's crowd. Never would have given me a second look. Just like all the rest, he'd have been too busy in the backyard studio where the magic happened. Where the piano he's currently playing sat. But that's a different life, one where my parents didn't die. Where I never set foot in Minnesota. Never married Grayson. Never met Zane.

Where I never promised not to fall in love again. *Remember?*

Zane looks up and his lips curve at the corners and the crease between his brow melts away. "Everything okay?"

I nod slowly, trying to bring my brain back to the present. "Dinner's ready."

He closes the fallboard with care and stands. If he knew who that piano had belonged to, I probably wouldn't be able to pry him away. But that's something he'll never know.

CHAPTER NINE

LYRIC

*J*stare hopelessly into my closet. Of all the things to stress out about, somehow what to wear to Zane's concert didn't make the list. Of course he didn't mention anything about what to wear, and Sacha is no help at all.

"What do you think?" I hold up a sweater for her approval. "With these dress slacks?"

I turn around and smooth out the gray wool slacks that will definitely need an ironing. Do I even have time for that? And is that a stain?

Sacha gives me a slow blink and drops down on the substantial pile of laundry in the corner of my closet. The pile of laundry that would be clean if my landlord had called the repairman on my washing machine. *Like he promised.*

I let out a quiet huff and scrape at the dark spot that's definitely a stain, and toss the wool pants on the floor. "You're right, these slacks are all wrong. What about this dress?"

The cold snap that moved in last night rules out the few spring dresses still hanging on the rod. Zane's fault. He mentioned snow last week and now they're predicting snow.

I reach for the wrap dress tucked in the back of my closet.

The thin layer of dust on the shoulders proves the purchase had been a mistake. An impulse buy. The pretty ocean-blue color had distracted me from the too-low neckline. Trying it on at the store might have been a good idea, but I'd been in a hurry. It wasn't until I bent down to help Ryan Carson with his shoelaces, the first time I wore it, that I realized how wrong the dress was for school. But tonight, with its long sleeves and nice thick wool, it's perfect. *Doubt if you'll be tying any shoelaces tonight.*

Zane's hungry expression has me questioning my decision. The minute he walks in the door, his eyes go straight to that daring neckline. "Wow."

He takes my hand and spins me as if we're on the dance floor, repeating his exclamation. A warm sensation fills my chest, and I can't help but smile. It's been a long time since a man appreciated my looks without criticism.

"It's not too much?" I ask once the room stops rotating.

"Too much *what*? You look amazing."

"But you're in jeans. I wasn't sure…" I smooth down the soft knit of the skirt over my hips with nervous hands. What if his mom doesn't approve?

"I have to change when we get home. Which we should do, now." He pulls my wool coat from the rack by the door, holding it out for me. "You're stunning, and once again I'll be stuck on stage." I slip my arms into my coat and he steps closer, his stubble brushing against my cheek. "When all I want is to be with you."

My body warms inside my woolly cocoon and my stomach free falls. I should be used to this sensation by now, but I'm so not. I've been waging a losing battle trying to control my attraction to Zane. Sometime over the past week I realized the futility in the fight.

It's still early days, but so far he's proven he's a good man, like Grace promised. The kind of man that holds open doors and helps little old ladies at the grocery store. The kind that allows his students to call at all hours—in desperation over a difficult piece of music or just to chat.

He promised we'd take this relationship slow, and he's a man of his word. But somehow the innocent pecks against my cheeks and the barely-there hugs he's been doling out aren't cutting it anymore. At least not compared to my nightly dreams where we're doing a hell of a lot more than hugging.

But I was impulsive once. And I bear the scars of that mistake. I shouldn't be with Zane at all. Maybe going slow with him is for the best.

Zane tugs me out of the house, and the stinging-cold rain and the warmth of his very real touch brings me back to my senses. He pulls my keys from my hand and locks my door, blissfully unaware of the argument swirling inside me.

ZANE'S MOM rushes down the stairs as we walk into the house. Her pretty paisley dress swishes around her legs when she stops at the bottom, a bit out of breath but looking nothing like the very ill woman I met less than a month ago. *Maybe she was having a bad day?* Tonight a healthy blush colors her cheeks, and her mascara-accented eyes are bright.

"Go change." She shoos Zane toward the stairs. "Tess is anxious to go. I can entertain Lyric."

Her small smile seems forced. Or maybe it's my imagination. *Nerves, probably.* On the way over Zane informed me that his older sister and her family couldn't make it—stomach flu—so *could you drive my mom?*

What was I supposed to say? Sorry, no? Take me home?

"Let's have a seat, Lyric," Janet instructs, with a wave of her frail hand toward the living room.

I'm sure she's perfectly nice—not judging me and my low-cut dress in the least. I smile back, realizing with a shock how tall she is. Even in my heels she towers over me by a couple of inches.

Zane plants another frustrating kiss on my cheek that does nothing to calm my anxiety. "Relax. I'll be back soon."

He disappears, and I follow Janet Cox into the living room. She sits, back straight, shoulders back, her formal bearing forcing me to do the same. Silence descends, thick and uncomfortable. I search for something to say to break the tension, but come up empty.

Zane reappears and all thoughts of conversation flee. I've already met Rockstar Zane, and Teacher Zane, but I'm not at all prepared for Formal Wear Zane. I like every version of him, but from the crisp white bow tie, to the white vest peeking below the hem of his high cut jacket with sweeping tails? *Holy hell, tails?* I'm pretty sure I'm gawking.

Zane kneels down in front of me, a grin on his face. "I'll have to wear this more often. I like the effect." He swipes a thumb across the side of my mouth and I swat his hand away.

"Ass."

Tess rushes in, and he's swept away in the chaos of gathering instruments and shoes and umbrellas and coats, then they're gone.

"I know exactly how you feel," Janet says in the vacuum of silence left in Zane and Tess's wake. "His father was just as handsome. I didn't stand a chance."

I breathe a small, uncomfortable laugh while smoothing the nonexistent wrinkles from my dress. "Zane said his dad died when he was little?"

The question slips out, making me wince. *Great conversation starter.*

Janet picks an invisible thread from her dress. "Mmmhmm. Brain aneurysm. Gone in a flash. There's a lesson in seizing opportunities in there somewhere, I suppose."

"I'm sorry—"

"Yes." She cuts me off. Folding her fragile hands in her lap, she pierces me with a direct look. "When your end date is given, beating around the bush is senseless. I don't know what your expectations are with my son, but I'd like to make some things clear."

"I'm sorry?" Confusion tugs at my brow and I huff out an uncomfortable laugh, remembering Zane's and my conversation a few weeks back about the word expectations. At the time, he assured me he didn't have any expectations and neither did I, but do we now? Either way it's none of his mother's business.

"I married his father three months after we met. Had Laura seven months later." She interrupts again. "I know how quickly these things can happen."

My brows lower further and a sarcastic comment sits on my tongue. The woman is crazy. Is she seriously suggesting what I think she's suggesting?

Forcing a smile, I swallow my initial acerbic response.

"Not with me, I can assure you."

She waves a frail hand in dismissal. "There are no assurances in life. If there were…" She turns her wrist to glance at the thin gold watch, then delicately folds her hands back in her lap like a couple of injured birds, giving them a grimace. "Zane told me about your ex. I'm sure whatever you went through, whatever you're looking for, Zane fills those requirements nicely."

I clear my throat as my lips grow numb. A trickle of fear creeps up my spine. How much did Zane tell her about me? My safety is only as secure as the trust I put in the people around me. How can I trust Janet Cox when I don't even know her?

"Excuse me—"

"Are you willing to move to New York with him?"

"New York?" I spit out. Did I miss something? I must have missed some vital part of this conversation. Why in hell would Zane move to New York? He just left there. "I don't—"

"He's only here temporarily. I honestly didn't want him to

move back at all, but did I get a say? Of course not. The fool found out about the cancer, and boom. Next thing I know he's taken a leave of absence and is on my doorstep like some ridiculous white knight." Those injured-bird hands take flight as she shakes her head. "Do you think I mortgaged this house and worked a second job to send him to Juilliard so he could become a high school music teacher?"

"Um, what?"

"He's brilliant, not that you'd know it." She continues, not noticing the shock certainly written on my face. "Putting his career at the New York Philharmonic on hold to teach some teenagers and hang out with his friends? To watch me die? This leave of absence he's taken could cost him everything. The idiot's throwing it all away for what?"

"I don't think he sees it that way," I defend, despite the betrayal burning in my chest. *Leave of absence?* Why didn't he tell me this was all temporary?

"Of course not. That's why I want to make things clear with you. Tess will be off to college in the fall. I'll be gone and Zane will go back. You can't stop him."

You can't stop him... Her words stab more than I want them to.

"I barely know Zane." *Obviously.* "I doubt I'll have any influence on his decisions."

"No, you won't, dear." She rummages through her purse for a second, then hands me a car fob with a Volvo emblem on it. "We should go."

I SHIFT IN THE DARK, my ass growing numb on the hard wooden seats, my head pounding in time with the bass drums. Six rows from the stage, the dark, crowded school theater is thick with nose-stinging perfumes, colognes, and a nauseating undertone of damp wool courtesy of the icy rain that decided to make this night even more challenging.

Janet Cox slumps in her seat, the perfect posture she maintained earlier gone. Numb terror settles in as I register the pain etched on her gaunt face. The music fades as I glance around. *Now what?* This was such a terrible idea, one I'm completely unequipped to handle.

I issue a silent curse to my good nature and place my hand on Janet's arm. "Are you okay?"

She glares back at me as if I've done something inappropriate. "Fine," she hisses, straightening her spine and giving me a cold smile before returning her focus toward the stage.

Closing my eyes, I count off the beats in the music. Four-four time, ten measures. One of the violinists comes in late on the seventh one, making me wince, but the distraction works. My pulse slows back to normal. Stupid, crazy, manipulative woman. See if I offer my help again.

You can't stop him.

Her earlier words come back, making my jaw clench.

Why would I stop him? Zane's future is his own business. He's made no promises. We've made no plans. He owes me nothing, and I don't owe him anything either. If anything, his mother's warning should come as a relief. When this is over there'll be no hurt feelings. Zane will have been a needed distraction, an escape from my mundane life, and I the same for him.

His presence on stage is magnetic, his conducting style engaging in a way I've never seen before. In between pieces he jokes and laughs with the audience and his students, telling stories about the music they're about to play and funny anecdotes about the composers. Zane has a sense of humor after all.

You can't stop him.

Janet's words burrow into my head, cutting through the music. Not that they should, but they do. Over the last few weeks Zane's had plenty of time to tell me about his past and his future.

That first night, when I revealed more of my life to him than anyone in this city, *why not then?*

The final applause breaks me out of my troubled thoughts. The stage clears and everyone stands. Except me and Janet.

"Sit and wait. It's going to be crazy for a few minutes," she informs, her bony hand digging into my arm to stop my escape. Tomorrow I'll have bruises for sure.

My foot taps an impatient rhythm against the carpeted floor. Happy families file out at a leisurely pace, stopping to chat with friends before moving toward the exit. I've had enough of this night. I want to go home.

"Zane said to meet in his classroom," Janet says, what seems like an eternity later, standing in the now-empty theater. But once we step into the hallway we catch up with the masses. And then some. Rowdy girls in blue and gold uniforms swarm past, cheering. A sports event of some kind—by my guess—must have let out, the participants merging with the theater crowd. It's absolute gridlock, the likes I haven't seen since the last time I drove the 101 at rush hour.

Zane's mom dashes forward, squeezing into a thin gap between two groups. I struggle to keep up, my eyes focusing on her pale green head scarf in the sea of bodies. For a sick woman she moves fast. This school is huge, the brightly lit halls twice as long as the grade school. Around one corner, then up a thigh-burning flight of stairs, I'm a mile behind Janet, cursing the poky elderly couple in front of me, my high heels, and Zane's mother's energy, when I spot a pale green scarf dart into the last classroom on the left. *Please let it be Janet Cox.*

I catch my breath and peek inside the classroom, spotting Zane immediately. Surrounded by a handful of students and parents, he gives me a halfhearted wave. A few kids are packing their instruments, but most are chatting and laughing. Bottles of soda and cups sit on a long table inside the door, as well as bowls of snacks and a few abandoned cake slices sitting on paper plates.

Janet has Tess cornered in what looks to be an unpleasant conversation by the expression on her daughter's face.

Mondale High is an old school, the main building an early twentieth-century gem with modern wings attached like ugly but necessary afterthoughts for a growing population.

The room is more rectangle than square, and at least twice as large as mine. On the far wall, a bank of ancient double-hung windows is a giveaway that we're in the original section of the school. By the doors on each side of the room and the odd gap between the center windows, this might have been two separate rooms at one time. The place is fairly spartan, no dress-up corner or reading nook here. Of course. Just a stretch of the original slate blackboard fills one wall, bisected in the center by a wide AV screen.

Conveniently located next to the far door is a stretch of lockers of various sizes; doors hanging open on a few reveal instruments resting inside. But it's the fourth wall that catches my attention. A collage of music posters covers every square inch. There's a lot of posters, and not the cheap Scholastic ones like I bought at the book fair this spring. No, these are glossy, high-quality art posters. Way more than a month's worth of grocery money is taped to this wall. More than two months.

A disgruntled Beethoven stares down at the class, as well as an overly serious Mozart. Bach, Vivaldi, Telemann, and others from the Baroque period as well as a few of the more modern composers, like Sibelius, Mahler, Holst, and Stravinsky. There are several artsy close-ups of instruments, their bold simplicity designed to catch the eye. An intricately gilded scroll of a double bass. The dark inverted S of a fret hole, surrounded by the glowing wood of a violin. The sensually feminine curve of a cello. But it's the wide-angled shots of the professional orchestras that draw me closer.

"New York Philharmonic…" I whisper, reading the bold font written across the top of one. The truth of everything Janet Cox said earlier weighs down on my chest. Not that I thought she was lying.

What do I do with this information? I mean, there's plenty I haven't told Zane. But this is different. Isn't it? If he's only here temporarily he should have told me.

The voices around me fade as I step closer. The poster is from two years ago, an aerial view of a performance. *A Night of Sibelius, conducted by Paavo Järvi*, it states in a smaller, but equally bold font at the bottom. I scan the orchestra, searching out a dark head and familiar set of broad shoulders. Searching for proof. Not that Janet Cox would lie to me, but—

"Hey, Angel," Zane whispers in my ear, causing me to jump at least a foot.

"Jesus." I press a hand to my chest and spin around.

"Deep in thought?" He holds out a slice of cake in offering, a playful grin curling the corners of his mouth. "Hopefully it's me on your mind. Thought you might like this."

"Thanks." I take the plate from his hand and set it on the low bookshelf on the other side of me. I'm in no mood for chocolate cake at the moment. Definitely a first.

His eyes narrow at the discarded cake. Then he gives my shoulder a gentle squeeze. "You okay?"

"Yep." I give him a sharp nod and pull out of his grasp, earning myself another frown.

"You sure?"

"Fine." The room has cleared out in the last few minutes. Zane's mother, his sister, and a group of three students standing by the door are all that remain of the earlier crowd. How long have I been staring at this damn poster?

"From my experience with women, a *fine* delivered in that tone never means fine."

"Your mother and sister are heading over."

His eyes linger on my face for a moment, concern creasing the corners, then he straightens and turns.

"I knew Caroline wouldn't show up tonight." His sister's brown eyes narrow. "And she almost stepped on my violin yesterday. She's a spiteful bitch. You need to do something. Expel her. Fail her—"

"You're not the teacher here, are you? How I handle my students is none of your business, Tess."

"God, I hate you." Tess growls at her brother and stomps toward the group of students.

Zane rubs a hand over his mouth and shoots me an exasperated look, and for a moment I pity his situation. Then I remember I'm just as angry at Zane as Tess, maybe more.

His sister storms back, hands on her hips. "Zane, listen—"

"I'm ready to leave," his mother says to me, cutting off her daughter—the woman has a real talent for taking control of a conversation—then turns to Zane. "Your sister is going out with her friends, but they said they'd help with the cleanup first."

Zane snorts, his eyes narrowing on his sister before shifting back to his mother. "She's going out? On a Thursday night? No way."

"What?" Tess snaps, her pale cheeks slowly flushing. "But—"

"Zane..." Janet sighs. "She's eighteen."

"And she has responsibilities. Like getting up for school tomorrow, and taking. You. Home," Zane says, enunciating the last three words slowly.

"I thought Lyric was taking. Mom. Home," Tess says just as slowly, mimicking Zane.

"I can—" I start.

"It's late and Lyric needs to get home as well." Zane cuts me off, then moves closer, slipping his arm around my waist. "Besides, Mom isn't Lyric's responsibility."

"I can take the bus—"

"No, you can't." Zane pivots to face me, his hand slicing the air between us, stopping my words. "You're not taking the bus at this time of night in the pouring rain."

"She can wait at the house until you get home, Zane," Janet interrupts, her voice slow and a bit slurred. Whatever energy she had earlier has seeped out of her. Her shoulders sag, and the dark shadows have made a return under her eyes. She leans heavily on the cane Zane had argued for her to take a couple of hours ago.

"Or, better idea, I drive Lyric home and Tess takes you. She has all weekend to go out with her friends." Zane's blue eyes flame hot with a look that would melt lesser beings. "Argument over."

"Fine," Tess huffs, throwing up her hands. "Run while you can, Lyric. My brother's an asshole."

Zane lets out a quiet laugh, his fingers rubbing at the crease between his brows. His mother sighs, watching as Tess stalks off toward her friends. I pull the car keys out of my purse and hand them to Zane's mom.

Janet frowns. "She might be right, you know."

"You're going soft, Mom. You never would have let me or Laura go out on a week night." Zane bends to give his mom a kiss on the cheek. "Go home. I'll be back shortly."

"I'm too tired to argue, Zane. And you got your way this time. Isn't that all that matters?"

Zane's mom sends me a challenging smirk that says I may have won this time but I won't in the end. Or maybe I'm being too sensitive, letting my imagination take over when I should be thinking clearly. Janet Cox isn't the enemy, just a messenger. She turns slowly toward the door, stopping a moment for Tess to say goodbye to her friends. The door swings closed and the room falls silent.

Zane tugs at his bow tie and the ends fall loose. "Well, that was pleasant. As usual. I've been called worse by Tess, though, so I suppose I've got that." His lips twist as he works to unbutton the collar of his shirt. Once undone, he lets out a quiet groan. "You're not going to take my sister's advice are you?"

He closes the small distance between us. A grin pulls at the corners of his generous mouth. "The illusion is over, right? You thought I was this handsome, amazing, talented guy, and I blew it. I should have waited until you were hopelessly in love with me before revealing the unpleasant side of my life."

"Stop." I back up, shoving my hands between us, and stare up into his self-professed handsome face. Then laugh, because if I don't laugh I'll cry. And I swore three years ago that no man would ever make me cry again. Even though Zane Brody's words are salt rubbed into the wounds caused by his mother's earlier advice. Falling in love with him? Never in my lifetime.

I turn away, giving my attention to the makeshift buffet table. There's a cluster of white bottle caps next to the two-liter bottles. They're all the same, no markings. Does it matter if they go on the right bottle? I grab one, deciding no, and twist it on. Then another, cranking it extra tight. The heady scent of the chocolate cake makes my stomach sour. Somehow this man has turned me off chocolate.

"Let's clean up and get out of here. I've had enough bullshit for one night."

Zane appears in my periphery. "Want to tell me what's wrong?"

"No." Done with the sodas, I wave at the bowl of chips between us. There's not much left, but maybe he wants to keep them. Have them with his sandwich tomorrow? What the hell am I thinking? Mr. Healthy doesn't eat chips.

"Do you have a bag for these?" I ask anyway. Maybe I'll take them home. Along with the soda he won't drink. And maybe that damn cake.

"Lyric." His brows lift and he raises his hand toward me, but I step back out of his reach. "Did I do something to piss you off?"

I lift the bowl between us. "Answer the question."

"Throw them out." He exhales heavily, his fingers pinching the bridge of his nose. "Keep the bowl, though."

I stifle the *duh* that wants to escape with his final instruction.

It's not an expensive bowl, just some flimsy dollar-store find. But still. Does he think I'm dumb? His trash can sits across the room, beside his desk. And of course Beethoven taunts me from his spot high on the poster wall, the New York Philharmonic photo credit practically glowing in neon. Anger blooms hot in my chest, and stupid, traitorous tears prick at the corners of my eyes.

I need to let tonight go. Get out of here and forget Zane Brody, his mother, and the last few weeks where stepping away from my boring life was a possibility. It was a dream and all dreams come to an end eventually.

Spilling the chips into the trash can, I gulp in a deep breath. Then another. It doesn't help, but I straighten my shoulders and turn around. Staring at the man's garbage won't get me anywhere. On the way back I manage to avoid Beethoven's piercing eyes, but Pachelbel's sneer lands a direct hit.

You can't stop him.

"I'm curious, when exactly were you going to tell me?" I'm not even halfway across the room when the words spill out. *So much for letting it go.*

Zane tips his head again, his tight smile and pinched brows saying I've lost him. "Tell you what?"

I wave my hand at the poster wall and walk closer. "This."

I'm at the same place I stood earlier, the wide aerial orchestra photo in front of me. Zane slowly makes his way over, his eyes wary like the first day he met Sacha. Maybe he thinks I'm about to bite too?

"Are you in here?" I stab a finger at the poster. "I looked, but then I realized I don't even know what you play. Anything with strings, isn't that what you said?"

He points to the cello section, second row. "I auditioned for two openings, cello and violin. They offered me the cello spot."

"Your mother's very proud." I try to keep the sarcasm out of my voice, but the muscle ticking in Zane's jaw, I've failed.

"What exactly *did* my mother say to you tonight?"

"That this is temporary. Th-that… you're only here on a leave of absence. That you'll be going back once… Why are you even bothering with me?"

I cross my arms, tucking my angry, shaking hands into my sides. Inches apart, Zane's expensive black dress shoes contrast with my soggy, rain-spattered heels—the peep-toes not the most brilliant idea with tonight's weather. But then brilliant ideas were never my strong point.

"You have every right to be angry." His fingers tug mine from their hiding place, and he raises my hand to his lips. "I should have told you everything that first night, or at least at some point before now. I should have realized my mother would say something to you. But you have to know I never would have started something with you if I wasn't sticking around."

I pull my hand back and shake my head. "I just met you a few weeks ago. Besides Grace's glowing recommendation, I barely know you. Obviously."

He captures my hand again, weaving his long fingers together with mine. "We've talked a lot these past weeks, Lyric. You know me. You know how much I love my family and my friends and teaching. You know how much tonight meant to me. Would it make any sense if I left it all for that?" He waves his free hand toward the wall above my shoulder.

I shake my head slowly, tugging my hand in an attempt to extract myself from his warm and comforting grasp. I can't think properly with the way his thumb is brushing soothing circles on my wrist. And I need to think. There are too many unanswered questions for me to be sure of anything right now.

"Maybe this would all make sense if you had been honest with me. But your mom was so… convincing."

"Then I'll have to convince you otherwise." He slips my fingers under his vest, pressing my hand against his hard chest, the heat of his body and the steady thump-thump of his heart seeping through the thin cotton of his shirt. Every hair on my arm rises, and a shiver of awareness travels under my skin.

"You feel that?" He pauses, and I jerk an unsteady nod. "It races out of control every time you're near. You make me feel alive for the first time in… ages."

"Zane—"

"Shhh. I'm not done." He presses my knuckles to his lips. "I can't stop thinking about you. Even from the first time I saw you in the grocery store, I knew you'd be my everything. I'd no sooner cut off my hands than walk away from us."

"Zane…" I have no idea what to do with his honesty. I don't need a boyfriend. Emotional attachments are foolish with the threat of Grayson appearing at any time.

Why did I go to Grace's birthday? If I'd stayed home I never would have met Zane. Never been tempted by his ombre-blue eyes. Never considered a life that didn't involve running from Grayson.

But now that I have considered the possibility, I can't stop my heart from wanting the impossible. *Stupid heart.*

Time slows. The world shrinks as I close the gap between us. Zane's eyes dilate, the darkness of his pupils eclipsing the pale blue centers. The slight stubble on his jaw scrapes against the fingertips of my free hand. His scent is stronger this close, a combination of cloves, leather, and cedar, along with an undertone of warm, salty exertion.

"This is such a bad idea," I warn as his hand comes up to cup my jaw.

"Reckless," he adds before bending down, teasing the corner of my mouth with light brushes of his lips, before taking my mouth properly, his tongue slipping in. A growl rumbles through his chest, guttural, impatient, and insanely sexy.

My fingers sift through his silky hair, my skin heating with desire as Zane deepens our kiss. His hand slips between the slit in my dress, his touch searing my bare skin.

A loud tap-tap echoes around the room, putting my need for this man on hold as effectively as an ice bath.

Zane stills, breaking our kiss with an audible pop. He darts a glance over my shoulder, then curses.

"Janitor?" I whisper, ignoring the ghost of his hand imprinted on my thigh.

"Principal."

My eyes widen and I squeak out a curse of my own while swiping a quick hand through his hair to tame it back in order—or attempt to. I may have gotten a bit carried away. There's little I can do with the ruddy stain on his cheeks or the hard ridge pressing against his dress slacks.

He smooths down my dress and places a hand on my waist, turning me around.

"Relax," he whispers, guiding me forward.

Outside the narrow window set into the solid door, Zane's boss leans back against the wall. He's shorter than Zane by a good three inches, a stocky build with wispy, slightly thinning blond hair and watered-down blue eyes bracketed with fine creases of age at the corners. He offers us a polite smile as soon as Zane opens the door.

"Brody, I was on my way out and saw your light on. Thought I'd offer my congratulations on your performance tonight." He holds out his hand, his eyes shifting from Zane to me and then back.

"Thank you. It was a pleasure." The two men engage in a hearty handshake, both smiling wide, his boss adding a pat on the shoulder for good measure. I keep my expression innocent. As if Zane's boss didn't catch us making out on school property.

"Everyone worked hard this year," Zane adds, then waves his hand in my direction. "This is my girlfriend, Lyric James. Lyric this is Mr. Iverson."

I dismiss the girlfriend label and offer Mr. Iverson my hand along with a greeting. The handshake he gives me is a toned-down version of Zane's. His slightly-moist grip is soft, as if he's afraid he'll crush my bones. Definitely no pat on the shoulder for me.

Zane slips his arm around me. "Lyric teaches kindergarten over at Grove."

Mr. Iverson crosses his arms and leans against the doorway, his eyes widening for a second, his smile warming. "You know when I first met my wife, she taught first grade at Grove. Now she stays home with the kids... which is where I should be right now." He straightens, taking a step back. "Heard plenty of good things from the parents tonight, Brody. Keep it up."

We both stand in the doorway watching Mr. Iverson disappear down the hall. A second later the heavy stairway door thuds shut.

I give Zane a wide grin. "That went well, I think."

CHAPTER TEN

ZANE

*T*he whole way home Lyric's quiet. I can almost hear the questions swirling around in her head. Questions I should have answered weeks ago. Questions I'd have answered earlier, if we hadn't been interrupted. Or distracted. That kiss was the mother load of distraction.

Her coconut and vanilla scent is embedded in my jacket, the taste of her lips lingers on mine, and the feel of her soft skin is burned into my memory. The thought of where things were headed if Iverson hadn't shown up has me hard all over again.

"Your boss was nice," she says once we get home—her home, which I'm beginning to like a hell of a lot more than my home. I give Sacha a vigorous scratch behind the ears in greeting and trail behind Lyric. "Sweaty palms, but maybe it's a condition. Some people have that, you know. Can't be helped..."

I lean against the kitchen doorway, watching Lyric put away the two-liter bottles of pop she refused to let me dump down the sink, along with the slice of cake she'd set aside earlier. When she'd been angry at me.

By the way she's babbling on, I have a feeling there's still some lingering resentment, and I'm not leaving until the tension between us is gone. I don't know exactly what my mother said to Lyric, but I have a good idea. And I'm just as pissed.

"Talk to me."

She gives me a hesitant glance over the refrigerator door. "There's nothing to talk about."

She bends forward, and I struggle to extinguish my groan. Despite the tension in the room, I'm still buzzing from our amazing kiss. I can't help but watch the way her dress slides up her toned thighs, lovingly hugging the luscious curve of her ass as she returns her attention to her fridge. If she were any other woman I'd have that dress hiked up around her hips, her panties down, and my dick buried balls deep inside her. But she's worth so much more than satisfying my base instincts. I'm destined for another fucking night in my basement shower, my hand and my fantasies for company when all I want is in front of me. But Lyric's worth more than a quick fuck against her appliance. When she finally says yes, I plan on spending all night showing her how much she means to me. Not the few minutes we have now.

"My mother laid a bombshell on you earlier. You have to have questions," I say, forcing my thoughts back to what's important. Thanks to my mom, Lyric's trust in me is shaken. I need to set the record straight.

The contents of her refrigerator clank together for a moment as she struggles to make room for everything. Sacha sticks her nose inside to investigate, but Lyric pushes her back. The dog turns and trots over, plopping her ass on the floor at my feet. Pressing her big body against my leg, she looks up at me with hope in her soulful brown eyes. I give her another rub that earns me a contented groan.

Lyric emerges from the fridge and shuts the door. "Fine. Why does your mother think you're on a leave of absence?"

I step forward and pull her into my arms, because now that I've had her in my arms, there's no place I'd rather have this woman. She goes pliant against my chest, and I'm calling it a win. If she was angry she'd be scratching my eyes out instead of leaning into our embrace.

I tuck a wayward lock of her golden hair behind her ear, and smile. "Because we spent my first month back fighting about it, and it was exhausting, for me, for her. Eventually I gave up. It's easier to let her believe what she wants—at least for now."

"Maybe your mom is right. You have too much talent to be a high school music teacher."

I groan, even though I've heard those words come out of my mother's mouth at least a hundred times. Probably more. "I love being a music teacher. And I love being home. New York was a soulless hell for me. I might have enjoyed the novelty of it in the beginning, but now... it's not the place I picture myself raising a family or growing old or even having a dog."

I reach down and give Sacha another scratch on her head. She's not my dog, but I wouldn't mind if she was. "This is probably more than you want to hear at this point in our relationship, but it's the motivating factor for why I'm here. I couldn't see any of my goals happening where I was. The noise, the attitudes, the cost of rent on my small apartment—that was huge by New York standards. When my sister called about my mom, it was all the excuse I needed."

"You really need to tell your mom that." A small smile tugs at the corner of her lips, and my heart flares with hope. Even though she'd been all over me earlier, I want more than the physical with this woman. Winning her trust is more important than winning a spot in her bed.

"I will. Soon," I say. Her smile wilts. "She needs to save her strength for fighting the cancer, not arguing with me."

"You talk about raising a family. I have to be honest, Zane. I've entered the whole death-till-you-part contract once and it didn't work out so well for me. If you're looking for a wife, you should keep searching. We could stick to the break-buddies thing."

Stupid break buddies. That bullshit might have gotten me in the door, but I'm not going back. Not when I'm so close to having her.

"I'm far from marriage material myself. I have a one-year contract with Mondale with a possible option for renewal—*if* I work out. I might be living off weekend gigs and any music lessons I can drum up. But the way I feel about you... no, the break-buddy thing won't work for me. And I don't think it'll work for you either."

"No." She shakes her head slowly as if struggling with some internal argument. "But Mr. Iverson likes you. I could tell that much. He'd be stupid not to renew your contract."

"Yeah, well, it's not completely up to him."

"But he has a say doesn't—"

I press a finger to her soft lips, silencing her argument. "I don't care about Iverson or Mondale High or anything right now but knowing if you're still angry with me."

She shakes her head in answer, her brilliant green gaze locked on mine, while her fingers slide up my lapels. "It's scientifically impossible to be angry with a man in a tux."

I can't help the grin that tugs on my lips. "I'll make a note of that."

My fingers cradle the base of her head, and I press my lips against hers. Her hands skate up my chest, and the feel of her touch is fucking electric. Even that first day when our fingers brushed as I passed her that bottle of tequila, her touch affected me. I feel alive for the first time in forever.

My hands cup her cheeks, holding her face as I deepen the kiss. I need the soft brush of her tongue against mine and the sweet sigh of her pleasure as much as my next breath. My dick hardens in my pants, my control pivots on a razor's edge. I'm so fucking lost for this woman, and once I'm inside her, I know she'll own me.

And for once that thought doesn't scare me.

In the next second everything unravels. I can feel the hesitation in Lyric even before she pushes me away. Sacha noses between us with a quiet whimper, furthering the divide.

"I'm sorry," she whispers. "I'm just…"

"Hey, relax. No pressure."

The look in her eyes guts me. Something between remorse and relief that makes my insides go hollow.

I capture her hand and kiss her knuckles, letting her know I'm not giving up. Not by a long shot. "You think I'd force you into something you don't want?"

Her eyebrow rises as if in challenge. And okay, I might have forced my way into her life, but I'd never…

"You can always say no, and I'll obey. You're in charge here. Nothing happens without your consent."

She nods, gifting me with a small smile that assures me I've been forgiven. "Okay."

"Good. Now I should go before Tess decides to come hunt me down."

I give her a brief kiss, because my lips are addicted to hers, then force myself to leave. Hardest thing ever, stepping out into the icy rain when there's a gorgeous woman waiting inside. But she said no, maybe not in so many words, but her message was loud and clear. I'm gonna have to work harder to win a spot in this woman's heart.

I climb into the car, the cold leather seats effectively dampening my desire. At least for now.

CHAPTER ELEVEN

ZANE

I pull into the fence-enclosed lot, slipping my Mustang into a parking spot between Dave's '67 Chevelle and Aaron's shiny new Outlander. Monday through Friday the lot is busy, but today the only other vehicles here are a late-sixties Corvette, a powder-pink '57 Caddy—both works in progress—and the sunshine-yellow company van that doubles as our equipment hauler on weekends. Dillon's Charger is nowhere in sight. *Maybe he's on a beer run?*

Getting out of the car, I grab my guitar from the back, repeating those positive thoughts while heading toward the two-story brick building. I can still picture Mrs. Mathers on a ladder, laughing, her blonde hair tied back in a bandanna, paintbrush in her hand as she stenciled the sign above the door. Mathers and Sons, Custom Auto Interiors, even though the *sons* were only kids back then. Wishful thinking? The sign is a bit weathered and faded these days, but by the time we were in our teens Mr. Mathers had all of us hand-stitching loose seams and working with Louise, his beloved industrial sewing machine that would happily make a pin cushion out of inattentive fingers. So maybe there was a bit of prophecy in those letters.

Inside, the smell of leather and glue is the same as the first day Dave and Dillon brought me over, back when my mom and Greg Cox first moved us to this side of town. I was an outcast, the new kid more than halfway through the school year, skinny as hell, and the target for every bully in our grade until Dave and Dillon told them to get lost.

Two vintage cars sit in the bays, waiting patiently for their restoration. The place is a little less organized than when Mr. Mathers ran it, but the essence of the shop is the same. I can still picture the three of us, rubbing conditioner into fresh leather seats or vacuuming carpets to keep our pre-pubescent asses out of trouble. And later working side by side with Mr. Mathers on my raccoon-ravaged Mustang that seemed more important to teenaged me than my college savings at the time.

I logged in enough time in this shop and at the Mathers home to be considered a son. During the Greg Cox years I ate more meals at their table than mine. Pretty sure Mrs. Mathers knew I had it rough back home, and there was always a plate for me. Always a bed if I wanted one, too. I'm not related in the normal, biological way, but Dave and Dillon are as much brothers to me as Laura and Tess are sisters.

My boots echo on the metal treads of the back stairway that lead to Dave and Dillon's apartment. Back when we were kids Mr. Mathers had rented out the space to one of his workers. Archie had been a cranky old guy with plenty of nose hair and little patience for kids. Dil swears his ghost still smacks him across the back of his head every now and then.

I push the heavy door open and step into the partially sunlit space, calling out a greeting.

"How's it going?" Aaron returns, waving a hand that almost conceals a beer, his hulking Viking body taking up a third of Dave and Dil's well-aged tweed couch. The brothers' decorating theme is somewhere along the lines of frat-house chic. A lot of stuff their parents didn't want to haul down to Arizona when they retired a few years back, some mismatched shit the equally decorating-challenged Archie may have left behind, and artwork courtesy of various magazine centerfolds and old calendars.

"Good," I answer, dropping my guitar on the far side of the open area designated as our practice stage, then grabbing my own beer from the fridge and settling into one of the chairs adjacent to Aaron's with a frown. "Where's everyone?"

Aaron tips his big blond head toward the back of the apartment, his lips twisting for a second. "Dave's trying to get a hold of Dil."

If Aaron's hard stare didn't clue me in, Dave's angry voice rising from the bedroom area does. A door slams, Dave's words muffle into incoherency, and I let out a curse. It's fucking Sunday. Every Sunday we hash out the following weekend's playlist. Introduce any new songs I've written. Dil knows today is crucial. Mandatory.

I let out a strangled groan as frustration burns in my chest. "We can't keep doing this. Why am I even writing new shit if we aren't going to practice it?"

Aaron shrugs. "Nothing personal, but I've got better things to do than hang out with you guys today."

"Same here, man. I'd rather be with Lyric."

Aaron's face splits into a grin. "Lyric, huh? You haven't scared her off yet?"

"Thanks for the vote of confidence." I shoot him a sarcastic look, then run a hand across my face. Last night had been close.

"Uh oh." Aaron's brows rise. "That look doesn't hold confidence. What happened?"

"My mom happened. Christ, I love her, but... Well, you know how she can be. Maybe it wasn't the brightest idea leaving her and Lyric alone, but I didn't have much of a choice last night. And she sorta went off about me. You know the whole *Zane has a bril-*

liant life in New York she's been giving me this past year. It was a total shock for Lyric. I feel like I've been shoved back three steps in earning her trust."

Aaron sets his beer down slowly on the crate-slash-table in front of us, his brows sinking. "You didn't tell her about New York? News flash, Zane. Earning trust is all about honesty."

"I was honest. Last night," I spit out the words through gritted teeth, my shoulders rising in defense. "My life out east is in the past tense, just like everything that happened there. Totally irrelevant to my future here."

Aaron breathes out a curse while shaking his head slowly, disapproving. Not that I don't blame him. If the tables were turned? Fuck.

"So what did you say to Lyric, you know, so I know what to say."

I wander over to the grimy stretch of windows and glance out at the dreary industrial landscape spread out in front of me. The dark, oppressive rain clouds are a perfect mirror to my mood at the moment. Was I actually looking forward to this practice session a few minutes ago? Now I'd rather get the fuck out of here. "Basically what I told you. I'm here to stay, and as soon as my mom gets better I'll be telling her the same."

Aaron tenses, his eyes sharpening. "You should tell her the rest. You know shit has a way of coming out when you don't want it to."

Of course he's talking about Lyric, but I play it dumb. "Her doctor says she has to keep a positive attitude."

"Zane…" He shakes his head, his voice holding an uneasy warning that irritates on every damn level.

There might be a few things I don't want Lyric to know about, but it's nothing like the shit she's keeping from me. Every time I turn around I'm running smack into a wall of secrets with this woman. I don't even know her real name for fuck sake. Lyric—

the name I thought of as some kind of destiny that first night—now feels like a bitter lie on my tongue.

Aaron's not standing on quite the righteous ground he believes—not that I can correct him in his assumption.

"Don't give me that. Tell me that there's zero you keep from Grace," I say instead.

He lets out a heavy exhale. "I'm in the middle here. You're my friend and Lyric's Grace's friend. It's totally fucked up, but if you hurt her, I'm the one who's gonna catch hell. So—"

"I'm not going to hurt her." I raise a hand in promise. "I swear. She's... different. She's—"

"Please tell me our boy is finally getting laid," Dave interrupts, clapping as he struts into the room. "You've been moping around, playing suffering-saint with your family ever since you moved back. No offense, bro, but it's about time you took care of your needs."

I give Aaron an exasperated look while taking a sip of my beer, instantly regretting that decision, and setting the can back down on the battered and stained wood surface. Dave's taste in beer could stand some improvement.

"It's not like that." Mocking my words, the memory of Lyric's sweet lips against mine, and my hand slipping inside her dress, drift through my head, along with the fantasies I conjured up later, fantasies of what could have happened if Iverson hadn't shown up.

Like I told Aaron, she's different. Fragile. If any other woman had responded to me the way Lyric had last night, I'd have taken full advantage of what she was offering. But the way she broke down that first night still haunts me, and even a month later I can see the fear in her eyes and feel her body tense when I touch her. It kills me to think what her ex-husband did to make her so fearful, but it would kill me even more if I were the one hurting her.

So before things get physical, I have to be sure. Even if my dick falls off from abuse.

"I think she's the one."

"What?" Dave sputters. "What one?"

"The one I want to spend the rest of my life with."

The sounds from outside filter in in the dead silence. The low hum of the cars on 94 a block away, a bird chirping in a bush outside, the tick of Dave's refrigerator, and the steady thump-thump of my heart in my chest. My inner voice suggests I may be out of my mind, but once the idea settles in, it feels right. Like we were meant to be.

Aaron's mouth hangs open and Dave starts laughing. Loud and obnoxious. "The rest of... You mean you're gonna marry her? That's a good one. You met her, what, how many weeks ago? Jumping the gun a little, don't you think? You haven't even slept with her. You don't even know what side of the bed she sleeps on. Or if she snores." He pauses, his eyes widening. "Or if she gives head. She may hate it, and I don't know about you, but that would be a deal breaker for me. You need to find that shit out before you go spewing this insanity."

Aaron reaches into the drawer of the table next to him and pulls out a strip of condoms, pressing them into my hand. "Go with God, man."

I shake my head and tuck the condoms into my wallet, because it's easier than arguing. Although the fact he knew Dave kept condoms in the drawer is a bit disturbing. "Did any of that matter to you?"

"Well..." Aaron rubs a hand across his jaw and chuckles. "Negotiating bed sides is a big deal, bro."

I exhale out a slow breath while raking my fingers through my hair. Nerves prickling with apprehension, I search for the right words. Sharing my feelings has never been easy, but I've known Dave since I was eleven and Aaron almost as long. If I can bare my soul to anyone without fear of judgment or disapproval, it's these two guys. "The minute I saw her in Lunds, I felt something. Some connection. And every time I'm with her... shit. I'm falling hard here and there's nothing I can do to stop it. And I'm not sure I want to." My heart's pounding out of my chest and my stomach—well, maybe that's Dave's crappy beer. Aaron has a shit-eating grin stretched across his face and Dave's eyes are about to pop out of his head. "All I know is when I look in her eyes, I see my future."

Aaron pats me on the shoulder. "Welcome to the club, buddy."

Dave drops down on the other side of the couch, beer in hand. "Yeah, well, you better write that shit down, 'cause those sappy words are gonna make all your fans weep."

"Speaking of fans, where's Dil?" Aaron asks, looking around as if he'll appear at any second.

Dave digs his fingers into his eye sockets and rubs. "Can't make it. Said something about a prior engagement."

"Prior engagement with what?" Aaron shoots a sharp glance at me, jaw clenched, his nostrils flared. "Dude, Zane can write all the fucking music you want, but if our bass doesn't know it—"

"I know." Dave drops his head against the back of the couch and throws his arm over his face.

I rest my hand on Aaron's shoulder and shake my head. Dillon's responsibility issues aren't Dave's fault. Taking it out on him won't do any good.

"Listen, this band, these gigs are important to me. I've got a whole summer without a paycheck, and I haven't heard from the school district about next fall. And fucking Greg Cox was pleased as piss to let me know his support payments for Tess would be stopping when she turned eighteen last month. I've got a mortgage payment and medical bills and a teenager who's heading off to college in a couple months and..." My jaw gives a painful twinge as I grind my molars, the angry pit in my stomach definitely having nothing to do with the beer. "A girlfriend to impress, *somehow*. So we need to figure this out, at least temporarily, until Dillon gets his shit together."

"I might have signed us up for a few concerts," Dave mumbles behind his forearm that's still covering his face.

"What?" Aaron straightens in his seat and turns toward Dave. "You did what?"

Dave pulls his phone from his pocket. "County fairs and shit. Wally suggested it. Sent me the links to the applications and all. I wasn't sure we'd get in, so I didn't mention it. But we did. Not all, but most. It's good money, better money than at Mill City. And you're gonna shit, because..." He trails off, a shit-eating grin plastered to his face.

Aaron and I both say, "What?" in a slightly-less-than-excited tone, and look at each other. Leaving my mother alone with my sisters every weekend doesn't sit well, and Aaron has a full-time job. Driving to the far ends of the state probably doesn't sit well with him either.

"We got into Summerfest," Dave's voice rises and he practically vibrates in his seat. "You know what this means? Exposure, agents, record deals, the fucking big time."

Dave's dream. Bright lights, screaming fans. When we were kids, he wanted to be the next Eddie Van Halen. When Aaron and I headed off to college, he hopped from band to band hoping to hit it lucky, ignoring the safe future waiting for him in his father's business. Always dragging Dillon along for the ride. Did Dil even want this in the first place? His absence speaks at painfully high decibels.

"You signed contracts already? We're committed?" Aaron asks. Dave nods in answer. The big blond drummer swipes at the loose strands of hair that have come loose from his ponytail with a heavy sigh, then yanks the leather strip from the back of his head, regathering his shoulder-length hair in his fist, before refastening the mass. "So what do we do about Dillon?"

"We need someone we can count on." My teeth sink into my bottom lip as betrayal eats at my gut. I don't want to be the guy who kicks one of his best friends out of the band, but someone has to be in charge. "I might know someone."

Dave stares out toward the bank of windows for a long beat. "Fine."

"I'll call him while Aaron calls Aunt Mary." I pull my phone and wallet out of my pocket, tossing my credit card on the table. "I'm starved. And have her throw in some decent beer. And a six pack of cola. Our new bass player can't drink."

CHAPTER TWELVE

LYRIC

*M*y teacher's aide, Mrs. Henderson, purses her lips together in her standard look of disapproval while I collect the math worksheet I just handed out. Okay, so it was the same worksheet we did yesterday, as little Joanie Keller so helpfully pointed out.

Shoot me.

It's Friday. I turn my grades in at the end of the day. Only a week and a half to go, filled with field trips, the class party, and the two-day chaos at the end of next week called the School-Wide Olympics. My bottom drawer is packed full of tiny T-shirts, all ready and waiting to be painted Monday with our chosen country's flag, along with a few fun lessons on Argentina. Does a worksheet really matter anymore? The look on Mrs. Henderson's face suggests it does.

I drop the papers into the recycling bin and ignore her. You'd think she's never made a mistake in her life.

I sink down in my desk chair, giving the older woman a stiff smile. "Who's ready for story time?"

It's been a day. Two temper tantrums, one bloody nose, the great Elmer's glue disaster of kindergarten room 2, and a lost hermit crab. *No, not technically lost.* Henry's scuttling around the room somewhere.

I'm off my game. Distracted by the man with ombre-blue eyes and enough talent to fill an orchestra hall. The man who ignited my world last night with a gold-medal make-out session before doubt extinguished my desire.

Stupid Grayson.

I stifle a sigh and hand Mrs. Henderson one of the kids' favorites, *Willa Wallaby's Wondrous Walkabout*—fitting at the moment with one of our class crabs off on his own walkabout, I suppose. The kids cheer as they rush over to the reading corner, completely oblivious to my fuckups. Unlike Mrs. Henderson.

"Remember to watch where you step... and sit," I call out as an afterthought, then glance under my desk.

I blow out a steadying breath and drop my pounding head onto the cool desktop. Mrs. Henderson's singsong voice fades. I spend the next few minutes adjusting today's lesson plan while keeping Henry's safety in mind. Monday's tango lessons will need to be canceled if the little crustacean doesn't show up before then. Have to remember to set out some food and water for the little vagabond.

An excruciatingly long time later, my morning class waves goodbye and Mrs. Henderson leads them out of the classroom for the day. I scramble around, searching all the low-lying crannies, but the elusive Henry is still on the lamb. My stomach interrupts the hunt, insisting it's time for lunch.

It's just me and Grace today. Which is fine. I'm not in the right frame of mind to put up with Zoe's incessant talk of the trivial. I'm being a bitch. It's not her fault I was too busy tiptoeing around Grayson's moods at her age to even think about nail polish colors, or the best self-tanners in order to look like you've spent a week in Cancún.

"You look tired," Grace says, her expression turning worried.

"Sleep has been..." If only I could tell her the whole truth.

That my ex-husband has started visiting me in my dreams again. *Not dreams, nightmares.* Violent, ugly, nightmares. "Elusive. I'm thinking of ending things with Zane."

Her eyes grow wide. "Why? I thought things were good."

"They are. I think. But..." How do I explain the guilt I felt last night for slamming on the breaks when Zane clearly wanted to keep moving forward? "I'm..."

Mr. Ogilvie from fifth grade eavesdrops from the table next to ours.

I lift a shoulder while focusing on opening the tiny cookie bag in front of me. It's one of those annoying packages that requires superhuman strength to peel apart the edges, but will likely give way sending the two delicious cookies flying if I'm not careful.

"You're what?" Grace prompts.

"Scared?" I whisper, mindful of the inquisitive ears in our vicinity.

Grace frowns. "Scared of what? Did he hurt you? If he did, so help me..."

I almost smile at my friend's fierceness.

Mr. Ogilvie chuckles, and I shoot him a sharp glance that causes him to start clearing his table. Or maybe he was about to leave anyway. My glare doesn't have that much power when it comes to humans over the age of five.

"No, Zane's been a complete gentleman," I finally answer in a quiet voice. Well, maybe not a complete gentleman last night, but I encouraged him. Until I didn't. Which was beyond humiliating. "It's all me. I'm messed up."

Grace levels a stern look at me. "You are not messed up."

Mr. Ogilvie slips out the door and the room grows quiet. It's the two of us and Karen manning the loud copy machine at the other end of the room.

"Yeah, Grace. I'm seriously messed up when it comes to men. And I'm not sure I'm able to give Zane what he *needs*." I send her a significant look, because talking about sex in the teachers' lounge feels inappropriate.

"Needs…" It takes her a second to connect the dots. But then, "Oh. Is he pressuring you?"

Fierce-mother Grace is back, and I have to shush her before Karen gets curious.

"Of course not." It's been a little over a month since we first met. Almost four weeks since the first time he took me to dinner. Most guys would be long gone if they didn't even get some hand action by now. And I'm not talking about what I did with his thumb. "But I think he's getting a serious case of sexual frustration."

And truthfully, he's not the only one. After he left last night, I intended to take an ice-cold shower. The same shower I watched Zane masturbate in four weeks ago. Next thing, I was turning the water temperature up and putting the shower wand to good use.

Which only fed my guilt.

Grace snorts. "If Zane doesn't think you're worth the wait, then I've seriously misjudged him."

"You haven't." The last thing I want is for Grace to hate Zane. He doesn't deserve that.

My friend sets her hand on top of mine and gives it a reassuring squeeze. "Then don't worry. Take as long as you need. Even if that means he has to stay frustrated until your wedding night."

My mouth drops open, causing Grace to laugh out of control. But somehow over the next twenty-four minutes of our lunch, she has me promising to not give up on Zane.

CHAPTER THIRTEEN

LYRIC

I wake alone, shaking, my stomach in knots. Grayson lurks in my dream. Again. I can still smell his anger, feel his hot breath on my face. I wake before his fist makes contact, and for that I'm grateful. Instead of our condo, he's here in my living room. Too real. It's been almost a year since the last nightmare. I'd hoped they were gone. *Guess not.*

Sacha's looking at me from the side of the bed, concern in her eyes.

I scratch her head, her relieved panting echoes around the room. The house retains the afternoon heat, but I refuse to breach the security of locked windows. I'm sweating in just a tank top and panties. Damn northerners and their aversion to air conditioning. My landlord assured me it wasn't necessary. Funny how he spent plenty of time praising the kick-ass heating system.

I walk to the kitchen and pour cool water into Sacha's bowl, then grab a soda for myself.

"Pop," I say aloud. Still sounds odd. Like a kid making a funny noise. *Pop goes the balloon,* I read in a book at story time.

The dream fades from my mind, but there will be no more sleep tonight. Experience has taught me this much—not just this past week, but years of Grayson's nocturnal visits. It's 12:22 according to the microwave clock. In eight hours I'm expected to corral forty-eight kids at the zoo. Today's going to be hell.

I flip the TV channels and settle in to watch an old black-and-white movie I don't recognize. But a second later, I'm shutting it off. Too restless, I pull my sweaty top away from my skin for some needed air circulation. Sacha watches from her chair as I run the vacuum. I don't disturb her, leaving her chair where it is, dust bunnies be damned.

The music Zane dropped off Saturday flutters to the floor as I move too fast past the piano. I gather everything up with a sigh and sit down, giving Sacha a warning glare.

"Let's not tell him," I whisper, putting my finger to my lips.

Scales are easy, not that I'd tell Zane. He doesn't need to know how well I can play. My fingers dance over the keys as sure as a lover's touch. I give the simpled-down Mozart minuet sitting behind the sheet of scales a dubious glance, then set it aside.

I stand and lift the music bench seat. My dad's music sits in a folder inside the storage compartment. I dive into the music my father gave me over a decade ago. Playing becomes a whole body experience, my eyes skipping over the notes, my fingers on the keyboard, the ball of my bare foot pressing the cool brass pedal. The music surrounds me in peace, and my tense muscles relax. I pay no attention to the sweat dripping from my chin onto the keys.

I'm immersed in a piece called "Summertime Sonata" when a knock on the front door pulls me back to the present. My heart lodges in my throat, threatening to jump out and splat onto the sheet music in front of me. I close the fallboard and stand on shaky legs.

From the slight gap in the curtain, I take in the tall dark-haired figure decked out in a familiar leather jacket standing on my porch. *What the hell?*

"What are you doing here?" I call out, opening the door wide enough to let Zane in. "Do you even know what time it is?"

"My apologies, Angel." He bows and stumbles, his words slurred. Stepping inside, he turns and closes the door, then twists each deadbolt with exaggerated precision.

He's drunk? I step back and he weaves toward me, his eyes bloodshot and unfocused. Sirens blare and red flags fly. My skin tingles and bile rises to the back of my throat. I've had plenty of experience with drunk men. Or at least one drunk man. It wasn't good.

"Don't, Zane," I beg as he steps closer.

"Why are you playing music in the middle of the night?" His breath reeks of something stronger than beer. It could strip the paint off the walls.

Sacha slips between us, her ears back, tail still. She's as leery as I am, until he coos sweet words to her while patting her head. Still, she drops down between us, sensing my tension. Zane hasn't assured me yet. It's gonna take more than a few honeyed words and a pat on the head.

"Couldn't sleep," I whisper, my muscles tense, ready to evade whatever's coming. "Why are you here in the middle of the night?"

"I needed to see you."

He looks like shit. His eyes are red, his pupils dilated. *Is he stoned too?*

"So you stopped at a bar first, or did your *need* strike after your first, second, or third drink?" I'm bating him. Black eyes and fat lips usually proceed from my sarcasm, but I've always spoken before thinking. Lessons never learned.

"And did you actually drive here in this condition?" I didn't see his car in the driveway, but I ask anyway.

His hand messes his already messed-up hair further. "I walked."

"And you complain about me walking. At least I'm not stupid enough—" My words die as a tear spills from his eye, making a path down his cheek and then hanging on the knife-edge of his jaw.

He reaches a shaky hand to cup my cheek and I flinch.

"Are you frightened of me?" his voice croaks out.

"I don't know."

He sighs like a leaky tire. "How do I get you to trust me? I want to be your prince, your knight. I want to slay your dragons, not be one."

"I don't know. Maybe don't barge in here at three in the morning, drunk?"

"I'm sorry. I really need you in my arms." His voice is desperate, a drowning man reaching for salvation.

"Zane. What's going on?"

"It's been a really bad night, and I don't want to talk about it." He presses his lips together for a moment. "I need you right now."

How can I ignore the anguished expression on his face? I can't. "I'm here."

He walks into my open arms, and a second later his lips are on mine, urgent, desperate. A fine tremor runs through his body. My name's a sigh he whispers like a prayer. "I need you. You know that?"

I try not to smile at his repetitive message. "Yeah?"

"If I lost you... I'd forget how to breathe."

My heart squeezes with the depth of emotion in his voice, his tears wetting my bare shoulder. "Well, that's not a bad option right now. Your breath is lethal. What were you drinking?"

He shifts his attention from my lips to the base of my neck. His tongue's warm on my sweaty skin, his heavy arms around me keeping him upright. My shoulders burn from the strain, and sweat trickles down my spine.

"Bourbon." He licks slow circles on my neck, and I can't help the shivers of desire sliding over my skin. "That's what... why I got you that bouquet. You liked that, right?"

"I liked that a lot."

"Romantic, but practical, all in one package. You're going to fall hard, future Mrs. Brody," he whispers, like it's a secret.

My lungs freeze at his words. "Shhh. Don't talk like that, Zane. I can't marry you."

"Someday. You're already mine. License or not, you're mine. I have fallen madly in love with you. Given you my heart. Can't give it back." He shakes his head slightly across my shoulder. "Wouldn't be polite."

"Oh, Zane..." He's wearing me down. Even drunk Zane is irresistible. A small part of me wants to let go, be free of my fears. Zane Brody's grown on me and it would be so easy to indulge in the idea of having him forever. "You're a sappy drunk, but tomorrow you're going to regret this."

"Sappy and love sick." He pulls back and reaches over his shoulder, removing his shirt in that crazy way guys have of pulling it over their head from behind. His voice is muffled under the cotton, and he doesn't quite make it, swaying on his feet. I jump in and help before we both end up on the floor.

His foul breath is forgotten as he claims my mouth again, slowly shifting us toward the bedroom. I take over steering after we bounce off the doorframe. Sappy, drunk Zane isn't coordinated Zane.

He fumbles with the button on his jeans. I shouldn't help him. I should send him back into the living room to sleep this off on the couch. But it's hot and he's going to feel miserable enough in a few hours. And I have nothing to fear from this man, at least not right now.

"We have work in a few hours, so this little sleepover is just that. A *sleep* over," I warn while dragging back the sheets and patting the mattress, choosing his side for him.

His lips curve up in a goofy grin. "I get the left side."

"Fine." I shut off the lights to keep from noticing his well-muscled thighs, or the way his black boxer briefs hug his firm ass. "Now get in bed."

"I love a demanding woman."

"And I love a man that doesn't vomit on my sheets."

He tucks me against his chest. "And I love you."

His breath evens out, and his whole body relaxes against mine. Sweat breaks out across my skin, having nothing to do with the warmth of the room or the hot man pressed against me. He's drunk. He doesn't mean those three little words. Will probably regret them in the morning—if he even remembers.

"YOU LOOK LIKE SHIT," his sister yells out her window as Zane and I step around the front of her car. Zane returns her comment with a rude gesture, then opens the front door for me.

"Lyric, this is my older sister, Laura Anderson. Laura, Lyric James. Be nice, please." He gives his sister a hard stare.

"I'm always nice," his sister returns his gesture as he closes my door. "So glad to finally meet you, Lyric. I brought coffee."

I thank her and then snag the cup of—oooh, vanilla latte. I think I may love Zane's sister already.

There's no mistaking Zane and Laura as siblings. They both share the same dark chocolate hair color and the same slight dimple in their chins. Zane's chiseled jaw and high cheek bones are softer on his sister, but those stunning blue eyes are even more unsettling framed in black mascara and subtle gray eye shadow.

"So no Black Sabbath at full volume?" his sister asks while passing the second cup of coffee into the back seat. "Damn, I was craving some vintage Ozzy this morning."

"News flash, sis. All Ozzy is vintage," Zane grumbles.

His sister casually flips him off while adjusting the rearview mirror and backs out of the driveway.

"Smart ass. Thinks since he was blessed with all the musical talent, I know nothing." Her gaze shifts to the rearview mirror. "News flash, brother. Mom called after ten last night to let me know you stormed out of the house. You want to tell me what happened now, or wait until I drop off your girlfriend? Although, since your car's still parked at Mad Jack's I can only imagine the condition you were in when you knocked on this poor woman's door at..." She glances at me and I mouth, *three a.m.* She shakes her head and continues, "I think Lyric deserves an explanation as much as I do."

"You two going to gang up on me?"

"Maybe." She flashes a bright smile my way. "Teasing my brother should be a national sport, especially when he's hung over."

Zane groans from the back seat. "She's giving up," he says, his voice gravelly with emotion.

Laura glances in my direction while stopping at the intersection at the end of my block, her brows furrowed. "Who's giving up?"

"Mom. She quit the fucking chemo. Says she's done fighting."

"Ahh." Laura nods, as if this is no surprise to her. "So you decided to get drunk?"

"No. I argued with Mom for a while, called her a selfish bitch, then stormed out of the house to think. Then I drowned myself in guilt while driving around, after an hour or so I found myself pulling into Mad Jack's parking lot, then I got drunk." His sigh is filled with regret. "Now go ahead and say it. I'm an idiot."

"I've known worse." The words are out before I can stop them, and the car goes silent. "Sorry."

"Shit," Zane whispers from the back. "I'm sure you have. But I'd rather you not witness me doing stupid things."

"So don't do stupid things, Zane," his sister says. "If you need help—"

"I don't need help." Zane growls. "One drink led to two, then three... Well, you get the picture. It wasn't pretty last night, but I don't make a habit out of it. I promise."

"I hope not. You're under a lot of stress right now. I'll give you a pass for last night."

The silence returns for the next couple of blocks.

"Why the fuck is she quitting chemo?" Zane asks, his voice rising.

Laura lets out a harsh breath. "She's accepted her fate. Now you have to respect that."

"I'd fight. I'd fight till my dying breath."

His sister shoots him a skeptical glance through the rearview mirror, then changes the subject to something slightly less uncomfortable. I think. "So, have you asked Lyric, yet?"

I almost spit my coffee onto Laura's wood-grained dashboard. Setting my cup back into the holder, I swivel in my seat and send Zane a suspicious look. "Ask me what?"

"Thanks, Laura. Obviously, that's a no."

The car slows as we stop at a red light.

"Ask me what?" I repeat.

"Ask her," Laura instructs, this time sending her brother an encouraging smile. "It's exciting. I know I'd say yes if I didn't have two kids and a husband that need me."

I shift my attention between the two siblings, my stomach sinking. I've had enough excitement in the past month. I'm not looking for more excitement. "Say yes to what?"

"I planned on telling you on the way home this afternoon, not with my big sister—"

"Tell me now," I say through gritted teeth. "Or I'm walking the rest of the way to school."

I glance out the window. We're maybe a half mile from school. I could easily walk there.

"Zane…" His sister prompts before pulling away from the light, then making the turn onto Snelling.

"Fine. Dave signed the band up for some concerts. Mostly local stuff. County fairs and festivals. Weekends only, obviously. We'll leave on Fridays and be back Sundays. Come with me? It'll be fun."

My eyes widen with shock while my pulse hammers inside my head. Fun? "What am I going to do with Sacha? I can't leave her home alone."

"Tess will watch her. She loved the idea, and honestly I'll feel a lot better knowing my sister won't be alone in the house. I know this is last minute, but Dave only told me and Aaron last week. I wasn't even sure I could go until I worked out the details."

"I'll be taking our mom on most of the weekends," Laura says, turning the car onto School Street. "But I'll stop in and check on Tess and Sacha."

My skin bristles. Zane worked everything out with his younger sister, his mom. Even Laura knows. Too bad he didn't let me in on this scheme.

"You wanted to stay busy this summer," Zane reminds, his hopeful expression practically begging me to say yes. I've yet to find the will to say no to his requests.

"Can I at least think about it? There's some things I have to work out." Like if the butterflies dancing inside my stomach signal excitement or fear. Like whether spending all weekend with Zane is a brilliant idea or a disaster. Like whether I'm ready for whatever *fun* he has in mind. *Pretty sure it means the kind of fun you have in a hotel bed.*

Laura pulls into the school parking lot, and I'm more than eager to get out.

"For the record, I like you, Lyric. Whatever you decide to do with this crazy man, let's have lunch."

I can't help but smile. "That would be nice. Have Zane give you my number."

"Not happening," Zane mutters, then opens his door. We meet on the blacktop, and he gives me an exasperated sigh.

"Happening," his sister calls out from inside the car.

"Be nice," I echo his earlier words with an encouraging smile. "I want to have lunch with your sister."

He groans. "Fine. I'll give her your number, but I'm warning you. She's inquisitive."

"Must run in the family. For the record I haven't tossed you out of my life." Even though I've tried.

Zane's gaze lands on the line of buses pulling into the lot, gracing us with their exhaust as they pass. A moment later a mass of kids swarm past.

"Look, I'm sorry about springing this tour on you." He breathes out a heavy breath of what I'm assuming is regret. "I don't recall too much of last night, but I do remember waking up next to you. If my life was my own, I'd want to see the morning sun dancing on your skin every day. But no pressure. Aaron is bringing Grace. I'm sure I can convince him to let the two of you share a room."

I nod, appreciating his no-pressure suggestion, although I'm pretty sure Aaron won't. Last night's sleepover was out of necessity—Zane was in no condition to walk home, and I was too tired to consider the ramifications of offering my bed. Every decision has consequences. But a part of me would be very receptive to a repeat of last night, without the passing out or the whiskey breath. A part of me has no trouble remembering the way Zane's chest pressed against my back, or the way his arm around me made me feel safe and secure. But am I ready to move this relationship in that direction, yet? My libido says yes, but the more logical me warns once I take that step there'll be no going back.

"I promise to think about it."

"That's all I'm asking." His smile suggests he thinks he's already won.

"Fine. Now go, Mr. Brody. I have a date with the elephants and giraffes and monkeys and..."

He leans forward and brushes his lips against mine. "And just so you know, I wasn't drunk enough to know the music you were playing last night wasn't the stuff I left you. You've been holding out on me, Miss James. Don't think we won't be coming back to this conversation in the very near future."

CHAPTER FOURTEEN

LYRIC

*S*acha wakes me bright and early Saturday morning, barking to raise the dead. I glance at the clock and let out a whimper. After the band's set last night, Zane insisted on taking a walk along the banks of Bde Maka Ska to wind down before heading home. A week ago I was contemplating breaking up with him, now I'm spending my nights running the pros and cons of accompanying him on the tour, while staring at the ceiling instead of sleeping. *At least you aren't having nightmares about Grayson.*

I've never been good at saying no, but this was more than accepting an invite to a lingerie party or volunteering to bring dessert to a dinner I'd have rather not attended.

Please don't leave me to face the groupies alone. Grace's desperate words from earlier last night played on repeat until I was too exhausted to think.

I stumble into the living room, tugging my robe closed and shushing my dog. Outside there's a hideous yellow van idling in the driveway. Pretty sure it's Zane, since Grayson wouldn't be caught dead in something that ugly.

"If you traded your car in for that hideous thing I'm breaking up with you," I call out from the porch.

Zane bounds up the steps with more energy than a person should have with what little sleep he's gotten. He hands me a bag of some savory-scented deliciousness and a coffee, then his hands cup my face and his lips are on mine in a slow, lingering kiss that has me struggling not to drop my bounty.

"Don't worry. I'm just borrowing this beauty from Dave. Now come and see what I've brought you." He flashes a wide smile and sprints back down the stairs.

Brought me?

"What did you bring me, Zane?" I follow at a slower pace while opening the bag with one hand. Inside is the most glorious sandwich I've ever seen. This beauty definitely didn't come from McDonalds. Even the layer of healthy spinach can't diminish the majesty of melty cheese and perfectly runny egg on pillowy-soft brioche.

I take a sip of hot coffee, warily eyeing the Mathers and Sons van as if it might contain a pony or a big screen TV. With Zane anything is possible.

The back doors swing open with a god-awful squeak and inside is… wood? Stacks and stacks of wood.

"What *is* this?" I mumble around a big bite of sandwich.

I do my best to ignore the way his arm muscles bulge, straining the sleeves of his T-shirt, as he balances three long boards on his shoulder as if they weigh nothing.

"It's your new deck."

Despite the muscle porn in front of me, I'm not smiling. Even with this breakfast fantasy in my hand—which I'm beginning to look at with suspicion—I'm the opposite of smiling. "I have a deck."

He turns with a "watch out." I duck a second before the boards he's holding slice the air above my head as he adds, "You have a death trap."

I chase him around the side of the house. "You're exaggerating. It's not that bad."

"Have you even looked at it?" He tips his head in the direction of the gate. "Can you open this please?"

Juggling my coffee and sandwich in one hand, I dial in the combination on the lock and shove open the stubborn wooden gate with my hip. *Have I looked at my deck?* "Of course I've looked at my deck."

Zane drops the boards in the grass with an all-mighty crash that makes me wince. "Come here, Angel."

He takes my hand and leads me to the wide structure that stretches along the backside of the house. I'll admit it's not the prettiest deck I've ever seen. The boards are a little warped and gray—okay, black—from being out in the weather.

Zane pulls a Swiss Army knife from his pocket and stabs the blade into my deck. I'm about to protest when he twists the steel into the wood and the board crumbles. All that's left is a small, jagged hole I can see straight through to the dark and dirty gravel below. "See that? That's rot. Luckily the joists underneath are okay. But I've checked a few places, and these boards are not safe, Lyric. One of these days you or Sacha are going to fall right through. Your landlord should have sealed this decking every year to prevent this."

I nearly choke on the bite of sandwich in my mouth. "Yeah, tell him that."

Zane turns to face me, his expression stone. "Give me his number and I will."

I wouldn't call Mr. Dunkelstein a slumlord, but he's not far off. But the rent is cheap and he minds his own business, so I'm not complaining. And neither will Zane.

"I might have to put you on a payment plan." A summer without supplemental income is going to be tight as it is.

Zane snorts out a laugh. "Like I'm going to make you pay."

"Don't be ridiculous. You're not footing the bill for *my* deck." I pop the last bite of sandwich into my mouth and chew as we stare each other down.

Zane's face cracks into a wide smile, and then he pulls me into his arms, burying his face into the crook of my neck. My skin tingles as his lips move. "You're fun when you're stubborn, but I know a way you could pay me back."

"And how's that?" I ask, all innocent, while my stomach bottoms out on this thrill ride called Zane Brody. My nipples pebble hard against the solid muscle of his chest. And a little lower... Well, let's face it, every part of me wants what he wants. If only I could turn off the part of my brain that's still telling me to be careful.

I'm tired of being careful.

"Join me on the tour," he whispers, his warm breath raising the hairs on the back of my neck. "I enjoyed waking up with you on Thursday morning."

"Even with a hangover?"

He pulls back with an uneasy look on his face. "Yeah, about that..."

"Don't apologize. I get it." I do. Zane's been in denial about his mother's condition. Accepting the unwanted truth sucks. "And I'm not saying no to the tour. I'm just..." Waiting for a sign that tells me this thing between me and Zane isn't a mistake?

"You're the boss. I can have Dave book another room if you want." He bends his knees and looks me straight in the eye. "I want you there any way you're comfortable."

I can't explain what happens next. It's like all the doubts and fears I've been harboring suddenly seem insignificant. Grace was right. Zane Brody is a good man. And I'm being an idiot holding him at arm's length.

He grabs his knife off the deck, folds it back up, and shoves it into his shorts' pocket. "You get dressed while I finish unloading the van. Dave and Dillon will be here shortly, and this..." He waves his hand in front of me, taking in the lack of bra under my tank top and skimpy panties, my open robe is doing little to hide. "...this view is not for them."

I refasten the tie on my robe because this view is not for my neighbors either. Then watch Zane as he heads back to the gate with long strides, while trying to reconcile this new mindset of mine with the one I'd woken up with up less than a half hour ago. It seems monumental.

"Zane," I call out and he turns, causing another flutter in my stomach. "I'll go."

SACHA STARES out the back screen door. I don't blame her. At some point today, Zane's taken off his shirt. Earlier, him, Dave, and Dillon ripped out all the old, rotted decking, but now it's just me and Zane.

Who knew carpentry work could be so entertaining? Sweat beads on Zane's bare shoulders and his muscles flex as he hammers in nail after nail, making the ink on his skin dance. Now I know why Grace and Zoe were always talking about those home improvement shows. A sweaty, muscled man working with his hands has to be the sexiest thing I've ever witnessed.

"How's it going over there?" he asks around the nails he's got hanging out of his mouth. He pushes back the heavy weight of his hair—liberally sprinkled with wood dust. The wicked glint in his eye lets me know I've been caught ogling him again. *Not my fault.*

I sit transfixed in front of a flower pot, its contents forgotten while I try to come up with other projects he can do around the house. Not that Mr. Dunkelstein would allow us to make improvements on this house. But if we bought a fixer-upper...

Reality crashes hard. My life here is temporary. *But does it have to be?* Grayson's been out of prison for almost two months. Surely I'd have heard from him by now if he planned to make good on his threats.

"Let me take *my* shirt off. Then we'll see who's distracted," I toss back.

Zane spits the nails into his hand. His eyes widen for a second as if contemplating such a thing. "Can we wait until I'm done with the power tools? I'd like to keep all my fingers."

"Good point." I shove the gardening gloves Zane bought me back on my hands. In front of me sits one of five monster-sized pots he bought, glazed in bright, happy colors, along with a combination of flower and vegetable plants. *To decorate my new deck.* "You're pretty good with a hammer. Did they teach you that at Juilliard?"

His smile falters. "No. Spent a summer working for Greg Cox's construction company while he was married to my mother."

My brows lower as I process his words. According to Zane, his mother and her second husband divorced not too long after Tess was born. But that would have made Zane, what, twelve, maybe thirteen at the most. What kind of work did his stepfather have a thirteen-year-old boy do? Not that it's any of my business.

I need to respect that there are parts of Zane's life I'll never discover just like there are parts of mine I'll always keep to myself. We both have skeletons best left buried.

I dig a hole in the dirt with my fingers and grab the last of three pots of white and yellow daisies. I'm already finished with the peppers and cherry tomatoes and the herbs.

"Don't forget to give them a good drink," Zane reminds with a smile that says he's forgotten his stepfather already.

Sacha lets out an impatient woof from her spot at the kitchen door, as if reminding me she's still waiting for me to let her out. Besides the walk we took at our lunch break, she's been in all day. *Poor baby.*

"Soon, Sacha. Zane's almost done."

"I am done," he corrects. "Want me to let her out?"

"Not until I'm done with the hose," I say. Zane's yet to see the crazy side of Sacha. "She likes to attack water drops."

"Better water drops than strange men you invite into your house," he says while fumbling with the circa 1970s folding chaise lounge chairs we found in the back of my garage.

"Ha ha. Very funny."

A warm, happy feeling settles under my skin. It's impossible to deny that Zane cares. He cares enough to remember my favorite flower. Enough to notice the dangers of a rotted deck. And also enough to put his wants and needs on hold while I figure out mine.

What guy would do that? Definitely not Grayson.

I head over to the side of the house where a bright blue hose with a high-tech nozzle hangs—courtesy of Zane—from a rusty, old hook that looks like it's been on this house forever. I can't even imagine what all this cost, much less pay him back.

By the time I return, Zane's got all his tools put away, and he's reclined back, hands behind his head, eyes closed. "All I need now is a cold beer and a hot woman."

"Beer's in the fridge, but I'm all out of hot women."

"You know what I mean." His eyes narrow in on me. "Come on over, Angel. Let's see if this rickety thing will hold both of us."

"You're filthy." Coated with sawdust that's stuck to his sweaty skin. *Gross.*

He lets out a low chuckle. "You have no idea." Then starts singing some Pink Floyd song about needing a dirty woman.

I give all the plants a good soaking and then send an arc of water in Zane's direction.

"Lyric," his tone is all big bad wolf. *The better to eat you with, my dear.*

I paste on a wide-eyed innocent smile. "Sooo sorry. I'm trying to get a hang of this fancy nozzle you got me."

His narrow gaze tells me he doesn't buy my excuse for one

second. I laugh, and because I can, because I know this won't end with a bloody lip or a dislocated shoulder, I shoot him again.

"Oops." I press my lips together while watching the water drip from his chin, dotting the fine hairs on his chest. It's an attractive look.

"You better run." He bolts out of his chair. I let out a squeal and leap off the deck with Zane close behind. Before I know it, the hose is tugged out of my hands and a second later I'm hit with a long, ice-cold blast of water.

Zane chuckles as I turn to face him, my hair dripping, my shirt sticking to my back. "Sorry. It got away from me."

"So funny."

"Yep." His grin is all mischief and sex appeal.

Another blast of icy water hits me in the chest. His smile doesn't even waver, and there's no offered apology this time. *Bastard.* I send him a waterlogged glare, then break into a sprint in his direction.

He mutters something that sounds like "oh shit" and takes off laughing.

He's so dead. I barely sprinkled him, but I'm completely soaked. The man obviously doesn't know what's fair. But when I catch him I'll be more than happy to teach him.

His long legs give him the advantage, but he's also tethered by the hose. He'll have to choose between standing his ground or dropping the nozzle and fleeing. Either way I'm ready.

The hose stretches taut and he turns, shutting off the water and holding his hands up in the universal sign of surrender.

I stalk closer, barking out a slightly out of breath and completely sinister laugh. Damn him, driving me to school every day. I'm out of shape.

"Lyric…" He gives me the same deep warning he gave earlier.

"Zane," I return sweetly.

He takes a step back, but the hose doesn't give an inch. "You got me and I got you. Let's call it even."

"Even?" I raise an unbelieving eyebrow while pulling my soaked shirt from my skin. *How can he call this even?*

He brandishes the nozzle in front of him. "Don't start something you aren't ready to finish."

"Could say the same thing to you," I taunt.

"Remember I didn't start this. But I'm more than happy to finish it."

Finish it, my ass. I lunge forward. Shoes squelching, my sodden-wet clothes hampering my forward momentum, I grab hold of the hose and pull.

Zane lets out a curse and pulls back. My wet fingers slide along the rubber, making me grunt in frustration.

Suddenly there's water everywhere. In my face, down my shirt, icy water chilling my damp skin all over again. And by the sounds of Zane's laughter, he's enjoying every second of his victory.

"I give up," I sputter, wiping water from my eyes.

There's a horrible crash, and both Zane and I turn to see Sacha barreling toward us, the screen door half off its hinges.

"Turn it off," I yell to Zane.

"It won't shut off," Zane shouts back. I stumble forward to assist in whatever the hell he's trying to accomplish—besides drowning all of us.

Ninety pounds of very excited dog bounces off my hip while she snaps at the spray of water. My foot snags on the hose, or maybe Zane's shoe. Whatever, my other foot slips in the wet grass and my fingers slide across Zane's slick chest in attempt to catch my balance. He swears, his fingers slipping against my equally slick skin, then I'm falling.

My body hits the soggy ground with a squishy splat and I stare up into blue sky for a fraction of a second, then Zane kneels down to offer assistance.

Sacha takes full advantage of our position, shoving a very

dirty plush bunny onto my chest and doling out doggie kisses equally between me and Zane.

"Stop." Her tongue lands in my open mouth, and I gasp and sputter, spitting out dog drool and mud and I don't want to think about what else.

"You okay?" Zane tosses the still spraying hose across the lawn and takes a second to inspect my face.

"Oh God." A slightly unhinged giggle bubbles up as I watch my goofy dog chase after the geyser.

"First time in three years a man has me on my back, and I'm covered in mud and grass clippings and…" I pick Sacha's plush bunny off my chest and pitch it into the grass. "God knows what else. I was hoping for something a bit more romantic."

"You look beautiful in mud and grass clippings." His fingers trail along my jaw and his thumb brushes across my bottom lip.

The playful mood quickly shifts with his touch, and his eyes—now more dark than blue—focus back on my lips. Somehow my hand finds its way onto the hard curve of Zane's bare pec, and I let my thumb trace over the constellation of stars inked onto his warm skin.

Then I press both my hands against his chest, holding him back. "Just so you know, I've recently been French kissed by my dog, who licks her ass and barfs up dead bugs."

"She kissed me too."

Does that make it better? Maybe? I'm not sure. But before I can decide, Zane seals his lips over mine, and I can definitely say the second tongue to invade my mouth today is much more welcome than the first.

More talented too.

His hands dive into my wet hair while his mouth takes mine with an urgency that has me forgetting about dirt and dead bugs, soggy clothes and the puddle I'm lying in. Or the show we're putting on for the neighbors.

I drag my bare foot up his hard calf—*what happened to my shoe?*

—and lock my leg around his thigh, pressing myself against his erection in the process.

Zane lets out a tortured groan, his hips pistoning forward. His kiss turns ravenous, lips bruising, tongue fucking my mouth the way his body clearly wants to.

My hands slip under the waistband of his shorts, exploring the smooth, firm curve of his ass, and urging him on. Even through my jean shorts he's hitting me perfectly.

He stills, pulling back a fraction to look down at me. "Definitely should take this inside."

"Definitely," I echo without pausing.

He lifts up on his hands and chuckles. "Now. We should go in, now."

"Don't want to stop," I mutter. Why does he have to be so insistent?

He dips down and places a soft, gentle kiss on my lips. Then another and another. "You're shivering. Let's get your crazy dog dried off and then let's work on that romantic stuff you were hoping for."

CHAPTER FIFTEEN

ZANE

"*D*amn, you're beautiful." I refuse to blink as I take in every inch of the woman sitting no more than a foot in front of me.

From her perch on the bathroom counter, she sweeps me with a scrutinizing stare, and my heart races. Clad in an innocent pale-pink bra and panties that are somehow sexier than lace, she sways one leg slowly off the counter edge, while the other foot's propped on the ugly orange marbled surface, her chin resting on her clasped fingers draped over her raised knee. Eyes narrowed a fraction, she chews on her bottom lip. The only sign that tells me she might be a fraction as nervous about this as I am. Actually, I'm fucking petrified.

Don't fuck this up, Brody.

There's so many ways that could happen, it's like walking a damn minefield. Our first-date panic attack flashes through my mind. With just a few careless words I almost lost her that night. I have to be careful. Her trust is fragile and precious. I've worked hard to get here; I don't want to lose this. I don't want to lose her.

She laughs. "A beautiful mess, you mean."

I've waited almost seven weeks for this woman—longer than

I've ever had to with anyone else. Weeks of tortured dreams and longing. Weeks of earning her trust and overcoming her fears. She's like a fucking drug in my veins. I'm addicted and helpless. And if I have to wait any longer I will, but it won't be easy.

The uncertainty in her forest-green eyes tells me I have to hold back, stay in control. This is for her. The woman with the scars both inside and out from the last bastard she put her faith in. I'd rather walk away than add any more.

Don't think you can at this point.

Not with the way the skimpy fabric covering Lyric hides nothing, not the dusky peaks of her hard nipples poking against the thin cotton, nor the shadowed paradise between her spread legs. My dick's rock hard and stretching obscenely against the front of my boxers. I can't think. Can't breathe. How do I take care of her when I'm fucking blind with desire right now?

"We can fix that." I crank the faucet knob on the shower and she returns my grin. At some point in this bathroom's life there was likely a tub crammed against this wall. Whoever replaced it with the walk-in shower deserves an award, a metal, a big fucking thank-you. The enclosure is nothing fancy, just some plain builder white tile, a glass door, and a shower head, but it's the perfect size for two people who don't mind getting close.

Lyric's big green eyes light up, and the corners crinkle in a way I'm beginning to appreciate. It's her genuine smile, the one she flashes when her guard is down, which is as rare as the vintage seventies counter she's sitting on—although a lot prettier.

The playful moment wavers as a knot of anxiety twists in my stomach.

Don't fuck this up.

"Anytime you want to stop, just say so," I confirm, lifting her off the counter and setting her back on her feet. My fingertips stroke the soft skin of her arms before weaving my fingers with hers.

"Zane..." She sighs my name, rolling her eyes with the same

impatience and frustration I've witnessed these past few days. Reaching up with our combined hands, I press my finger to her lips, flashing her a stern look. I've got too much to lose by rushing ahead without thinking.

"Just listen, okay?" She tips her head a fraction and nods, and I lower our hands, giving hers a reassuring squeeze. "I do anything to make you uncomfortable. Tell me. I want this to be good—wait, not good, *amazing*." I grin wickedly, because I can't help my confidence. I may have made more than my share of relationship mistakes, but I've never had any complaints in bed. And pleasing Lyric is my ultimate goal. "So fucking good you forget—"

Her hands tunnel into my hair and she pulls me to her lips, cutting off the rest of my words with a kiss. A really nice kiss, infused with the flavor of minty toothpaste and enough eagerness to shock the hell out of me and relieve some of my fears.

Of course she insisted we brush the doggie kisses off our teeth. After we toweled off her dripping wet and squirming dog. After she insisted we strip down and deposit our sodden clothes in the washing machine. After wiping up the muddy footprints from the backdoor.

Twenty minutes later my desire to have this woman is only stronger. Her kiss severs the last thread of my willpower. There's no holding back. Not with her tongue in my mouth and her fingers gripping my ass. Her soft curves press against my bare skin, her hips rocking against the hardness in my boxers, making me groan with a mixture of pleasure and agony.

I blindly walk backward, my fingers curling around the shower doorway, guiding us in the right direction. With my free hand I make quick work of the clasp on her bra, slip the thin straps off her shoulders and let it fall to the floor. Another step back and my fingers hook into her panties, sliding them over her generous hips and letting the sodden fabric drop as well. My hands skate down her sides, over the curve of her ass, then back up to her breasts, assuring myself she's finally naked.

"Zane," she starts to pull away, her labored gasps matching mine. I chase after her lips, not wanting to sever our connection. Not wanting to give her time to think. "Don't you need to breathe?" she pants. Her eyes are dark pools in a sun-dappled grove. Verdant and lush with a sparkle of sunshine. Fucking gorgeous.

"I can breathe later. Right now..." I dart my tongue out to lick the corner of her mouth. "I only need you."

I pull her closer, kiss her harder, deeper. Her cool fingers slide inside my boxers, her knuckles brushing against me, causing me to shudder. Then she tugs the sodden fabric down my hips. Blessed gravity takes over and they splat against the shower floor, leaving me naked with just enough mental capacity to remember to close the glass door before guiding Lyric under the hot spray.

My back hits the cool tile wall with a thud while I devour Lyric's mouth. Lips, tongue, teeth. Her hand wraps around my cock and all the blood in my head rushes south, making me dizzy. Making me forget for a minute why we're in here.

I've lost count of the number of times I've dreamed of pinning her to the wall behind me and sinking into her hot flesh. The temptation to do just that is powerful, but I have other plans. Plans that include tasting every inch of her body, making her scream my name over and over while I discover all the ways to make her come. To worship her body *properly* on a soft mattress, not against the shower wall. At least not the first time.

I take my time soaping up every inch of her slick body, her soft feminine curves that I'm reading like a map. Every moan, every gasp gets recorded for future use.

She returns the favor, and I have to grit my teeth when her soapy fingers slide up and down my granite-hard length in a way that's guaranteed to have me spilling into her hand in seconds. Does she even have a clue what she's doing to me right now? By the wicked smile curving her lips, I'm thinking she does.

I reach down and unwrap her fingers before I lose control, then guide her hands to my shoulders.

"Hold on," I instruct, then lift her legs around my waist, pinning my eager cock between us. Shut the water off and open the door. I can't wait any longer.

She frowns, her eyes squinting a fraction as she scrubs her fingers through my hair. "Wait. Your hair. There's still some shampoo."

"Don't care." I set her back on the vanity and grab a bath towel off the shelf. She probably has a thing about wet sheets, so I do a thorough job of drying both of us off before carrying her into the bedroom.

The late afternoon sun still shines on the opposite side of the house. But inside her room shadowed pools claim the corners while dust motes sparkle in the few lingering beams of sunlight by the window.

A handful of steps into the room and I set her on the edge of her tall brass bed and peel back her towel to reveal everything. I press slow kisses down her neck, my tongue collecting the sweet drops of moisture from the shower. The heavy weight of her breast fills my hand, my thumb stroking over her already hard nipple, making her sigh.

"Zane…"

"Tell me you want this. That you want me," I whisper, then dip down and close my lips over the puckered skin.

Her fingers slide through my damp hair while mine glide through her soft, slick folds. "Want…" she gasps out as I scrape my teeth across the hardened bud of her nipple. "God yes… want you."

I take her mouth again, my tongue making slow passes against hers while I guide her down onto the mattress. I drive two fingers into her tight heat while my thumb draws slow circles around her clit. Her hips arch off the bed, and I can't help but groan at the way she feels and the needy sounds she's making.

My dick is painfully hard and dripping, but I shove my need aside.

I slide my free hand down her leg, hooking behind her knee and spreading her legs apart. Time stops and I take in a slow breath, locking in the details of this moment. Lyric's eyes, dark and hungry, her breasts heaving, her skin a rosy pink. The soft plain of her stomach and her silky thighs. My fingers buried deep inside her.

"Beautiful..." She has to be the most beautiful woman I've ever laid eyes on. But her beauty is more than physical. She's beautiful for the way she's dropped her defenses. Giving me a chance I probably don't deserve, making me want to be a better man for her.

I drop to my knees, spread her thighs open further with my shoulders, letting my slick fingers peel her open. She rises to her elbows, her eyes wide. She issues a shaky protest. Begging me to take her, to fuck her.

"Shhh," I whisper, gripping my cock hard, her dirty words almost my undoing. Sliding my hand down to her foot, I cup her heel and guide her leg over my shoulder. "Not yet."

"Oh my God, Zane." A blush creeps across her cheeks and down her throat, and her eyes flutter shut as I place her other leg over my opposite shoulder, opening her up to me completely. She's so fucking gorgeous with her neatly trimmed curls and glistening pink flesh.

I drive my fingers back into her heat, then retreat only to plunge back again. A few more strokes and my hand is drenched. Her thighs tremble with every sweep of my thumb over her clit, her hips rocking in time with my fingers.

"Zane... I'm... I'm..." she cries out, her muscles squeezing my fingers as she comes, her legs shaking.

I barely give her time to come down before replacing my fingers with my mouth. Her cries are all the encouragement I need. My tongue delves inside her cleft, licking up the nectar from her orgasm. I'm fucking ravenous, and she's just as sinfully sweet as my dreams promised.

"Zane... oh fuck," she gasps, her fingers digging into my scalp, pulling me closer, pulling me exactly where she wants me despite her protest. "I—I can't."

"For me," I whisper against her soft flesh. "Come for me."

My lips close around her clit and I suck her into my mouth. My fingers curl, dragging against her inner walls as I slow my strokes. She comes apart again, beautifully, spectacularly, her sweet voice crying out in a breathtaking crescendo.

I ease her down slowly, relishing every twitch of her muscles, every gasp from her lips. Then stand. Sheathe myself with the condom I put in my wallet almost two months ago just for her.

"Please..." Lyric scoots back against the pillows and reaches for me, a lazy, satisfied expression on her face that makes me want to celebrate. "I need you, Zane Brody."

I press a soft kiss to her lips, then drop my forehead to hers and drag her leg over my hip. Then pause for a second and stare into her eyes, searching for any trace of doubt or fear. Finding none, I press forward. Inch by inch, I slowly sink into her exquisite heat, filling her, until I'm completely inside her.

Her mouth drops open, her breath coming in harsh gasps that match mine. Our bodies tremble and my heart thuds loud in my chest. I still, relishing in the feeling of her surrounding me. Then she lifts up and kisses me, and I let go.

My hips roll forward, my pelvis grinding. Her lips on mine, her hands in my hair. I surge forward, again and again. Cradling her knee in the crook of my arm, I pull her leg higher, diving deeper. I lose myself in her.

With every thrust, I give a little more of myself to her. Losing the fight to keep something back. There's no going back. Only forward, and only with her. She's my truth and my reason and my music. My forever.

Her body pulses around me, my name the sweetest cry on her

lips. I follow her, letting my pleasure pull me under. I'm lost without a care, swept up in the surge, vanishing for one perfect breathless moment.

We come down slowly, breaths harsh, lips and hands still exploring with languid strokes, like we can't get enough of each other. I pull back from our kiss and roll to my side, taking her with me. Taking in the flush of her cheeks and the shine in her eyes. Her swollen lips curve into a smile that has my heart lifting.

"Oh my God, Zane," she whispers, her voice drowsy.

"Yeah…" I can't help but agree.

Reluctantly, I slip out of bed and dispose of the condom and then return, sliding across the sweat-drenched sheets and settling in close to Lyric, breathing in her soft scent mixed with the warmth of her skin. I tug the blankets over our now-chilled bodies and pull her closer, pressing a kiss against her shoulder.

Sacha scratches at the door, and I let out a resigned sigh and start to shift away from Lyric. She grabs my arm and pulls me back.

"Don't. Sacha will climb between us and ruin everything. I want to enjoy this for a little longer."

As if she understands, Sacha drops to the hall floor with a loud groan of protest making us both chuckle.

"Me too," I say, tucking a strand of hair behind Lyric's ear with a satisfied smile that might be permanently affixed to my face. "Maybe I should cancel tonight, so we can enjoy this a lot longer." Like all night.

"And maybe Dave will skin you alive."

I let out a groan of agreement while pulling Lyric closer, nuzzling the sensitive spot at the base of her neck. "You're probably right. But we have a little time. And I think I know how to spend it."

After a sleepless night, I should suggest a nap. I'm going to be dragging in a few hours once this incredible high dissipates. But now that I have Lyric, I can't get enough.

"Yeah?" She giggles, her body squirming against my pursuing fingers in a way that tells me she feels the same.

She's warm and wet and... fuck. I roll her back against the sheets, the feel of her soft curves filling my hands, making me instantly hard all over.

"Yeah." I rock against her while reaching for the spare condom I set on the bedside table.

CHAPTER SIXTEEN

LYRIC

"Oooh dessert. Thank you." Laura's grin threatens to split her face in two as she takes in the bags from Durango Bakery that Zane handed me before dropping me off at his sister's house in St. Paul. Her flowy print top and navy shorts scream comfortable, and expensive. In my discount capris and tank top I feel like the poor relation, but within seconds Laura pulls me off the wide front porch of her stately bungalow and into her home, giving me a warm hug. "I'm so glad you're here."

Zane had instructed me to *behave* before taking off for practice. But by the way his sister links her arm in mine with a "we have so much to talk about," I'm thinking his instructions might have been aimed at the wrong person.

We head through her expansive home and out into a lush backyard complete with swimming pool. A child cannonballs off the diving board, cheered on by a half dozen other children already in the water.

"Thanks for agreeing to come over," Laura's voice rises above the shrieks and laughter, motioning to an umbrella-covered patio table, set for lunch, on one side of the deck. "I'd have loved to have gone to a restaurant, but with the start of summer vacation, my time is theirs. And we have more privacy here than at a restaurant table. Iced tea or lemonade?"

My attention is pulled toward the happy chaos going on behind me. "Ice tea, please. Zane said you have two?"

She laughs while pouring fragrant tea—that's definitely not Lipton—into two pretty, cut glass tumblers. "Biologically, yes, but the pool is a magnet for all their friends. It keeps them busy and out of our hair for a while, so I'm not complaining. Now, help yourself before they get hungry."

She waves her hand toward the pile of prepared sandwiches sitting on a floral platter along with a couple of matching serving bowls filled with pasta salad and chips.

I watch as Laura grabs a ham sandwich. "I take it you're not a vegetarian?"

"I like bacon too much. And burgers and steak," she replies, spooning some kind of Italian pasta, complete with strips of salami and chunks of mozzarella, onto her plate. "And junk food, but don't tell my brother that."

"Your secret's safe with me. We've had words about my Ho Ho addiction."

She groans. "Ho Hos... God, aren't those the best? I sometimes steal one from the pantry. Okay, maybe more than sometimes."

We spend the next few minutes discussing our favorite childhood foods while eating something a bit more nutritious. I wax on about the merits of anything covered in Nutella, and Laura fills me in on where to get the best chocolate chip cookies in the Twin Cities. I might have met my sugar soulmate in Zane's sister.

A comfortable warmth fills my chest. After the whole disaster at the high school, I'd been reluctant to meet any more of Zane's family. Dreading another cold reception and another confrontation. But Laura's nothing like her mother.

"Now tell me how you two met."

We're both wheezing with laughter by the time I finish telling her the grocery-store tale, then the bar story, complete with his whole break-buddy idea.

"My God, I thought he was smoother than that. No wonder he's still single," Laura snorts out another laugh, dashing away the tears from her eyes with the back of her hand. "This information is the perfect ammo for the next time he gives me crap. But thank you for not running away, like I probably would have."

"Believe me, I tried," I say before taking a bite out of my roast beef—real roast beef, not the packaged kind—and Havarti sandwich.

"Well, I'm glad you stuck around. He needs some happiness. My mother can be... difficult. And Tess... well, let's just say I'm glad it's not me living in that house again. I'll take my two maniacs over them any day."

I follow her gaze to the pool where the kids are playing some kind of water version of tag, while silently agreeing with her assessment. "I'm sure your mom's life isn't pleasant right now."

"You're too kind. And truth is, she's always been a little caustic. When you're family, you kind of overlook her cutting remarks, but..."

I take a sip of tea, perfumed with lavender and mint, while formulating a sympathetic response. "I understand. And I'm sure she means well. Zane's incredibly talented."

"He is talented. And I've told Mom numerous times, what he chooses to do with that talent is up to him."

"She wants the best for him. You can't fault her for that." Jesus, I should get a Nobel Peace Prize or an Academy Award for the bullshit coming out of my mouth.

"Possibly." She exhales a slow breath. "Excuse me for a second. I'm going to pop those empanadas into the oven, and there's something I need to show you."

"Kids, sandwiches," she calls out, then heads inside.

The kids rush over, wrapped in colorful towels, each of them snagging a sandwich. A little girl lingers, her inquisitive blue eyes and dark brown hair giving away her identity. "Hi. I'm Mia."

"Nice to meet you, Mia. I'm Lyric."

Her smile widens. "Uncle Zane's girlfriend?"

I nod my confirmation as Laura returns.

"Mom, this is Uncle Zane's girlfriend." The girl squeals. "She's so pretty."

"I know. Your uncle is very lucky."

The little girl drops down onto the chair next to me. "Uncle Zane is my favorite uncle."

"Don't let Uncle Charlie hear you say that." Laura sends me a smile and sits down, setting a small framed photo of Zane and the band in front of me.

Or wait. It's definitely Zane, but his hair is longer, and thank goodness I've never seen the hideous plaid shirt he's wearing. The other three men in the photo are definitely not Aaron, Dave, or Dillon.

"Uncle Charlie is nice, but Uncle Zane gives me piggyback rides." Mia rises up on her knees and points a small finger at the photo. "That's my Grandpa Ian."

"Uncanny, isn't it," Laura adds with a smug smile.

"Wow," is all I manage to say.

"Mommy, are me and Ollie twins?" Mia asks before biting into her sandwich.

"No, sweetheart. Your brother is two years older than you. Now why don't you take your sandwich and hang out with your friends? They have juice boxes." Mia slumps back in her chair and shakes her head, then takes a big bite of sandwich. Laura sighs. "So much for privacy, I see."

I laugh while Laura pours a glass of lemonade for her daughter.

"I was only seven when he died, but my mom was never the same." She smiles at the photo, then props it up on the table. "She packed up everything that reminded her of him and put the boxes into the attic. Pictures, his clothes, his instruments. From what Aunt Mary says he was just as talented as Zane. He could play any instrument within seconds of picking it up."

"He'd have been proud of his son."

"Probably." Her smile fades. "He was a lot of fun, but we struggled financially. I remember going to school in secondhand clothes, jeans too short and shirts too big. I remember a few times going to bed hungry. Playing music in a bar doesn't pay a lot, and that's all my dad wanted to do. My mom worked two jobs so he could follow his dreams. I definitely remember the shouting after I'd gone to bed."

"Zane's not like that, though."

"No, he's not. But I remember my mom's expression the day he dragged my dad's old guitar from the attic. Remember him and his friends practicing in the garage." She shakes her head slowly while sipping her tea.

"She thought he was going to turn into his father?"

"Who knows what would have happened if Mom hadn't convinced him to apply to Juilliard. Teenage Zane was all about the band, and the girls that came with the band. Pretty sure if Mom hadn't gotten pregnant with me, her and Dad never would have married."

"This explains so much." I pause to sip my tea. "So, do you think he should go back to New York?"

"I think he's happy here. He's got friends and you and a decent job, and family. I didn't like having him so far away, so my opinion might be a bit prejudiced."

"From what I've seen, his students love him."

"He's easy to love, but then that's just my opinion." She pours more tea in our glasses, then stands. "Let me get those empanadas."

Laura disappears inside and I turn to Mia. "What grade are you going to be in this fall?"

"Third grade. I'm hoping for Mrs. Brown. She's so nice. She

gives out prizes on Fridays for the bestest of everything. Bestest reading, bestest math, bestest behaved. Are you going to marry my uncle?" Her smile is so wide it must hurt.

"Usually you have to get to know someone for a while to be sure. And it's kinda up to the guy to ask."

"Ask what?" Laura inquires, setting the plate of warm empanadas on the table.

"If Uncle Zane marries Lyric, will that make her my aunt?"

Laura rolls her eyes. "If you want cupcakes, you need to go back to your friends. Now."

Mia lets out a little huff and climbs out of her seat. "I'm going to call you Auntie Lyric anyway."

She squeals with happiness, then bolts from the table. "Ollie, Ollie. Auntie Lyric is gonna marry Uncle Zane and we will have baby cousins to play with. Ollie, Ollie…"

"Sorry about that." Laura shakes her head slowly, watching her daughter join her friends. "She's going to be that gossipy girl in high school no one likes."

Despite Mia's proclamation, I can't help but smile. "She's adorable."

"Sometimes. Now grab one of these empanadas before I eat them all. They're apple but have enough sugar in them to make them unhealthy. Then tell me if you ever decided on the whole band tour thing?"

I nod while snagging one of the warm hand pies. "What do you think? Does anyone ever say no to your brother?"

CHAPTER SEVENTEEN

ZANE

"You look gorgeous," I say the minute I walk into her house. She's a knockout in her mint-green dress that nips in at her slender waist and flares out at her gorgeous hips. A mess of sexy straps crisscrosses down her back. If we weren't expected at the high school in a half hour, I'd be peeling it off her right now. But that will have to wait until this evening's over.

"Thanks." Her voice shy, her skin pinking at the compliment. Her hands tug at the lapel of my suit and my dick responds. "You look amazing yourself."

"I owe you." I capture her hands and kiss each of her knuckles before things get out of control. "If I were you, you know after the concert, I'd probably never want to interact with my family again."

She pulls away to slip on her sexy-as-fuck high-heeled sandals that show off her cute pink toenails. "Laura and Jason will be there to protect me."

Once again I'll be on a damn stage, shaking hands with the entire graduating class. Not that I should complain. One of those seven hundred sixty-two hands I'll be shaking belongs to Tess. I'm fucking proud of my little sister. And I'm pretty hyped for myself as well. As of nine o'clock this morning, I'm a permanent part of the faculty at Mondale High.

"And we have a lot to celebrate tonight." Lyric lifts up on her toes and kisses my jaw. Then wipes her lipstick from my face. "Oops. Congratulations, Mr. Brody."

"The kind of celebration I'm planning can't start until after my sister's graduation dinner." I take her lips completely, demonstrating the kind of festivities I have in mind.

"We're going to be late, Zane. And you're now wearing more of my lip color than I am."

My dirty mind goes to all the places she could leave her lipstick. *Shit*, we definitely need to get the hell out of here.

I give Sacha a goodbye pat and guide the woman I'm quickly losing myself to out the door. Then into my car.

Graduation is as long as I expected, and dinner longer. But my mother behaves as promised, complimenting Lyric's dress and engaging in pleasant conversation with her. Maybe she's coming around to my version of happiness.

On the way back to Lyric's, we chat about the tour. Another reason to celebrate—she said yes to coming along. I might have hated the idea at first, but now I see only opportunity. We're booked in every fair and festival from International Falls to Summerfest in Milwaukee. Six weekends spent showing Lyric around my home state and a good part of Wisconsin.

Only off note is Dillon. Technically he quit the band, but my ultimatum of clean-up-or-get-out was a factor in his decision. Or maybe not. Maybe this is what he wanted all along. Maybe he's silently thanking me. Or maybe I'm just looking for ways to assuage my guilt.

So, everything's set. A different city almost every weekend, except for Tess's graduation party the weekend after Summerfest.

It was the only productive thing to come out of Lyric's afternoon with Laura.

I pull into her drive and turn to face her. "Did I tell you how much it means that you and Laura have bonded?" Even if my sister and Lyric exchanged enough inside info about me to make me nervous.

"Your sister's awesome." She unbuckles, crawling into my lap as I slide the seat back. "Both of them, actually. But I have to be honest... I like their brother the best."

My hands slide under the hem of her skirt in a way I've been fantasizing all night. "Playing favorites, Miss James?"

The sun dips behind the horizon in the rearview mirror, its remnants bathing the interior of the car in dusky pinks and oranges. A soft breeze blows through the open windows, cooling my heated flesh. Lyric fits perfectly in my lap, her soft breasts pressed against my chest, the heat of her core making me swell in my dress slacks. She rocks her hips, her green eyes darkening with desire. My fingers breach the edge of her panties, finding her slick center.

My hands are in her hair, pulling her lips to mine. Tipping my head, I angle my mouth, plunging my tongue into her sweetness. A thought sits at the back of my brain. Something about this being a bad idea, but I can't recall why at this moment. I can't recall anything but the taste of Lyric's lips on mine and her hands working my zipper.

A horn blares and headlights shine bright in my mirrors. Lyric jumps, her eyes wide as she looks over my shoulder. In the mirror, I watch my mother's Volvo S60 pull in behind me, Tess behind the wheel. Then Laura's Audi Q5 behind that.

And fuck, they're both getting out.

The woman in my lap mutters a curse and climbs back over to her side, then hops out, leaving me alone to deal with the situation she provoked. Outside it's a fucking family reunion in

Lyric's driveway. My dick's definitely not invited, but damn if it didn't get the memo. Tucking myself back in, I barely get my zipper up as Laura leans on my door.

"Are we doing this, or are you just going to play with yourself all day, little brother?"

CHAPTER EIGHTEEN

LYRIC

"Zane..." I sigh, watching the sisters back out of my driveway, his mom's Volvo left behind. The keys burn into my palm, promising freedom and danger in equal measure. "I can't take this."

"She wants you to have it." Hand on my back, he guides me up the walk. "You can't walk to the shelter, and don't even think about taking the bus."

Two buses, actually. But Zane's concern about the shelter job is no secret. The neighborhood is less than ideal, and the danger of angry exes showing up is real.

"I'll transfer the title—"

"No!" I bury my shaking hands into the crook of my arms. "Zane... I... I can't have anything in my name. Nothing on record. He'll find me."

I'm neurotic. I know. But Grayson's money can buy the best private investigators. I can't slip up. No records. No titles, no credit cards. No insurance, even though the school district provides it for free. The less Grayson can find on Lyric James the safer.

I eye the black car as if it's a bomb. Explosion imminent.

"If I get pulled over… My name is on my license, Zane. I'd have to move, and neither of us want that." Not when I'm just beginning to like my life. I turn away from the dilemma in my driveway.

"This is your home. Don't let some asshole chase you away from it. I promise I'll always protect you." Zane circles an arm around my waist, pulling me into his warmth. It would be so easy to give in to this man, but I know that would be a fatal mistake for both of us.

"Not to disparage your manliness, but you're no match for my ex." I unlock the door and greet an excited Sacha. Her stubby-tail wave is all for Zane.

"Don't count me out," Zane says, on his knees, the recipient of doggy kisses. "The tux and tails may tell one story, but I've seen my share of trouble."

The scars on his knuckles confirm his statement, but at the moment he looks far from trouble, wrestling with my dog. Whatever he thinks, there's no way he can win against someone the size of Grayson.

"You're taking the car. No arguments. I promised you wouldn't be walking to school this winter. We won't change the title until necessary. Then we'll deal with it."

I blink slowly. I'll never be able to repay his family for this gift even if I worked three jobs.

"Hey." After disentangling with my dog, Zane slips his arms around me. "I want you in my life. Today, tomorrow, next year, and many years after that. You're stuck with me."

I don't know what to do with that. I keep telling myself to trust Zane, and I want to. So bad. My heart says he's a good man, but the small voice of the battered woman inside my head is harder to convince.

He bends down to kiss me, but I pull away, heart pounding, head spinning. He's moving way too fast for me to keep up, and by the expression on his face he realizes as much.

"Go wash the slobber off your face," I say to soften my rejection.

He wipes the back of his sleeve across his lips. "Better?"

Sacha butts her head between us, reminding us she's ready for her walk.

CHAPTER NINETEEN

LYRIC

Thursday I show up at the shelter promptly at eight. It takes a few minutes of anxiously driving around before I find a parking spot down the block from the large four square with dingy windows and peeling paint that matches its neighbors.

Opening the front door, nothing's changed much in the past two years. The gnawing fear and desperation that was a constant companion two years ago seeps into my bones for a second as I take a step inside. A deep breath sends the feeling away. This isn't my reality anymore.

"I'm here for Ellen," I say to the young girl staring at me from behind the desk on the one side of the stairway when I realize she's waiting for me to step inside and close the door.

"Let me get her," she replies, heading toward the kitchen in the back.

A baby cries upstairs. Talking, raised voices, the sounds familiar and yet not.

Ellen's in her forties, brilliant red hair tied back, freckles across her nose and cheeks. Stick-skinny because she never stops moving. We share a big smile and a hug. "Lyric! So good to see you." She pulls back, beaming. "Let me look at you. It keeps me going to see my success stories."

Ellen's a fast talker.

"Good to see you, too."

"I was thrilled when Kelly said you wanted to volunteer. Never turn down a willing hand, but experience—your kind of experience—is invaluable. Let me give you the tour."

I FIND Zane lounging the backyard when I get home. Half of me is happy to see him, the other half... ugh. I'm tired and... I don't know.

Today hit me harder than I expected. I need to process, maybe with a pint of ice cream and a bottle of wine, not whatever healthy shit Zane has burbling on my stove.

Slinking around the kitchen sliders so as not to disturb him, I head into the bedroom. Shower off the day and change into pajama shorts and a tank top, because no matter what Zane has planned, I refuse to go out tonight.

Back in the kitchen, I pause at the door for a second. Zane slips a pencil between his teeth and strums the beginning of a catchy melody on his acoustic guitar, then pauses to scribble something on the pad next to him.

I'd given him a set of house keys for emergencies, but at the moment he's made himself at home on my deck, shirt off, bottle of beer half empty on the table.

Sacha's on her side in the grass, long legs straight out, one paw twitching. Either Zane's drugged her or worn her out with whatever doggy games the two have been playing, for her to not realize I'm here.

I drag the sliding door open. My dog perks up and Zane turns, giving me a stunning smile that makes the day go away faster than that ice cream and wine ever could. "What's the emergency?"

"Peace and quiet. Tess had friends over. Loud friends. Loud music. Loud feet up and down the stairs. I couldn't concentrate." He slips the pencil back between his teeth and strums. "Just need to finish this, then I'll get dinner ready."

"Okay." I head back inside to investigate tonight's menu. Something curry, from the smell of it. My stomach growls.

"Didn't you eat?"

I turn, congratulating myself for not jumping at Zane's proximity. "I thought you needed to finish?"

My attention shifts out to the backyard. Sacha's intent on chasing a butterfly, ignoring the angry chatter from the squirrel in the neighbor's tree. For now. The smell of fresh cut-grass drifts in through the screen door.

Zane's hands close around my waist and he drops a kiss against my bare shoulder. "Changed my mind."

I smack his hand away from my breast. "I don't want to be a bad influence."

"Your influence is completely good." He snakes his other hand inside the back of my bottoms, running his calloused fingers down the curve of my bare ass. My body wakes with his touch. "I find inspiration in the sight of your tits. I'm at my most creative when my tongue's between your legs."

Do I argue with his logic?

"Being your muse is such hard work," I mumble behind the fabric of my tank top as its pulled over my head.

"I missed you," he whispers in my ear before nibbling on the lobe, making me shiver with anticipation.

"I missed you too."

His tongue dives into my mouth, and I barely notice my shorts sliding down my legs, leaving me naked. My nipples pebble against Zane's bare chest, the light sprinkling of hair providing the perfect friction.

"Turn around, Angel," he whispers, guiding me to face the table and pressing me down against the scarred wood surface. I turn my head to the side, resting my cheek against my hands. From the corner of my eye, I watch Zane.

"Is this okay?" he asks. So considerate.

Just for a second I'm back in LA. The sting of wood against my face as Grayson slams me down against another table. Then the moment's gone.

"Lyric?" Zane's concerned voice whispers in my ear.

"More than okay," I answer, then moan as his teeth nibble the edge of my earlobe.

"Spread your legs for me."

"Zane..." Who am I kidding? I want this as much as he does. Maybe more.

"You're gorgeous like this. So perfect..." He traces the outline of my body with his hands. My breath hitches as his fingers skim over the outside of my breasts. "You take my breath away, you know that?"

I hum an incoherent response, too distracted by the slow glide of his hands over my body. I can't help but shiver as he traces a line down my spine, then lower, his finger following the crease of my ass before delving between my folds. "Already so fucking wet for me."

"Zane..." I gasp as he slides two fingers in deep, and then out. Then pumping back in, hitting that spot inside me that has my body sparking with pleasure. Truth is, I was wet the minute I spotted his car in my driveway. Anticipated this moment—well, maybe not the kitchen table part, but his hands on me.

He pulls his fingers away and sucks them between his lips with an appreciative sound. I almost cry in frustration at the loss of his touch, but I know he's far from done.

Then he's down on his knees, arms wrapped around my legs, his warm hands curling around my inner thighs. He pulls me back against his face and I gasp. His hands hold me still while he flicks his hot tongue across my clit before spearing into me. I cry out, and he does it again and again. Each pass has my thighs trembling, my body squirming against his hold. The feel of his scruff scraping against my sensitive flesh is almost too much. Too perfect.

God, he's so good at this.

He sucks me into his mouth, his teeth scraping over the tiny bundle of nerves, making me explode with a cry loud enough for my neighbors to hear through the open back door. Sacha lets out a woof, her nose pressed against the screen. Zane says something I can't quite comprehend at the moment. Whatever it was, she turns and plops down in the grass.

The sound of his zipper has my insides clenching like the bell to Pavlov's dogs. I watch as he drops his shorts low enough to release his heavy and colorful cock, which I've yet to find the nerve to inquire about.

The table screeches across the tile floor as he thrusts into me. Skin to skin. No barrier. He feels amazing, and I trust him. He's not Grayson. No need to hide the small compact of pills on my bathroom counter I've been taking for the past two years to regulate my erratic periods.

All thoughts of tattoos and birth control flee as he buries himself deep inside me, then pulls back and presses home again.

"Damn, you feel good. So perfect." His hands close around my hips, anchoring me, pistoning forward, dragging the head of his cock along my inner walls. Pleasure heats inside me again.

It's insane how well he knows my body in such a short time. It's like he was given a manual. One Grayson never had—and likely no other man will.

I shove the thought of my ex-husband and all other men out of my mind and concentrate on the way Zane's pumping into me, muttering sweet-filthy words I pray like hell never end up in a song.

He drags me up, one hand on my breast, the other pressing

the spot where we're joined. His mouth closes over my shoulder, leaving marks I'll have to work to hide tomorrow. Not that I care at the moment. The change in our position has his cock hitting the place inside me that lights up with every stroke.

"Zane!"

"Yes," he hisses, pressing kisses against the side of my neck, spewing more dirty-sweet words.

"Fuck, that's it, Angel. So. Fucking. Good when you squeeze me like this. When you come all over my cock."

His sinful words and the sexy gravel in his voice push me over the edge. My orgasm rips through me, the pleasure so intense it's almost painful. My vision darkens around the edges. I'm in a free fall, held up by Zane's arms alone. His breath comes out in gasps against my shoulder and the scorching heat of his orgasm fills me.

A voice in my head whispers a warning. I'm not supposed to fall. It's not a good idea—the worst idea possible—but it's too late. I can't fight my feelings for this man much longer.

The sun soaks into my skin as I stretch out on the couch with Zane behind me. We're watching some documentary. Something to do with, um, I'm not exactly sure. We've been talking. And touching. Which would be way more comfortable in my bed, but it's only a little past seven.

"So, how far off your schedule did I put you?"

Zane presses a kiss to the juncture of my shoulder and neck. "Not at all. Song's done, just have to finish the music before practice tomorrow."

"Can't wait to hear it," I mumble over a yawn.

"Come over to my place after work tomorrow. I was thinking of picking up our girl in the morning, if that's all right. Tess will be gone all day. No sense in the Sacha being alone. Mom might enjoy her."

"She used to be a watchdog before you came around." As if hearing her name, Sacha trots over and shoves her snout into my face. I shoo her away. No ass-licking kisses, thank you. "Fine. Take her."

"She'd guard you with her life. I guarantee it. I'm just a play-mate." Sacha sets her head on my hip and Zane automatically scratches it.

"I thought you were my playmate." Truth is, I'm secretly enjoying their bond. We're like this little family.

"You're my *special* playmate." Zane chuckles. "So, tell me about your day. You've been quiet about it."

"It was good, I guess." No way am I telling him about the dread I felt walking in, or the woman who wept with relief after receiving a phone call from her attorney, or the little girl with the haunted eyes. Thank fuck Grayson never got me pregnant.

I yawn again as the exhaustion of the day threatens to pull me under. A troubled night's sleep and the two more orgasms Zane gave me after dinner, along with a long-ass day, have me worn out. I'm boneless and content to lie here until morning, despite the scratchy old fabric against my bare skin.

Zane's chuckle comes from far away. "Sleep well, Angel."

"Mmm hmm," I agree as my heavy eyelids slide shut and whatever Zane says next is lost to the inevitable pull.

HANDS PIN DOWN MY SHOULDERS. A scream bursts from my throat. My heart's threatening to choke me, and I can't breathe. "No, please. Not again," I gasp.

"Lyric, it's okay," a voice whispers, and I focus on the blue eyes staring down at me. Blue not gray-green.

I'm shaking, gulping lungfuls of air. Blinking back tears, my reality comes into focus. Zane's wide eyes reflect my fear.

"Oh God," I gasp.

"You were whimpering." Zane wipes my tears with his thumbs. "I tried to wake you. I'm sorry."

"So damn real." I sit up, hugging my knees. The sun has set, leaving the living room in shadows. Zane pulls me into his lap, his warm arms surrounding me.

"Tell me."

I shudder. "God, I can still smell his anger."

"Maybe this volunteering isn't a good idea. Dredging up memories." His arms pull me tighter. "I don't want you reliving this shit every day."

"It's not the shelter." The nightmares have been back for weeks, not that Zane needs to know. "And I'm okay now. Really. It's…"

I try to give him an upbeat smile, but by the frown pulling at his lips, I'm not doing that great of a job.

"I used to wake screaming every night, reliving the day my husband was granted bail after the first time I'd pressed charges against him," I start, gauging Zane's reaction. "You sure you want to hear more?"

"I want to know what you've been through. So I don't trigger your memories. Like I did that first night at Sarapelli's."

I can't even guess what might trigger my memories most of the time, but I continue because Zane has a right to know what he's signing up for.

I share with him the night Grayson stumbled upon the little compact of pills hidden deep in my underwear drawer that explained why I'd yet to become pregnant. I was no stranger to angry Grayson, but that day angry didn't even come close to describing the state my husband had been in. It was like whatever restraint he had up until that point had vanished.

I was sure I was about to die. Genuinely surprised to wake in the hospital covered in bruises and sporting an incision where they removed my ruptured spleen. The policewoman sitting by my bed told me I was lucky. Convinced me to press charges because the next time *I might not be so lucky.*

Zane's arms tighten around me. "Shit, Lyric."

"She was right. The next time I wasn't so lucky."

Grayson made bond thanks to his hockey buddies, then showed up at our house despite the restraining order that promised me safety. What happened after that will be seared into my memory until the day I die. From the first punch to the moment I smashed through the plate glass sliders that separated our patio from our family room. But I keep the details vague because by the way Zane's body goes still and tense, he's heard enough.

"Thank you for trusting me." Zane's hands stroke my bare shoulders in an attempt to comfort me. Which is sorta funny because at this moment it's him that needs comfort. "Promise me you'll quit volunteering if it gets too much?"

I easy his worry with a bright smile. "Of course."

CHAPTER TWENTY

LYRIC

*T*he fairgrounds are clogged with all forms of humanity, every one of them sweating. Including me. It has to be over ninety, and the scent of hot cooking oil and body odor hangs on the stagnant air. People scurry everywhere, seemingly with no destination in mind on this stifling summer day. Except Grace and me. We're targeting the funnel-cake stand. After the mini doughnuts, after the corn dogs, after the native version of empanadas filled with venison and wild rice. Our goal is to consume every fried food available before Zane catches up with us. I have no idea what he plans on eating. Everything here is unhealthy in the best sort of way.

About an hour ago, we left the guys to set up. A bit of a challenge, because every band's setting up at the same time. All their equipment sits on stage ready for the night's three bands. Grace and I wisely left the tangled spaghetti of electrical cables and frayed nerves, planning to meet them later by the Ferris wheel— the tallest and brightest structure for probably twenty miles in the farming region of southwest Minnesota.

My phone bings a text from Zane.

"They're done." I show Grace my phone, laughing as I read it.

She cringes. "I thought guys didn't use emojis."

"He does."

Grace laughs, patting me on the shoulder. "You two are so cute."

I press my lips together. There's definitely a bit of gloating in that statement.

The Ferris wheel is in sight, along with a thickening crowd. I grab Grace's hand and plow through the mass of damp bodies.

We spot the guys, followed by a group of scantily dressed girls. Zane plants a possessive kiss on my lips, and I swear I hear the breaking of a dozen teenage hearts.

"Have you heard from Tess?" The whimpering sound behind me reminds me of my baby. Tess is home watching Sacha. Haven't decided who Zane is more concerned with.

"Everything is good. Our princess may need some longer walks when we get back. I might have wanted to be more specific with the cookie rationing. Sounds like she's taking advantage of Tess's good will." He pats my ample ass. "But by the end of this weekend we're all going to need some exercise."

"Hey!" I smack his hand and walk away, slipping my arm around Noah—the band's new bass player and recent graduate of Mondale High—and giving him a playful wink. He's looking especially adorable today. Taking a page from Zane's book, he's gelled his auburn hair into a sexy mess. He's in black jeans that look exceptionally fine on his young bod. Pretty sure the fan crowd isn't just for Zane today.

"Stick with me, Noah. The sharks are circling. You don't want to get bit."

He looks down at me and laughs. Zane hooks his finger through my belt loop, pulling me back to his side. "Back here, James."

I lift my chin in an attempt to look down on the man tethering me to his side. Not that I'm successful. Not without a ladder. In his boots, Zane's got a good eight inches on me.

"I happen to love your ass," Zane whispers while nuzzling my neck.

I giggle as he finds a particularly sensitive spot, then steers me toward a baked-potato stand where he instructs the vendor to throw whatever vegetables he has on his. *Gross.*

Back in the concert area, Grace and I worm our way through the growing crowd, settling in a few rows back from the stage. A mass of giggling girls huddle around beneath Zane's microphone. Their traditional rock sound has a mixed following, but the guys looks draw in the women. *Don't think about it.*

The crowd cheers as Aaron, Dave, and Noah come out. Noah looks nervous, his eyes wide as he scans the large crowd. Dave waves to the fans, riling them up as he plugs his guitar in.

Some girls behind us notice Noah. "Ooh. He's new."

"And gorgeous," another one adds.

I roll my eyes at Grace. She giggles. While Grace deals with the obnoxiousness with humor, I'm struggling to control my gag reflex.

Grace leans in and whispers in my ear, "Relax, Lyric. We both know who our men will be going home with tonight. None of this matters."

"I'm so getting a piece of that tonight," I mimic one of the girls, clutching my heart and batting my eyelashes. Then give her a look that asks if she approves.

It's Grace's turn to roll her eyes, and we both collapse into laughter.

"Come on. Let's go, boys," she shouts, still laughing a minute later.

Then the crowd goes crazy. I can't even think. Zane walks on stage. No, he struts onto the wide platform like he owns it. Shirt off, tats, pecs, and abs on display for the crowd. Okay, the night is sweltering, but seriously? His sex appeal is off the charts, and the fire in my gut says this is a part of him I'm not willing to share.

He scans the crowd, then a smile breaks his face in two and he waves at me.

"Holy fuck," Grace yells, looking at me. "He's hot. Did you know?"

"That he was coming on stage half naked? No!"

"I love you, Zane," the girl behind us screams, then lowers her voice to something a fraction less ear splitting. "Rumor has it he has a donkey dick."

Grace eyes widen with shock, and I can't help but laugh. *Okay, it's ridiculous.*

Suddenly a hand clamps down on my arm, accompanied by a hot, sharp pinch as she digs her nails in, spinning me around. "Are you laughing at me, bitch?"

She's in my face. Her eyes unfocused and bloodshot. The smell of pot wafts from her clothes.

"Ow, fuck," I yell, shaking her hand off my arm. "Back off, crazy."

Grace gets between us as a couple of security guys turn our way from the sidelines. "Yeah, bitch. Back off."

"Grace..." I motion to the men in orange vests who are currently watching us.

"Hello, everyone," Zane shouts, quieting the crowd and distracting the woman who was seconds from getting us kicked out. Grace moves us a few feet away and signals to security all is okay.

A girl up front screams, "I love you, Zane." It seems to be a theme.

Zane's smile widens. "Thank you... Are you ready to rock, Minnesota?"

The crowd cheers. Zane shakes his head. "Come on. I know you can do better than that." He spreads his arms wide. "Who wants this?"

I'm deaf. They can probably hear this crowd all the way down on the interstate a few miles from here. Zane turns and nods.

Aaron taps out the beat. Noah and Dave come in one measure after. Then Zane blows everyone away.

GRACE and I stand aside while the guys sign autographs and take pictures. Well, it's mostly Zane. Aaron dragged Noah off to the side because things have gotten out of control. Zane put his shirt back on, but it doesn't seem to have any effect. The line of women willing to do anything to get his attention is crazy and it's his own damn fault.

This is our summer. Like it or not.

Jealousy serves no purpose, I remind myself. Grayson was jealous all the time, and look where it got him.

A cold chill that has nothing to do with the dropping evening temperatures skitters down my back. My skin itches with the eerie feeling of being watched. I spin around fast and scan the crowd in hopes of catching... who? Definitely not Grayson. If he was here, he wouldn't be lurking around. He'd be in my face.

But a private investigator? Or a loyal fan?

Grace's voice pulls me out of my paranoia. "Jesus, Lyric. You're trembling. Are you cold?"

"Yeah. Too much sun, maybe." I've no other way to explain the goosebumps on my arms.

Grace motions to Aaron to wrap it up. To my surprise, he does. Pulling Zane from the crowd despite the boos and whimpers.

"Everything okay?" Zane's warm arm around me settles my nerves.

"Fine. You were awesome."

"Yeah?" Zane picks me up, spinning me around and around. He's hyped on adrenaline. Performer's high. His eyes glassy, his smile bright. "God, that was fun."

"We killed it tonight," Dave shouts as we head back to our cars.

"I'M GOING TO KILL DAVE," Grace mutters as we walk into her and Aaron's motel room sporting the same musty, smokey scent as mine and Zane's. "This is gross, Lyric. *Gross.*"

"Maybe the owner has a thing for retro. It's very *in* right now." I glance around the room, doing my best not to laugh. Dave couldn't have booked a worse motel if he tried.

We're talking rusty-orange industrial carpet, a giant floral-patterned bedspread in a similar orange and mud brown, and shaggy brown curtains. Not to be outdone, Zane's and my room boasts an avocado-green and dusty-blue color scheme.

"If this is *in*..." She waves a hand at the ceramic monstrosity sitting on the nightstand.

"At least you don't have a used condom under the bed," I point out while pulling back the bedspread to reveal what I'm guessing was once crisp, white sheets similar to the ones in our room.

"Oh God, Lyric," she shouts from the bathroom. "I'm going to kill Dave."

"Ew." Black mold has staked a claim in the corners of the shower, and the toilet seat has no lid.

The guys took off after handing me and Grace the keys, promising to return with dinner. But now? I'm not sure I will ever be hungry again. Which is saying something.

"We had cleaner bathrooms at summer camp," Grace mutters.

"Tomorrow, you and I cancel all of Dave's reservations and book something better."

"No. Today. Right now," Grace replies.

Back in the bedroom, Grace checks for bedbugs but thankfully comes up empty.

Between the two of us, and the trusty reservation app Grace

has on her phone, we book every weekend with nothing less than four-and-a-half-star hotels that include king-sized beds, complimentary breakfasts, and daily housekeeping. Our Milwaukee hotel even has an indoor waterpark.

We both flop down on the ugly bedspread and stare at the water-stained ceiling. "Give it to me straight. Is this one of those places that charges by the hour?"

"Probably?" I grimace. "But next week we get clean sheets and unlimited waffles."

"And a pool. I'm buying a new bikini." Grace flips onto her side, bumping into my arm. I let out a yelp.

"What's wrong?" she asks, her brows lowering in concern.

"That skank at the concert got me with her nails." I lift my arm above my head and point with the other hand at the spot that feels like fire.

"Oooh. She did." Grace squints at the underside of my arm and then sits up. "It bled a little. Let's clean it up and get a Band Aid."

"It bled?" I follow her into the bathroom and stare at the two-inch-long-gashes in the streaky mirror. "What the hell?"

Like all teachers, Grace's purse is stocked with supplies for every minor emergency. The voice of the doctor who removed my spleen warns this scratch isn't minor. The Neosporin and bandage Grace has on hand will have to do for now. But, I'll need to call my doctor first thing Monday. *Damn you, Grayson.*

"So tell the truth, does Zane have a donkey dick?" Grace asks with a straight face, distracting me from her ministrations.

We both burst out laughing, but mine dies the minute the cold antiseptic spray hits my raw skin.

"Shit. No. It's a very nice-sized dick, but... fuck." I wince at the pain lancing down my arm. "You ever see a donkey's dick?"

"No." Grace frowns as she dabs at the cut with what I hope is a clean towel. "Have you?"

"No, but I can imagine, and I'll pass thank you very much." I let out what I think a donkey bray sounds like and then do an imitation of the squeaky-voiced fan. "Oh Zane, give it to me with your donkey dick."

Grace and I laugh until we're wiping tears from our eyes and gasping for breath. Once we recover, she presses a superhero Band-Aid to my arm with an apology when I wince. "Keep it covered with an antibiotic ointment. Nail scratches can be nasty."

"Will do, Mom."

Back in the bedroom, we settle down on the bed again and wait for the men to return. We chat about the upcoming school year, Zoe's dating adventures, then round back to the men in our lives.

"Zane's happier than I've ever seen him. And you can't stop smiling. You can thank me anytime."

"I think I'm falling in love with him, Grace," I confess while my heart lodges in my throat.

Her smile grows. "Then my work here is done."

"I didn't say it was a good thing." I let out a sigh of frustration and confusion. "He's got a lot going on."

"You mean besides finding pants to fit his donkey dick?" Her brows lift and her eyes dance with the joke.

I grin back. "I'm sure it's difficult." I pause for a second. "I hated watching him interacting with his fans tonight. The way they felt entitled to touching him. It brought out some really ugly feelings in me."

"Did your ex cheat?" It's not the first time Grace has probed me for information on my past, but this time I consider telling her everything.

"Yes, but this is different," I say, then seal my lips shut. Not that I don't trust Grace with more. But I know once she knows who I really am, she'll look at me differently. Treat me differently. And I don't want to lose what we have right now.

She stares at me. Expectant. But when I stay silent, she says, "Zane would never cheat. You know that, right?"

I nod but refuse to say more.

"Good." Her lips curve up at the corners into a small smile. "Just keep reminding yourself, this is only temporary. Zane and Aaron are letting Dave have his fantasy for the moment, but neither of them want this to become an every-summer thing. Whatever these girls think, it's you Zane wants to sleep next to. Even if that bed is covered in a circa 1970s bedspread."

THE NEXT MORNING we all stop for breakfast on the drive home. A cozy diner sits off the interstate a few miles out of the tiny farming town we'd spent the night in. A truck stop of sorts, with a sign proclaiming it serves breakfast twenty-four hours.

Being late Sunday morning, the trucker clientele is sparse. A few big rigs are parked outside, their baseball-capped drivers hunched over hearty portions of food at the long counter that brackets the wide pass-through window with a view of the kitchen. A few families fill several other tables—probably the after-church crowd. Little ones stuffing whipped cream-topped pancakes catch my eye. *Am I too old for the kiddie special?*

The waitress shoves two tables together to accommodate our group, slaps down menus, and promises coffee. My stomach growls as I peruse the menu. It's extensive for such a small place. My mouth's watering as I debate whether I'm in the mood for a salty or sweet meal. The waitress returns, pours coffee, then takes our order, starting at the other end of the table.

"Steel cut oatmeal and fruit," Zane orders once she gets to our end.

I roll my eyes at Grace. We've discussed his healthy eating habits ad nauseam.

"I'll have the Belgium waffle supreme." I don't look at Zane, but I can feel the heat of his disapproval. *Too bad.*

"Chocolate sauce and whipped cream?" the waitress asks.

"Yes, please." I press my lips together as I glance at the man next to me. Zane rubs a furrow between his brow.

"Headache?" I ask after the waitress leaves.

"Chocolate sauce *and* whipped cream?" his voice is stern, but there's a twitch at the corner of his mouth telling me he's doing his best not to smile.

"Oatmeal and fruit?" I throw back, faking a yawn. "Am I dating an eighty-year-old?"

"Zane has been acting like he's eighty for as long as I know him," Aaron informs. "Live a little, brother."

"Is it wrong for me to want to live a long, healthy life with the woman I love?" Zane asks while staring at me.

I still, my eyes narrowing at the man seated next to me, the one who's just dropped the L-word for the first time. Sober. In front of everyone.

The table falls silent, and I'm too stunned to comprehend what I should say. Sure, I told Grace I thought I was falling in love with Zane, but saying it out loud? With everyone staring at the two of us?

Zane scowls at his friends. "What?"

The guys avert their eyes, looking at anything and everything but me and Zane. Dave glances up from the tiny white sugar packet that suddenly has his rapt attention. "Not a thing."

"What, a few little words of affection freak you big boys out?" Grace leans back in her chair and glares at Aaron. At the moment he's studying his fingernails like his life depends on it. "Congratulations, Lyric. You found yourself a real man."

Aaron looks up, his eyebrows raised almost to his hairline. "I love you," he whispers so quietly, a pin dropping would be louder.

Grace glances at me and shakes her head slowly, then looks at Aaron with a sneer. "Nice. Try."

The guys all "uh oh," until each one is silenced with Grace's glare. All except Zane, who's smiling at Aaron. Aaron smiles back and winks. In the next second Zane taps a simple beat on the table. Aaron stands and captures Grace's hand. Her eyes widen as Aaron starts to sing Harry Styles's "Love of My Life."

Every head in the restaurant turns. Grace's blush grows by the second, but Aaron keeps on, making a few alterations to tailor the song to her. His voice is smooth, and if it weren't for Zane's rich baritone with that hint of gravel that makes every hair on my body stand, Aaron could easily slide into the lead-singer slot.

The thought sits unwelcome in my mind. Is that what would happen if Zane's mother coerced him to move back to New York? He swears it would never happen, but I don't trust his mother.

Zane smiles and slips his arm around my shoulder. I push the thought away along with a million others in my live-in-the-moment philosophy I adopted sometime over the last couple of weeks. I've got too many things to stress about. My relationship with Zane isn't going to be one of them.

Aaron finishes up his sappy love song and sits as the waitress brings our food. He waves a hand at the healthy round of applause from the diners and our table, then turns to Grace.

"Do I get my man card back now?"

CHAPTER TWENTY-ONE

LYRIC

*T*uesday morning I pull the Volvo into the only open parking spot down one of the side streets and walk the three and a half blocks to the shelter, giving the neighborhood a critical eye, hoping Janet's Volvo will still be here when I come back. I'm nervous as hell behind the wheel, so it took me a few tries to wedge it into the gap between a rusty truck and some tiny compact that's also seen better days.

The day isn't starting well. A nasty storm knocked out power just before I woke. My shower was cold and my hair dryer was useless. So was trying to apply makeup in the semi-dark. Then Sacha barfed her breakfast as I was about to leave. I'm running late. Third week coming here and I'm late.

I walk in and almost immediately a crying baby is shoved in my hands, followed by a bottle.

"Thanks, thugar. I have a dentith appointment a little later. Need to thower. Maybe you can watch him while I'm gone?" At first I think this woman has a speech impediment, then I realize her two front teeth are broken almost to the gum line.

"What's his name?" I ask before she gets too far up the stairs.

"Devon. I'm Shirley." *Shirley* comes out *Thurley* because of the teeth. She turns as an afterthought. "Don't forget to burp him. He geth the colic if you don't."

Devon looks up at me with big brown eyes, all innocent and trusting. His short corkscrew curls are soft on my bare arm. I know nothing about babies, but he's adorable, and how hard can it be to feed a baby?

I plug in the bottle and his eyes close. His chubby cheeks suck with single minded determination. "Okay, Devon. Let's see how long you make that last."

In the chaos of the kitchen, one of the other women hands me a tea towel. "Devon likes to spit up," she informs me, letting me know how much formula stains. I like this top. Tossing the cloth over my shoulder in preparation, I thank her for the information.

The bottle is empty quicker than I imagine possible and Devon's quiet snores tickle my ear. He's fallen asleep before I can burp him. Now what? Do I wake him? Let him sleep? Of course the kitchen's cleared out. There's no one to ask.

Oh shit.

ZANE'S HOUSE has a wide fenced-in backyard, thick with bushes and a couple of mature trees. Sacha is in her element exploring every nook and cranny of this new world as I exit the back door. She doesn't even notice me as she sniffs under a bush like it holds the secrets of the universe. Or maybe some furry critter.

"Oh, hello," his mom says when I step onto the patio.

Zane strums a few chords on the guitar in his lap, scribbles something on his ever-present notepad, then sets the guitar aside.

"I brought lunch." I smile and hold up a bag filled with falafel sandwiches.

Zane runs inside to grab plates and drinks while I help his mom to the table. Her color looks better. Her doctor still has her hooked up to an oxygen tank, but her last appointment was positive.

"How was your day?" Zane asks, moving his work aside.

"Exhausting. A baby is way more work than a classroom full of kids." I groan as I bite into my falafel. I may not be one hundred percent on board with this vegetarian thing, but the combination of warm spices and cool sauce, crunchy fried goodness on pillowy-soft pita is heaven.

Zane tips my chin up, looking into my eyes.

"Want to talk about it?" he asks, wiping a smudge of sauce off the corner of my mouth with his thumb, then sucking it off.

I shrug. "Devon's six months old and likes movement. Sitting down wasn't an option. My shoulders ache and my legs are rubber from all the pacing. I'm not sure I'm cut out for babies."

"Zane was like that," Janet says with a laugh. "Never any rest."

I return her laugh with one of my own. "I can see that. He never—"

"Hey," Zane cuts in, shooting me a mildly offended stare. "I'm here you know."

"Completely different when it's your own," she says, ignoring Zane's comment, then looks off in the distance as if lost in thought. "Somehow you find the energy."

We eat in silence. Well Zane and I eat. Janet picks. Her appetite is minuscule. Birds eat more. I clean up when we finish and throw the leftovers in the fridge.

"So what are you up to?" I snag a comfortable lounge chair next to Zane. Sacha finally realizes I'm here and trots up to greet me. "Hey, baby. Daddy treating you good?"

"No barfing," Zane informs with a shrug. "Tossed the ball around a bit. I think she's fine."

"Probably ate too much grass this morning." I scratch behind her bat-like ears and she groans. "How's the music?"

Zane's on a mission to write a few new songs for the next

concert. Mix things up since there's a lot of regulars following the tour. *Don't want our playlist getting stale.*

"Almost done." He smiles and grabs his guitar and strums a few pretty chords. Then stops. "Sorry, James. This one's a surprise. You're going to have to wait like the rest of our fans."

A WEEK later I'm back at Zane's. He's hesitant to leave his mom alone. Her balance is precarious at best, and her pain meds make her dizzy. The change in her from last week to this week is alarming. She's lost weight, if that's possible, the oxygen tank sits by her side, and the cane she's been using has been replaced with a walker.

Despite that, Zane and his mom still argue a lot. Most of the time she treats me as if I'm not there. Other times with outright disdain. It's not pleasant, but Zane feels guilty leaving her on weekends, so here we are.

"You're hovering, Zane," his mom snaps from her spot at the patio table. I look up from my book, squinting as I lower my sunglasses, but refrain from commenting. It usually makes things worse, so I've learned to keep my mouth shut.

"Go out with Lyric. I'll let you know when I'm about to die."

Zane flinches. It's painful to watch, and I have to bite my tongue as I struggle not to jump to his defense. Dying shouldn't give people the right to say whatever's on their mind, but Janet does. I want to smack her for the pain shadowing Zane's face.

"I'm not hovering. Lyric and I are happy to be here." He looks to me for help.

"Sacha is much happier in your shady yard. And it's convenient for me to come here since Zane watches her while I work."

"I can watch the dog. Go out. Have fun. See your friends. The clock is ticking down. You'll regret wasting your time with me when you're back in New York." Her words make my stomach curdle. Or maybe that's the nasty antibiotic my doctor prescribed for the scratch on my arm.

Zane's voice hardens. "Mother, I'm not discussing this."

"Ignore the inevitable. You—"

"Not discussing this, I said," Zane cuts her off, and walks into the house.

Janet sighs. "He doesn't want to accept reality."

"Bludgeoning him with your opinions isn't going to make him change his mind." Okay, sometimes it's impossible for me to keep quiet. Not when Zane's hurting. "I'm not sure what your goal is here, but he's gonna need a lot of therapy to get over the guilt you're laying on him."

"Nonsense! I'm making sure he doesn't make any mistakes after I'm gone."

"The only mistake is the regret he feels for arguing with you when all he wants is to tell you he loves you. When all he wants is to be with you." I get up, my queasy stomach having nothing to do with the medicine I'm on. I can't be here to witness this anymore. "But obviously that's not important to you."

I call Sacha and go inside. No way am I leaving my dog with Zane's mother. I find Zane in the kitchen talking to Tess.

"I'm sorry, Zane," Tess says, her eyes reflecting his sadness.

"Yeah. Well, she doesn't want me here right now, so me and Lyric are leaving." He huffs, looking up when he notices me. "We have things to do."

Tess gives me a small smile. I don't know her well. Except for her graduation, I haven't seen much of her. I don't think she's avoiding me, but she makes herself scarce when I'm around. Or maybe she's just a busy teen.

"Go. Have fun. I'll call you if I need you." She hugs Zane, then heads out to the backyard.

"Come on," Zane says to me, or maybe Sacha. I'm not sure. "I have to fix your window problem."

He snaps Sacha's leash on and heads out the front door, a

large bag in hand. I chase after him while hopping into my shoes. "I don't have a window problem," I want to tell him, but he's already backing his Mustang out of the driveway. I sprint to the Volvo to follow him but give up when he leaves me in his dust.

By the time I get home Zane has let Sacha out back and has opened all the windows in the house. There's also a big square fan humming away by the patio doors.

"It's a furnace in here," he says the minute I walk in. "I can't do much immediately, but it'll cool off this evening."

I grab a soda, lingering in the coolness of the open fridge longer than necessary. "I'm not leaving the windows open overnight."

"Relax," he whispers in my ear. My heart still trips, but I'm not jumping out of my skin like I used to. "Your safety is my number one priority."

He ducks under the sink, retrieving the toolbox some former renter left behind.

"You better talk to my landlord before you make any holes," I yell at his retreating back.

"No holes necessary," he says, and my mouth drops open as I follow him into the bedroom. Then climb on the bed to watch him pull some kind of hardware out of the bag. "These things just clamp on."

"It's a temporary fix, but when we get our own place I'll install something more permanent." He throws that bomb out there nonchalantly while busy working on the window.

"Our place?" I ask while watching him fiddle with my bedroom window.

Moving in together? It's been less than three months. He's *moving* way too fast for me. I don't even know his middle name or his shampoo preference. I haven't even gotten up the nerve to tell him how I feel about him. Every time those three little words form in my mind, I choke.

"Relax, Angel. When the time comes we'll both be ready. Until then I'm gonna do my damndest to make sure you're comfortable here." He takes my hand, pulling me up off the bed. "Starting with locks on your windows that allow them to be opened a crack at night."

He shows me how to work the little clamp that stops the window from opening more than a couple of inches. It looks flimsy to me, not something I'd bet my life on, but I keep my opinion to myself.

"Thank you."

"Let me do the rest, then I'm taking you out. Wear your prettiest dress and heels. You have around an hour and a half to get ready."

I give him a narrow glance while considering what my prettiest dress would be, and whether it's clean. A little forward notice would have been nice. But he's taking me out, and that means I don't have to cook.

Collecting my bra and panties from my dresser first, I continue on into the bathroom while Zane heads back into the living room, the toolbox swinging at his side.

CHAPTER TWENTY-TWO

ZANE

*L*yric walks out of the bedroom and my heart stops for a second. Do I really want to go out, or turn her around and spend the rest of the night in bed? The thought of other men looking at her in that dress has me lean toward option two.

She's fucking stunning. Her golden hair is pulled up in some kind of pretty twist, baring her long graceful neck. The caveman in me considers leaving a few marks on that delicate skin. Claim my territory for all to see, like a big fucking neon sign saying *Taken*. Something to distract admirers from the sexy-as-hell dress she's wearing.

I told her to wear her nicest dress, but shit. I might have wanted to lay some ground rules, because I'm about to lose my mind over this short black-lace number with some kind of skin-toned lining making it look like she's not wearing anything under it.

If this were Tess, I'd send her back to her room to find the other half of her outfit, or ground her for even buying it.

Funny, I've seen most of Lyric's dresses, been in her closet once or twice, and I don't remember this one.

Not that I don't like it. I do. I even like the leg part. Did I mention low cut? Shit, yeah. And honestly, I mean, black's my favorite color, which Tess informed me one time isn't actually a color. But whatever.

Fuck, I'm sweating.

Lyric frowns and looks down, her hands smoothing the fabric that hugs her like a second skin. "Something wrong?"

I realize I've been staring for at least a few minutes, not saying a word. She twists her hands in front of her, her teeth sinking into her bright red lips. I definitely don't remember her wearing that lipstick.

"Yeah." I nod. "I think my heart stopped. You may need to call an ambulance."

She laughs and walks over, wrapping her arms around my neck.

Yep, I'm dead. Looking down I can see all the way to her stomach. Oh, hell. She's not wearing a bra. My dick swells, approving of the view no one else should have the privilege to see.

"You look pretty amazing, too. Where'd the suit come from?" she whispers.

I'm swimming in a fog of lust and her perfume. It takes a minute for her question to sink in. "Suit, right. Hung it in your closet after graduation. Never took it home." I consider the logistics of diving between the luscious curves of her breasts, painting her with my come.

Lyric clears her throat, snapping me out of another fantasy.

"Um, Zane." She taps on my shoulder and I look up into her grin. "Did you forget dinner?"

"Right, dinner." I'm so fucking hard it hurts. Resting my head on her shoulder, I groan. "You're killing me, James. Tell me something tragic or horrible, or we're never getting out of here tonight."

She laughs until I drag her hand between us, pressing her fingers against me.

"If you don't feed me soon, I may barf."

HER WIDE-EYED SURPRISE when I pull up to the valet stand is worth the extra money. The other night at Mill City, I realized that in the two months we've been together we've barely gone out. Between Lyric's whole hermit-lady routine and all the fucking bills back home, I've neglected my boyfriend duties. Tonight I'm changing that.

She frowns at me as we walk past the giant portrait of a bull inside the entrance. "A steakhouse?"

"Best steakhouse in town," I tell her. At least that's what Aaron says. White tablecloths, real napkins, ninety-dollar steaks—not that I eat them, but Lyric does. According to my best friend, Lyric was green with envy when Grace told her about their anniversary dinner here a few weeks back.

"Relax, Angel, tonight's about you."

Her eyes dart around, taking in the restaurant beyond the hostess stand. The place is dark and romantic, with high-backed booths and candles on the tables. The hostess leads us to the back of the restaurant to an intimate spot that's private enough to satisfy Lyric's reclusive nature. At least, I hope it does. At the moment, the tension vibrating off this woman is making me nervous.

"Enjoy your meal," the hostess says after dropping off menus and promising our server will be along soon to take our drinks order.

"You okay?" I ask while perusing the wine list.

She lowers her menu and frowns at me. "Zane, you do know this is a steak place, right?"

"I think the bull-themed artwork kinda gives it away."

"What are you planning on eating?"

I can't help but be touched by her concern. "They have pasta and salads. Don't worry. I won't starve."

"I feel bad. After the last few weekends of fair food, we should go someplace both of us can enjoy," she says before turning her eyes back to the menu.

"A little bird told me you like steaks. If you're enjoying yourself, I'm happy." I smile when she looks back up, her eyes overflowing with so much emotion. I can almost see the words I've been dying for her to say in her expression. *Say it, Lyric.*

Our waiter, Raymond, returns as Lyric opens her mouth to say something, maybe the thing I've been waiting to hear. And fuck, I want to tell him to get lost. To rewind time and give Lyric the opportunity to finish her thought. But the moment is lost.

The man isn't winning any bonus points when I notice him hovering too close to Lyric. I clear my throat and shoot him a glare, letting the guy know his tip is heading as far south as his eyes. He takes a wise step in my direction and proceeds to inform us of the specials.

Lyric orders the petite filet, then consults the menu with a frown.

"I can't decide between the asparagus with hollandaise or garlic creamed spinach," she sighs.

"The sides are meant for sharing. The portions are quite large, miss," Ray informs in his professional, yet still-irritating way.

"Then we'll share." I drop my menu and give Lyric an encouraging smile. "Order whatever you want."

She looks up at Ray, biting her cherry-red lip. "We'll have the spinach, the loaded mashed potatoes without bacon, and macaroni and cheese. Oh, and a side of grilled mushrooms."

"Would you like some gorgonzola or marrow butter on your steak?" Ray asks.

She frowns, biting her lip again.

"Can she have both? On the side?" I ask, solving her internal struggle.

The waiter leaves after I order the pasta Alfredo and a bottle of Burgundy. *Finally.*

"Will it gross you out to kiss me after I've eaten animal flesh?"

I stifle a laugh. There isn't much that could keep me from kissing Lyric, but she's sweet to ask. "I think I can manage."

She leans back in her seat, hands folded on the table. "So tell me about this vegetarianism thing. You've skirted around the issue for almost two months of vegetable curry, meatless pizzas, and pastas. We've moved way past break buddies, so I'm going to be blunt here, because as your girlfriend I have the right to be curious, and I may want to make you something fancier than omelets or grilled cheese. So where do you draw the line?"

The thought of Lyric cooking something fancy is laughable. She scrambles eggs to death and calls them omelets, is a whiz with a can opener, and does a fair job with grilled cheese as long as she doesn't get distracted. An actual dinner would be interesting, but her narrowed eyes and crossed arms prevent me from saying so.

"I prefer not to eat anything that breathes or has a face. Anything that can look me in the eye." I glance at the pictures of beef cattle that hang around the restaurant and shake my head. "Can't go there."

Lyric tilts her head as she stares at me. Probably thinking me as odd as I'm thinking everyone here consuming an animal while staring at its picture. Maybe not the exact picture, but the idea is there. "So when did you stop eating meat?"

"You really want to know? It's not the most enjoyable story." She nods, so I continue, my skin tightening. Talking about my stepfather is never pleasant, but Lyric deserves this glimpse into my past. "I was eleven, close to twelve, when my mom married Greg Cox. Plain and simple, the guy is an asshole. Decided the day he moved in he'd be the disciplinarian, and I guess I was more than happy to give him a reason to apply himself. Not that Greg Cox complained. Far from it.

"In his opinion real men knew how to throw a football, shoot guns, and drink beer. They didn't play music—they definitely didn't play in an orchestra. So he enrolled me into sports, canceled my music lessons, forbid me from hanging out with my friends. When I was almost fourteen, he decided I was old enough to join his annual hunting trip. His friends took their sons, and as far as he was concerned I was his son. I tried to get out of it but no luck. Embarrassed the hell out of him when I refused to shoot a deer. In front of his friends and their sons."

Lyric slaps her hand over her mouth. "Oh no. Zane..."

"Let's just say he made sure I'd think twice before embarrassing him again."

Lyric's face falls as the story ends. "He hit you?"

More like beat the hell out of me, but I keep that to myself. "And he forced me to watch while he butchered the deer he shot. My mom wondered why I couldn't sit for a week after we returned. When she found out what happened, she kicked Cox out and filed for divorce. Worth a sore ass in the long run."

"Oh Zane," she whispers, her eyes shining.

I reach for her hand, giving it a light squeeze. "In a way it proved my mom loved me more than him."

Before our conversation can get any heavier, the waiter brings our salad, then a short time later enough food to test a less-sturdy table.

Lyric digs into her steak, and I forget about the plate of food in front of me. Whether she's tearing her grilled cheese into crouton-sized bites and tossing them into her soup, or slowly unrolling one of her Ho Hos, watching Lyric eat is never boring. At the moment she's dipping tiny pieces of steak alternately into the small ramekins as if trying to decide which sauce she likes better. We're going to be here forever, but I don't mind.

"Maybe my time with Gray was worth it too."

I abandon my Alfredo in favor of listening to her theories. "How so?"

She takes a sip of wine and sets her glass down. "Well, I mean, if I had to go through it again I'd probably take a pass, but without Gray I'd never have left LA, never moved here, never met Grace and Zoe, never ended up going with them to Mill City the night I met you."

She's quiet for a moment her eyes locked on mine. I'm thinking she's not gonna say anything, but then she smiles.

"I think... No, I know—"

"How's everything here, folks?" Ray says, making Lyric jump. Interrupting another moment. "How's the steak, miss?"

Lyric answers while I contemplate driving her steak knife into our waiter's eye. After he leaves the moment's gone. Once again.

We finish dinner, and I pay the bill. Then head out for our next adventure of the evening, leftover cartons in tow. Lyric frowns at me when we bypass the valet stand and continue walking down the sidewalk.

"Come on. I have a surprise. You okay to walk in those shoes?" I glance down at those sexy-as-hell heels she wore the night I met her.

"How far?"

"Two blocks." I gesture ahead to our destination.

"Easy." She grins and takes my hand. I can't help but smile back at this beautiful woman. There's no fear in her eyes, no tension in her shoulders. This moment may not last forever, but for now I bask in this perfect snapshot of what our life could be.

Two blocks down, I stop in front of the modern glass and steel building, the large block letters above the entrance spelling out the words Orchestra Hall. Lyric gives me a confused frown.

"We're going to a concert?"

"Possibly." I wink and knock on the darkened door, ignoring her exasperated sigh. "Relax, this will be fun."

CHAPTER TWENTY-THREE

LYRIC

a security guard opens the door a crack. Except for the emergency lights, the place is dark and silent. Zane gives him his name while I continue to frown. I'm not good with surprises, but Zane seems to have a penchant for throwing me off guard. At the moment I'm very off guard and not overly happy, my very full stomach clenching with apprehension.

"Yes, Mr. Olensky is waiting," the uniformed man says, then opens the door wider for us to enter.

"Who's Mr. Olensky?" I whisper as we follow a couple steps behind the security guard, barely paying attention to the tall, smooth columns rising to the high ceiling above us, or the street lights shining into the darkened, glass-enclosed space. I spent half my childhood in orchestra halls similar to this one, but that time of my life ended when my parents died.

The guard opens one of the double doors and waves us forward, and whoa. *Okay.* For a moment I forget this is a really bad idea and take in the space. As concert halls go, it's not the largest I've been in, but the acoustical cubes, that appear poised to fall from the ceiling and tumble down the wall behind the stage are definitely different. And beautiful. *Way to go, Minneapolis.*

Piano music drifts from the grand piano centered on the stage. Tchaikovsky's Piano Concerto No. 2. Zane takes my hand, leading me down the side aisle.

"Zane…" I whisper-shout, my feet pausing. I'm not taking another step until he explains. "Who is he?"

Zane backtracks to my spot in the aisle. "A friend."

A friend… Of course. Zane probably has friends in every damn orchestra around the globe. Not that his short explanation helps my anxiety one bit. Friends of this caliber could blow everything for me.

Zane pulls me through the stage door and up a short flight of stairs. The stage comes in view, bathed only by the soft light of the utilitarian sconces high on the side walls. From this vantage point the seating area is dark, just a faint outline of the forward balconies is visible. Anyone could be sitting out there, but I wouldn't know.

My mouth dries and my stomach suggests that second helping of spinach wasn't a stellar idea.

The last notes of the music fade, and Zane applauds, alerting the pianist—Mr. Olensky, my guess—of our presence. The man leaps up from the bench, a wide smile on his face.

"Brody," he shouts, making quick strides across the stage. In faded jeans and a plain T-shirt, wispy, platinum-blond hair, and glasses, and a gold ring on his left hand, he doesn't appear to be a threat. But then neither did the friendly woman in the first women's shelter who tipped off the fucking paparazzi.

"Carl." The two men meet in the middle. Zane clasps the man's hand and pulls him into a hug.

"A fucking year," Carl growls, pulling back with a grin. "It's taken you a fucking year to finally come say hello?"

Zane runs a hand through his hair, grimacing. "It's been crazy with my mom, and Tess, but I apologize."

"Heard about your mom. Shit, I'm sorry." Carl's gaze shifts to me, his eyes widening with curiosity. At least, I hope it's curiosity.

Zane crooks his finger, beckoning me forward and out of the shadows. I take a slow deep breath, begging my stomach to settle. The second round of antibiotics my doctor prescribed are as nasty as the first and don't seem to be helping the puffy, oozing, redness on the inside of my arm anymore than the previous one. If given the chance, I'd happily rip the talons off that skanky bitch, or maybe castrate Grayson for taking my spleen. But at the moment I'm too focused on not barfing on Carl's loafers.

"This is Lyric. Lyric, Carl Olensky. Carl and I were in the high school orchestra together—"

"And then Juilliard," Carl finishes. "This asshole stole my spot in the Phil."

Zane laughs. "You never would have married Jill if you stayed in New York. High school sweethearts," he tacks on the last bit of information while glancing in my direction.

"True…" Carl offers me his hand. "Nice to meet you, Lyric."

I smile and return the sentiment. My stomach settles a little with the man's lack of recognition.

"Carl's the director of the youth orchestra here," Zane informs, slipping his arm around my shoulders.

"And you're teaching high school, now?" Carl shakes his head and sighs. "What the hell happened to us? Weren't we supposed to be touring the damn globe, stealing hearts and getting rich?"

"Does a bunch of county fairs count?" Zane chuckles.

"Fuck no." Carl laughs back. "And neither does playing in an empty hall to impress a pretty woman, not that I don't appreciate being an accomplice to another one of your crazy plans. Remember when you bribed the pianist at Macy's to let you play?"

My eyes widen with shock. "You're going to play?"

"Well, I'll be in my office if you need me." Carl slaps Zane on the shoulder and heads off the stage. Turning back, he adds, "Call me sometime. The four of us should have dinner."

"Definitely," Zane replies, then takes my hand, pulling me toward the beautiful instrument sitting on center stage.

My eyes dart out into the audience, and I assure myself we're alone. No one's watching. No one's paying attention. *Cue the paranoia.*

"What are you going to play?"

Zane slides onto the bench and motions for me to take the spot next to him.

"You've been curious about the piece inked on my skin, so I thought I'd start with that." He dances his fingers over the keys in a playful crescendo, giving me a wink.

"Start?" I can't help but glance over his shoulder toward the vast darkened space beyond the stage again. *Is that movement?*

Shit. I try to calm my imagination, because the slight shift in the darkness is definitely my imagination. My eyes playing tricks on me.

Zane starts the first movement, a slow whisper of notes, and oh… it's even more heartbreakingly beautiful than I thought. By the time he runs through the reprise—this time in C-sharp—Zane's hands blur behind the tears flooding my eyes.

His mother is right. He should be on stage, one with an audience who'll appreciate his music, not teaching high schoolers. Four months ago I'd have sent him off with a pat on the back and a "good luck." But now I'm selfish. The thought of him leaving guts me. And I hate Janet Cox for being right.

"Hey. This isn't the reaction I was hoping for." He brushes at the tears coursing down my cheeks, his gentle touch causing me to sob. His arms surround me, pulling me into his warm embrace. My tears soak into his suit jacket, bringing out the faint scent of the fabric.

My stomach lurches in warning, and I shove him back. Clapping a hand over my mouth, I mutter, "Bathroom."

Zane's eyes widen, but he's up and guiding me off the stage. Behind the curtain I spot the glow-in-the-dark restroom sign and bolt for it.

Two or maybe ten minutes later, I flush the toilet from my spot on the floor. It's fairly clean, as bathrooms go. No unidentifiable stains or wet spots. Zane knocks on the door and I mumble for him to enter, too exhausted to care how I look.

"Hey, what's wrong?" He slips between me and the wall and slides down onto the floor.

"I'm sorry I've ruined this." I snag a handful of toilet paper to blot my face. Okay, maybe I do care a little. Zane takes the wad from me and gently wipes the tear tracks and mascara smears from my cheeks.

"Don't worry about it. I'm more concerned about you." I flush the toilet a second time and Zane settles me sideways onto his lap. "You okay? Dinner not set well?"

I shake my head.

His hand settles against the back of my neck, his fingers kneading at the knot of tension. "Are you pregnant?"

I jerk back, my eyes wide with horror. "No! God no."

Zane holds his hands up and chuckles. "Okay. Sorry. I had to ask."

I lean back against his chest and breathe out a slow exhale. "Definitely not pregnant. It's just the antibiotics for this scratch." He frowns as I point at the injury he thinks I got from roughing around with my dog. Time to fess up. "Actually, I got this from one of your rabid fans that night at the Scott County fair. While you were on stage."

His eyes widen with shock. "Why didn't you tell me?"

"Because you have enough to worry about. And it wasn't a big deal."

Zane levels me with a dark look. "It's obviously a big deal. You're on fucking antibiotics."

"That…" I suck in a deep breath. If Zane's angry about some

random fan, he's going to love what I'm going to tell him next. "People who don't have a spleen are more prone to infections."

He stands, then offers me a hand up. "Fuck, Lyric. You should have told me."

I turn on the faucet and dip down to rinse out my mouth with tap water. Zane gathers the loose hair from around my face, holding it out of the way as I spit out the foulness.

"I'm fine, Zane. I follow the doctor's orders. Get my flu shot every year, watch for any fevers, and I guess I need to avoid jealous fans." By the tick in Zane's jaw, my joke has fallen flat.

"I had you working in the garden. And we were washing my car yesterday. And... maybe you shouldn't come to the concerts. Wait at the hotel."

I cup my hands on either side of his face to get his attention. "Stop. It's a slight risk. I'm not going to stop living because I might get hurt."

He traces a finger down my cheek, his lips curling into a small smile. "Too bad you don't have the same philosophy about your ex."

Zane's right. Since May, I've stepped so far out of my comfort zone, but I'm still watching my back. Am I ready to let my past go? The answer comes in a heartbeat. "I should. If he knew where to find me, he'd have been here already. Maybe it's time to stop looking over my shoulder."

CHAPTER TWENTY-FOUR

ZANE

*M*y phone wakes me sometime in the middle of the night. The piercing ring pulls me out of a pleasant dream. Or maybe the sound was part of the dream? Lyric lets out a breathy noise of frustration, grounding me where I am. And the stupid argument between me and my mom the minute I walked in the door yesterday after making the two-and-a-half-hour drive from Pine River. The phone rings again, this time in the here and now. My gut sinks with dread. I need to stop letting her get to me.

Will I get the chance? Or is it too late?

I spring out of bed and mutter a string of curses that have nothing to do with my foot connecting with the sturdy dresser leg.

Lyric's bedside clock reads 2:28. I find my jeans and then wrestle my phone from the back pocket. No one calls at two-fucking-twenty-eight on a Monday morning with good news, and the thought sends a wave of anxiety rolling through my stomach.

My phone rings again as I contemplate whether to answer.

Selfish, I know. And stupid. Whatever's happened has happened. Ignoring this call won't change that fact.

Anxiety turns to confusion as I stare down at my screen. It's not Laura or Tess but Aaron.

"Aaron? What's up?"

"We're at Abbott. Shit, man, you need to get down here. Dil's fucking OD'd." Aaron raises his voice to be heard over a siren blaring in the background.

"No. Fuck no." I squint as Lyric turns on the bedroom light. Then she's tossing me my clothes from yesterday while shoving her legs into a pair of shorts.

"Dave's a mess. Me and Grace just got here… he was afraid to call you, you know, with your mom and all." His voice lowers to a whisper, but there's all kinds of noise in the background. Raised voices, crying. Another piercing shriek of a siren makes it hard to understand everything Aaron's saying. "…doesn't look good from what I'm hearing so far."

"Shit. I'm on my way. Let Dave know I'm coming, okay?"

"Yeah."

I turn and grab my jeans, underwear still inside from when I peeled them off, before sinking into Lyric's sweet body only a few hours ago. *If only I could go back.*

"Dillon's…" I clear my throat to dislodge the guilt that threatens to swallow me, then repeat what Aaron just told me. My hand brushes over my stubbled jaw. "I thought it was my mom."

Tears sting my eyes. Am I the worst friend in the world to be a little relieved it's not my mom? Not that I wish this on one of my oldest friends, but—

Lyric's hands cradle my face, her gaze steady, pulling me out of my dark thoughts. "I'll drive."

ARE funerals more solemn on rainy days or sunny ones? At the moment the sun shines down on our tiny gathering. Dillon had a small family. His brother, parents, a couple of cousins, an aunt and uncle. And the band. According to Aaron, the friends responsible for his drug addiction aren't here. *Probably best.*

The service is quick, to the point. A life cut short, a remembrance of a man's time on this earth. Aaron and I each say a few words about a good friend who enjoyed every minute of life. Maybe a little too much enjoyment, but no one mentions that.

CHAPTER TWENTY-FIVE

LYRIC

*T*he day after the funeral we're on the road to Milwaukee. Dave refused to even consider canceling Summerfest. Eight hundred bands, eleven stages. An opportunity of a lifetime according to Dave. I've been to Coachella a few times, but this... It's overwhelming. Massive. The world's largest music venue, according to Aaron. Grace and I are given wristbands and a map because getting lost is a real possibility.

Enthusiasm is low. Energy nonexistent. Everyone's sleep deprived after sitting around the clock by Dillon's bedside, hoping for a miracle that didn't come. Of course, Zane blames himself. *Maybe if I hadn't forced him out of the band?*

Grace and I head into the crowds while the guys head off to the South Party Pavilion where they're set to play at five. After that, the plan is to grab something to eat and head back to the hotel for the night. Tomorrow morning, we return to Minneapolis. Which is too bad. Milwaukee looks like an interesting place to explore.

But this trip's a fine line between respecting Dillon's memory and not wasting the money the band's sunk into it.

We check out one of the famous headliners, then an up-and-coming-band, then head for one of the many food pavilions, grab a couple of beers and a fried sampler platter and then find a spot to sit.

"It's so hot," I whimper from the grassy spot where we've crashed.

"It's not that bad," Grace replies, looking fresh and cool, while I'm dripping sweat.

Shit, am I running a fever again? I've finished this latest course of antibiotics—which did a number on my digestive system—but I'm still not one hundred percent. But that could still be the antibiotics. Or something else. At least the cut on the inside of my arm looks a little better.

I drain half the plastic cup of beer in one go while making myself a promise to call my doctor come Monday morning just to be safe.

Grace and I hit a place that serves, I kid you not, s'mores empanadas. If it was possible I'd bring some back for Zane's sister Laura. Instead, I send her a picture. Then laugh when she replies with a gif of a slobbering dog along with *You are cruel, sister.*

I can't help but smile. When I was little, I always wished for a sister. Now, maybe…

Before I can dive too deep in my fantasy world, Grace notes the time and we head off to locate Zane, Aaron, Dave, and Noah.

The crowd for Heartattack is bigger than anything we've seen so far. It looks like all of the Twin Cities has shown up. A few people I recognize from Wally's yell hi as we pass through the entrance. Inside we're packed like sweating sardines.

"Thank you, Milwaukee," Zane shouts, and the crowd screams their approval. "And thank you Minneapolis, St. Paul!" I cover my ears and yell as the cheers around us turn deafening.

"We'd like to dedicate this song to Dillon Mathers, a talented bass player. Dil, wherever you are, we love you." Zane's voice cracks at the end, making my heart ache. Then he turns and Aaron taps in the beat of the first song.

"MEN SUCK!" I exclaim, sipping my third mai tai by the pool. Or is it my fourth? "We didn't even get to stay for the fireworks. I love fireworks."

"Me too." Grace nods, the straw from her margarita in her mouth. "So much. Let's finish these then, we'll conquer the lazy river."

"Roger, that captain." I salute. "I call dibs on the pink inner tube. The orange ones clash with my bikini."

Grace's sharp laugh echoes through the large enclosed space. "No rogering allowed, LJ. It's not proper during a mourning period."

"Who knew guys took mourning so fucking seriously." I look around, but it's sometime close to midnight and we're alone and quite possibly the most drunk I've been in ages. "I mean, I didn't know the guy well. But you'd think he was a saint, not the band member they kicked out."

Grace nods like a bobblehead. "I know. Aaron's all broken up about it. He's guilted…" She frowns. "Guilted? Guilting? Himself into celibacy."

I let out an unladylike snort, polish off my mai tai, then signal Daniel, our trusty waiter, for another round.

Our hotel rooms are sweet. Plush king-sized beds, steam showers, spa tubs, and fully loaded mini fridges in the seating area. But this adorable water park tucked into the basement is the best feature, hands down. Grace and I are alone—the guys chose to continue to grieve in the rooms. Which I get. But…

"Zane hasn't even looked at me since last Wednesday. That's a whole week and a half without an orgasm. I'm atrophying here.

My prime is slipping away." I wave my hand in front of myself in case there's any question as to what I'm talking about.

Daniel lets us know the pool will be closing in ten minutes. Grace and I groan. The thought of going back to the room sucks all the joy out of my rum buzz.

Grace slurps the last of her margarita and pats my shoulder. "Come on. Let's be mermaids for ten more minutes."

CHAPTER TWENTY-SIX

LYRIC

*T*he door swings open and I stumble forward despite the red light flashing on the stupid card reader for the third time. My eyes widen and my mouth drops open when I'm greeted by Zane's backside as he walks back to the bedroom. It's like I don't exist at the moment.

"Never was good with those things," I explain with a sad sigh. "Did I wake you?"

"No." He slides back under the blankets while I head into the bathroom. My bladder's letting me know in no uncertain terms that four mai tais are way beyond its limit. Or was it five?

I take in the crisp white-marble tile floor, veined in pale gray, the large soaking tub that I won't have time to enjoy. *When was the last time I had a nice bath?*

The room tilts as I stand, and I grasp the darker marble counter with both hands. The woman staring back at me blurs for a second, then comes into focus.

"What the hell do we do now?" I ask her, not that she appears to have any better ideas. It's been almost a week since we were called to the hospital for Dillon Mathers, and we both agree

Zane's pulling away. A few months ago this would have been exactly what I'd wanted from him. But now...

"Missed you at the pool," I say, taking in the man in bed. His eyes are closed, but the tension in his jaw tells me he hasn't fallen asleep. "Grace and I were mermaids."

One eye peeks open. "Hmm?"

I give the string at the neck of my bikini top a slow pull and the fabric drops to my waist. Zane loves my boobs, but at the moment he doesn't react.

"We enchanted all the men," I add, untying the bow at the back and letting my top splat against the carpet.

"Hmm."

My wet bikini bottoms follow, but, again, no response. Nothing. Not even a twitch. *Fine.*

I plaster on a smile I don't feel. "We sucked their cocks. Grace wasn't sure if that was a mermaid thing, but I said what the hell. I need the practice."

"What the fuck?" Zane sits up like a jack-in-the-box, his expression letting me know he doesn't appreciate my banter. *Too bad.*

I breathe out a satisfied chuckle at his response—the first damn response I've gotten from him in a week. "Was wondering how long it would take you."

"Lyric, I'm tired," he says as I rip the sheets back and climb on top of him. "And you're drunk."

"Um huh. And you're not in the mood." I run my hand over the substantial evidence of that lie hiding beneath his underwear, giving it a nice tug. "But it's the Fourth of July. I want fireworks. And I think you do too," I sing the last sentence.

He stills my hand. "You're naked in my bed. The physical has nothing to do with the emotional."

"You're emotionally tired?" I shake my head and sigh in frustration.

"It's been a bad week." Zane yawns, scrubbing his face with his hand. "I'm exhausted. Could we please sleep?"

"You know, from what I've heard from the male population, sex cures all." I raise my eyebrows and give him a seductive smile. "We have an amazing room…"

"No, Lyric." He lifts me off him, dropping me on the floor beside the bed. I dig my toes in the plush carpet as the room does a lazy spin.

"My nipples are kiiiilling me. I need your mouth." I cup the tender flesh, offering them no satisfaction.

Zane rolls over, ignoring me.

"Fine. Have it your way." I huff out a frustrated growl and roll out the desk chair. More of an upholstered arm chair with wheels. I spin the thing around to face the bed and sink down onto the green print fabric I hope is somewhat clean.

Zane punches his pillow and drags the covers back over his shoulders, settling in. *Yeah, we'll see about that.*

A hiss escapes my lips as I cup my breasts. The damn things really are tender, and the heavy ache in my uterus tells me my magic birth control pills won't be holding this month's period back. *Last chance, buddy.*

My hand drifts between my legs, and I can't help sighing in pleasure. I'm so fucking horny I want to cry.

Slipping my leg over the arm of the chair, I'm spread wide for him—if he wants to look. He doesn't.

Whatever. I close my eyes and pretend my fingers are Zane's. I'm so wet, it's ridiculous. My fingers are coated the minute I slide them between my folds, parting my flesh, before plunging into my slick heat. I pull out, then slide back in on a gasp as the base of my thumb presses against my clit. My head falls back and my eyes close and I moan, finding my rhythm. I'm not Zane, but I can get the job done.

"Fucking hell," Zane whispers, his voice hoarse.

My eyes fly open. He's sitting up, his eyes dark pools locked on me.

Maybe it's the alcohol, or I've had enough of his guilt and self-pity. I should be embarrassed, but I'm not. I'm staring directly at him, my juices dripping down the crack of my ass. I'm not stopping.

"What the fuck are you doing?"

My teeth sink into my bottom lip, and I moan as sparks of pleasure dance in my belly. My pussy tightens around my fingers. "It's been over a week, Zane. If you're not interested, I'll take care of myself."

He fists the sheets, his shoulder muscles tense. Our gazes lock as I continue sliding my fingers in and out of my pussy. The struggle in his eyes is as clear as day. He just needs a little push to make him snap.

My head falls back and my eyes flutter shut. I'm so fucking close, my thighs trembling, sweat beading on my skin. My fingers, Zane's fingers, it doesn't matter anymore.

"Oh God," I pant out. My hips rock into my hand as I increase my pace.

"Fuck, no." Zane's fingers clamp down on my wrist, stilling my movements. My eyes fly open, and I'm met by an angry blue stare.

He drags me up from the chair and our mouths clash in a way that might be painful, if it wasn't for the forty-proof rum coursing through my veins. I dive my fingers into his soft hair, careless of where they've been or what's on them. *He can shower in the morning.*

At the moment I'm not letting go. I'm not submitting. Tonight I want control.

Pushing Zane toward the bed, I slide his boxers down his hips, freeing his erection. Before he can stop me, I wrap my fingers around him and give him a slow stroke, letting my thumb caress his crown. Just the way he likes it.

"Fuck, Lyric." My free hand on his chest, I shove him onto the bed. He goes easily. With one finger I push him all the way back and join him. "What are you doing to me? You're driving me crazy."

"We drive *each other* crazy," I tell him as I climb on top of him, rubbing myself down the hot length of him and coating him in my wetness.

He reaches for my waist, but I'm not giving him a chance to pull me off. I grab his wrists, pushing his arms over his head.

"Nuh-uh, hands on the headboard. You have to earn the right to touch me."

He pauses a second, his eyes dancing with curiosity, before he wraps his fingers around the blond slats above him. "I like this bossy side of you, James."

"I do too." His cock glistens under me, slick with my arousal. I piston my hips forward then back, dragging his hot skin against my clit. His tattoo winks at me from between my thighs.

"I have so many questions, Brody."

He chuckles, his surly mood taking a leave of absence for the moment. "Was wondering when you'd get the nerve to ask."

I skim my fingers along Zane's length and his breath hisses out. "Did this hurt?"

"Too drunk to remember."

"So what made you decide to put a tiny dragon on your p-penis?" I stumble over the word *penis*. Even lubricated with alcohol my tongue has difficulty with that word.

"No fucking clue. And for the record, it's not tiny."

I move off him and lie down on my side, my head resting against his hip to get a better look.

"Hmm. In the realm of dragons, it's pretty small."

His fingers dance on my shoulder, disobeying my order, but at the moment I'm too busy to care. The detail of this thing... each scale on the dragon's body is a different shade of blue, from turquoise to navy to sky blue. Its eyes are fire red. I trace the path it twists around the shaft of Zane's cock.

"How many of those girly drinks did you have by the pool?" he rasps. "I'm pretty sure they affected your vision."

"I'll have you know, mai tais are serious drinks." I point my finger at Zane. "Now let's get back to your dragon."

"Let's," he breathes.

"So why a dragon on your…" I fumble again with that word.

"Penis. I love that you can't say it." He chuckles.

"Can too. It's just… penis… look every time I say it, it twitches." I pause, watching it do just that. "It's a bit unnerving."

"It's like a dog. You call its name and it wants to… come." He grins at his joke. "Your lips only inches away don't help."

"Oh." I lean in and close the gap.

Zane groans and his hand grips the back of my neck. His flesh is warm, so very warm, under my lips. I close my eyes and breathe deep. He must have showered before bed. The smell of his body wash lingers on his skin combined with my scent. Spicy, piney, with a hint of female. Very masculine. I dart my tongue out for a taste. Nothing foul, just clean skin and me.

Zane's hand threads through my hair, and I refrain from scolding him. His hands on me are as natural as breathing at this point. I can't imagine not feeling his gentle touch.

I trace the path of the dragon from its tail at the base to its flared nostrils at the top with the flat of my tongue. Pressing his crown between my lips, I bring him into my mouth.

"Fuck," Zane whispers.

I smile in satisfaction and take him deeper into my mouth, deep enough to nudge the back of my throat. My ex-husband once paid a thousand dollars for a blow job, and in the short time of our marriage I learned all the tricks. But somehow I don't think Zane would appreciate me shoving my finger up his ass as much as Grayson did. I could be wrong, though.

I play it safe for now and keep my fingers wrapped around his base, dragging my tongue over his sensitive crown before taking him all the way down. His hips thrust up and his fingers tighten in my hair.

Zane issues a gruff curse before pulling me off with trembling hands.

"You need to stop or this is gonna be over really fast."

"Oh, sorry," I say, not at all sorry. "I got carried away."

He drags me up his body, rewarding me with a slow kiss. "I love when you get carried away. You're so fucking good at getting carried away."

His tongue invades my mouth and all talking ceases for a while.

I love this man. I didn't want to. Fought it hard. But he won. I love everything about him, and I don't know what to do with that.

I swallow a sob that threatens to break me. I can't go there. Not now. Not here, in a romantic hotel room, with Zane naked under me. His cock twitches against my thigh, reminding me of his need. My need. Reaching down, I guide him to me. In one quick move I impale myself upon him to the hilt.

Zane sucks in a breath. "Shit."

I don't want the slow, gentle connection we've shared the past few months. I don't want to make love. I need a hard fuck. Something to distract from our uncertain future and my dangerous past that will forever linger in my nightmares. I want to focus on the here and now for tonight.

I slam myself down on his steely length over and over. Zane's hands close over my hips, driving me down and slowing my reckless pace. I lean forward, dragging the crown of him over the secret places inside me, making me tremble with my approaching orgasm.

His eyes smolder, dark and hooded, as he watches me. Arching my back in invitation, I silently beg him to touch me. His warm hands cup my heavy breasts, and thank God, the damn things have been aching for him.

"Harder," I beg, needing the flash of pain that comes with the pleasure of his talented fingers.

Sweat rolls down my back, sheening Zane's skin. My legs burn, and it's a race to come before the things give out.

Zane slides his hands back to my hips, his fingers dig into my flesh, guiding my rhythm faster, harder, as if he knows exactly what I need. "Come for me, Angel."

My body tightens like a spring and then I'm off, my body quaking. I cry out as the world ceases to exist, this supernova threatening to destroy me.

Waves of pleasure course through my body, and the words spill out. "I love you."

Zane pulls me down, and in one move has me pinned under him, kissing the breath out of me. The hard length of his cock presses into me with the roll of his hips, letting me know he's not done.

He rises up, kneeling between my thighs, setting my ankles over his shoulder. His hands slide under my ass and he lifts me to him. In one quick motion he thrusts forward, driving deep. Sparks light up the back of my eyelids, bright like lightning in the dark sky.

I gasp for breath between each punishing stroke, my pleasure climbing higher but somehow still out of reach.

His arms bracket the side of my head and he stretches out above me. "I love you, Angel. So fucking much it drives me crazy."

"I love you so much. I didn't want to, but I do." My gaze locks onto his, my heart hammering against my ribs hard enough to hurt.

His tortured expression and his quiet "Please, let me love you" breach my last defenses.

"This scares me," I whisper softly, but in the quiet room filled with the sound of our harsh breaths, it sounds like a scream.

"I've got you. Nothing to be scared of."

His hips roll forward and his pace slows. The sound of his sweet words, of love and promises of forever, extinguish the cold fear coiling in my gut. I want an eternity with this man.

He slides his hand between us, brushing my clit with his calloused fingers. In seconds another orgasm rolls over me like an ocean wave. My cries mix with Zane's as his rhythm turns erratic before he comes.

Our breaths and heartbeats mingle and compete for dominance. He's heavy as hell. Fully expanding my lungs is impossible, and my bladder isn't too happy either.

"Marry me," Zane mumbles into my neck. *Mr. Romantic.*

"Ask me when I'm not drunk, Brody." Chances are I'll still say yes because... I don't know why. Three years ago, I swore off marriage. Swore off men altogether. But this one's grown on me, and life without Zane is unthinkable. But for right now, I give him a poke on his chest. "Get off, stud. I need to pee."

CHAPTER TWENTY-SEVEN

ZANE

*L*yric hops out of bed as the sun streams through the sheer curtains covering the window of our hotel room, highlighting the fine hairs on her body like frost. I should have closed the heavy drapes, but it's too late and we should be getting up anyway. The guys will be waiting in just over an hour according to the bedside clock.

"Going to shower," she says with a smile that has only one meaning. *Don't wait too long.* After last night I know she'll start without me, and just the thought, just the image of her spread on that chair is enough to get me off my ass. I'll be hard for days thinking about that.

What had I been thinking? Denying myself her body for over a week. Stupid, and worthless. Like abstaining from sex would bring Dillon back or relieve my guilt? He's probably calling me all sorts of names for my stupidity at this moment.

The guilt over turning my back on my friend will always be there. But this morning I want to move on.

You asked Lyric to marry you. Pretty big move.

She didn't say no.

Maybe the next time have a ring to go with the words?

A couple of weeks back, Aaron and I went shopping for an engagement ring for Grace, and one caught my eye. Square diamond, with emeralds flanking the decent-sized stone. Probably not as big as her ex gave her, but it's not a contest. And even if it is, I'd win because I'd never lay a violent hand on Lyric.

The shower turns on and I can't help the goofy grin that pulls at my lips. She trusts me. She fucking trusts me. I want to dance, maybe let out a victory cry. Write a song in her name. Instead, I slip out of bed and head toward the bathroom with thoughts of pinning this beautiful woman against the marble walls. Maybe licking her until she screams, first. We still got to pack, but I'm gonna make every minute of the next hour count.

The instant my hand lands on the bathroom doorknob, my phone rings. Breathing out a harsh sigh, I glance at the damn thing. Not Aaron and Grace. They're probably just as wrapped up in each other as I want to be with Lyric at the moment. More likely it's Dave and Noah wondering if we're coming down for breakfast. The temptation to ignore it is strong, but by the sound of the third ring I'm turning back to answer the damn thing.

"Yeah," I say before my throat dries up and my entire body goes numb with the sound of racking sobs.

"Tess? What is it?" I sink down on the bed, knowing this is bad.

"Zane…" She barely gets my name out before she loses it again.

"Breathe, Tess. Slow down and breathe." I grab a handful of hair and pull. Of all the fucking times… "Where's Laura?"

"She's on her way. Zane… I need you."

"What's wrong?" I pace across the room and stare out at the city skyline. I'm in fucking Milwaukee, hundreds of miles away from home. Useless, and there's not a damn thing I can do about it.

My hand swipes at my stubbled jaw as I wait for Tess to pull it together enough to tell me what's going on. I'm pretty sure I know, but I need to hear the words.

"Tess. Come on, honey." I sigh, pacing across the small room like a caged animal. I should alert Lyric, have her ready to leave, but I need to stay on the line with my sister until I know she's okay.

"The bottle was empty, Zane. I forgot the pain meds in her room last night. I'm so sorry."

"Fuck me." My feet stumble as every muscle in my body freezes at my sister's words. A pain-filled picture settles into my mind. "She took them all, didn't she?"

My baby sister's sobs fill my ears and it's answer enough. Fuck.

"Not your fault, Tess." More likely mine for leaving that kind of responsibility to an eighteen-year-old girl. For leaving period.

My forehead presses against the window until it hurts. Stupid. I'm so fucking stupid. I should have never agreed to this trip, or this crazy-ass tour.

Mom has been pushing me away since I moved back, and over the past few months I've been too happy to comply. Spending nights at Lyric's and days practicing with the band. I'd lost focus, and now…

"I'm on my way, Tess." I groan at the hollow meaning in those four little words. *Five fucking hours.* I won't be home for five fucking hours.

"Okay," she whispers, her voice cracking, breaking my heart. "Hold on Zane."

"Hey, honey," Laura says, her voice tired, strained.

"Shit, Laura," I laugh quietly, bitterly, while dragging my hand through my dirty hair. "Why?"

She laughs back, but it's more a strangled cry. "You know Mom. Was there ever a why to what she did?"

I turn away from the window. "Shit. We've got to pack, then we'll be on our way."

"Take your time. Drive safely. I love you, baby brother."

"Yeah." I sigh and hang up, or try to. My hands shake so bad I give up and toss the phone onto the bed, then my ass hits the floor as my legs give out.

I'M LOST inside my head. It's a world of razor-sharp pain I'm pulled from when I open my eyes. Lyric kneels in front of me, her eyes wide with fear and concern. How long have been sitting here? How long has she been watching me?

"Zane?" She frowns, her cool fingers tracing the path of my tears.

"She's gone." I don't even recognize my voice. "My mom killed herself last night."

Her arms go around me and I'm trying to remember how to breathe, but I must be doing something wrong. It's like sipping air through a fucking straw, and the weight on my chest is excruciating. I'm dying. My sisters don't deserve this much grief in one weekend.

"Shh, Zane. Slow breaths." Her fingers sift through my hair, forcing a sob from my lungs. "It's okay, Zane. You're not alone. I'm here. I'll take care of everything," Lyric whispers in my ear while I cry on her still-damp shoulder. The coconut-vanilla scent of her wet hair grounds me. I don't have time to cry like a fucking baby, but there's not a damn thing I can do to stop the tears.

"Don't leave me. Please," I beg.

"Never, Zane. I love you."

My breath comes in shudders and gasps, but it's an improvement from moments ago. And it's all because of the woman in my arms. If my sisters weren't waiting, I'd lock us in this room forever, avoiding the pain that waits outside the door.

I blink as Lyric pulls away, her hands still on my face. She looks directly into my eyes. "I'll never leave you."

Despite her assurance, fear grips my heart. What we've had has been too perfect. The perfect bubble. Protected. Safe. Now reality has returned and we're plunging straight into a maelstrom. Will we survive?

My hands weave into her damp hair and I kiss her back. Hard and deep. Like with this one desperate kiss I can forge a strong enough bond to carry us through the dark future we're about to face.

Whatever happens, however hard these next few days or weeks may be, I need to let her know she is everything to me. Lyric is my soul. Without her I can't see my way forward. There's no way forward for me alone. Without her I don't exist.

"Don't ever forget how much I love you," I whisper against her lips.

She pulls away, a sad smile on her face. The farther she gets the colder I feel. We have to go—I know that—but a sense of dread settles in my bones as I watch her run around the room.

"Stay there. I'll call Grace, then pack. We'll be out of here quick."

A quiet fog descends, and I settle into the numbness, happy—if that's the right word—to let this sense of detachment replace the pain and anxiety that threaten to break me.

I BREAK out of the fog and look down at clothes I don't remember putting on. The rumble of my Mustang engine tells me where we are, but I don't remember getting into this seat either. Lyric's hands clench the steering wheel. The tiny crease between her brows tells me she's not comfortable driving my car. I want to reach out, place a steadying hand on her knee, or tell her to relax, but the words are out of reach, and so is she.

The perspective from this side of the car is off, but everything is off, the whole fucking world tilted on a different axis. I stare out at the farm fields and towns as we speed by, fucking envious of all the people we pass who are completely unaware of my sorrow and loss.

Lucky bastards. Fuck 'em all.

LAURA AND TESS smother me with love I don't deserve. Mom's gone, her room empty. The bottle of Exalgo on her bedside table, empty. The bottle I'd had refilled like the good fucking son I am, just before I left. I'd basically given her the loaded gun to kill herself.

I hurl the bottle across the room with a curse as Laura walks through the door.

"Zane." She pulls me into her arms. I'm supposed to be the strong one, but I can't even do that right. "You've been in here too long. Lyric said you didn't have breakfast. Let's go get something."

"I'm not hungry. You go."

"Don't do this, Zane. It's not your fault. She would've done this whether you were here or not."

I give her a nod in hopes of pacifying her need to mother me. I had a fucking mother and now she's gone. "Let me be for a while. I need to think."

She presses a warm hand against my cheek. "Not too much, okay? I'll bring something back for you. And get out of this room. Oh, and Lyric called, said to come home. Sacha misses you."

Laura locks the room behind me. She knows me too well. Maybe.

When I got home I discovered a small envelope on my pillow, my name written in Mom's flowing cursive. I stuck it in the top drawer of my dresser, knowing the dagger-filled message could wait for a quiet moment like this.

Was this the last thing she wrote, or had she penned this sometime earlier? I'll never have that answer, and I'm not sure I want it.

Door closed, I settle on my bed and open the envelope, my heart beating loud in the quiet room.

My darling boy,

You're probably really angry with me right now. I can't blame you. From your perspective this must look like a selfish act on my part. And maybe it is. Maybe wanting to spare you and your sisters the inevitable task of watching me painfully succumb to this stupid disease is selfish. I'd like to think your last memories will be of happier times.

"But you didn't fight, Mom. You fucking gave up," I scream into the cold, empty house.

I know what you're thinking, Zane. To stop fighting isn't the same as surrendering. But, I'm tired and I have better things to discuss with you, my love.

And I do love you, Zane. Hard as it was at times, I love you more than you will ever know. Sometimes love requires sacrifices. Whether we make the right sacrifices, only time will tell. But my last request is for you to make one for me...

The note paper crumples in my hand like the trash it is. *How can she ask this of me?*

"Fuck you, Mother," I yell, tossing the ball of selfish words across my room. I reach down, my hand landing on the cold weight hiding under my bed. The cap is off and the bottle to my lips. I don't want to think and the burn of the amber liquid going down my throat promises an easy oblivion.

MY HEAD'S fucked the next morning, but it suits my mood when I finally drag my ass out of bed a little before ten.

The house stands quiet, empty. In the kitchen I stumble over to the full coffee pot—thank fuck for small favors. After I polish off half the contents, I feel almost human. At least the timpani in my head has taken it down a notch or two and my stomach's not ready to turn inside out.

A shower helps even more until my eyes land on the picture of my dad's band on my nightstand. I throw it and my mom's crumpled letter I'd fished off the floor sometime in the night into my desk drawer. I'll think on her words later.

The house is still empty two hours later, and I'm running through where everyone is. I reach for my phone. Didn't Laura say something about calling Lyric? The temptation is there, but I can't bring her into my pain.

Glancing out front, I stare at my Mustang for at least ten minutes while fighting with the pull to drive across town to the little two-bedroom house where all my happiness lies. I don't deserve even a shred of happiness, but I'm a weak motherfucker. My keys are in my hand, and I'm out the door.

I need my suit from Lyric's closet, but I need her even more.

I PULL into Lyric's driveway and stare at the empty space in front of me where my mother's Volvo usually sits. Lyric's Volvo, I mentally correct while stepping out of my car.

Inside, Sacha greets me with her usual enthusiasm—on her back, legs in the air—and I can't resist a quick—okay, not-so-quick—belly rub. I'm in no hurry and maybe Lyric will show before I have to leave.

It takes two trips to grab all my shit. Thank God Lyric's been doing my laundry, because I haven't. Everything at home needs to be washed. I even had to use Tess's strawberry shampoo since I'm out of that too. It's a testament to how much I've neglected my duties at home, but I shy away from that painful thought.

Wearing days-old clothes and smelling like fruit, I do the few dishes sitting in the sink, toss Sacha's mangled squirrel for her, then wipe her muddy paws and let her back inside when her tongue starts dragging the ground. I grab a beer. Park my ass on the couch and scan the TV channels since Lyric's still not back.

After a couple of hours, Laura reminds me I'm needed at home.

I leave a note for Lyric. Maybe she's with Grace. She's not with Laura and Tess; I've asked. I've lingered as long as I can, now back to fucking reality.

CHAPTER TWENTY-EIGHT

ZANE

*C*ompared to Dillon's funeral, my mom's is a fucking circus. I don't recognize half of the people bawling around her casket like it's the end of the world, patting my shoulder like I give two fucks that they're trying to console me.

Inside, I'm screaming, *I don't even know who the fuck you are.*

If we're so damn important, where have they been all my life? Where were they when my mother's second husband was making my and Laura's lives a living hell?

And speaking of...

"Who the fuck invited Greg Cox," I growl into Laura's ear, my fists curling in my pockets.

"He's Tess's dad, Zane. Mom had a list. He was on it." Turning, she gives me a narrow look. "Behave. It'll be over soon."

Over? It would have been over days ago if we weren't waiting for everyone on Mom's list to arrive. But here we are, me and my sisters, our lives still on hold almost a week after our mother decided we weren't worth sticking around for.

I give Laura what I hope is a polite smile. "Better? But if Cox says one fucking word to me..."

"Zane..." Laura sighs. "Come, let's sit down. The service is about to start."

I'm being an ass. We both had to deal with that man.

Laura's on one side of me, and Tess's on the other. I haven't spoken with Lyric since the morning in the hotel. The longest time I've gone without hearing her voice since the week after we met. Turning around in my seat, I spot her in the back of the church with Tess's boyfriend, Connor, and Oliver and Mia. My nerves settle a fraction as our eyes meet.

The minister drones on forever about the miracle of life and the glory that awaits us in the end. Bullshit that means nothing to me. Probably meant nothing to my mom either since she didn't believe in the fantasy of heaven and hell and a benevolent god watching over us. But for the two women on my left and right, I make an effort to pay attention and look moved by the whole spectacle.

The service ends and we're stuck at the entrance of the church, thanking everyone for coming and accepting condolences. *Again.*

This time I capture Lyric's hand and pull her to my side. "Stay with me, please."

Her hand squeezes mine and everything's more bearable, even when Greg Cox walks up.

I give him a stare guaranteed to freeze his balls but keep my hands to myself. At twelve he seemed so tall, so frightening. Now he's an overweight old man. My icy expression lets him know I haven't forgotten the years of his bullying and abuse.

He walks on and Lyric gives me a look that's full of questions I can't answer here. Not here.

"My beloved stepfather," I whisper, answering the question in her eyes.

She lets out a tiny sound of outrage, and I have to tug her back to my side. I'd laugh if it wasn't so inappropriate at the moment.

"Easy, tiger." I give her hand a light squeeze in solidarity. "Maybe I'll let you take a whack at him later."

THE PROCESSION to the cemetery takes forever. Me, Tess, Laura, and her husband, Jason. are in a limo just behind the hearse. The hip flask in my pocket taunts, but my sisters would have my balls if I got drunk before they dropped our mom into the ground.

It's fucking hot at the cemetery, blazing under the stupid dark blue awning that holds back any breeze and traps the heat as well as my car roof. I'm sweating my balls off, looking forward to getting home and getting out of this equally hot suit.

But Laura has other ideas when I start loosening my tie on the ride home, what feels like hours later. "Mom would want you to look your best, Zane."

I give my older sister a tired look before staring out the window, while she reminds me of the importance of being social for the next several hours. *Who the fuck decided you had to throw a party when someone died?*

Walking in the back door, I take in the kitchen island covered with catered trays of lasagna, bowls of salad, and garlic bread that were meant for Tess's graduation party that had been scheduled for today. And of course, enough fucking hotdishes covered in melted cheese and studded with tater tots to feed a small army.

Fucking hell, I need a drink.

"REMEMBER the Christmas after Zane was born?" Aunt Mary asks, a twinkle of laughter in her voice. "Hard to believe something so tiny can grow into—"

"You're embarrassing the man, Mary," Uncle Joe laughs back anyway. We've all had a few too many drinks. Besides heading to the makeshift bar in the kitchen, I've been sticking with my aunt and uncle most of the day, ignoring the rest of the crowd, despite Laura's urgings to be social.

"Zane," Laura interrupts. "We're going home. Tess left with Connor."

I take a sip of my bourbon, ignoring the frown marring her face. "Fine."

"We put all the food in the fridge," she adds, pulling my glass out of my hand. "You might want to eat something."

"Will do, Mom." I let out a laugh as her face falls. "Too soon?"

She walks back into the kitchen with my drink, and silence closes in on her wake.

"We should get going too," Uncle Joe says, standing.

I stand and grab the arm of the couch as the room shifts. "Nooo. The party's just getting good. Don't let Laura and that stick up her ass scare you away."

Aunt Mary gives me a hug. "I think you need some rest, too,"

"I'm fine." And I am, now. Greg Cox left almost an hour ago, and this buzz I've got going on has erased all the guilt I've been cultivating this past week. "Really. Where's Lyric? Have you met her?"

Aunt Mary lets out an uncomfortable laugh, her eyes sliding to my uncle. "Months ago. Remember you brought her into the restaurant?"

"Oh, right."

I trail behind the older couple as they head out the front door. They're leaving, and I don't want to be alone with my self-loathing. *Fuck.*

"Zane."

"Lyric." I tamp down the thrill at the sound of her voice. I don't want to be alone, but I don't want to suck her into my misery either. "You should go home. I don't want your company tonight."

"Zane…"

I can feel her behind me as I head into the kitchen. The food's been put away and the counters cleaned. Leave it to Little Laura Hostess to take care of everything.

Of course she put away the alcohol, but I find it all inside the corner cabinet. I shake my head at her incompetence. If she really wanted to stop me she'd throw this shit down the drain like last time.

"What?" I ask. Lyric has the same frown of disapproval as Laura on her face.

"Let me heat you up some food. You've had too much to drink already. The veggie lasagna is—"

I pull a fresh glass from the upper cabinet, then turn and point a finger at Lyric. "Can you believe that bastard Cox tried to talk to me? Right here in my house."

She closes the distance between us, and her delicate hand cups my jaw. I stare into her beautiful eyes wishing I could hide away in them.

"You want to talk about it?"

My stomach clenches and I turn away, but she's persistent, following me around the island to the place I left the bourbon. "No..." I whisper. "Go the fuck home, Lyric."

She's quiet for a minute. I've probably stepped over a line, but at the moment I don't care.

"I know what it's like to always be wondering when the next fist would strike. I recognize the fear in your eyes."

"Don't want to talk about it." I concentrate on pouring the amber liquid into my glass. What does she mean fear? I don't fear anyone, least of all Greg Cox.

"Come home with me Zane." She places her hand over mine, her other fingers still wrapped around the bottle. "You shouldn't be alone."

I shake my head and bark out a bitter laugh and reach for my glass with my free hand. "I *need* to be alone."

She closes her eyes, rubbing the cute little crease between her brows. "I'm not leaving you alone to drink yourself to death, Zane."

Grabbing the bottle off the counter, she walks over to the sink and pours the aged bourbon straight into the drain.

"What the fuck are you doing? That's expensive."

She snatches the glass out of my hand and tosses the contents down the drain as well.

"Saving you from yourself," she yells back, her eyes inches from mine. "I fucking love you, you idiot."

My hand sweeps across the counter, knocking the empty bottle and tumbler to the floor. Glass shatters everywhere. Lyric flinches, but I don't care. *Why the hell is everyone trying to save me?*

She heads to the cabinet where my sister stashed the liquor, but my hand wraps around her arm, stopping her.

"You love *this*?" I point a finger at my face with my free hand and stare down at her. I don't need to look in the mirror to know my eyes are bloodshot from not enough sleep and too much alcohol. I lean in closer despite knowing I'll regret this moment come morning. But right now I can't stop myself. Lyric needs to go before I self-destruct any further. "Tell me."

"Zane, stop," she whispers, the compassion in her eyes just about killing me.

"Don't love me." I growl between my teeth. "Just go the fuck home."

I watch the tears in her eyes spill over, watch the tracks form on her soft skin, watch her love for me dim. "Zane, please, don't do this."

My thumb brushes over the rapid pulse in her throat. "If you stay, you'll hate me." I drop my hands and step back. "Now fucking go."

Her fingers go to the spot on her throat tracing the path of my thumb. She nods before I turn away, pressing my hands on the edge of the sink. Outside the window, it's as dark as my mood.

"Go Lyric," I whisper, hating my words. Hating the way I've hurt everyone I've loved. "I'm not good for you."

"Zane." The sound of her footsteps tells me she's moving toward me, but I hold up a hand to stop her approach.

"Call me when you sober up. I love you."

The front door closes and I squeeze my eyes shut. *Have I destroyed the last bit of happiness in my life?*

CHAPTER TWENTY-NINE

LYRIC

a week goes by with no word from Zane. *Probably best.* He's shaken my trust, and I need time to process what happened. Over the past few months, I've convinced myself he's not Grayson, but that night in his kitchen has tested my conviction.

He's hurting. He never would have acted the way he did if he hadn't been drinking, or if he hadn't lost two people he loved in the span of a week. If Greg Cox hadn't provoked him. Hollow excuses, every single one of them. Like the excuses I made for my ex-husband years ago when he first started with the verbal intimidation. Not long before the first time he hit me.

Do I want to go down that road again with Zane? the woman in my bathroom mirror asks.

He probably wasn't aware of what he was doing, another voice *excuses.*

So fucking familiar.

I lift my arm over my head and remove the bandage under my arm. Then wince at the ugly sight. It was getting better, but now...

After a few more days of silence, I change my mind about

leaving Zane alone. I'm moody and irritated, and full of self-doubt. No matter what happens between me and Zane, I'm a shitty friend for not recognizing his cry for help. However quiet it is at the moment.

His car isn't in the driveway when I pull up. I curse under my breath when Laura and the kids pull in behind me as I'm about to back out.

"Hey, Lyric." She taps on the window. "How are you?"

I'm stuck, so I get out. "Tired." I give an honest answer, too tired to sugarcoat my frustration. Grief, stress, and bad sleep habits with nightmares of Grayson leave me exhausted. "Is Zane expected back soon?"

She pauses and the look on her face has my stomach bottoming out. Whatever she's about to say, I'm not going to be happy.

"Um. Come in." She gestures to the bag of groceries. "I need to put these away for Tess."

"Okay," I drag out the word. A yes or no answer is all I need, but I follow her into the silent house.

Laura putters around the kitchen putting away the groceries while the kids head into the backyard. "It's been really weird here. Too quiet. I offered Tess our spare bedroom, but she insists on staying here alone. I guess once she's off to college I'll put the place on the market."

I lean in the doorway. "Where's Zane?"

Laura's expression of shock and sadness has my stomach twisting into a painful knot. "He didn't tell you? He left. Went back to New York the day after the funeral."

"No," I gasp out, my throat constricting with emotion.

Laura pulls me into her arms as a harsh sob breaks from my chest. "I'm so sorry. He didn't even tell us. Just left a note. I've tried to call, but it goes straight to voicemail."

I give her a shaky nod and back away.

"I'll call you if I hear from him," she adds, and I nod again.

Then rush through the house and out the front door before vomiting into the bushes while hot tears course down my face.

"You stupid bastard."

I stare at the Volvo for a second. Even if Laura hadn't blocked me in, I wouldn't take it. It's not mine, and whatever ties I had with this family are gone.

I dry my eyes and leave the keys on the seat. Exiting this relationship with as much as I entered it.

A few blocks over, there's a bus stop. Somehow I muster the energy to walk that far, ignoring the strange looks I get from two teenage girls once I arrive. *Like they've never cried over a boy before.*

My world has turned black and white. In the course of a few months, Zane has brought a technicolored vibrancy into my life. Colors I hadn't noticed until he left. I recognize the life I had before him for what it truly was, a shell, empty and barren of joy. With my only concerns surrounding my safety, I had been satisfied just to exist. But Zane showed me more.

I'm exhausted and cranky, and my arm hurts like a son of a bitch. I'm jumping every time my phone rings and sobbing when it's not Zane. Even the packages of Ho Hos sitting in my cupboard have me in tears, not to mention the disgusting bag of quinoa Zane gifted me.

I find Sacha staring out the living room window at all hours. Watching. Waiting. Hoping.

"He bewitched both of us," I tell her while attempting to coax her onto the bed that night.

She whimpers while nosing the blankets back. It's a new habit. Like she thinks Zane's hiding in the sheets.

"He's not here, baby."

She wanders out of the bedroom, her nails clicking on the floor as she checks each room, then gives up and comes back to lie down next to me with a mournful groan.

"You've broken my dog's heart too, you motherfucker," I whisper in the dark before crying myself to sleep.

"Oooh. That's nasty," Dora, the clinic nurse says when I peel off the bandage under my arm.

I'm subjected to a lengthy lecture on neglecting my health while she takes my blood pressure, checks my pulse, my temperature—slightly elevated on all three. I've gained almost six pounds —probably all the fried fair food. She pulls a paper gown from the drawer in the exam table and hands it to me with a tsk. "You haven't had a physical in over a year. Doctor'll want to do a pap."

I stifle a groan, but just barely. Without health insurance, this visit will drain my damn savings.

"Everything off. Doctor'll be in shortly." She shuts the door behind her, leaving me to stare at the ugly green pile of paper in my hands.

Several minutes later, Dr. Grove steps into the room after knocking. She's not much older than me, but, with prematurely gray hair, she always gives off a maternal vibe. I expect hugs but never get them.

"Let's have a look at that arm first." Her frown deepens as she presses on the puffy skin around the wound.

"Hmm. How did this happen again?"

I give her the shortened version of the events at the concert. My breath hisses out with her every touch.

"Sorry, dear." She steps away and has a seat at the desk. "How long has it been this inflamed?"

"Um..." I have to think a moment. Time has blurred with everything that's happened. "A week, I think."

Doctor Grove lists off the antibiotics she's prescribed, staring at the information on her computer screen for what seems like forever. Then pulls a vial from the cabinet and gloves from the box. "Fingernails harbor all kinds of bacteria. I'll send a swab to the lab so we can figure out what we're dealing with." I suck in a breath as she dabs at the wound with an apology. "Until then, I'm going to prescribe dicloxacillin. Your arm should start looking better within forty-eight hours. If not, by then we should have the results of the culture."

"Sounds good." It doesn't sound good. It sounds expensive.

"Now let's check the rest of you. Any complaints?"

"Tired." I fill her in on the events of the past few weeks while she checks my eyes and ears and throat. "I think the weight I've gained settled all in my boobs."

She motions for me to lie down, one of those thoughtful frowns creasing her forehead."Hmmm. Are they tender?"

My grimace at her touch should be answer enough, but I answer, "Yes, but maybe once I buy larger bras…" If I can afford them after this visit. Might be cheaper to stop eating.

I trail off and she peppers me with questions I'd rather not think about. "Are you sexually active? When was your last period? Have you been using any backup birth control?"

I give her a short rundown on my relationship with Zane, and how I'd had cramps a couple weeks ago, but it'd been a false alarm.

"Why would I need backup birth control? I've been on the pill for years."

My last answer seems to crack her calm bedside manner. Her eyes go wide for a second as she motions for me to sit up.

"You do know antibiotics reduce the effectiveness of the pill. Okay. From that answer, I think it would be prudent to do a pregnancy test."

"No…" *No way.*

I stare at the specimen cup she hands me like it's cursed. This can't be happening. A few minutes later, I leave the cup on the designated shelf in the bathroom with a prayer. I'm nauseous. *Psychosomatic, power of suggestion*, I tell myself. I've felt fine, no symptoms. *I'm not pregnant.*

A few minutes later the doctor's face says it all. "You have a lot to think about, Lyric."

How am I going to afford a baby? I can barely keep Sacha supplied with her favorite kibble and the fancy dog treats Zane got her hooked on. I can barely afford this doctor's visit. How am I going to pay for months of doctor's visits and a whopping hospital bill in the end? Then years of diapers and formula and clothes and…

The doctor hands me a pamphlet outlining all my options. The easy way out settles heavy on my chest. The prudent option. But when will I get the chance to be a mother again?

"I'm keeping it," the words slip out without thought of how I'm going to pay for food and a crib and college.

She smiles and nods. "Congratulations, then. I'll write a script for prenatal vitamins and an ultrasound. Let's get a look at this baby as soon as possible."

I walk out of her office in a haze.

"You ordered a salad. Are you okay?" Grace laughs, noticing my sudden deviation from all things fried and greasy that now make me want to puke.

I sit across from her in a quaint little restaurant not far from school. Calling Grace had been a difficult decision. She's my best friend, but she's also dating Zane's best friend. Can I trust her to keep my secret? Not that this pregnancy will be a secret forever.

"Yeah. I decided to take better care of myself." My lips curve into a crooked smile as I try to convince myself that I don't want a juicy burger and fries. "A summer of fair food has taken its toll. I have three weeks to fit into my school clothes."

"Tell me about it," she says while pinching her side. "It's double yoga sessions for the next few weeks."

Grace's eyes go soft with sympathy once our server walks away. "How are you?"

All the air leaks out of me. "I don't know."

"I'm so sorry. I feel responsible. If I hadn't introduced you two—"

"It's okay. I don't blame you. He was hard to resist."

"Aaron is pissed." Grace grimaces while doctoring up her herbal iced tea. "Dave had to cancel the rest of the tour. I can't believe he up and left, no warning, no goodbye."

"He hasn't even returned Laura's calls." I shake my head slowly. "A part of me is worried about him, but the other part…"

"Would like to castrate him?" she fills in the words I'm thinking. "I don't blame you. I thought so much better of the guy."

"Well, the castration thing would be a little useless at this point." I breathe out a quiet laugh. "I'm pregnant."

"What?" She sets her glass of tea down slowly.

"That was my reaction." I explain the whole crazy situation with my arm, my spleen, and the antibiotics.

"So that deranged bitch is the reason you're pregnant? That's insane. Have you tried to contact Zane?"

I shake my head as the waitress brings our lunch. "Why should I?" I ask after the waitress leaves. "I owe him nothing. He owes me nothing. We had a few months of fun. He's moved on."

"He might want to know. Be a part of his child's life."

I watch as she shoves a couple of fries in her mouth, then focus on my salad before the nausea kicks in.

"I'm not dragging him back into a life he doesn't want. He made his decision. I have to respect that." My voice cracks and my eyes fill with tears. This admission is like a stake through my heart. I'm bleeding out at the table.

Grace takes my hand. "I'm here for you."

"Thank you. Please, you can't tell Aaron. He'll tell Zane, and… the way we left things, I'm not sure Zane deserves to know."

"I don't think he's spoken to Zane, but I swear I won't say a word. It'll be our secret until… well, until you won't be able to hide this anymore."

"I need time." My lip trembles. Having someone to trust

means everything. "And help. Could you go with me for my ultrasound?"

Grace beams. "I'd love to."

MY PREGNANCY SEEMS abstract until the ultrasound. Grace holds my hand as the technician guides the wand over my stomach.

Suddenly a whoosh, whoosh, whoosh comes from the machine.

"You got a washing machine in there," Grace jokes.

"That's the baby's heartbeat," the technician says, turning the wand. "And here's the baby. It's still early, maybe a month? It'll be a few weeks before the baby looks like a baby."

She points to a blob on the screen. The blob looks nothing like a human. But that's exactly what it'll be. A human, with feelings and needs.

"Oh God." Tears leak down my face for the billionth time since Zane walked out of my life, but this time they're happy tears. "It's real. Shit, Grace, how am I going to be a mother?"

The technician prints off a black-and-white grainy screenshot of this little human. My first baby picture.

"Hi, Olaf," I whisper to myself, tracing his blobby body.

"You'll be fine." Grace giggles. "I have faith in you."

"I'm glad someone does." I sob. More tears. I don't know why I bother with makeup these days. I've turned into a faucet.

I DON'T KNOW if it's a boy or a girl, but in my mind it's a boy with dark hair and stunning blue eyes that will someday win girls' hearts. And I'll teach him not to break them.

I talk to little Olaf constantly, telling him whatever's on my mind. I catch odd looks from strangers, but I don't care. We have this private world only the two of us can share.

I've picked up my phone so many times to call Zane. Grace is right. He deserves to know. But then what? What if he doesn't want us? What if he does, but he refuses to stop drinking? To recognize he has a problem? Our child deserves better than an alcoholic father.

There were so many little warning signs I ignored. The night he passed out on my bed. The many times after a concert when he and the guys let loose. How Zane always let a little more loose.

My heart still aches for him, but I have a responsibility to Olaf now.

These are the thoughts that follow me through the days and torture me at night. School will be back in session soon, along with plenty of distraction. Before I know it, I'll be on maternity leave in March. The parents are going to hate that.

I'm going to need a car. I can't walk to school this winter pregnant. Would Laura give me back the Volvo if I told her she's going to be an aunt?

"Auntie Laura, will you let me have the car back to drive little Olaf around?" I practice saying into the mirror one morning. Not that I can ask her. She'd tell Zane in a heartbeat. And I'm not quite ready for that.

I'm deep in thought as I walk home from the grocery store early one evening. The sky is painted in oranges and reds and purples. Summer's winding down. My arms are weighed down with sacks of groceries, and my legs are ready to give out. And I still have to walk Sacha in the remaining minutes left of daylight.

In the last couple weeks, my legs have gotten used to walking again, which is good since I want to eat everything. But I swear, my bladder has shrunken to the size of a pebble. I'm familiar with most of the public washrooms in the city.

Right now my bladder's screaming to get home before it

bursts. I fumble with pulling out my keys and almost step on them.

Flowers. A bouquet of white roses sits on my doorstep. My blood chills and my grocery bags slip out of my hands and tumble down the steps. My heart is in my throat as I search the neighborhood.

Nothing. I ease my shaking legs back down the steps and rush from the house. Across the street, I tuck myself behind a huge oak and pull out my phone.

"Lyric, how are you?" Ellen asks, all happy to hear from me.

"He's here." I force the words out of my constricted throat.

"Take a deep breath. Are you sure?" Her voice calms me. I don't have to explain. Ellen knows.

"There's a bouquet of white roses on my doorstep. He always bought me white roses when he apologized."

"Get out of there." Her calm voice turns forceful. "I'm on my way. I'll pick you up at the corner of Hiawatha and Lake. Can you get there?"

My heart leaps into my throat. I've prepared for this possibility, have a bag in the back of my closet in case. But the reality of the situation leaves me shaking like the leaves in the tree above me. "I need to get my dog first."

"Make it quick. Don't stay in the house longer than you have to."

I watch the house for several minutes, searching the street for any unusual activity or unknown vehicles. Everything seems safe. Except for those roses. *What if Zane sent them?* Not a chance, my conscience tells me.

The neighborhood is quiet, the house still. I can't wait any longer. My bladder is bursting and so is Sacha's. I step out from behind the tree and head across the street, ready to face my demon.

CHAPTER THIRTY

LYRIC

Kicking the roses to the side, I slip my keys into the deadbolts, one by one. Taking one last look behind me, I open the door and slip inside. Slam the door shut and engage the locks. Then I allow myself to breathe.

My lungs freeze as the overpowering scent of roses hits my nose. I turn and whimper. My knees threaten to drop me where I am. I close my eyes hoping when I open them it'll all be gone. A bad dream. But no.

Every surface has a vase bursting with white roses. The coffee table, the end tables, the piano. *He's been inside my house.* The thought makes every hair on my body stand stiff. I need to leave, now. Grab Sacha and go.

Where is she?

She should have been in the window watching for me. Should have been at the door greeting me. Most times I can barely get in the front door with her enthusiasm.

"Sacha." My stomach clenches as the silence stretches on along with my dog's absence.

"Sacha!" I yell louder, not that it's necessary in this tiny house.

Forcing myself away from the door, I step further into the living room. I'm dreading the answer at the end.

My dog lies on her side behind the sofa. I drop to my knees and pet her still form. A quiet snore escapes from her lips and my lungs remember how to breathe. She's not dead, but she doesn't wake, even when I shake her.

"Fuckin' oath, Faith, you look like a cool glass of water on a hot day."

I glare in the direction of my ex-husband's voice.

Grayson Thorpe leans lazily against the bedroom doorway. His voice rich with that Aussie accent that at one time I thought was so sexy, but now only makes my blood run cold. He hasn't changed much in the past three years. Maybe a little thinner, a little sharper around the edges. He's still gorgeous—golden blond hair, now streaked with hints of silver, gray-green eyes, a chiseled jaw sparkling with stubble from the afternoon sun coming in the front windows. His once alluring tribal tattoos peeking out from above his shirt collar. But his allure is marred by the ugly he hides inside him, waiting to come out when provoked.

"What did you do to my dog?" I growl through clenched teeth. "Whatever. We're taking her to the vet. Now."

"Careful, Faith," he says, his voice low and dangerous. "She's just taking a little nap."

"Nap. What do you mean, nap?" I ask in a calm voice, heeding his warning. A tiny voice begs me not to provoke him. *I need him compliant, not angry.*

"I slipped her a Xanax in a tidbit of steak. Your girl will do anything for a bite of meat, even let a nasty bloke like me in the house." He sends Sacha a skeptical look. "Not a very good watchdog if you ask me."

"Xanax." Fear settles into my stomach at the thought of Grayson drugging my dog. "Do you even know if that's safe for dogs?"

"Perfectly safe. Don't worry your pretty little head, I haven't killed your dog."

I stroke the fur on Sacha's chest and take a couple of deep calming breaths to clear my head. *Think rationally.* Grayson hates when I get emotional, and making him angry won't help me or Sacha. "How did you get in here?"

"Told your landlord your husband wanted to surprise you... Surprise!" He laughs and the sound burrows its way under my skin, making me shiver. There was a time I used to love his laugh, but not anymore.

"I knew you'd come."

He closes the gap between us in two steps. His hand twists painfully in my hair, bringing my face to his. "Blonde? You thought changing your hair color would be enough to keep me from recognizing you? Thought you could move on?"

"Let me go, Grayson." I clench my teeth against the oh-so-familiar pain.

"Not on your fuckin' life." He sneers, his nostrils flaring. "Now tell me, Mrs. Thorpe, who's the fuckin' galah?"

My heart lodges in my throat. Galah—idiot. *He knows.* Somehow he knows about Zane. "What galah?"

For once I'm thankful Zane isn't here.

His hand tightens in my hair. I suck in an uneven breath, my eyes watering. "Don't fuckin' lie to me, Faith."

My scalp screams as he pulls me to my feet, then drags me into the kitchen and shoves me onto a chair.

Spread out on the table are pictures. Me getting into Zane's car. The two of us sitting close at the band's table in Mill City. Zane and I holding hands at one of the county fairs. I swallow the lump in my throat as I take in the image of Zane and me in what could only be described as a passionate kiss the night we walked around the lake after his set at Mill City.

"Now. Who's. The. Fuckin'. Galah?" His spit hits my face, but I refuse to give him the satisfaction of wiping it off.

"He's—he's gone. Moved to New York. I haven't seen him in weeks."

"Fuckin' cunt touched something that wasn't his."

"This is between you and me, not him. Please leave him out of this."

His smile is one of pure evil. "Fuckin' right this is between you and me. I warned you what I'd do if you let another man touch you."

His hand is an iron band around my arm, his fingertips digging into my flesh, but I'm certain they won't be the only bruises he'll leave on me today.

"How many times did'ya fuck him in here?" Grayson pulls me into the bedroom and tosses me onto the bed. "In this bed? Did'ya enjoy it?"

I scramble back to my feet. "Don't touch me."

"Faith, Faith, Faith," he whispers in that calm, cold voice that has me trembling. "Before morning I'm going to reclaim every inch of your lovely body. If you're repentant, I might even let you enjoy it."

"Fuck you, Grayson Thorpe."

I barely see his fist coming before pain blinds me, like a direct hit from a freight train. There's a momentary sense of weightlessness before the floor comes up to greet me and then everything fades to merciful black.

I wake some time later, my face sticky with blood. I groan in a combination of frustration and agony. White hot, throbbing pain encompasses the entire left half of my face, telling me Grayson hasn't lost his touch. After all these years you'd think I'd have learned not to fall face first, but no.

Every. Fucking. Time.

The room's dark and Grayson is gone. Small miracles. He's

not far. I'm not fooling myself. He's here for me and he won't leave without me. This is my fate. The one I've been expecting. I had a little over three years' reprieve for good behavior, now I'm back in hell.

I raise myself up with difficulty. The room spins. My head feels like a hollow melon. Concussion, my brain supplies. My stomach revolts as I attempt to get up. I cover my lower belly with my hand and send a prayer to whoever will listen for Olaf's safety.

Silence blankets the room. I glance out into the hall, but nothing. *Where the hell's Grayson?* Not knowing is frightening. I need to find a way out, but if he catches me...

A tug on my shoulder reminds me that my purse is still with me. My phone's inside. It's not much, but it's a plan. Or a start of a plan.

Crawling into the bathroom, I shut the door with a quiet click and hold my breath. Then curse myself for not adding a lock when I fixed the damn thing. After a moment that doesn't bring my raging ex-husband, I flip on the light and rummage my purse for my phone.

It's not there. *Shit.* It must have fallen out when I fell.

I don't want to, but I stand and look in the mirror. I shouldn't recognize myself, but I do. The side of my face is swollen and red. *It'll be even prettier by tomorrow.*

I muffle my cry behind my hands. Telling Zane that Grayson sent me to the hospital twice didn't tell the whole story. There'd been at least a half dozen or so times Grayson brought the nurse who lived three doors down over to patch me up after handing her a wad of cash to keep quiet.

I wiggle my jaw, testing for loose teeth. Then prod my cheek and wince. Spots dance across my vision. *At least he hasn't fucked you, yet.*

That thought sends a wave of nausea through my stomach. I

groan and look back into the mirror. Too bad this look never turned him off.

Forget the damn bruises. I need to think about Olaf. And Sacha. I refuse to believe Xanax is safe for her. Truth is, the longer I'm in this house the less likely we're all getting out alive.

I rummage through the bathroom for any kind of weapon but come up empty. Although bludgeoning him with a hair brush would be satisfying. *I'm a fucking survivor.* I've survived Grayson Thorpe once, I can do it again.

I shove the prenatal vitamins under the sink, behind the cleaning products. God only knows what my ex-husband would do if he finds out I'm pregnant. Then take one last glance into the bathroom mirror, gather my courage, and open the door.

From the bedroom I hear voices. I can't make out the words, but I recognize Grayson's deep rumble. I follow the sound to the living room.

Lights flash across the walls. Red, white, red, white. Out the front windows, beyond the glare of floodlights, police cars line the street. *Ellen.* Of course Ellen called the police when I didn't show up.

"No. I'm not coming out… she's my fuckin' wife. I have every right to be with my wife…"

His voice comes from the kitchen. My bruised body tells me to turn back, but I force my feet forward and walk into the kitchen.

"Faith." He shakes his head, setting my phone on the counter next to a vase filled with at least two dozen roses and closing the distance between us. I flinch as his fingers touch my face. "I'm so fuckin' sorry, baby. Why do you keep makin' me do this? All I want…" He trails off, his gaze shifting to the front windows. "For some reason the cops think I'm holding you hostage. Can you believe that?"

My gaze lands on the gun sitting on the counter and my blood goes cold.

"I won't go back to jail," he says, his tone hardening with a finality that makes my heart race even faster. *He has nothing to lose.*

My hand automatically goes to my stomach. To Olaf. *Think before you speak.* "Of course not. This is just a huge misunderstanding."

My breath rushes out of me at the lost look on Grayson's face. I should hate him. I do hate him, but... I despise the vulnerable man standing in front of me almost as much as his angry side. At the same time my heart squeezes with some weird, misplaced sympathy. Three years of therapy and I still don't understand the complicated feelings I have for my ex-husband. He needs help—more help than I can offer. More help than he received in that jail cell I put him in.

"I can talk to the police. Make them understand," I say with a breezy confidence I don't quite feel. Then I kneel down and set my hand on Sacha's chest. It rises and falls in a slow rhythm I convince myself is normal.

"We had a plan. It was me and you and our children. It was a life together. I just kept fuckin' it up." He waves the gun around, gesturing with the damn thing.

I force myself to step away from Sacha with reluctance. She's alive for now, but for how long? What I do over the next few minutes could decide her fate. And Olaf's. And mine.

"You know I hate guns. Just set it down and let's talk like we used to. Remember when we were dating, how we'd sit and talk for hours?" I gesture to the sofa and take a seat. "Please?"

He nods and sets the gun down next to my phone, and my lungs start functioning again. On the sofa, he slips his arm around me and nuzzles my neck. "Like old times."

"Yeah. Like old times." I nod, doing my best not to stiffen as his lips slide up to my jaw. The voice in my head warns of the dangerous game I'm playing, but do I have a choice?

"I've missed you so much, baby. I know things went bad really fast there. It hurts to think about what I did to you. I wasn't... I wasn't in my right mind. I love you, Faith. I never want to hurt you. You have to believe me." He strokes the fresh bruise on my face. Pain and guilt flood his eyes. I believe his words, but I know he can't control himself. At the moment he's remorseful Grayson, but I know from experience how fast his moods can change.

"I believe you. I really do. But you have a lot more work to get better. You need to see that." I take his hand in mine. So large—almost twice the size of mine.

"I do. I've been in therapy. Giving talks on domestic violence. I've changed. All for you, Faith." His accent thickens with emotion. "I've been planning. Whatever you want. We'll take it slow. One day at a time. I just can't live without you. And you can't possibly be happy here." His lips brush against mine and I force myself to kiss him back. "Don't you miss LA? Fuckin' oath, babe, you can't be serious about this place."

"I've made friends here. I like my little house. I like being independent. I think if you want to prove that you're getting better you need to respect my decisions."

I send up a little prayer that I haven't pushed him too far.

"Have you fallen for someone else?" Grayson's voice sharpens, his tone dangerous. My mouth dries as the line I'm walking thins. "That musician?"

"No, Grayson."

"You don't trust me?" His voice turns small, like a hurt little boy.

"I don't trust anyone. Not just you."

"So you're happy here." It's not a question, but I nod anyway.

My phone rings again. He stares across the room at it, his hands clenching and unclenching, until the ringing stops.

"What do I do now, Faith?"

"I can talk to them. Let them know this is all a big mistake." I offer him a sad smile and take his face into my hands. "Let me help."

"I've fucked up again, haven't I?" he whispers, his hands covering mine. "I can't go back to jail. I won't. I've broken parole to come here. They're going to send me back."

"No, Grayson. I'll work it out. I promise." I press a kiss to his stubbled cheek.

I expect him to walk over to my phone, but he heads to the door instead, and a flicker of uncertain hope blooms inside my chest.

"Please go. I love you, Faith." His hands gently cup my face, then his lips are on mine. Tender. So like the handsome blond man that swept me away years ago. With therapy, maybe we could have worked through our problems in the early days, but now it's too late.

I kiss him back while a trickle of fear skitters down my back. This feels an awful lot like goodbye.

"I promise I'll come back when I've fixed things, Grayson. Just wait here. Okay?" I glance toward Sacha for a second. *Please be safe.* Then open the door. "I'll come back to you. I promise."

Blinding lights hit me in the eyes as I walk out the door. Instinctively I raise my hands and stumble down the first step.

"It's the wife, hold your fire." I hear someone shout as I fumble for the porch railing, trip over the bags of groceries I abandoned earlier, and land on my knees.

A gunshot rings out behind me and I scream until my lungs give out. My heart tells me what my mind refuses to accept, like a connection has been severed. I turn, ready to sprint back up the stairs when hands grab me.

"No, no, no…" I sob, fighting the arms that pull me away as police rush the house. "No, Sacha… Grayson…"

The arms tighten around me, and everything goes black for the second time today.

CHAPTER THIRTY-ONE

LYRIC

I wake to more bright lights and a myriad of aches. My brain struggles to put my thoughts together.

"Just relax, ma'am. Everything's going to be all right," an unfamiliar woman in some kind of uniform says. "Can you remember anything?"

My mind connects the fuzzy images of the day. Shopping. I was grocery shopping, and... A frown tugs at my brows, triggering a deep throb on the left side of my face. The memories connect. Grayson, Sacha, the gun. *No.*

"My dog," I answer, my voice clogged with emotion.

"Can you tell me your name?"

"Where's my dog?"

A man, just out of my line of sight, says something and the woman looks in his direction. Memories flood in while I wait for an answer. *Grayson's dead.*

"One of the police officers drove her to the emergency vet. I don't know any more."

"Grayson gave her Xanax. Let the vet know. Please."

"Her BP's increasing, 162 over 108," the man calls out. "You're in an ambulance, miss. We're on our way to Abbott. You just relax. Stay calm. We'll let the vet know about your dog. But right now, you're our priority."

"I'm pregnant."

The man gives the woman a look I can't decipher. "Thank you. That's important information. Is there anything else we should know?"

I spend the next few minutes giving them a rundown on my medical history, the name of my doctor. Insurance information? *Shit.*

The ambulance stops and the sirens quiet. Seconds later the back doors of the vehicle fly open and I'm swept into a vortex of chaos. My stomach protests the uncontrolled movement of the gurney I'm on, but I'm helpless to stop it. Nurses, doctors, a whole army of hospital personnel in different-colored scrubs shout questions and bark orders. I pick out the calm voice of the man from the ambulance, giving answers as we enter the hospital. He's not close, but he's obviously following the nurses that wheel me into some kind of exam room filled with too-bright lights and the smell of disinfectant.

I catch Grayson's name on a whisper. DOA. Suicide. Brains everywhere. Someone shushes whoever is speaking, but it's too late. I'm only getting one word out of ten, but the image of my husband's head blown apart in my living room proves to be too much for my stomach. There's almost nothing in it, but it doesn't care. A quick nurse shoves a tub under my chin, patting my back in comfort as I spew the little I've eaten today.

I let out a whimper of self-pity. I hate hospitals. They're a backdrop to all the painful moments of my life and every single one of them crashes down on me at this moment. Grayson dropping me off with a ruptured spleen, the agonizing days after his second attack. My parents, Dillon. I close my eyes as they fill with tears and my breath shudders.

Too familiar. Doctors, nurses, X-rays. This will be the last time, I remind myself as I drift off to sleep. At least Grayson can't put me here ever again.

"Hey, you're awake," a familiar voice chirps as my eyes flutter open some unknown time later.

"Grace?" I widen my eyes, confused.

"You bet." She smiles wide. "You really need to tell your birth partner all your secrets, missy. How am I supposed to help when I don't even know your real name?"

"Hey, you two okay in here?" Aaron asks, poking his head between the curtains.

"We're fine," Grace snaps, rolling her eyes. "Keep your eyeballs in the waiting room. Lyric could be naked in here for all you know."

"Fine... I'll get some coffee, maybe see when they plan on releasing her," he says from somewhere beyond the curtains.

"You do that." She smiles at me again. "He's been barging in every fifteen minutes. You'd think he was your father. He's so worried." Her smile evaporates. "We all are. You should have told me. Jesus, Lyric—Faith?—to get a call again in the middle of the night. After Dillon..."

Her voice trails off, but she doesn't have to say any more.

"I'm sorry. It all happened so fast." My eyes flood with tears as my mind goes to Sasha. "He drugged Sacha. Do you know..." I can't finish the question. One more heartbreak and I'm done.

"I was told she's going to be fine. Groggy but fine. Officer Julius waited all night for her to wake. I think you may have to give him visitation rights. Did I mention he's cute?" Grace wraps her arms around me as my relieved sobs shake both of us.

Aaron barges in and she glares at him.

279

"Doctor's coming. I think we're busting her out of here." He grins and retreats back behind the curtain again.

"I have nowhere to go, Grace. I can't go back to my house." Just the thought of the mess there has my stomach doing flips.

"Don't worry about it. You'll stay with me until we get things sorted out. We have so much to talk about." Grace pats my hand while giving me a reprimanding stare. I've kept so much from her. I don't blame her. "Aaron talked to the police. They'll let him know when they can get inside the house. He's gonna rent a storage unit once they open today for all your stuff. When you're ready to find another place, him and Dave will help you move in."

"You haven't told him about…" I rub a hand over my stomach.

Grace shakes her head. "Of course not. It's our secret, like I promised. But if Zane finds out about last night, he'll probably show up. Then it's up to you."

"Aaron can't tell him about Grayson." I shake my head and wince as pain lances across my entire face. "Zane's made his decision. I don't want him coming back out of some misplaced guilt."

"I'm not even sure Aaron's talking to him, but the death of Grayson Thorpe will be splashed all over the news. Zane would have to be living in a cave not to find out." Grace gives me a sympathetic smile. "Rest now, worry about Zane later. I'm so damn glad you're okay."

I LOOK around Grace's guest bedroom with a sigh. As guest bedrooms go, it's nice. Queen-sized bed covered in giant pink lilies, reminding me of a Georgia O'Keefe painting. A large dresser on one wall, and closet that will hold most of my clothes on the other—once Aaron and Dave bring them, that is. Nothing to complain about, and I should be grateful. I'm really tired of being displaced by my ex-husband.

I plop down in the small blush-colored armchair in the corner of the room and stare at the dark TV on the dresser. I'd turn it on, but it's been a tribute to the great Grayson Thorpe since the nurse at the hospital switched it on sometime this morning. There are no details on the cause of his death, yet, but I know it's just a matter of time.

Last time I left him with the clothes on my back. This time I don't even have those, having vomited all over myself at the hospital. I walked out in scrubs and a face full of bruises, looking like something from a horror film. Now I'm sitting in Grace's sweats. I'm five-three and she's five-eight. The results aren't cutting it. I look as homeless as I am.

My best friend walks into the room, biting her lips, trying to hide her smile. Sacha gets up slowly, still groggy from the drugs Grayson gave her. According to Aaron, the vet promised she'd be fine by tomorrow.

"We need to get you some better clothes." Grace chuckles while scratching Sacha's head.

"I know, I know." I return her laugh, wincing as it pulls on my face. It feels good to laugh even if it hurts. Laughing means I'm alive.

"Aaron's calling the police again to see if they can get your stuff. He said they've roped off the place and security's fierce. From what he's heard the NHL is keeping everything vague, but that can't last forever. Might want to brace yourself."

"Oh God." My thin laugh is full of pain and sarcasm. "I can't wait."

She drops down on the floor next to me. "You've been through a lot. Stay in bed for a few days."

"How does someone get over this? First Zane, now this? I didn't want Grayson to die."

"You always had this quiet strength I admired. Now, I see why. I don't think I could have survived what you've been through. You're the kind of role model all little girls should look up to."

I can't help but scoff. "Not really, Grace. In those final

moments with Grayson, I don't know, he had me. He drugged my dog, he hit me hard enough to do this, but then he talked about his therapy and how much he loved me. I was buying it. I didn't want to, but when I walked out that door, I think I'd have done anything to save him. What does that say about me?"

Grace shrugs. "That you're a really good person?"

CHAPTER THIRTY-TWO

LYRIC

*G*race orders me to stay in bed for the next two days. She tries to convince me to rest longer, but I can't. Somewhere inside my friend is an amazing mother waiting to get out, but she needs to stop practicing on me. I'm restless and tired of being stuck inside. From her guest bedroom windows I can see the trails of the Riverwalk that follow the Mississippi. I'm itching to stretch my legs and get some exercise before this baby turns me into a blimp.

I'm planning my escape over breakfast when my phone rings with an unknown number. My internal voice tells me not to answer it, but I do anyway. Grace is gone and I'm lonely. This telemarketer will be sorry they called me.

"Is this Faith Asher-Thorpe?" the voice on the line asks.

"Um, yes." I look at my phone in confusion. No one's called me that in years.

"This is Dee McNichols. I'm with the Hennepin County coroner's office. I was informed you're the next of kin for Grayson Donald Thorpe. Is that correct?"

Blood rushes from my head, and my breakfast threatens to

make a return. I put my head between my knees and breathe as I hear the woman on the other end asking if I'm still there.

"I'm sorry." I slide down on the floor and tuck my knees into my chest. "Not every day you hear from the coroner. A little shocked here."

"My apologies, ma'am. I'll try to make this as brief as possible. Can you confirm that you're Grayson Donald Thorpe's next of kin?"

I breathe out a tired breath while Sacha noses my face. She's as confused as I am. "I suppose so. His parents live in Australia."

"He had you down as his medical contact. We need to know where you want his remains sent."

"I'm sorry. What?"

"We can only keep remains so long at our facility. We need the name of your funeral home so we can coordinate the transfer with them."

"Oh," I say, because what can I say? Grayson will have to forgive me for such mediocre planning—short notice and all. I haven't planned a funeral since my parents' and that was in LA. Shipping him back there would be astronomical. "Do you know Williamson's?"

It's the first thing that comes to mind. They took care of Zane's mother. Did a nice job, I suppose. Not that I have the money for such things.

"Oh yes. From what I hear they do lovely work."

"Good, although Grayson wanted to be cremated, so I don't think they'll get to do much to him." I grimace at the phone. If someone told me this morning I'd be casually discussing funerary work with a coroner today I wouldn't have believed them, but here I am.

"I'll get an order into them, then," she says. "My condolences, Mrs. Thorpe."

I'm about to correct her. I'm not Mrs. Thorpe, but she hangs up.

IT'S a day of phone calls. After a week of silence, the world has discovered that I have sole responsibility of the great Grayson Thorpe's remains. Somehow my number has gone public. *Thank you, Dee McNichols.* There's nothing on the news yet, according to Aaron, but I know it's a matter of time. Reporters are relentless. The same ones that called me every name when I ruined my husband's career now want information on his services.

I'm about to disappoint them again. There won't be any. Grayson may have given me control over his remains, but I don't want them. First chance I get he's going home.

It's only my respect for Grayson's family that's keeping me silent. The stories I could tell. A picture of my face to shock people out of their idol worshipping.

Instead, I silence my phone and start my lesson plans for the coming year. School's only a couple of weeks away. I normally have everything organized by now, but this summer has been some other kind of special.

By the end of the day I groan at the messages. Fifty-eight in total. Wishing there was a delete-all button, I wade in.

"Hello, Mrs. Thorpe, this is Ed Barber from the *LA Times*..."

Delete.

"Hello, Mrs. Thorpe, this is Nora Jenkens from the *San Fran—*"

Delete.

After twenty-something, I lose count and keep deleting.

"Hello, Mrs. Thorpe, this is Arthur Summerton, Esquire," the man says. Punch drunk on deleting reporter's messages, I barely stop myself in time from erasing this one. "I'm legal council for Grayson Donald Thorpe. I received word that my client has recently passed. If you're Faith Anne Asher-Thorpe, former wife of Grayson Donald Thorpe whose previous address was 2925

Brentmire Drive in Los Angeles, please give me a call. You're the executor of my client's will."

I replay the message three times, stunned. Why the hell did Grayson make me his executor? Next of kin, now this? *Jesus, Grayson.*

I dial Mr. Summerton's number. He answers on the third ring.

"Mr. Summerton, this is Faith Asher."

"Thank you for returning my call, Mrs. Thorpe."

"Just Faith Asher," I repeat. "I dropped the Thorpe over two years ago. Why would Grayson make me his executor, Mr. Summerton? Don't people usually inform the person they involve in these things ahead of time? I'm sorry if that sounds rude, but it is a bit of a shock."

"I'm not aware that Mr. Thorpe didn't inform you, Mrs. Thorpe. I'm sorry to be the bearer of bad news, but—"

My control slips. Can't the guy get my name right? "It's *Ms. Asher*. And you aren't bearing bad news. Grayson did that when he shot himself in my home three days ago. You're an asterisk. Now what does this whole executor-thing involve?"

I envision doling out all of Grayson's shit to his friends and writing checks to his family. The second part I wouldn't mind—I love his mother—but seeing his friends isn't on my top-twenty-things-to-do-before-I-die list. This could be Grayson's final revenge, forcing me to confront all the people who ignored my pleas for help.

"My sincerest condolences, Ms. Asher. You're not only the executor, but the sole beneficiary of Mr. Thorpe's will."

Besides Sacha's snores, the room is so quiet you could hear a feather drop.

"I'm sorry, could you repeat that?"

"You're the sole beneficiary of the Grayson Donald Thorpe estate, Ms. Asher."

"I...That c-can't be," I sputter. "He has parents in Australia. A sister, too. They deserve every penny of Grayson's estate, not me."

"As executor of the will you may choose to disburse Mr. Thorpe's estate at your discretion, but this was his wish." He pauses. "Ms. Asher, are you aware of the size of Mr. Thorpe's estate?"

"I was his *wife*," I spit out the word wife as if it's poison. Grayson was never frugal. Before we married he lived an extravagant life. There might be a few million left in his bank account if his family is lucky.

"Let me send you a copy of the will. It would be good to meet in person sometime soon. Documents to sign and whatnot. I can wire you funds to pay for his funerary expenses and for upkeep on his properties until they can be disposed of. If you choose. You may not want to give everything away. I'll enclose my card. Please contact me with any questions. Mr. Thorpe's managers will continue to work for the estate until you direct them otherwise."

Properties? Managers? Mr. Summerton hangs up, leaving me wondering what secrets Grayson kept from me.

A DAY later a fat Fed-Ex envelope arrives containing Grayson's portfolio and will. His investments are jaw-dropping, too many numbers lined up in a row, too many commas in between. The condo in Brentwood and another home in Malibu? Property in Airlie Beach, Queensland? And there in black letters, beneficiary, Faith Ann Asher-Thorpe. I need a lawyer to make sense of everything he's left me. And a therapist to help me understand why.

"I don't want this," I repeat to Grace after showing her the documents. Technically, overnight, I've become a very rich woman. "What the hell am I going to do with all of it?"

"You could give it to charity," she suggests, shrugging. "What did his lawyer say?"

I groan with the intricacies of Grayson's estate. "It's going to take a while to go through probate. If we had still been married everything would have transferred automatically. So, he said not to do anything until then." I glance over at the granite box on my dresser, cursing the man inside for the umpteenth time. "I've booked a flight to Sidney on Friday. I have to take him home before school starts."

Grace's eyes widen. "Sidney? Australia? That's a long flight. You should check with your doctor first."

"I plan on calling her. But I have to take him home, Grace. I can't ship him through the mail. That would be heartless. My in-laws are good people."

"I understand. If you want, I'll go with."

I shake my head. She and Aaron have fun plans for the last week before school starts. I'm not getting in their way.

MY DOCTOR GIVES me the okay to fly to Australia, with plenty of walking breaks to keep my circulation healthy on the long plane ride. Good thing I've got an extended stopover in LA. While there, I plan to see Mr. Summerton, sign some papers with regards to the will.

I look forward to a couple of days in the California sun. According to Summerton, Grayson rented out our Brentwood condo and moved into a place in Malibu. I'm curious to see the house. Our condo was nice, but comparing Brentwood and the Bu is laughable. If Grayson gave me everything, I now own one of the most exclusive properties in the state.

Grace plans a nice dinner for the night before I leave. I offer to help, but she points to one of her dining chairs.

"Sit. Everything will be ready in a second. I want this to be perfect," she says, setting a salad bowl in the middle of the table. "Talk to Aaron."

Aaron takes a seat across from me and watches Grace run back into the kitchen.

"She does know I'm coming back, doesn't she?" I ask Aaron.

"Minneapolis is pretty boring compared to California and Sydney. I think she's worried."

"I have no one there, though. No family, no friends. Everyone's here. Why would I leave you?"

He lifts his shoulder in an awkward shrug. "Hey, I'm not saying you would. I'm saying she's worried. You two have gotten close over the summer."

"I know. She's like the sister I never had." I smile as she walks in, bringing the smell of garlic with her. Aaron stands and takes the heavy platter from her and sets it on the table. "And you're like a brother."

"Maybe brother-in-law?" Aaron turns Grace's hand to face me. A large diamond sits prominent on her ring finger.

"Oh my God!" I squeal, jumping from my chair to hug Grace. "Congratulations."

Grace beams. "Thank you."

"When?" I ask. "You didn't have that on yesterday, did you?"

She shakes her head. "Aaron asked a few nights ago, but..."

"Jesus, Grace. If you hid this because of me, I'm gonna smack you."

Grace glares at Aaron. He shrugs. "Told you."

My best friend rolls her eyes and groans. "Okay, okay, you're right. I didn't want to rub my happiness into my best friend's broken nose. But obviously Aaron knows better than me. Let's eat."

I place my hand over Grace's and give her a tender smile. "I love that you wanted to protect my feelings."

"Maid of honor?" She smiles back, tears glistening in her eyes.

I give her an enthusiastic nod, emotions choking me.

"Should we group hug or just eat? I'm starving, so whatever. Let's just get it over with and eat," Aaron says. Grace and I laugh, wiping tears from our eyes.

"Men," she grumbles.

Grace is an amazing cook, and her garlic shrimp is no exception. Aaron will never have to worry about starving. If I stayed with her longer I'd be tempted to take a few lessons from her. But at the moment I'm too hungry to worry about how she was able to achieve the perfect brownness on the garlic without burning it or why her shrimp is so tender and mine's always the texture of a rubber ball. It's just delicious.

Grace gives Aaron a look that would scorch lesser men when his phone rings toward the end of the meal. It must be important, because Aaron holds up a finger and answers.

"Hey, man. You're still alive." He laughs and looks at me. I swallow my food with difficulty, and my skin prickles with unpleasant goosebumps.

"Yeah. Grace is gonna take my balls. You're calling at dinner, but it's okay." Aaron pauses for a second, then says, "Sure. Hold on."

He sets the phone on the table and presses the speaker. "You're on, man."

I shut my eyes tight and shake my head as the voice that haunts my dreams comes across the speaker, "Hey, Grace. Congratulations!"

She gives Aaron a wide-eyed look of astonishment. Zane's voice is a knife in my chest. The last month of healing is gone in an instant. I can't talk to him. I can't even listen to him. Raising my hands, I shake my head at Aaron.

"Thanks, Zane. We've missed you." Grace frowns at Aaron and mouths, *What the fuck are you doing?*

"Yeah. I miss everyone there too." I close my eyes as his words rip me to shreds. "I've been busy."

"Too busy to give a heads up?" Aaron asks. "You left us high and dry, man. Dave is pissed, I'm pissed."

"Listen, I'm truly sorry, brother. That's why I'm calling. Two weeks. I'll be back in two weeks." My stomach plummets. What do I do with this news? He's calling Aaron, not me, and his message is loud and clear. I don't matter.

Zane sighs out a heavy breath on the other end. "This has been really hard. I've had to think on a lot of things out here. Clear my head of a lot of shit. The perspective's been good. I realized I want to be back home. My lease is up. I'm out at the end of the month. I've talked to the principal there, my job's still mine. And the Dani thing is settled."

Aaron's eyes widen and he reaches for the phone, but I'm quick to grab his wrist.

"Zane," he warns while looking at Grace. Her narrowed eyes and the angry flush coloring her cheeks says she's as out of the loop as I am. "Um…"

"No, man. You were right. I should have cleared that up last year. It wasn't cool leaving her hanging, but it wasn't like I could have flown back once I committed to helping Tess and Laura. And it would have been a dick move kicking her out of my place."

Aaron covers his eyes and groans.

The world falls silent except the roar in my head. The pain of hearing his voice a moment ago is nothing compared to the punch in the gut I'm experiencing at the moment. Grace's mouth drops open showing she's in as much shock as I am. Hot anger rushes through my brain and my chair screeches on the tile floor as I stand.

"You son of a bitch," I yell, not caring that he hears me anymore.

"Lyr-ic?" Zane's voice cracks on the phone. "What the hell, Aaron?"

"What the hell, Zane. You fucking cheater!" My voice seems to know only one volume, and it shakes the windows and sends Sacha scrambling to find out what's wrong.

"Wait. I can explain—" he starts, but I'm having none of it.

Janet said he had a life in New York, but I didn't listen. I foolishly believed we had something good here. All the time I was the other woman. *Oh God.* How many times will I trust a man before it sinks in that they're not worth it? Men lie and cheat and treat women like garbage to be disposed of whenever their needs are satisfied. *Never again.*

"You can shove your explanations up your ass, Zane Brody," I spit out before walking out of the dining room.

Minutes later Grace walks into my room and hugs the life out of me.

"I didn't know. I swear."

"I believe you," I assure her as I grab another suitcase out of the closet and set it on the bed. I've already packed two, and Grace eyes the third with suspicion as I pack my dress clothes.

"Faith, what are you doing?" Her sad look breaks my heart. I haven't had too many best friends over the years, and Grace is the best.

I sigh and sit down. "I can't be here with him, Grace. Every time I see him my heart… and the baby. He's gonna want to be involved. I can't do it. It'll tear me apart. I have to go."

"No. We'll figure something out. Aaron said things between Zane and Dani were bad before he left last year. She was just subletting his place."

"I don't care. It's a secret he kept from me, after I shared so much with him." I shake my head in frustration. "She's living at his place? The place *he's* been staying for the past month? This is so fucked up, I don't even want to know what he's doing anymore."

"What about Sacha?"

I let out a strangled sob as my dog rests her nose in my lap as if to remind me she's still here. Not that I'd forget. She's been clingy ever since Grayson. It breaks my heart to leave her, but she can't come with me. Not yet. There's no way I'm shoving my baby into the cargo hold of an airplane.

"Watch her for me?" I plead with Grace. "For a few weeks. I'll buy a car and drive back to get her."

"He loves you." Grace stands and shuts the bedroom door. "What about the baby. He has a right to know about his baby."

"Someday, but not now. I have to be stronger, and right now—"

"Don't go," Grace pleads. "At least give him a chance to explain."

I shake my head. "I have tickets. I can't… I can't trust him again. I have to go."

CHAPTER THIRTY-THREE

FAITH

I know I've made the right decision the minute I step off the plane. The sun caresses my shoulders like a lover, and the scent perfuming the breeze is as familiar as my reflection in the mirror. I'm home, and I'm free.

Even without Gray's inheritance, I can make it here. When my parents died, I had my own investments from the sale of the house and my parents' savings. I barely touched it while in school, had no need to while married to Gray, and if I had withdrawn one penny after the divorce, Gray would have found me like a bloodhound. Over the past six years my own worth has grown considerably. Tacking on Gray's, it's mind boggling.

Arthur Summerton's office is on the twenty-eighth floor of 611 Place in the downtown financial district. *Fancy.*

I'm pointed to the elevators by the nice security guard and then a minute later I step out of the lift into a bright hallway. The brass plaque on the wall tells me Summerton's office is to the right.

His receptionist gives me a narrow look as I maneuver my two suitcases and the tote carrying the stout granite box containing Grayson's ashes.

"I'm off to Sydney in the morning," I explain to the middle-aged, dark-haired woman for some reason. "It's winter there."

"Do you have an appointment?"

Before I can answer, a blond man in a custom-tailored Italian suit and a chunky gold watch interrupts, "Faith Asher-Thorpe?"

I spin around, ignoring the receptionist and her now-inquisitive eyes. "I dropped the Thorpe a few years back, but yes."

We head back to an office as fancy as the man who inhabits it. I'm tempted to stare out the window but refrain.

"Have a seat." He motions to the two chairs in front of his ebony and glass desk. "I have a few documents for you to sign. Nothing too complicated..."

An hour later I'm released from a lawyer's version of *not too complicated*. It's after three and I'm starving. And nauseous.

"You're lucky I don't bury you in your backyard after all the trouble you're putting me through," I mumble to Grayson while heading toward the blue Honda that waits for us, ignoring the people glancing at the crazy lady dragging two suitcases and a tote bag, and talking to herself. It's fucking LA, for Christ's sake, and I'm not the looniest of the loonies on this block.

Okay, maybe I am.

Before I can blink, Bret, my Uber driver, hops out of the car and has my suitcases stowed in his trunk. *Someone's not afraid to work for his review.* Unlike my previous driver, this guy's dressed to impress in an eye-catching ensemble consisting of a deep-purple button-down, paisley vest in shades of plum and pink. Chartreuse tie, dress slacks, and matching alligator loafers complete the ensemble. I like him already.

He reaches for the tote containing Grayson's urn, but I shake my head. My relationship with my ex-husband might seem a little odd to some, but I'm making the most of it. I'm finally getting to speak my mind without repercussions. I'm finding it very therapeutic.

Maybe I've lost it, but with all of Gray's money I'll find myself a good therapist when I get back from Australia. Until then, Grayson stays with me.

Bret gives me a wary eye but verifies the Malibu address. It's an intimidating number on Cliffside Drive. I've never seen this place, have no idea when Gray purchased it, but I'll be spending the next few days living like the rich and famous.

"Any chance we can hit a drive-through on the way?" I smile into the rearview mirror as Bret frowns back. His car is pristine, and I'm the crazy lady talking to her dead husband.

"Drive-through?" he asks like I've suggested driving to Tijuana.

"No?" I ask, then add, "I'm pregnant," hoping he'll take pity on me.

I'm here for only two days so I chose not to rent a car. My thoughts are that there might be something waiting in my Malibu garage. Grayson was a car nut, so the options could be interesting.

He sighs. "My husband will kill me."

I hold up my hands. "Totally understand. Guys and cars. It's just I get nauseous when I don't eat."

He gives me a narrow look from the rearview mirror. "How nauseous?"

"If we take the 101 North, there's an In-N-Out on West Sunset." I smile wide. "It's sorta on the way."

Bret sighs.

"I'll pay you an extra fifty. And treat you to lunch, dinner, whatever," I offer while digging into my purse. Bret hums. I make eye contact with him in the mirror. "A hundred, but that's my final offer."

It isn't. I've got a wad of hundreds in my wallet, courtesy of Grayson and the ATM on the first floor of Summerton's building, but years of pinching every penny are hard to forget. Lyric would have stretched that hundred to last an entire month, but here I am with a Benjamin Franklin in my fist, ready to hand it over in order to buy a twenty-dollar meal.

Bret laughs as my stomach growls loud enough for the guy in the car next to us to hear. "Fine. We'll stop. Forget the hundred, just buy me a milkshake."

"You're a saint."

He rolls his eyes with all the drama of a teen girl. "No, I'm not. Just a guy with a conscience. If Carl asks why the car smells like fast food, I'll tell him I was saving a damsel in distress."

Thirty minutes later, I'm in the front seat. Probably so Bret can keep an eye on me. Grayson's heavy stone box is now a table, and the tote bag—along with a dozen or so napkins—are spread around me. To catch any drips from the animal-style fries Zane Brody would definitely have a few things to say about.

Guilt tempers my appetite. Am I doing the right thing in running away this time? It's not like my life depends on escaping Zane. Only my heart.

With Bret's blessing, I turn on the radio to silence my thoughts. Plenty of time for that after I return from Sydney. Before long we're singing—Bret horribly off tune—to the oldies on Carl's favorite radio station and laughing like old friends.

Not for the first time, Bret gives the urn sitting on my lap a significant look. "So what's the story with that? If you don't mind me asking, that is."

I give him pared down version of the truth. My ex-husband died and I'm returning him to his parents. Nothing more.

A little while later we pull up to something out of a dream. And it's only the gate. I rummage through my purse for the instructions from Summerton. There are two codes. The gate's my birthday—0927. I get out and punch it into the keypad and the modern steel beauties glide open on silent hinges.

I hop into the car and Bret drives down the curving path that opens onto a sprawling glass-and-steel mid-century structure that blows my mind.

Grayson bought this?

"Holy Moses," Bret whispers as he gets out of the car. "Who was your ex-husband? Some movie star?"

"No." *Just a former left wing for the LA Stars. You know, the one who got kicked out of the NHL for almost killing his wife?* There's no way I'm sharing that. No matter how much I like Bret.

I walk toward the door on numb legs. "Can you bring my bags in?"

He stops at the trunk. "You sure? I could be an axe murderer or something."

I laugh. If Bret's an axe murderer, I'm a bank robber. He's about five-six and a hundred thirty pounds of quirky fashion. I think I'm safe.

"Last week I planned on returning to Minneapolis after sending my ex-husband home. Plans changed and I'm staying. I need friends. You're at the top of my list, unless you have somewhere else to go."

"At your service, ma'am." He laughs, tipping an imaginary hat.

The second code is our wedding date. *What the fuck, Grayson?* I punch in 0716 and the door swings open. I hit the same numbers on the keypad inside to disable the alarm. My house has a fucking alarm.

Bret whistles as he follows me in. "Baby, you hit the jackpot."

"No shitting." I stop and gawk in the space between the entry and the living room.

The place is stunning. Decorated in hues of blue and pale greens that compliment the views that wait outside the windows. I had no idea what to expect, but this isn't it. It certainly isn't hockey-boys-club decor or the comfortable casual style we lived in. It's modern and chic and contemporary. A decorator had their way in here.

I wander into a gourmet kitchen that's useless for a person like me who can't cook. The shiny stainless steel ovens would probably be offended if I put a frozen pizza in them. Canned soup seems like a sacrilege on the six-burner stove, but since I live here that's what the menu will be.

"Holy shit." I wander toward the foldout wall of glass that opens to a deck that stretches over the edge of the cliff this house sits on. Off to one side is a pool that makes me happy I packed my suit.

"If this was my place I'd be living out there," Bret mutters.

The glass sliders fold back with little effort. Which is good. After a four-hour flight from Minneapolis, an interminable amount of time at the lawyer's, then another almost two hours to get here, I'm in need of a nap.

Outside, the sound of the waves crashing pull me to the railing. Good thing I'm not too afraid of heights, because shit. It's a long way down.

A chill runs down my arms. Driving in, we passed other gated entrances. There must be neighbors, but from my vantage point there's not a soul around.

First time he got angry, Grayson would have tossed you over the cliff. Not that I'd have moved in here with him.

"Pretty, but too quiet," Bret says, reflecting my thoughts.

"Yeah. I'll have to give this place some thought. The life of the rich and famous isn't my thing," I confess as I turn to head back inside. "Let's have a look around, though."

"No complaints here. Give me something to tell Carl tonight."

Down a long hall we discover five stunning bedrooms. The last is the master, and it doesn't disappoint. It's bigger than my whole house back in Minneapolis, and has the same foldout doors that line the back of the house leading to the deck. To the side of the massive king-size bed is a sitting area that rivals the living room, with a breakfast bar that makes the kitchen almost obsolete. It's all done in shades of grayed-down plum that make it look like Bret planned his wardrobe around this visit.

I squeal when we walk into the master bath. "A tub." I'm

bouncing on my tired toes in delight. "I haven't had a real bath in years."

Bret laughs. "That's not a tub. That's another swimming pool."

He's right. The tub is massive. It would easily accommodate a couple, which is... I don't know. *Grayson bought this for me?*

The whole bathroom is stunning. Miles of counters, a shower with more sprays than I can count, and the soaking tub from my dreams.

Grayson's things are all here. Razor, shaving soap, shampoo... everything. I open every cabinet and door, my heart squeezing with grief. *It's like everything's waiting for him to return, but he won't. Ever.*

Back in the master bedroom, the door opposite the bath hides a walk-in closet the size of my old bedroom. Grayson's suits hang on the rods lining the one side, and his clothes are folded in the drawers. The scent of his signature aftershave lingers in the still air. If I had any doubt he lived here, I don't anymore.

We head past the kitchen, and I convince myself maybe I could learn to cook more than pre-made frozen stuff. At the garage door, I hit the light switch before stepping down into Grayson's playground.

Bret erupts in hysterical laughter behind me. "Wow."

All three bays are filled with Grayson's *toys*, and I can't help but giggle.

"I can't see you driving that," Bret says, stepping down into the garage as if he's drawn to the vehicles like a magnet.

"I don't ride bikes, that's for certain."

I walk past the red-and-silver death-machine with the name Aprilia stenciled diagonally in huge letters. I don't know much about bikes, but this thing looks like something from a sci-fi movie.

And speaking of sci-fi movies... I roll my eyes at the silver-and-black Aston Martin parked in the middle bay. With its curving, bold lines it looks like an insect who decided to grow wheels.

"Collectors are going to have a field day when I put this thing on the market. I'm keeping the Jeep, though."

I walk over to the bright orange beast that's so much more than a Jeep. Big knobby tires, a rack of lights above the top. Not one, but two winches hang off the front. The customization probably cost more than the vehicle. But if I put the back seat down, there's plenty of room for Sacha.

I'm coming baby. Just give me a few more days.

I circle the two-seater convertible for a second before attempting to locate the driver's side door handle. "Can't picture a baby seat in here. Or my dog."

"You'd definitely stand out, though." Bret depresses a latch placed behind the front wheel. The door glides up and we both laugh. My new friend hops into the sleek car the second I offer him the chance. Then I snap a photo for him to show his husband.

My feet head toward the row of colorful surfboards that are calling my name. Up close, I recognize the short board with the triple fins that sat unused in our Brentwood garage. *Why is it here?* By the last year of my marriage, I wasn't allowed to step foot out of the house in anything as skimpy as a swimsuit. Much less go to the beach. Had Grayson changed that much?

The question is irrelevant at this point. Grayson's gone and I can do whatever I want.

Think my doctor will let me surf?

BRET LEAVES after we spend some serious time basking in the warm sunshine on the stunning deck. He talks about the love of his life, and I tell him about Sacha. In just one day I miss her something fierce. It'll be a long trip back to Minneapolis, but there's no way I'm leaving her behind.

Bret gives me his number with the offer to get together when

I'm back in town. I smile as he drives away. It's not much, but he's one friend more than when I stepped off the plane. It's a start.

I need friends. The thought reminds me of my one back home-not-home-anymore. I've been keeping my phone off to save battery, or so I tell myself. Truth is, I don't know if I can trust myself to ignore Zane's calls much longer.

I force myself to delete the few texts he's sent me without reading them. And the same with the voicemail he left. I remind myself he's broken my trust and that can't be forgiven. This time there will be no sweet talking, no showing up after school begging me for a date. I'm almost two thousand miles away at an unknown address.

It feels wrong keeping Grace at arm's length, but I have no choice. She'd tell Zane where to find me in a heartbeat. I'll have to speak to him at some point, but for now I'm not ready.

I snap a few pictures and send them to Grace, letting her know I've made it here okay. Her one-word reply is *Wow*. I agree, then call her for an update on Sacha and Aaron, and ignore her sales pitch regarding Zane.

I change out of my travel-weary clothes and head out in the Jeep. *My Jeep.* My beach calls. The waves are too choppy to surf at the moment, but I need the feel of the ocean on my skin.

Heading back the way Bret brought me in, I hop on the Pacific Coast Highway. The next town over is Ventura, but I'm not going that far. In Malibu the PCH swerves inland in deference to the wealthy that staked claim to the ocean property, but just past, the road hugs the coast again. The views are breathtaking even for someone who's driven it all their life. I've missed this so much.

A stop at Sunlife Organics for a strawberry and avocado smoothie to help soothe the beast in my belly. I'm constantly hungry, and over the past week, I've discovered the hard way that the consequences of ignoring the warning signs aren't pretty.

I pull off the road twenty minutes later. The beach is surprisingly empty for a Friday afternoon. For now we have it all to ourselves. I'm feeling a bit like a pack mule as I balance the tote with Grayson in one hand, my smoothie in the other, and a towel over my shoulder as I climb down the steep, narrow trail that leads to the sand.

Besides the call of the shore birds and the roar of the surf, it's quiet. Enjoying the hot sun, cool ocean breeze, and good food is exactly what I need after the past weeks of crazy. I curl my toes in the warm sand, enjoying the long-forgotten sensation.

"Remember Traci Lawrence? We used to come to this beach every morning. I wonder whatever happened to her?" I muse, looking down at Grayson. "If it hadn't been for her, we never would have met. She dragged me to that awful party I met you at. I often wonder what would have happened if I had stayed home that night. I should have, you know, Grayson. I failed my psych exam that Monday. I really should have stayed home and studied. But I met you instead and that whole weekend was shot. My whole life, really."

Collapsing back onto the warm sand, I breathe out a long sigh.

"But that was you, Grayson. Everything always on your schedule. The warning signs were there if I had read them. You took over my life from the start, consequences be damned. And here I am, still letting you control everything. I should leave you on this beach. If I didn't love your mum so much, I would."

I close my eyes and smile.

"I often wonder about you, me, fate. If it wasn't for you, I wouldn't be pregnant right now. That's a real kick in the teeth, huh, Grayson? You always wanted kids and here I sit pregnant with some other guy's baby. All because I ran from you. Funny how life works. If it wasn't a curse, I'd name him Grayson."

The sound of the surf taunts me. Swimming alone would be stupid, for me and the baby inside me. If it weren't for this baby... I'm stuck. A fucking incubator to a child I don't need, by a man who doesn't want me. If only I could surf over the pain like a wave, ride over it until I hit the shore, but instead I'm drowning in it.

Damn you, Zane Brody, and the child that will remind me of you for the rest of my life.

ON THE WAY back I stop for fish tacos and some provisions in a small strip mall I remember from before. The food's good. Not Pinks or Cali Tacos, but I'm not in the mood to fight traffic again. Minneapolis made me soft. I need to get used to the snail's pace of the LA freeways again.

I throw milk and soda into the fridge that's almost empty. There's some food in the cabinets, cereal and—thank you, Grayson—Nutella. I add bread and some snacks to the shelves, then close the doors on the still barren kitchen. I promise myself when I get back I'll look into some real shopping.

While at Summerton's office, he gave me a file folder for each of the properties Grayson owned. Security codes, copies of deeds, insurance, all sit inside. Inside the file to the Malibu property is the name of Selina and Jorge Gomez, housekeeper and caretaker. Once a week they come to clean and maintain the place. When I get back from Australia, I'll get a chance to meet them.

I wander down to the basement. It's a hockey lover's dream. Grayson's memorabilia and collections are displayed in a rec room worth millions. This room gives me the willies. As soon as I return, I'm putting it all up for auction and giving the money to a worthy cause.

Of course I can't sleep. My eyes close for about fifteen minutes, then my bladder wakes me. I should go back to bed, but I'm wide awake. I wander out of the guest bedroom and down the hall, contemplating the realities of living here. This is way more house than I need, but the unending view of the ocean is hard to resist.

I curl up on the sofa for a minute and listen to the silence. Bret was right; this is a lonely house. Not even the sound of Grayson's ghost to keep me company.

In the master suite, I flip on the lights and the wall of glass goes black as the night and the ocean beyond. My skin prickles. Anyone out on the water could be watching me. Not that there is, but still... I flip the switch back off and the sense of exposure vanishes. Grabbing a seat on the chaise, I watch the far away lights of a ship until they wink out of sight.

Selina must have stripped the bed, because beside the clothes in the closet there's not a trace of Grayson's masculine scent in the house. Among the racks of clothes, the ghost of my ex-husband is strong, as if he could walk out from behind his custom suits any second.

Only half of the room is full, though. Even the drawers on one side are empty. I slide them all open to check, but there's nothing inside. Except one. An envelope addressed to me sits inside the last drawer I open. I sink onto the plush carpet and take in the strong bold script of Grayson's handwriting.

To my darling wife, Faith,

Shit.

If you're reading this, things didn't go as planned. I'm truly sorry for that, and for any suffering I'm putting you through. God knows I've put you through enough. I never meant to. Honestly. And I hope this all makes some kind of amend.

I've made some good investments. Don't go buggering them up, will you? And don't go giving everything away. I've taken care of my parents as well, so don't worry about them. This is all for you. You deserve it. I may have had a fucked up way of showing it, but I love you, Faith. Have a good life.

I hope someday in the far future I'll deserve you in heaven.

Grayson

My heart's in pieces. I was a fool to think Grayson could never hurt me again. His fists may never touch me, but he still holds the power to slice me. Everything makes sense. He knew the risks of coming for me. Planned for every possibility, even failure.

I wake sometime later still on the closet floor, still a mess. Wondering if I'll ever get over the two men who have scarred my soul. My body's stiff, but my heart is frozen.

I wander past Grayson's urn on the dresser as I leave the bedroom.

"I wasn't worth it," I mutter.

CHAPTER THIRTY-FOUR

FAITH

*W*here is home?

The thought sits uncomfortable in my mind as I wake up in Grayson's bedroom. It's two in the afternoon, the first day of September, and I'm still in bed. Tomorrow a new class of kindergarteners will walk into Grove Elementary, Room 2, but I won't be there to greet them.

Since coming back from Sydney I've barely left the cocoon of a thousand-thread-count sheets and cashmere blankets. The sorrow on Lillian Thorpe's face when I handed her the granite box with her son's ashes will haunt me the rest of my life. *How could he have done this to them?*

The silence of the room has me throwing open the glass wall and letting the crash of the surf in. Still, it's lonely here. I'm totally dependent on my daily calls to Grace, to her updates on life back in Minneapolis, the weather, the pre-start staff meeting she attended on Friday.

"Zoe says hi, and so does Kelly and Karen from the office."

"Tell them hi back." My eyes grow hot with tears. I miss my class and the sense of purpose my students gave me. I miss the feel of belonging. Miss Grace and Zoe, Karen in the office, and nurse Kelly. I didn't even say goodbye. Just like the men in my life, I left without warning.

You need to go back. The thought has me out of bed and reaching for my still-packed suitcases. Being here is a mistake. At least in Minneapolis, with my dog and my house, I knew who I was. I'm as adrift as an unmoored boat, lost to the currents and winds.

My thoughts turn to Zane, and I freeze as the gut-wrenching pain of betrayal returns. *I can't avoid him forever.*

I was the other woman. The tears that used to accompany that thought have dried, but the fact still makes me nauseous. Or maybe that's hunger.

Grace's voice brings me back from my thoughts. She's been talking for some time, but I've drifted off into misery.

Her voice is panicked in my ear. "Faith, come back."

Scrubbing away my tears, I curl up on the wool rug and grab the cashmere blanket that's become my constant companion. "Maybe."

But then what?

The silence between us lasts only a moment, then her long sigh breaks the quiet.

"This is stupid. We all miss you. Zane's crazy for you, if you'd give him a chance—"

"No!" I don't want to yell, but I have no choice. "Grace, please tell him to stop the calls, the texts. I need space—"

"But if you'd let him explain," she interrupts. The last few conversations have ended this way and I can't keep doing this.

"See. This is the problem if I come back. This pressure. *Zane's a good guy. He's crazy for you. Just give him a chance to explain.* It's too much for me right now." I'd never know if I forgave him because he deserved it or because this roller coaster of hormones convinced me to. I can't have that uncertainty.

Grace's quiet for almost a minute. Of course, I've hurt her feelings. But whatever guilt I'm feeling vanishes when she says,

"I'm sorry, but you are pregnant with his baby. He deserves to know."

"And he will. On my terms. You promised not to tell him." She did, but I'm not sure I can trust her because she wants what's best for both me and Zane. And maybe those things aligned at one time, but they don't now.

MY BRAIN WHISPERS this is just a dream, but it's so real. Grayson's standing behind me as I look out toward the ocean. "You like our place, darling?" he whispers, his lips brushing my neck, making me shiver. "I bought this for you. You're gonna love it."

"Why Grayson?" I ask, turning to face him. "Why did you do it? Your family… me… we love you so much. You had so much to live for."

"Shh." His warm hands mold to my hips and his lips claim mine. I can't remember what I was wearing when the dream started, but the silky smooth heat of our bodies coming together tells me we're both definitely naked now.

This is the husband I want to remember. The man who took his time to show me he loved me. It feels so right when he pulls me against him. So right to feel the strength of his desire hard against my stomach. A small voice in my head tells me something's wrong, but I ignore it.

"God, Grayson." I shudder with pleasure as his fingers dive into me. "Why couldn't it have always been this way?"

He shakes his head, his teeth dragging across my shoulder. "I'm sorry, Faith. I just wanted to make you happy."

"You have. Many times," I remind him as the dream shifts and Grayson's incredibly muscled body presses me into the soft mattress of his bed. "I forgive you."

He's making me very happy at the moment. His eyes soft and

loving, drinking me in as our bodies slide together in a slow sensual rhythm as if we're underwater.

My orgasm is bright and sharp, rolling through me like the storm clouds in Grayson's eyes, flashing with lightning. He pulls away and the distance chills my skin. I follow him out of bed, needing his warmth. Needing his arms around me. He stands at the glass wall, looking out. His back's to me and I press against him.

"Grayson?" My breath mists in the cold air. Frost spreads across the window, silvering my ex-husband's shoulders. The trickle of his icy release slides down my inner thighs, burning my skin.

Grayson turns and I look up into his eyes, but everything is… *Oh God, his beautiful face.* There's nothing left, just blood and bone and nothing.

A scream climbs up my throat as I back away, averting my eyes from the gore that's all that's left of the man I once loved. I glance around the room, terror gripping my heart like a vise. The beige walls, my secondhand sofa, the worn tables. We're no longer in Malibu, but in my house in Minneapolis.

My gaze lands on the spray of blood that spreads along the long wall and part of the ceiling above.

He moves closer, but I back up until the back of my legs hit the sofa. "Grayson, no."

"See what you made me do?"

A cry of fear, fresh and raw, tears from my throat as I dart toward where the front door should be, but in this dream it's a blank wall.

"Shh, baby. I've brought you something. A surprise. I know how much you love surprises."

My eyes widen on the huge purple-and-orange snake that appears in his arms. It's as wide as his biceps, and I can't even see how long it is. He's reeling it out like yarn, or a magician pulling out handkerchiefs. It just keeps coming.

My lungs struggle to take in a breath. "Grayson... I hate snakes."

"No. You'll like her. She's special. She eats mice and unwanted babies." He walks toward me in slow motion.

"No! I want this baby." I glance around as my heart pounds through my chest. Zane's on the sofa, his expression blank. "Please, Zane. This is your baby. You have to help me."

Chills raise the hairs on my arms, my body. I'm so cold. "No, Grayson. Please."

Zane doesn't budge. He's watching Grayson with detached curiosity as my ex-husband moves closer. My back's against the wall and I've got nowhere to run. "Help me, Zane."

"Touch her." Grayson grabs my hand and places it on the snake. A scream forms in my throat, but it's trapped. I close my eyes, blocking out the dry scaly feel of the snake under my fingers, the undulating muscles under the skin as it moves.

"Grayson, stop."

"She likes you. Look."

I open my eyes with reluctance and the scream breaks free. The snake has wrapped itself around my waist. Squeezing. Tighter and tighter. The pain is unbearable, excruciating.

I wake panting, grabbing at my waist with shaking hands, trying to remove the horrible dream snake. It's not there, but the pain is.

I cry out, doubling over as a knife slashes through my body, waves of pain cutting me in two.

I stumble out of bed and hit the lights. Blood. The pristine white sheets are dotted with bright red blood. A fresh wave of pain grips my stomach and I double over.

"No..." I moan.

Everything is a blur of pain and anguish. Blood on the sheets, blood on my thighs. Sobbing, I drop to my knees as another wave of agony hits. I scramble to the bedside table and my phone. *But who do I call?* Bret the Uber driver? Selina, who's basically a stranger? I'm all alone here on my cliffside estate. I have no one.

AMBULANCES, hospitals, doctors, nurses. Pain. Loss.

A continuing nightmare that loops through my life with agonizing frequency. Voices murmur just out of my hearing, faces grim. I've been prodded and invaded, but by the evasive looks I'm getting, no one's ready to break the awful news to me yet.

They don't have to, I feel it in my bones. Olaf's gone. Another goodbye I don't want, but I have no choice. Another man who's left me.

My situation sinks in. I've isolated myself here on my clifftop home, my need to run from my problems making me more vulnerable. But now that I have nothing tying me to Zane, I can go back. Once I get out of this room, I'll book a flight, leave this nightmare behind.

What seems like days later, a doctor comes in. I'm prepared for the worst. It's been hours at least, and the empty feeling inside me lets me know what's coming.

His lips move, but the words…

"It's not that uncommon for there to be light bleeding in the first trimester. It occurs in about twenty percent of pregnancies. Although since you're expecting twins, I'd advise taking it easy at least until you can schedule an appointment with your obstetrician."

"Twins?" I shudder. "You must be mistaken. My ultrasound never showed twins."

"This one did. You're right around nine weeks. Development of the fetuses looks normal. Congratulations." He looks at his chart and the door, eager to move on. "Any other questions, Ms. Asher?"

"But the pain. Are you sure everything is okay?"

He smirks. "Gas. Your bowels are a bit impacted. Pregnancy can cause constipation, holding it in makes it worse. I'm sure the long flight back to the states contributed. The nurse will give you a stool softener. A good diet helps, too. Fresh fruits, whole grains. Stay away from processed foods and chocolate. Chocolate constipates."

"Thank you," I reply with a grimace. Over six months without chocolate? No way am I giving up my chocolate.

He has to be wrong about the chocolate. And the twins. Neither can be possible.

A nurse comes in as dawn breaks. I can go home as soon as the doctor signs my paperwork. An hour later, Bret meets me at the entrance, car door open, a decidedly pissed-off expression on his face.

"You should have called me. Why didn't you call?"

I spend the next half hour getting lectured about friendship and trust. *Men...*

CHAPTER THIRTY-FIVE

FAITH

*A*voidance, I've found, is a great way to keep from answering the important questions in life. Questions like, *what the hell do I do now?* And, *am I ready for two babies?* The thought of two helpless infants depending on me to eat and burp and have their diapers changed—and a million other things I can't even contemplate—is enough to keep me in bed for another week.

"Twins," Grace shrieks when I call to tell her the news and beg for advice. Not that I don't know what her advice will be. The woman is a broken record when it comes to Zane. But I need to talk to someone, and besides Bret—who wouldn't understand the whole twin crisis—Grace is all I have.

She laughs as if my news is the greatest thing ever and fucking hilarious.

I drop back into the soft pillows on Grayson's bed with a frustrated growl. "Not funny, Grace."

"Of course not." A short burst of giggles follows, making me sigh. "But you have to see it's time to come home. Two babies, Faith. You're gonna need help. Do you really want to do this alone?"

"I can't go anywhere right now. Not until my doctor agrees it's safe to travel." The shocked expression on the ER doc's face when I asked about a cross-country road trip doesn't give me hope for the near future. "I need you to watch Sacha for another couple weeks, maybe longer. Please."

Her "Ummm. About that..." has my heart racing.

I sit up and grasp the phone between both hands to keep it from dropping out of my trembling fingers. *"About what?* Is something wrong with Sacha?"

"Sacha's fine. Now."

"Now? What happened that she wasn't fine before now?"

"She wasn't happy here. Not without you. She wasn't eating and she just—"

"Just what?"

"I was worried about her. And, well, then Zane stopped by. And she seemed so happy for the first time since you left." She pauses for a beat, and I can almost predict what she is about to say. "So he took her."

"Grace, no," I yell, then take a deep breath, letting it out slowly. My babies need me calm. But Sacha's also my baby, and I'm furious with myself for leaving her behind, and with Grace, but mostly I'm so angry with Zane my head's about to explode. "He took my dog?"

"Maybe you should call him."

I SPEND the next few days imagining all the ways I could kill Zane. The man had no right taking my dog. But then the man had no right barging into my life when he had another woman living in his New York apartment. He has no boundaries. He makes his own rules.

I know exactly what he's doing. I didn't answer his calls, didn't return his texts. He's stepping up his game, increasing the odds in his favor, using Sacha as bate to lure me in. But I'm not going to bite. Even if that's the easy way out of this.

Panic hits hard.

I'm going to suck at this parenting thing alone. Let's be real. I'll be the mom who forgets playdates, who's a pariah at bake sales, the one sitting alone in the stands at their soccer games, graduations. But with one phone call, I could change everything. Kids should have two parents.

Alone, the kids are going to gang up on me. Manipulate me into eating crap, allowing late bedtimes, dating too early. Unsafe sex.

Without Zane, there'll be no one to hold my hand while I deliver these kids. I'm going to be the only single woman in Lamaze classes filled with happy couples. No baby shower, giving birth alone in an empty room.

Tears pool in my eyes. Going back to Zane makes so much sense. *But no.* Taking him back just because I'm scared isn't the solution. How many times did I stay with Grayson because the alternative was too scary?

For the moment, avoidance is my friend. A comforting blanket I wrap around myself to insulate from the pain and confusion. Lounge in the sunshine, binge watch movies from the massive TV across from my bed, gorge myself on Selina's delicious cooking.

Grayson's ghost is probably having fits over how much weight I've gained.

"Get used to it, buddy," I call out in case he's listening.

The house is too quiet, but I'm done with TV for the day. And sunshine. And thanks to Selina, the place is spotless. I'm losing my mind sitting around doing nothing. *What the hell do rich people do all day?*

And this house. It always comes back to this house. The problem with being so isolated was evident the night I waited forever for the ambulance to show. *What if one of my kids gets hurt?*

This definitely isn't a house for kids. Just the thought of a toddler—toddlers—racing around the cliff is the stuff of nightmares. Not to mention the swimming pool that would be nearly impossible to block off. Slick floors and sharp-edged furniture, the combination asking for disaster.

I make an appointment with a realtor for the same day as my doctor's appointment. Kill two birds with one stone. Then crawl back in bed for the rest of the week.

My DOCTOR CONFIRMS my twin diagnosis with more cheer than necessary in my opinion.

"Yep, there they are. I count two," she chirps when I argue the point, pressing the wand over my lubed belly. The machine makes a rhythmic whoosh, whoosh, whoosh. "Two heads, four arms, four legs."

"But how did they miss it the first time?" I scoff. "You'd think it'd be obvious."

"Not necessarily. Early ultrasounds are sometimes hard to read."

I whip out the picture. Like Perry Mason, I show her the evidence. I've been watching too many vintage detective shows. "I still have it."

"Hmm. I can see the difficulty, but there it is." She points to a light shadow behind the bean. "One's shy. Hiding behind her sibling."

"Her?"

"Her, him. It's too early to tell, but the odds are good it will be one or the other. Or maybe one of each." She grins at her joke while wiping my belly off. *Great, I have a comedian for a doctor.* "We'll know more next month. Heartbeats are good and they look healthy. I'd still limit activity. No heavy lifting. The early bleeding isn't too concerning usually, but it is your first, and with twins... let's play it safe."

"So no travel?" I ask with a heavy heart.

"You can drive to the store and things like that. But I wouldn't suggest anything more. You don't want to end up on bed rest for the duration of your pregnancy." She scrunches up her face at the unpleasant thought.

I leave the doctor's conflicted. The temptation to call Zane is overwhelming. I miss Sacha. And Zane.

I end up at my beach. Surfing is out of the question, but I shove my toes in the sand, let the waves crash at my feet. Then pull out my phone and call Summerton, because if I'm doing this —calling Zane—I need to know my options.

Summerton paints an ugly picture. What if Zane wants them but not me? Visions of shuffling my tiny children off on flights, spending holidays away from me. The stress, the worry. The constant contact required between me and Zane. It'd be like ripping a scab off a sore every time I saw him.

I want to believe he loves me, but the growing silence between us is unsettling. It's been weeks since his last attempt to contact me. Is he obeying my wishes to give me space, or has he given up and gone back to his girlfriend in New York?

In the end, I tuck my phone back in my purse. I have five months. I don't need to decide until the birth. But can I wait that long for Sacha? I shove the image of her playing with Zane, getting closer to him, from my mind with difficulty. Will she forget me in the next five months?

I wade out into the cool, late-September water. The waves tugging at my legs, coaxing me out further. The hem of my sundress dips in the foam as I head deeper. For one brief second I contemplate swimming out, not stopping. The cool, soothing water of the ocean my grave. The pain ending here, now. I can almost understand Grayson's final thoughts. But I carry life. And those lives force me to head back to the beach and sit in the warm sand.

The hot sun warms my back, the soft ocean breeze cools my face. I close my eyes. My breath syncs with the waves. In... out. In... out. I fold my legs into a half lotus wondering how long I'll be able to do it. The tiny bulge under my ribs warns not long. My hands rest naturally on my knees, and for the moment, I let go.

It's been years since I meditated. Breathing in peace, breathing out stress and pain. My muscles relax and my mind goes blank. It could be minutes or hours, even days later. I open my eyes. A man sits a few feet away. I should be wary, but for some strange reason I'm not.

"Howzit," he says in a soft voice, tipping down his Oakleys for a moment to look at me, then pulling them off as if the view is worth it. His smile's as bright as the sun, and I can almost hear his thoughts. "Did I disturb you?"

California grows men gorgeous, but this one is something special. His high cheekbones, tapered jaw, and dark intense eyes. His warm brown skin suggests a lot of time in the sun, or maybe it's his default skin tone. Thick, dark brown hair sticks up in messy spikes, the perfect length for me to grip with my fingers.

He's shirtless. In lime-green board shorts that leave his muscled body open for viewing. And what a view. My body hums with appreciation. I've been so horny, it's ridiculous. Pregnancy hormones suck when you're alone.

"No." I answer him in a surprisingly calm voice.

"I didn't want to frighten you. You looked so peaceful. I'm Jackson Abe."

"I'm F-aith. Faith Asher," I stumble.

"Twice the Faith. I like that," Jackson sends me a teasing wink. "Or are you unsure?"

I laugh. Probably for the first time in weeks. "I'm not sure about a lot of things."

"Buyer's remorse? I know I'd be questioning a decision

like that Jeep up there." He tips his chin toward the parking lot behind us and the orange behemoth I'm beginning to love.

"Ha ha. I happen to like that Jeep. I never lose it in a parking lot."

"I can imagine. I spotted it a mile away."

I glance up at the cars parked at the top of the hill again. Next to mine sits a black Bug convertible. *Cute.*

I give him a playful smirk. "You sound jealous. Maybe 'cause my car's more masculine than yours?"

"Ha ha. I happen to like German engineering, and I'm not pretentious enough to splurge on a Porsche."

What would he think of the Aston Martin in my garage?

"I also spotted that orange behemoth in my neighborhood earlier, if I'm not mistaken. There can't be two of them." Jackson's words carry a barely-there-hint of an accent, an intonation in his voice I can't place.

"If your neighborhood is the Pacific Palisades, then yes. I was looking at houses."

His eyes land on my empty ring finger and his eyebrows rise along with his grin. "Solid. We'll be neighbors, then."

"Maybe." I laugh, because this is so my life. A hot guy's hitting on me and I can't do shit about it. "Oh, Jackson, you don't want me. I'm pregnant... with twins."

His severe slash of dark brows draw together. "Congratulations. You and the father must be very excited."

I sigh. Why am I spilling my secrets to this guy? "He's not involved. It's... complicated."

"Oh, shit. I'm sorry..." He gives me a slow shake of his head, his sympathetic expression warring with the less-than-sorry tone of his voice.

"So... the Palisades?" I ask, changing the subject to more neutral territory. "You live there long?"

"A few years. So this guy... the father... is he local?"

I groan. This guy sure is persistent. Sort of like another guy I know. "I just moved back, so no. He isn't local."

"Running away?" At this point, he relaxes onto the beach, stretching out on his side, elbow propped, his head resting in the palm of his hand. The view of his long lean body is distracting.

"Came home." I shake my head to clear the thoughts that want to take over. Bad thoughts that have me under this man, knowing the texture of that crazy hair and the taste of his warm skin. "Jackson, my life is so complicated we'd be burned to a crisp sitting here while I explain everything."

"Better idea. Let me make you dinner. I can tell you all my crazy stories about my family and my mom's goal to have me marry the perfect woman. And you can tell me why you moved back home without the man who got you pregnant. Might be the start of a great friendship."

"Tell you what... you're clearly here to surf." My eyes drift to the lime-green board lying a few feet from him with envy. "Let me watch. My doctor forbids me. At least let me live vicariously through you. If you're any good, you got a deal."

His laugh is distinctive, and not exactly masculine. On anyone else it might be called annoying, but somehow it fits his unpretentious style. "You like mahi mahi? I make a mean mahi mahi crusted in macadamia nuts. You're coming over, sistah."

NEVER QUESTION a Hawaiian's surfing skills. *Yeah, Hawaii.* The man spent his childhood in a small town on Oahu before his parents split. His mom lives in Santa Barbara and his dad's place is just a stone's throw from the Banzai Pipeline. Jackson's dad was a champion surfer, and he's still one of the most sought-after teachers at the island's best surf school, according to Jackson. What he's doing at my little beach is the question. There are way more challenging spots to surf.

He also makes great fish. Served on a bed of rice with a pineapple salsa. Why the guy's not married is another mystery. The tiny gold ring I spotted hanging from a chain around his neck might hold the answer, but I'm respecting his privacy for now.

His condo is two blocks from the house I'm considering. In this price range it's not going anywhere fast, so I have time to decide.

I wanted an actual house, but Jackson's condo is pretty sweet. It's off Sunset Boulevard near where it hits the PCH. The ocean views are stunning from his small deck, and the aptly named street is living up to its reputation as the sun slowly sinks into the water amid a kaleidoscope of colors.

"God, Jackson. I may have to come over every night for this show."

"It never gets old and you're more than welcome," he says, handing me a glass of water. He sets a beer with a Japanese label down on the table and then sits next to me. "So you need to give me the scoop on your life. You've been stalling."

"You sure you want to know?" I brush a strand of windblown hair off my cheek. "I feel like a complete idiot."

He nods.

I still don't know why I'm opening up to him. Maybe I'm lonely. Bret and his husband, Carl, have been cool, but I'm the third wheel in their happy life. I don't want to be the third wheel and, right now, with Jackson, I'm anything but the third wheel. He has this quiet strength—a complete opposite to Zane's brash cockiness—that's drawing me in. I need someone to trust, and Jackson seems trustworthy.

So, I tell him everything. Everything about Grayson. Not who he was, at least not yet. I'm not sure Jackson would look at me the same if he knew I was worth millions. Although clearly he's running a close second. This place isn't cheap.

Then I tell him about my whirlwind romance with Zane.

322

"Chee! So the yolo had two women on the line at the same time?" He rakes his fingers through his hair making the spikes even more messy.

I nod, then shrug. "His friend Aaron said he was planning on breaking up with her—"

"No." He cuts me off. "Don't try to defend him. I might think you should let him know that you're pregnant, but the bakayarou is still way wrong. You're either with someone or you're not. You make that shit clear."

"Bakayarou?" I stumble over the pronunciation of the word and laugh. "Is that a Hawaiian swear word?"

"Nah. I save all my really foul words for Japanese. Except for when I'm around my mom. She'll box my ears." He raises those expressive eyebrows, making a truly frightful face.

"You're adorable, Jackson."

"I'll show you how adorable I can be," he says wiggling his eyebrows in a suggestive way.

"I need a friend more than a boyfriend. Plus you were going to tell me about your mother's matchmaking."

"Ah, yes." He groans. "My curse. She has her heart set on me finding a nice Japanese girl. When you get all nice and round, I'm gonna take you over to meet her."

"That's terrible, Jackson."

"No. It really isn't. She calls me once a month at least. 'Jackson, my son, I found you the perfect girl. You must come for lunch,'" he says in a high-pitched voice I assume must be his mother. "I go to appease her, but it's awful. Ugliest girls I've ever seen."

I laugh hard, tears pricking my eyes. "That really *is* terrible. You're mean."

He laughs too. "Next time she invites me, I'm bringing you. You can fend off my mother and my future bride."

"Deal." I give him my hand. And our friendship is sealed.

Over the next hour he tells me all about his summers with his dad. Learning to surf. Traveling to competitions all over the world. It was stupid of me to wager a bet on his skills, but dinner was far from a loss. And neither is Jackson's company.

He sold his first software company when he was twenty-two and still studying at Stanford. Not happy to join the idly rich, he and his best friend started another company, combining their love of video games to help disabled children. *Swoon.* The man's handsome as fuck, loaded, and has a heart of gold. Too bad I'm stuck incubating another man's babies.

CHAPTER THIRTY-SIX

FAITH

*A*fter a flurry of phone calls and texts from Zane in the first few weeks after I escaped to LA, the line has gone uncomfortably silent. My feelings about this change as frequently as my clothes. One day I'm a sobbing mess, wondering how he could have given up so quickly. Then I'm angry at his gall for stringing along two women. The next day I'm bawling again over Sacha. Pregnancy hormones suck and so does Zane.

Somehow Jackson sticks by me no matter what my mood. We've quickly become best friends. A few weeks of shared meals, his amazing dinners and my Nutella-and-jelly sandwiches at the beach, cement a bond I may not have allowed years ago.

Tonight, I'm finally inviting him to my home.

I've hesitated. It's not that I don't trust Jackson, I do. It's just knowledge can change people. Jackson's more than comfortable in his multimillion-dollar condo and his programming business. He's found the good life, that's for sure. But there's a difference between what he has and my thirty-million-dollar Malibu estate, the Aston Martin in the garage, and everything else that my ex-husband left me, but Jackson doesn't know about. Guys tend to freak when women can buy and sell them ten times over, and I don't want to scare Jackson away.

But I can't hide from him anymore. Even three weeks seems like I waited too long. The gate buzzes and I hit the intercom button. Jackson's laughter comes over the speaker.

"Hey, Jackson, drive on up," I say, then hit the control that opens the gate. A couple of minutes later there's a knock on the door, then the door chimes ring.

"You've been holding out on me, baby girl," Jackson says with a laugh the minute I open the door.

My stomach flip flops, but I tell myself it's nerves. It has to be. The way he's looking around all wide-eyed with shock is the reaction I feared.

"Don't you have a butler or something to answer the door?" he asks, laughing again.

I hold Jackson's face in my hands, forcing him to look at me. "Grayson left me this place, Jackson. If you know anyone with the funds to buy it, please send them over. Preferably before the taxes are due. I think my ex is laughing right now watching me try to figure out how to manage this place."

"Who the hell was your ex?"

Pictures explain better than words, so I take his hand and head downstairs. Jackson gasps when we reached the bottom.

"Hockey nut?" he asks, looking around. Every inch of wall space is covered with Grayson's stuff.

"Kind of," I answer, walking over to his team picture. Looking at him still hurts.

"Haven't won the cup since," Jackson says over my shoulder.

"Nope. Grayson was so happy that year." I touch his face behind the glass. "It was the year after when things started getting ugly."

"Thorpe was your husband." He's not asking, but I nod anyway. God, I'm getting so sick of telling this story. Jackson turns me, folding me into his arms. "You deserve a lot more than this house for what you went through."

"Thanks, Jackson." I blow out a heavy sigh. "I just want to be a normal person."

"You're so much more to me."

"I know." Over the past few weeks Jackson has made it clear he'd be happy to explore something more than friendship. But if it all goes to hell, where would I be? "Let's eat. I'm starving."

Upstairs, Selina's famous enchiladas wait in the oven. Everything my housekeeper makes is amazing, but her cheesy enchiladas are my favorite. I take the entire baking dish out to the deck where the table is already set. Jackson brings out the beer I bought for him and water for me.

"Man that smells good," Jackson comments with a frown. "Thought you couldn't cook."

"I can't." I laugh, dishing out a large portion on his plate before setting some on mine. "Selina likes to leave me food. I think she's afraid I'm going to starve without her."

"Selina?"

"The housekeeper. She keeps this place in *Architectural Digest* condition. It's another reason I want to move. I feel like leaving a mess in this house is like screaming in a church. I'm not a slob, but I've never been so obsessed with keeping a place this spotless."

"Well, you know I'm not an obsessive cleaner." Jackson's house is tidy but lived in. A place you can put your feet up on the coffee table without feeling guilty. "But I could get used to this view."

"It is pretty spectacular," I agree after swallowing a healthy bite of food.

Jackson has two more helpings of enchiladas before we're done. I don't know where he puts it in his lean body, but the man can eat.

"That was pretty awesome. You need to keep her when you move."

"I plan on it. With two babies... I don't know how I'll live without her and her husband, Jorge. The two of them run this place." I walk to the railing and sigh, rubbing the growing swell of my belly.

Jackson follows me, his eyes watching my hands. "You're showing."

"Want to know my dirty secret?" He smiles and I continue, "Sometimes I take an entire tray of those enchiladas and climb in bed and eat the whole thing. I'm going to be as big as a house soon."

Jackson steps closer and flames dance on my skin. His hand is in my hair, tilting my face toward his as he bridges the gap between our lips. My stomach flutters in a way it hasn't in a long time. I let go and kiss him back, delighting in the way our mouths fit together, the way his tongue slides against mine, bitter from his beer.

An image of Zane flashes across my mind, unbidden and unwelcome, extinguishing my libido as effectively as a bucket of ice water. I step back from Jackson with reluctance.

"I'm sorry."

"You need to call him. Get closure or whatever it is you need. You won't be free until you do."

I look up into his dark eyes. "I'm scared Jackson. He'll want joint custody. I can't even think about shipping my babies halfway across the country."

He shakes his head, his eyes reflecting a world of pain. "They have a right to know their father. You're taking that away from them, not just him."

I step away, not wanting to hear anymore. "You don't under-stand, Jackson. He left me. And he lied to me. He had another woman in his apartment in New York. He had no right starting something with me in the first place." I don't mention Zane's alcohol problem, but it's another point against his character. Probably the biggest one and the main reason I haven't called him. "How can I trust him with my children after what he's done?"

Jackson's hands close around my shoulders. "He may have left you, but did you leave him? You need to do this for yourself too. Until you get rid of the guilt, he'll always be with you."

JACKSON HELPS me move on a nasty Saturday, late in October when the Santa Anas are giving it their all. My small ranch house in the Pacific Palisades, a couple of blocks from the beach and Jackson's place, is perfect. Three bedrooms, for when the kids decide they want their own space, a small backyard to play in, and a nice master bedroom for me. It's an area I wouldn't have been able to afford without Grayson.

There are several schools in the area, but none are looking for help. Even if they were, who would be eager to hire someone in my condition? No one, I find out fast. Instead, I take on a volunteer position teaching ESL a couple of afternoons a week at a rec center. It's not kindergarten, but it's rewarding. The students appreciate my help. And it keeps me busy and feeling useful.

I have to laugh every time I think about my life. I'm indebted to a dead ex-husband I hate, I'm pregnant from a man who stole my dog and lied to me, but who I can't seem to forget, and I have a best friend that I'd give anything to feel more for, but I can't. Fate sucks.

I wish I could give Jackson what he wants. I see the longing in his eyes, the way he watches me when he thinks I'm not looking. I know he's in pain, but he still sticks by me. Before long, his friends are my friends. We celebrate Thanksgiving. And even though Jackson's not Christian, he drags home a mangy-looking Christmas tree after finding me crying over some sappy holiday commercial. On New Year's Eve we binge-watch TV until our eyes blur, then fall asleep together on the sofa way before the clock strikes midnight.

He makes me laugh when all I want to do is cry. Someday he's going to give up and a piece of me will die. He's going to make a great husband, and I'll lose my best friend. It'll hurt like hell, but I'll let him go because I can't keep him. I can't give him what I don't have.

My heart.

Today he's taking me to his mother's. As promised long ago, she's invited him for lunch. A Japanese American girl awaits, and my two babies are more than noticeable at six months.

"Are you sure you know what you're doing, Jackson?" I ask as he turns onto the ramp for the 101 toward Santa Barbara where his mom lives. "She doesn't have any heart problems, does she?"

"Nah. She's fine. Hopefully this will stop her meddling." He glances over at me and smiles. It's a wicked smile. "Hele on, baby girl."

Convertible top down, wind in my hair, I smile back and shift in my seat to watch him drive. He's a beautiful man. Elegantly built. His long slender fingers drape casually over the wheel, his dark hair shining like obsidian in the sun.

He's a catch. The thought constricts my heart, a ribbon of jealousy wrapping around the organ. Hypocritical, I know, but I can't help it. My feelings for Jackson have grown into something I can't quite define. My fluctuating hormones make me vulnerable to his quiet charms.

He turns in my direction, probably sensing my stare, and his lips curve up. "What?"

"Nothing... Tell me about this girl."

"Not sure. Mom wouldn't say."

I stare at him in shock. "She wouldn't tell you? Kinda scary, isn't it?"

He lifts a shoulder in a casual shrug, then links his fingers with mine. "It's always scary. That's why you're with me this time."

I let out a laugh. "Oh, I'm your protector, am I?"

"Sure." He glances over at me and my stomach dips as our gazes meet. Even the polarized lenses of our sunglasses can't protect me from this pull.

I look away and take a long, deep breath to settle my feelings. I have no right to these feelings. "Keep an open mind. Maybe you don't need a *protector* this time."

He lifts my hand to his lips. "I'm always going to need you, baby."

"Jackson..." My heart squeezes tight as my own babies start getting restless from the long car ride. I can't be someone else's baby with this constant reminder of Zane inside me.

"Faith..." he returns.

The side of the road moves along for a few minutes, and my lungs struggle to take in every breath as my two kids stretch out.

"But what if this girl is really special? What if she's the one, Jackson?" The thought fills me with sadness. I don't want to lose this man, but it isn't fair to hold him back from happiness, either.

"What if I've already found the one?"

The traffic loosens and we accelerate with the cars around us before I have a chance to answer. *How do I move on?* How do I let go and give Jackson what he wants?

QUITE A WHILE LATER, we pull up to a neat ranch-style house similar to mine, except for the meticulous landscaping. My house is still a work in progress, but it's obvious Jackson's mom is an expert gardener.

Running my fingers through my windblown hair, I give Jackson one last leery look. He takes my hand and walks me up the curved walkway and into the cool air-conditioned home.

Past the entry is a living room. A woman glances up from the sofa that's visible as soon as we walk in. Her eyes widen and she jerks back, bracing her hands on either side of the sofa. "Fucking hell," her lips say loud and clear from one room away.

Jackson's own eyes have widened as well, and his face has flooded with some kind of strong emotion.

What? I mouth to him, pulling on his arm.

He shakes his head and nudges me forward, his arm around my waist.

"Mom," he yells, making me jump.

"Jackson?" His mom appears around the corner. Her wide smile melts as she sees me. Her eyes scan my body, her face going instantly pale when they hit my very pregnant belly.

"Jackson?" she repeats, frowning by this time. A dark blush rushes to her pale cheeks.

"Mom. This is Faith." His voice is strained, and his small smile is in stark contrast to the stiffness in his voice.

"Jackson…" Her eyes never leave my bump, as she continues speaking in what must be Japanese, her hands flying to emphasize her words.

"Sure, Mom." He leans down and kisses my cheek. His mom lets out an anguished sound. "Have a seat, baby."

I slip my sandals off at the door and walk into the room, eyeing the stunning woman who's eyeing me with what might be curiosity. Or possibly hostility.

She's not even close to the quiet, mousy girls Jackson described months ago. Even though she hasn't said much yet, I get the feeling this woman's anything but quiet. She's definitely not mousy with her crimson-streaked jet-black hair, tattoos, and eyebrow piercing.

She has perfect skin and a perfect figure, petite and elegant, while I've turned into a beached whale in the past few weeks. Jackson's going to take one good look at us together and say sayonara, Faith. I know I would.

I give her a small polite smile and a cautious "Hi, I'm Faith."

"Hi. Kimika," she says, and my eyes widen.

"Ryan's sister?"

Over the past few months Jackson and I have gone out with his best friend Ryan Yoshido and his girlfriend Hallie Reynolds. The one time Hallie mentioned Kimika's name, Ryan quickly shushed her. Between that short exchange and the steely look on Jackson's face when we walked into his mother's house, I have the distinct impression this woman sitting next to me has a complicated history with Jackson.

Her eyes narrow and she gives me a hesitant nod. In the next second we both flinch as shouting starts in the other room. It's in Japanese as well. Loud and fast, as if delivered via machine gun.

I glance in the direction of the altercation even though I don't understand a word, then back at the girl. "You understand?"

"Enough." She grimaces. "You?"

I shake my head.

"Probably better." She scrunches her nose, and the diamond in the crease sparkles in the light. And it's hard not to notice the flash of gold embedded in her tongue when she talks. "Congratulations. I'm sure you and Jackson will be very happy... eventually."

I glance toward the argument again. "Yeah. I don't think so." Her eyebrows join together in confusion. I wave my comment off. "Never mind."

A few minutes later Jackson comes out as if shot out of a cannon, fumbling to slip his shoes back on. "Come, Faith. We're leaving."

His mom follows behind him, still yelling.

I struggle to stand. Kimika offers me a helping hand. *Beached whale rising.* I've got a few inches on her, and not just around the waist, but she's stronger than she looks. I give her a grateful smile and a thank-you while Jackson waits by the door, his face dark, the muscle in his jaw pulsing.

He glances toward the woman in the living room for a second, breathing out a harsh breath. "Mika."

"Jackson." She grimaces and gives him a small wave with her delicate fingers.

He takes my hand, pausing as he opens the door. His arm curls around my waist, his hand resting lightly on my stomach. "I love you Mom but this time you've crossed a line."

"What was that about?" I ask once we're settled in his car. Somehow I don't think this is how Jackson planned today.

His free hand swipes at his jaw, before turning the ignition. "Nothing."

The argument between Jackson and his mom didn't look like nothing, and the voice in my head is telling me this Kimika is a whole lot of something. But I keep quiet. Jackson will tell me in good time. Or not.

The ride back is quiet. Too quiet. Jackson's making a mistake. Probably. Setting all his hopes on a future I can't guarantee. I should let him go now. Set him free. I wish I had the strength to, but with the babies... I need him. I need to be selfish for a little longer.

In my driveway, Jackson gives me a pained smile. His fingers lace with mine, resting on my distended stomach. Some unidentifiable limb stretches inside my belly and Jackson's smile turns warm and sunny.

"They're active today." He chuckles. "Must be fun."

"You have no idea." I roll my eyes and laugh. My fingers squeeze his tight with solidarity. Maybe for now I can give this beautiful man something. "I can't do this alone, Jackson, but if you want out—"

He shakes his head, his eyes softening. "I'm not going anywhere, Faith."

I nod, relief flowing over me like warm chocolate. "Would you like... would you be interested in being my birth partner? I need someone—I need you. I want you to go to Lamaze classes. To be there—"

"I'd love to. If you're sure." I start to nod, but he places his finger over my lips. "The father, he should be here. You should call him."

I shake my head once. "No. He hasn't tried to call me in months." Not since the end of August. I've almost convinced myself it doesn't hurt anymore. But maybe letting Jackson into my heart is just what I need.

"You have to know I want you."

"I don't want to lose my best friend."

He leans over and his warm lips find mine. It feels right, it feels good. After a moment he pulls back and traces my face with his fingers.

"Silly girl. You'll never lose me."

CHAPTER THIRTY-SEVEN

FAITH

*J*ackson takes his role as my Lamaze coach seriously. He's constantly reading up on pregnancy, giving me advice and support. In short, being a pain in the ass. He's perfect.

A few weeks before class starts, he surprises me with a shower disguised as a block party. He organized the whole thing with the help of all my wonderful neighbors. By the end of the day I have a handful of phone numbers, everyone offering to babysit or give advice or just be a friend.

I wake often in the middle of the night petrified. I can't pretend this isn't happening anymore. The two cribs crowding my nursery prove that, if the giant beachball in my stomach doesn't.

"You're not sleeping on your stomach are you?" Jackson whispers while I practice the breathing our Lamaze instructor demonstrated. I give him a sharp look. *Has the man seen my belly?*

"No," I whisper back.

"I read that can be dangerous. Make sure you prop a pillow to keep from rolling. Or I could sleep with you."

I stare at Jackson. His expression is all serious. "No." *Yes.*

Seven months without sex is wearing on me. My dreams have turned against me, becoming extremely erotic. I should be grateful that Grayson no longer haunts my nights, but he's been replaced by dark eyes and a surfer body that leaves me panting when I wake.

Just thinking about Jackson in my bed starts a throbbing between my thighs, and my skin flushes with desire, leaving me hot and sweaty in this air-conditioned room.

"You okay?" he asks with a grin that says he knows exactly what I'm thinking.

Since the kiss in the driveway, Jackson hasn't pushed for more and that's fine with me. Even if I'm horny as hell, who'd want to have sex when there's a kicking watermelon blocking the way? *I can wait a few more months.*

"I'm fine."

"Keep breathing, moms," the instructor yells. "Partners, keep them focused. Encourage your mommies."

Jackson snorts, setting off my giggles.

"Come on, mommy, be serious." His voice cracks with suppressed laughter.

"Fuck you, Jackson."

"Practicing your foul language? I hear that's common delivery-room talk." His laugh earns us a censured look from the instructor.

"Remember, I'm not to blame for your condition," he whispers in my ear while wiping the imaginary sweat from my brow. "So no damaging the man parts, okay?"

I close my eyes, trying not to think of his *man parts*. My body flushes hotter. God damn him and God damn Zane. I should be enjoying my pregnancy and everything that comes with it. Including the increased sex drive. Why the hell am I playing the virgin Mary with the hottest guy in LA?

Once this pregnancy's over, I'll work my ass off getting back in shape, and Jackson… I open my eyes and take in the gorgeous man next to me.

He'll be mine.

"MY MOM WANTS to know when we're getting married."

Jackson gives me a solid whack in the middle of my back as I choke on my mango smoothie. I barely manage to avoid spraying the peach-colored beverage all over his pristine white sofa.

"What the fuck, Jackson?" I wheeze.

He shrugs, grinning. "I might have sort of given her the impression the babies are mine. It's been the quietest three months of my life. I should marry you just to thank you."

"Ha ha. I'm fat and ugly. You could do so much better." Today my libido has been overshadowed by my insecurity. My mood swings over the past week have been spectacular. One minute I'm so looking forward to being a mother, the next I'm crying with self-doubt. Sacha has probably forgotten me. Probably happier with Zane and his organic dog treats and expert belly rubs.

Today I'm uncomfortable and grumpy. My feet are swollen, not that I can see them. And I have three more weeks to go. *Ugh.*

Jackson drops his smoothie on the coffee table with enough force it splashes over the rim of the glass. "You're the most beautiful woman I've ever seen."

I give him a skeptical look. The twins have given me a physique not much different from the mangos Jackson cut into the blender minutes ago.

I rest my smoothie on top of my belly, taking advantage of the convenient shelf. "I'm as big as a house, Jackson. I'm not sure you've noticed."

Maybe he hasn't noticed my size with the big muumuu dresses I've been wearing. My bikini is wedged in the back of my dresser drawer collecting dust. I haven't worn it in months. Probably won't again for years.

"You. Are. Beautiful." He stresses every word while setting my smoothie next to his before taking my fat hands in his. He guides me toward the wall of windows that look out onto his balcony and the amazing view beyond.

Reaching down, he lifts the hem of my dress and, before I can stop him, pulls it over my head.

"Jackson!" I cover what I can with my hands, which isn't much. My stomach bulges and squirms with my touch. I don't even remember what underwear I put on this morning. Beyond my massive belly could be pretty lace or dirty old cotton for all I know.

"Shhh."

Jackson replaces my hands with his. His smile grows with the movement under my skin. The kids are less active today, but the warmth from Jackson's beautiful hands stirs the babies inside me. His dark skin tone contrasts against my pale belly, and for a moment I wish these children I'm carrying were his.

A wave of guilt washes over me, then anger. These babies belong to a man I haven't spoken to in months.

"You're pregnant," Jackson says, breaking me out of my thoughts. "And magnificent."

I exhale an uncomfortable laugh, trying to push my feelings away. "Magnificent like a mountain? Maybe like the sun? Big as—"

Jackson's hands cup my face. Then his lips cover mine, silencing me.

Oh God, his lips.

I love his kisses. Every single one has felt like water in the desert. Like something I never realized I lost until I found it again. Like something I needed, but didn't know it until it was given to me.

His velvety tongue strokes mine, unleashing a firestorm in my body. It doesn't take much. I'm hot and needy, my skin tight and sensitive, so ripe I'm going to explode. I'm tired of what little satisfaction I've been giving myself. I need the feel of a man inside me.

Why the hell have we waited?

"God, I want you so bad," he whispers against my lips.

"Please, Jackson." I gasp at his words. "Please touch me."

I'd give anything not to be pregnant, not to have this belly between us. The logistics of my body won't make this easy.

Jackson steps behind me, as if reading my thoughts. His fingers on my chin guide me back to continue our kiss. A thrill settles in my belly as he bends me forward over the back of his chaise lounge, our bodies molding together. An ache builds inside me, calling for the hard ridge of his cock pressing against my ass. Like sex-crazed teenagers dry humping, this feels naughty and good, and wrong and yet so, so right. Every inch of him through his thin athletic shorts promises satisfaction.

"Take me, Jackson. Please."

His hands... oh, God, his hands. I moan as his fingers brush my nipple through my bra. Then he yanks the fabric down and my heavy breasts spill out into his hands. Breasts that have ached for the past nine months sigh at his touch.

"Please..." I beg, greedy for more. For everything.

He slips a hand inside my panties and I shudder as his fingers breach my core.

"God, you're so fucking wet," Jackson growls into my ear. His teeth scrape my shoulder and I shudder again.

My knees tremble as he fucks me with fingers I've been dreaming of for months now.

"I know this is wrong. But I can't wait any longer, Faith. I've wanted you since I first saw you."

"Shh." I pull his mouth to mine, silencing him.

I don't want to talk. Talking leads to thinking, and thinking

SECRETS WE KEEP

will make me second-guess what we're doing. And I don't want this to stop.

I press his hand harder against me, pushing his fingers deeper. I'm going to come. My body tightens around him.

"Oh God, Jackson. I'm coming."

Blinding heat and pleasure rip through me. An orgasm so strong it's painful as it rushes over me in waves from my core out and back, stealing my breath and making me tremble. My legs shake with the intensity, threatening to give out as the pleasure-pain goes on for what feels like forever.

"Should I get a condom?" Jackson asks, dragging his shorts down his legs.

I let out a laugh. He's kidding right? But before I can answer him a wave of something that has nothing to do with pleasure and everything to do with pain grips my belly.

"Oh my God." I cover my face in horror, as a trickle of liquid courses down my thighs and dribbles onto his wood floor. "I'm not peeing myself. I swear."

"Pretty sure this means we should stop now."

341

CHAPTER THIRTY-EIGHT

FAITH

*J*ackson's still laughing about the untimely break in my waters, telling the story to anyone who'll listen. I should be embarrassed, but since everyone he talks to has had a good look between my legs, I became immune to any feelings of shame hours ago.

"I should offer my services to pregnant women, you know," Jackson says, sitting back in his chair, one foot balanced on the other knee, offering his latest nugget of wisdom since my doctor made her first appearance this evening.

I can still hear Dr. Keller's laugh when Jackson told her he was glad he didn't have his face down there at the time. She agreed and the two of them got into a detailed discussion on the virtues of a good orgasm for bringing on labor. Except for her checking my progress, I might as well have not been in the room.

Jackson's taken her professional opinion and is now running with it. "As a superhero, should I be called The Labormaker or The Laboranator? I like the sounds of Laboranator, but it's a bit ambiguous."

"I like the sounds of labor coach, but someone seems to have forgotten that," I snap at Jackson, then whimper as I'm caught in the jaws of another contraction.

I pant as the pain rips through me while I stare at the monitor, watching the contraction's progression, hoping for some detachment. It's not working and neither is Lamaze. Whoever thought breathing through the excruciating pain of labor was a perfectly good substitute for modern drugs should be drawn and quartered. I've stayed valiant for over a dozen hours, remembering our instructor's words on staying strong, and the virtues of natural childbirth, but this is bullshit.

"Breathe," Jackson instructs, rubbing my back. "You're doing great."

"I want an epidural."

"You told me no. Your words, Faith. You said, 'Even if I beg, don't let them pump drugs into my body.'"

"I was wrong, Jackson. I had no idea what I was talking about. I *need* an epidural."

"Sorry. I promised the rational you." He shrugs like it's no big deal. It isn't to him. He's not the one whose body is being torn apart one contraction at a time. Lamaze breathing is about as effective as giving someone an aspirin before surgery.

I collapse back onto my pillow. "Fuck you, Jackson."

He grins and winks. "Raincheck, baby."

Funny. Not.

He hasn't sat here for what feels like days as the contractions get stronger and the pain reaches a level that has me gasping for breath. No one tells you that when you're calmly sitting in Lamaze class—that the pain will make breathing impossible, that you'll think someone is ripping out your kidneys straight through your back, that the time in between will feel like seconds and your whole world is pain and you'll want to curl into a ball and disappear but you can't because this is your reality.

I whimper as my stomach hardens and another contraction takes hold. Jackson resumes his back rub and his positive words.

Oh, fuck.

"Epidural," I cry, my eyes pleading with Jackson.

"Breathe, Faith. It's too late. The nurse said so about an hour ago."

"Fuck the nurse." I whimper, panting through pain I never thought possible. Pain worse than a ruptured spleen or a fractured jaw. Jackson's back rubs aren't helping. Breathing. Isn't. Helping.

"I didn't hear the nurse. It doesn't count. Tell her."

"Baby. Did you see her? I'm not messing with that bitch. She'll take my man parts."

"Jackson…" I plead, the pain slowly receding like a wave. "No more kids. This is it. Okay?"

He's almost as pale as me. "I'm good."

Nurse Scary is back. Jackson's right. She looks like some of the Stars' defensivemen I used to know. Tall, wide shoulders, arms that—

She snaps on a pair of gloves, making me shiver. "Let's take a look."

Jackson pales further as he peeks between my legs. Whatever she's doing, it hurts like a son of a bitch. Then another contraction builds and nothing exists outside my bubble of pain.

"Stop looking down there, Jackson." I glare at him once I can think again. "Don't look… when they come out. Promise me."

He holds his hands up with a look like I'd have to be crazy. "Don't worry. I only want pleasant memories the next time I look at your pussy."

"Looking good," the nurse says while walking away. "Gonna call De. Keller. Don't push yet."

I gawk at her for a second before she disappears down the hall. "Did she actually fucking say that? 'Don't push yet?' Why the hell would I push?"

"Breathe, Faith," Jackson reminds, like I'd forget. Like I have a choice.

Then I forget as another contraction twists me into a pretzel. Suddenly, the need to push isn't an option, it's non-fucking-negotiable. "Oh God, Jackson... I'm gonna push."

Jackson's eyes widen. "No! No, no, no, Faith. No Dr. Keller. No push. Not qualified to deliver a baby here."

"Need to, don't want to. Don't have a choice."

"Oh fuck..." He grabs at his hair and pulls. "Blow. That's right. You need to blow." Jackson starts blowing like a kid with his first bubble wand. "Come on, Faith. Blow. Don't push. Please."

At that moment Dr. Keller strolls in. "How we doing, kids?"

"She needs to push," Jackson says.

"Great. Let's take a look." She pulls up a stool and guides my feet into stirrups. "You're good to go, Faith. On the next contraction I want you to push."

Next contraction?

"I change my mind. I don't want to push." Pushing hurts like the fires of hell.

"Come on, Faith. Only one way out of this situation," Dr. Keller advises of my harsh reality with an encouraging smile. New rule. There should be no smiling in the delivery room.

"Thanks," I snap before another contraction locks me in its teeth.

"Push, baby," Jackson yells along with Doc Keller and Nurse Scary, and some other woman who might be the pediatrician. Or possibly another nurse. "You can do it."

"The baby's crowning. Maybe two more good pushes. Come on, Faith."

It's three, but who's counting. I fucking am.

The third push rips me in two. It must. The pain is indescribable. But in the midst of the fiery agony Dr. Keller yells, "Stop."

Stop?

"Okay. Slowly now. Push."

Everything happens at once. I push, there's a flurry of activity at the foot of the bed, and everyone cheers.

"Jackson, come here," Dr. Keller instructs.

Next thing I know he's holding a baby. *My baby.*

"Faith. We have a girl." He laughs, tears in his eyes.

"Take a breather, Faith. Say hi to your daughter, then we'll get ready for round two." Dr. Keller's reminder has tears flooding my eyes. I don't want to do this again.

Jackson lays my daughter in my arms. She's beautiful. Dark fuzzy hair covers her head. She's beet red, but her little nose and those bright blue eyes are gorgeous.

A fierce contraction reminds me her sibling wants out too. She's whisked away and it starts again.

Twelve minutes, fourteen seconds later, Zane Olaf Brody is born. Jackson names his sister Kayla Rose. They're perfect. The moment their ombre-blue eyes stare up at me, the decision is made. I don't know when, but sometime when I'm ready I'll have Summerton contact Zane. I'm too exhausted to think beyond that. Right now my world is in this room.

"Faith?" Jackson whispers.

"Yeah?"

"I looked. It was fucking amazing."

CHAPTER THIRTY-NINE

ZANE

A year ago I met the love of my life. The sun rose and set in her eyes. And I was an idiot. I thought she'd always be there. I should have been truthful. I should have explained everything from the beginning. Now it's too late. I've lost her and nothing has been right in my life since.

Pen to paper, I can't even describe the highs and lows in the last year. It would sound like a really bad country-western song. No one would believe the shit I've been through.

In the end only one thing matters, I can't find Faith. Somewhere in Los Angeles my heart sits in the hands of a woman who probably doesn't care if I exist.

I'm free to leave. Leave her behind. Start fresh somewhere new. But everything tells me to pack up my shit and move to LA. Search for the woman with the golden hair and the smile that haunts my dreams. In a city of 3.8 million people, she can't be that hard to find, *right?*

Sacha noses my hand and I scratch her head. I keep telling myself even if she doesn't want me, she wouldn't abandon her dog. But the months of silence tell a different story.

My phone rings an unknown California number. I hold my breath and say a small prayer as I hit answer.

My hopes dash with the sound of a man's voice.

"Zane Brody?" Fuck, another reporter. I should hang up.

"Yeah," I answer, my voice hesitant, wary.

"Is your middle name really Olaf?" He has the kind of laugh only an insane person has. I pull the phone away and squint down at the screen like it might give me some clue as to who the hell this guy is. It doesn't.

"Who the fuck is this?"

"My name is Jackson Abe. I had to call you." He pauses and I tell myself to hang up. Either he's a reporter or he's some lunatic with a grudge. I've had my fair share of both lately.

The silence stretches on, testing my patience. "Hello?"

"Congratulations, man. You're a dad." His voice is thick with emotion or something.

"What?"

"Faith, man. We're here at the hospital. She's going to kill me, but… man to man… this is too big. A fucking miracle. A guy can't not know he has kids."

I swallow the lump in my throat. I've been through too much. If this is some sick joke, I'll hunt this Jackson Abe down and gut him with my bare hands. "Kids? What the hell are you talking about?"

"She said you didn't know, but ask Grace. Faith had me call Grace. She'll probably kill both of us, but I'm here. Anyway… Kayla Rose, born five pounds two ounces and Zane Olaf, four pounds twelve ounces. And they're fucking beautiful, like their mom."

My mouth opens and shuts. It takes me a second to do the math, but when I do, I know whoever this guy is, he speaks the truth.

"Fuck," I finally rasp past the lump in my throat. I'm gonna fucking kill Grace, and Aaron. I'm sure if she knows, he knows too.

"I know, man. Bawled like a baby myself. Don't tell anyone, though." He exhales a heavy breath into the phone. "Listen, got to go. She needs some time. Emotional right now. Feel me? I'll call you soon. You need to fix this. One way or another."

"Wait," I yell into the phone, desperate not to break this connection, my only connection with Faith.

There's a moment of silence, then, "Yeah?"

"Tell her I love her."

There's a heavy sigh. "Figured... Tell her yourself. Talk again soon."

He hangs up. *Fix it one way or another?* Who the fuck is Jackson Abe? Then it sinks in. Holy shit, I'm a father. Of twins.

CHAPTER FORTY

FAITH

$\mathcal{T}$ime is a strange concept when you have kids. There's no constant. It's not metered out in precise amounts, like sand dropping through an hourglass. A night with two fussy babies can last forever. As one settles, the other starts again, disturbing the first. They tag team me like that. Nights that slowly leach into dawn as your eyes struggle to stay open and you beg theirs to close. Then other times go by in a blink. A perfectly timed nap ends right when my eyes close.

My days are measured by the amount of sleep I get. Some days blending into the next in a bleary haze. There's never enough rest.

Jackson's been supportive, but he has to work. His life moves forward with meetings and business trips, while mine seems stuck in molasses. I miss him when he's gone.

I have to double-check my calendar when I notice my six-week checkup. Where did the time go? My babies have grown so much I have a hard time remembering the scrawny little things they were forty-two days ago.

Jackson smiles at me from his spot in Dr. Keller's waiting room. "Howzit?"

"Everything is good." I take a moment to make my yearly appointment, then take Jackson's hand as he leads me out of the office. "Are my babies okay?"

Jackson's neighbor is watching the twins. First time. I'm more than nervous. My mind picturing every horrible scenario possible. I'm questioning my decision to go back to work. How can I leave them with strangers?

"They're fine." He squeezes my hand in reassurance, then drops it. "Mrs. Garcia has, like, eight kids and a million grand-kids. I've never seen her without a baby in her arms."

"Dr. Keller said I can resume all normal activities."

Jackson grins. "We should go surfing."

"Maybe…" I take a deep breath. I don't have surfing on my mind. "I think we have unfinished business."

He tilts his head, his expression unreadable. "I see."

He's been distant since the birth. Maybe he's freaked out by what happened. Maybe he's changed his mind. Or maybe it's my sleep-deprived brain. Either way, I don't want to push him. But I miss his kisses. I miss his touch.

I place my hand on his leg. "I want us."

Jackson closes his eyes tight and nods. "You need to think on this a little longer, baby. Your hormones are still out of whack. I want you to be sure."

"I'm sure, Jackson." I lean across the console and place a kiss on his jaw. "Come over tonight. I'll make dinner. After the kids are asleep, I'll show you how sure I am."

His eyes shine with tears. "I love you, Faith."

CHICKEN'S IN THE OVEN. Rice is done. Salad's in the fridge. Table's set—nothing fancy. The fine china sits unused at the Malibu house, but I have candles and wine glasses.

Wine. *Shit!*

I uncork the wine to let it breathe. Jackson will be here soon. My nerves jump with anticipation. This is right. Or so I keep telling myself. This. Is. Right.

Zee's asleep in the playpen, and for once Kayla isn't trying to wake him. Thank God. One down, I think as I lay him gently in his crib.

Two cribs in their room is a squeeze but necessary.

Kayla's my little hellion.

"Aren't you baby?" I ask the fussy girl whose eyes refuse to close. "How about a snack?"

She latches on with gusto, making me wince. "We have a big night tonight. Try to be gentle. Someday I'll let you date the hot guys too."

A few minutes later, she's done. Zee's always up for a hearty meal that knocks him out for hours. Kayla is good after a few minutes, but comes back for more an hour later. If I'm lucky. How they could be so different amazes me.

She fights sleep. Her tiny hands restless, rubbing her face.

"Come on, Kayla," I whisper. "Mommy needs to change and get ready for her night. I don't want to look like I've been spit out of your diaper bag."

I feel him in the doorway as I start singing "Frère Jacques." "Be done soon. There's Sapporo in the fridge. Help yourself," I sing to the melody as Kayla's eyes start to close.

Footsteps edge closer and I hush him in warning. She's so frickin' close, if I have to start over I'll cry.

Taking a breath, my body stills. Not Jackson's crisp cologne, my nose tells me. Spicy and warm and oh so recognizable.

"She's beautiful. Just like her mother," he whispers while rubbing a lock of my dark brown hair that's only a couple of shades lighter than his between his fingers. "I had a feeling you weren't a blonde."

I swallow hard, gasping out a breath. Kayla senses my tension and her eyes fly open, her focus past my shoulder and up. I turn and look into matching ombre-blue eyes and start to tremble. "Zane..."

"Our babies." He slips his hands under my arms. "Let me take her."

I relinquish my hold, and he slowly slides her to his shoulder as if he's done it a million times.

"Daddy's got you, Kayla," he whispers, and I lose it. My tears fall faster than a Minnesota rainstorm. Zane catches the stream with his thumb. "Go. Do what you need to do."

Jackson's in the kitchen, leaning against the counter, one hand wrapped around the Japanese beer I got him and the other scratching Sacha behind the ears. He looks up with so much pain in his eyes it kills me.

Sacha trots over, her tail wagging something fierce. I drop down on my knees and give her a hug worthy of the long separation, then stare up at Jackson.

"What have you done?"

He shrugs like it's no big deal. "When you love something, set it free. If it comes back, it's yours. If not..." He heaves a heavy sigh. "...you were never mine, baby. Every day I could see it in your eyes."

"And what, I'm his?" I stand and whisper-shout, waving my thumb over my shoulder. "You know the story, Jackson. It's been ten months."

I move toward Jackson on instinct and slip my arms around him. "I'm more yours—"

"No." He interrupts, pulling me tight against him in a warm embrace. "As much as I want that. No, Faith. You need to hear him out. The man's been through hell."

My laugh is filled with bitter irony. "And I haven't?"

Jackson pushes me back, tipping my chin up to look at him, his dark eyes shining with emotion. "Hear him out. Promise me."

"And then what?" My lip trembles at the thought of Jackson leaving. "What about you?"

353

"I'll still be around. Ohana, remember? We're family." He kisses the top of my head, then says, "Maybe I'll call my mom. See if I can get Kimika's number. Don't worry about me."

The front door closes with a quiet click and I'm alone. With Zane. And Sacha. And two kids. This is how it should have been. Easy. But it's not.

My stomach twists with ten months of trapped emotions. What do I say? What's Zane going to say? Wounds that have scarred over may rip open tonight, leaving me bleeding. I can't bear the pain again. This time the jagged pieces of my soul won't fit together at all.

I pull the chicken out of the oven. It's perfect, but my appetite is gone and Zane won't eat it. I wrap it in foil and throw it in the fridge as he appears in the doorway, his eyes red. He's lost weight. A lot of weight. His cheekbones are hollow, and his clothes hang off his frame.

He looks hungry, so I plate the pineapple rice meant for me and Jackson. Toss the salad one last time and set it on the table. Zane sits and I grab the wine.

He halts my hand as I go to pour. "Just water." The serious look in his eyes says it all.

I nod and set the bottle on the counter, then pull a couple of mineral waters out of the fridge. Our conversation stays safely on neutral topics. The weather, LA traffic, nothing substantial. Everything we need to say hangs over the table like a dark cloud. I want to get this over with. Send him on his way and call Jackson back. He couldn't be serious about calling Kimika, could he?

I pounce as soon as he sets down his fork.

"Jackson says we need to talk." I stand and grab our plates and head to the dishwasher, looking at Zane over my shoulder. "Are you sick?"

He shakes his head. "I've wanted to see you so bad."

I shrug. "You need to start further back than that, Zane."

I'm being a bitch, but I can't help it. Jackson should have warned me. *No.* Jackson never should have contacted Zane.

"Can we sit down, Faith?" He motions toward the living room. "This is a pretty long story. I've driven straight through."

"You drove?"

"Yeah."

I freeze halfway into the living room. My piano sits on the far wall. Outside, a strange SUV sits in the driveway with a small trailer attached to the back. "Where's the Mustang?"

"Sold it." He groans as if in pain when we sit down, his eyes drifting shut for a moment. "I'd have come sooner. I would've come last summer. I never planned on leaving you. You have to believe me. Shit just happened."

"Start with your *girlfriend*, Zane. You know, the one in New York? The one that should have prevented you from starting something with me in the first place," I hiss, mindful of my volume. The last thing I need right now is screaming babies.

Zane shakes his head and sighs. "I really wish Aaron had let me know you were in the room when I was talking to him. I'd have told you, but not that way. A week before I planned on returning home for my mom, I found out she'd been cheating on me. We were way over before I even met you.

"Look, call me stupid, call me soft. You don't know how hard it is to find affordable housing in New York. I told Dani she could stay at my place until she found something. I assumed she was looking while I was gone. I assumed wrong. I also assumed that she realized we weren't together anymore, but she didn't get that message either."

I narrow my eyes. Can I believe him?

He sets his phone in front of me on the ottoman. "Call Tess, call Laura if you don't believe me. They'll both tell you as much. I'm not a cheater, Lyric."

My insides clench at the betrayal. Everyone knew?

"Faith," I correct with a huff. "You don't even know me

355

anymore. Grayson's dead. Shot himself in my living room while you were gone. I'm Faith Asher now. Again. Whatever. Lyric James is gone."

Zane nods his head while breathing out a quiet laugh. "I know. Brian Asher's daughter. Grayson Thorpe's wife. Seems like I'm not the only one who hasn't been honest in this relationship."

I suck in a sharp gasp of indignation. "Ex-wife. And don't you dare. Not sharing who my father, who my ex-husband was, isn't the same as not revealing your not-so-over relationship. I was protecting my life with my lies."

"Jesus, Lyric. Faith. Your father was a world-famous pianist. And here I was teaching you fucking scales. Bet you got a good laugh about that."

"Zane—"

"Fuck that. I don't care about your father or your ex-husband. You kept your pregnancy from me," he lowers his voice to a whisper when I shush him. "You denied me the last month and a half of my kids' lives."

The heavy weight of guilt presses on my chest. He's got me on that.

"You didn't miss much," I say to lessen my shame. Not that it works. "It's been nonstop screaming and pooping and exhaustion."

"I would've helped." Zane runs his hand down his face, his body sagging. "I'm sorry, Faith. I should never have left. I should have protected you—"

"No, you shouldn't have. You'd be dead. Grayson would've sh-shot you," I say, my voice breaking. "He had pictures of us. Had someone watching me for God knows how long."

"I should have been there, regardless of the outcome. I promised to protect you." His Adam's apple bobs as he swallows with effort. Guilt. We're quite a pair. "I let you and Sacha down."

Over the last ten months I've tried to block that night from my mind, but it all floods back. Zane shifts next to me, pulling me into his arms as a sob breaks loose in my chest. "I was so scared I'd lost her. And then I did."

"I was afraid we'd never see you again," he whispers into my hair. "I've missed you so much."

I sniff. "Your calls stopped. I thought you gave up."

He breathes out a heavy breath. "I stopped calling because I didn't want to drag you into my drama."

I scoff as we pull apart. He gives me plenty of space, reminding me of that first night so long ago. "Drama? You mean your drinking?"

"No. Not my drinking. You don't watch the news much?" He rubs his hand over his face as I shake my head. He knows me. I hate watching the news. "I better start at the beginning."

CHAPTER FORTY-ONE

FAITH

"*I* had booked a flight to come out here over Labor Day weekend. Grace gave me an address—not this address—"

I let out a growl of frustration. "Of course she did."

"Yeah, she warned you might not be happy, but I figured I had three days to beg your forgiveness." He pauses for several beats, then swallows audibly. "I never made it to the airport. Never got a chance. The day before my flight, one of my students, Caroline Reese, accused me of... well, a lot of inappropriate things."

My eyes go wide. Of all the things I expect him to say, this isn't on the list. "Oh, Zane."

"So, instead of packing for my flight, I was arrested. Charged with sexual misconduct with a minor."

"Obviously you're here and not in jail, so..." I prompt when he's silent for too long.

He clears his throat and runs a hand through his hair in a way that tells me he'd rather forget it all.

"Zane..." I squeeze his arm. "It's okay. I don't have to know the details."

"Yeah, you do. No more secrets." His face hardens as the

words come out. Pretty sure his statement goes both ways. "My brother-in-law posted my bail. I sold my car. We mortgaged my mother's house to pay for an attorney. It was scary as shit. The possibility of spending the next decade or so behind bars."

I place a comforting hand on his shoulder. "But you're here. You're safe."

He spends the next few minutes reliving his days in court. The accusations. The humiliation. He lets out a snort of bitter laughter. "I've never been so thankful for that stupid dragon tattoo."

He laughs hard, shoulders shaking. Tears stream down his cheeks, the levity of the situation evaporating. Without hesitation, I wrap my arms around him and cry for the both of us. For the fucked up lives we've both been subject to.

"Fuck, Lyric..." I don't correct him this time. The poor man's been through hell. *God damn you, Jackson.*

Once Zane regains his composure he goes on. "I had no choice but to tell my lawyer about the tattoo. Embarrassing as hell, letting a stranger photograph my junk, then letting my lawyer pass the picture around the courtroom for all to see. But the judge immediately threw out the case, so..."

"If it's any consolation, I lost count of how many people had a look between my legs," I inform. "So, now what?"

"I'm not going back to Minnesota, if that's what you're expecting me to say." It's exactly what I expect him to say. "I have nothing to go back to. I might have been found innocent, but the stigma..." His gaze travels around the room, stopping on the wall of photos I've amassed of the twins. Sacha noses Zane's hand while whimpering. "My career's gone, the band, gone—"

"The band?" I sputter, louder than is wise if I don't want to wake Zee and Kayla.

"Can't really blame them—"

"I can," I spit out between gritted teeth. How dare his friends turn their backs on him? And why the hell didn't Grace tell me?

"It doesn't matter." He points down the hall to where my babies are sleeping. *Our babies.* "My life is with our kids. I want to be their father. Maybe your husband? I'm gonna suck at a lot of things, Faith. I don't know what kind of job I'm gonna get out here. I'm hoping the shit in Minneapolis doesn't follow me, but I'm probably not going to teach. Hell, I don't think I ever want to again."

Husband? I take a good look at Zane. Beyond the sunken cheeks and dark circles under his eyes. The dirty hair and soiled clothes. Will I ever be able to trust him again?

But his eyes lock on mine, and that old swoop in my stomach reminds me of everything we once had.

"I start teaching in the fall," I tell him for whatever reason.

He gifts me with a smile. "Good for you."

"Yeah, well, I'm thinking maybe you could watch Kayla and Zee? Save me the cost of day care." It's an olive branch I'm hoping won't bite me in the ass.

Zane's smile widens. "I'm in."

"You looked like you handled Kayla pretty well in there."

I catch a slight sparkle of the old Zane in his smile. "Unlike most thirteen-year-old boys, I loved helping my mom with my baby sister. Funny, it was one of the few things Cox didn't harass me about."

"I'm sorry." How did I not see the extent of pain he was carrying around before? It's impossibly obvious to me now. "You know, it's very LA to see a therapist."

"Very New York, too." Before I can respond, he stands, wiping his hands on his rumpled jeans. "I'll always love you, Faith. Whatever you decide, you need to know that won't change. But I'd like the chance to prove I'm a good father and maybe a good partner. If you're open to that. But no pressure."

"Are you staying somewhere?"

He scrubs his hands in his hair again. "Jackson offered me his spare room, but I'm thinking that might get complicated."

Jackson. I have yet to decide whether I'm pissed at his involvement in this. Stupid selfless idiot.

I stand as well, fighting the impulse to keep Zane here longer. To talk, and maybe see where the night leads. Which is reason enough to get him out of here.

His keys jingle in his hand as he points out the front window. "Mind if I leave the trailer here? At least until I find a place to keep my stuff."

I nod like a damn bobble head. "Yeah. Come back in the morning and we can talk more."

AFTER ZANE LEAVES, I brush my teeth, change into my pajamas, and crawl into bed. Then stare at the ceiling.

If only there was a magic pill to make the last ten months of anger, hurt, and resentment disappear. Seeing Zane... so damaged by his own troubles. If I had been there. What would it have been like? Better? Worse? I can't imagine being pregnant and dealing with his legal problems at the same time. *Maybe this happened for a reason.* Maybe it's better this way, as selfish as it sounds. It would have been a strain on us, on the babies.

And damn, Jackson. While I'd planned a romantic evening, complete with dinner and music and sexy new underwear, he'd had a different plan. And now the heavy weight of guilt is almost unbearable. I called Zane a cheater, but am I just as bad?

Accepting that sleep is unlikely, I toss the covers back and get out of bed. Back in the living room, Sacha greets me with her wet nose. "I've missed you too."

My gaze goes to my piano. On top is a small picture of Zane and Sacha. One I took last summer. She's smothering his face in wet doggy kisses. Without her easy approval I don't think I would've let Zane in.

On the other side is a larger picture in a simple silver frame.

This one I don't remember, but my heart aches with the image. I'm sitting on Zane's lap. It's like there's no one else in the world —our eyes are locked on each other. The love in our gaze is so powerful it's staggering. Do I want that back? A quiet voice says *yes*.

Sacha noses my elbow and I smile down at my first baby.

"Daddy took good care of you," I whisper while petting her soft fur. Her warm brown eyes look up at me in confusion. "I know. He'll be back tomorrow. I promise."

It's late and I'm bone exhausted, knowing in a few hours Zee and Kayla will need me at least semi-alert. I curl up on the floor next to Sacha and wait for her soft snores to lull me to sleep.

Kayla shrieks, waking me first. She always does. A moment later, Zee joins in. *Let the fun begin.*

Sacha's right there, pacing back and forth between the cribs, sticking her nose between the bars. Kayla squeals when she licks her tiny toes.

"You like the babies?" I settle down into the cushioned rocker and situate the twins, one on each breast.

Sacha gives each tiny foot a sniff and then lies down at my feet with her usual groan. I didn't realize how much I missed that sound until this moment.

"We don't get a lot of sleep around here, so take advantage of it when you can."

Kayla goes down first. Somehow I get her in her crib without waking her or disturbing her brother's dinner. Zee's a fussy thing when his milk supply is cut off prematurely, but tonight luck is with me.

I snag the diaper bag off the floor, then close the nursery door and head into the living room. Sacha follows a few steps behind before claiming the doggy bed Zane brought.

Zee is slowing down, but the grunts and pops coming from the other end tells me he's about to test the metal of his diaper. I've learned the hard way not to buy bargain brands. His sweet face turns five shades of red. It'd be amusing if I didn't have cleanup duty. And of course stripping him down wakes the little man up completely.

Sacha trots out of the room as he exercises his lungs. I don't blame her.

We start walking. Exercise, I remind myself. My ass almost fits back into my size six jeans, so I'm not complaining too hard.

He likes it when I sing. "Twinkle Twinkle," "Frère Jacques." Before long it's whatever pop songs are in my head. Eventually I cave and sing Heartattack's songs. *Zane's songs.* It feels a bit traitorous. Zane should be here singing them to his son. Maybe tomorrow. Tonight we're dancing to the beat in my head. He's not sleeping, but he's not screaming either, so I call it a win.

"You like your daddy's music, huh, little Zee."

He gives me a wide toothless grin. His first real smile that isn't gas. Or maybe it is. Either way it's glorious. If it wasn't two in the morning and my hands weren't full, I'd take a photo. Save it for all those bad nights that I think will never end. His smile makes everything worth it.

Zane should be here. This is only the first of this little boy's milestones, but my heart breaks for his father's loss. Zane needs to be here to witness all the other firsts to come. I can't be selfish with his children. They need his love as well as mine.

And I can't lie. There's a part of me that needs his love too.

CHAPTER FORTY-TWO

FAITH

*Z*ane shows up early in the morning, looking like hell. I'm pretty sure he didn't sleep in Jackson's spare room. His beard is well past a four o'clock shadow, unless it was four o'clock three days ago. His clothes look ready for the trash. *Is that sand in his hair?* I don't care. No, that's a lie. It breaks my heart to think of him sleeping on the beach like a homeless person.

Our babies are having tummy time in the playpen. Fed and changed, they have maybe an hour until they get bored.

"You look like hell." I state the obvious. "Didn't Jackson let you shower?"

"Overslept. Didn't want to waste time." His gaze is stuck on our children in the playpen.

"Go. Shower." My memory calling up the first time I said those words. I'm in a different robe today. Somewhere between Minneapolis, Sydney, and here, my silk robe vanished. This one's terrycloth, and a bit too warm at the moment. Or maybe it's the sexual tension humming between me and Zane that has me all heated up.

Zane gives me a playful wink. "Is that an invitation?"

A trickle of sweat makes its way down my spine. My granny

panties grow wet, and so does the thick padding in my nursing bra. *Damn leaky boobs.*

"For one. You want to hold your kids? Clean up." I turn away and head into the kitchen. Whatever desire I have for this man will have to wait until… I don't know what, but if he thinks we're going to pick up where we left off, he's mistaken. *That place wasn't so great, from what I remember.*

"I'll make breakfast," I call over my shoulder.

"Just gonna run out and get my bag," he yells before the door closes.

I roll my eyes as one of the twins fusses at the noise. Then force my shoulders lower.

A minute later I hear the door again. Sacha goes nuts, barking and bouncing with enthusiasm as she bolts toward the front door. You'd think Zane's been gone weeks, not less than a minute.

I turn, my mouth gaping.

Zane stands in the doorway, a leash in his hand. On the other end is a too-skinny red Doberman, doing a good impersonation of a wriggly worm, while Sacha gives them a good sniff.

"Meet Garth," Zane says, a small smile curving his lips.

"Garth?" I ask with way less enthusiasm than my dog.

I tell Sacha to settle, then kneel down and scratch the newcomer's ears, while attempting to dodge his inquisitive tongue. "Tell me you've taken up dog walking as a side hustle, Zane."

"Not quite. Met Garth and his owner on the beach yesterday while walking Sacha. He's being deployed overseas and his wife said the dog had to go. He's well trained. Garth, that is."

"I see that." I smile as Garth licks my face while Sacha noses in. "But we have a dog, remember? And two kids. And a just-over-a-thousand-square-foot house."

I silence the voice in my head reminding me I'm still in possession of four thousand feet of ocean-front property in

Malibu. I like my little house. It doesn't have a frickin' cliff for the kids to plummet off.

Zane kneels down next to me, and Garth lies between us. "The guy was desperate, and Sacha and Garth hit it off within seconds. I couldn't say no."

Sacha lies almost on top of the poor guy, but he doesn't seem to mind. "You're a softie, Zane Brody, but you stink. Go shower. I'll take care of him."

A half-empty bag of discount dog food sits by the door along with a dog bed. Sacha investigates the strange dog bed while I find a couple of bowls suitable for dog food and water. Then rummage through the fridge for something equally suitable for the picky man in my house to eat.

I take my time mixing up a batch of pancake mix, while thinking through all the positives and negatives Zane's presence creates. The possibility of shaving both legs at once overrides any negatives I can come up with.

Both Garth and Sacha hang by the stove, noses twitching, while the smell of bacon drifts through the air. I can't help but smile at the happy pair.

Zane wanders back into the kitchen as I'm done flipping the last batch of berry pancakes. I pull the rest out of the oven and set everything on the table. Zane peeks over my shoulder as I grab the orange juice out of the fridge.

"You actually have healthy food in here. Where's your beloved pop? Your pudding packs?" His minty breath wafts across my neck, causing all the hairs on my body to stand at attention.

I'm frozen in place, his body heat soaking into my back, his clean-man scent making my head spin. "I... uh... Did you use my toothbrush?"

Out of the corner of my eye, his grin is off the charts. "Brought my own. How can I help?"

I turn and look up, taking in the dark shadows under his eyes, the hollows of his cheeks. Zane was always lean, but at the moment I can count every one of his ribs.

A trickle of water runs down his temple. I watch its progress down the side of his face, over his freshly shaven jaw where it hangs suspended. Despite the stress the past year has taken on him, he's still beautiful. Maybe more so.

The impulse to kiss him is almost too strong to resist. But one kiss would lead to two. Then three. Then he'd strip me of the little clothes I'm wearing and I the same of him. And then—

No.

I grab the orange juice and duck under his arm, while giving myself space to calm my racing heart and will away the heat in my cheeks that are a dead giveaway to the direction of my thoughts.

Grabbing two glasses from the cabinet, I set them on the table, filling each one with juice. "Hope you're okay with orange juice. If you'd given me a heads up, I'd have bought almond milk. But, I guess you and Jackson wanted to ambush me."

He takes a chair, folding his arms over his chest. "Tell me about Jackson."

His voice is casual, but his intent is crystal clear. *Who is this man who has filled in while I was gone?*

"Jackson's a friend." I take a sip of my juice. It's not a lie. At least after last night it isn't.

"Don't insult my intelligence, Faith," he says, his voice low with warning. "I want the truth. No more secrets."

I tip my chin up. "That goes both ways."

"Agreed."

I nod my head. "Fine. I met Jackson last September, the same day my doctor confirmed I was pregnant with twins…" I tell him everything. That first dinner at Jackson's, the kiss on my balcony, the visit to his mother's, Lamaze classes, and the twins' birth. "He lives in the condos a couple blocks down the street, but then you know that, I assume," I finish.

"What I don't know is your feelings toward him."

Something inside me bristles at Zane's tone, but I ignore it and go on. "He was there for me when I had no one else. He's a good man. He's seen my highs and lows. He made me laugh and handed me tissues when I cried."

"I agree, he's a good man." Zane's eyes shift toward the living room, where Kayla is yelling at her brother. "Called me from the hospital. Told me about the twins. Don't know if you knew that."

Dammit, Jackson. I answer with a shake of my head, doing my best not to scowl.

Zane's blue eyes blaze. "I'll be forever grateful to him for that, and for setting this up. But I'm not giving him the keys to my kingdom."

"I think last night made it clear he doesn't want *your kingdom*," I say with more bitterness than intended.

Zane's eyes sharpen. He misses nothing. "Do you want him to have this kingdom? Because I sense that if I fuck this up he'll be waiting in the wings."

"His mother hates me. She wants him to marry someone—"

"And my mother expected me to move back to New York after she died—"

"You did, Zane. You moved back with your *girlfriend*." I spit out the word like venom.

"She wasn't my girlfriend anymore." His chair screeches on the tile floor as he stands.

I stand as well, rushing around the table and poking a finger into his chest. "Did you share a bedroom? Did you two have one last fuck before she moved out?"

"No. I've been faithful to *you* since the day we met. Can you say the same?"

My silence speaks volumes.

Zane blows out a heavy breath, his eyes closed, his jaw hard. "You made a nice dinner last night, but you didn't know I was coming. That chicken you put in the fridge certainly wasn't for me. Neither was the makeup and perfume you were wearing. Unless that was for the kids."

His voice drips with sarcasm.

I blow out my own calming breath. "You left me, Zane. No note, no phone call. What was I supposed to think?" I swallow the lump in my throat, watching the darkness shadow Zane's eyes. "Jackson and I... we had a moment. It... it might have turned into more than a moment, but circumstances conspired against us."

"I see." Zane rubs his eyes and turns away stiffly.

"You're angry?"

"Of course I'm angry! You had a *moment* with another man. I don't even know what the fuck that is, but if *circumstances* stop conspiring against you, then what?"

"They won't." Kayla lets out a shriek, letting me know she doesn't appreciate my tone.

"Are you sure?"

Our daughter's frustrations reach a peak and I head into the living room, grateful for once for her interruption. I hand her her favorite rattle, but she's so worked up she tosses it back at me, almost hitting her unaware brother who's happily gurgling to his stuffed bunny.

I scoop Kayla up, but Zane takes our wailing daughter from me.

"I'm sure." I spit out the answer to his question. "You should be proud of my restraint. I was celibate for seven months. Seven months with a willing man waiting for me to say yes, and my pregnancy hormones begging me to make a move. There were so many times I wanted to, but every damn time I thought of you."

Zane's eyes shine with unshed tears as he presses his lips to his daughter's head while rocking her against his chest. Her ear-splitting shrieks settle down to the occasional whimper.

"You thought of me?" he asks, his voice hoarse.

I sigh like a leaky balloon. "All the time, you stupid man."

He looks so perfect holding his daughter. She nuzzles her

head into his neck and coos. This *should* be perfect. Maybe someday it'll be. It's a chance I have to take.

"You're right. Last night's dinner was for Jackson. I had given up on you. Decided it was time to move on. Then you show up and… and… *God, Zane.* I love Jackson. He's good and kind, and he's been here for me. But I was *in* love with you, and I know the difference."

Kayla's attention shifts toward my voice, her eyes wide, her bottom lip trembling. I pull her from Zane and give her the reassurance she needs.

"*Was* in love?" Zane's expression is almost as despondent as his daughter's.

"Up until the day of your mother's funeral I never thought you… I trusted you." I shake my head, the pain of that day fresh again. "After everything, I trusted you. I had to find out you had left from your sister. Do you know how that felt? I don't think you could have hurt me more if you'd used your fists."

Zane flinches with that last harsh statement, but it's true. Bruises fade and bones heal, but heartbreak lasts forever.

I set Kayla back in her playpen, before the growing tension in my body sets off her alarms again. Then wrap my empty arms around myself, sending Zane a look that summarizes all the pain and insecurity that surrounds me, and give him the honesty that's written in my heart. "I want to trust you, for myself, for them, but what happens when the next crisis comes around? What will I tell our children when their daddy disappears?" *Inside a bottle*, I silently add.

He pulls me into his arms, and despite the warning voice in my head, I can't help but relax into his steady embrace. "I'm so sorry, Faith. I fucked up. The mess I made of my mother's funeral, the way I treated you. Drunk or not, I have no excuse for any of it. And I left because I needed to fix myself before I could be worthy of you."

"Okay." I pull away, because being this close to Zane isn't good for my self-preservation.

"The first night in New York, I attended an AA meeting. I've been going ever since. Don't think I could have made it through the past year without my sponsor, because honestly, the urge to drown myself in a bottle was so fucking tempting.

"Last night, I went to my first AA meeting here in LA. I'm an alcoholic, Faith. Always will be, and I can't guarantee I won't fuck up ever again, because forever is a long time, and there's no guarantees in life. But I'm committed to staying sober for myself, and you and the kids."

"I can't give you guarantees either, but for the kids I'm willing to try. Because they deserve to have a father. As for me..." I shake my head. Do I want to give Zane another chance? "I don't know. I need time."

He gives me a small smile. "All I've got is time."

This would be so much easier if he wasn't so damn sexy. Standing there in worn jeans that hang off his hips, exposing the hard muscles at his waist and that trail of dark hair that leads to—

No, no, no.

Keeping Zane Brody at arm's length will be torture. My body is throbbingly aware of the fact I haven't had sex in almost a year. Zee's sound asleep and Kayla isn't far from dreamland herself. It would be so easy to drag Zane off to my bedroom right now. But am I ready for what comes after?

Zane steps back as if hearing my thoughts. "According to Laura, the best gift you can give a new mother is time to shower. So go. I'll keep an eye on these two and clean up the kitchen."

I don't have to be told twice. I walk away, looking forward to hot water, freshly shaven legs, and clean hair. *And maybe a little one-on-one time with my shower head?*

"Don't put her too close to Zee. She hits him with her rattle."

Zane smiles, sending a ripple of awareness to places already too aware of him. "Zee? Got it."

"And he had a big breakfast. I'm expecting imminent destruction of that diaper," I add taking another step toward the bathroom.

"Destruction. Got it."

"And—"

Zane's on me in a flash, his hands turning me toward the bathroom door. "Faith, I've got it. Relax. Unless aliens invade or the sun burns out, I've got this covered."

CHAPTER FORTY-THREE

ZANE

*I*n the past three months I've learned a few things about California. It's expensive as hell. Jobs are hard to come by. Sunshine every fucking day.

What I wouldn't give for a nice thunderstorm. Or snow. Who knew I'd miss shoveling a driveway?

Today I'm not minding the weather. After our usual walk on the beach, me, the twins, and the dogs are spending some quality time on the back patio as usual.

A couple of weeks after showing up here, Faith offered me her spare room. It's small. Barely room for a twin bed and my collection of musical instruments, but I'm not complaining. The alternative, a hostel that was almost an hour's drive away, had eaten a good chunk of my minuscule savings in the two weeks I'd stayed there after leaving Jackson's spare room.

Sacha shoves her wet nose into my face while I attempt to settle Kayla on her freshly diapered butt in her playpen with an assortment of toys that are destined to be on the stone pad outside the pen at some point, and in one of the dogs' mouths even faster.

Garth gives my daughter an impatient woof while waiting for

the first volley. Kayla's laugh puts a smile on my face. It's their favorite game, that keeps me busy chasing the dogs, and washing dog drool off toys until my little princess gets bored or falls asleep.

Zee babbles to his stuffed rabbit he calls Raaah—right now everything is raaah to him—from the second playpen.

I settle down on my lounge chair and grab my guitar, giving it an experimental strum. I can't even remember the last time I took my acoustic out of its case. Sometime last summer before the world turned to shit?

Being arrested silenced the constant soundtrack of notes and bits of lyrics that have always played in my head. Or maybe it was losing Faith.

Until this morning my head had been empty. But then I woke today to a new song begging to be set free.

A breeze flutters the petals of the bougainvillea clinging to the pergola above my head, sending its sweet perfume into the warm September air. Some kind of bright yellow bird flits from branch to branch in a nearby tree, singing a pretty song.

Kayla squeals as I pluck at low E while turning the peg. A year in the guitar case has done nothing for the tuning of this instrument. *Have to give the others some attention later.*

Zee chimes with his own sweet squeal by the time I get to the G string, and I'm serenaded by both of them through the last two strings.

"You want to sing along?" I ask, then strum a few chords from the song that's been aching to come out since the early hours of the morning. The dogs plop down in the shade, their game of chase-the-toys temporarily on hold.

One-handed, I pull up my recorder app while strumming a simple tune with the other. Pausing to jot down the notes isn't an option with my adoring audience cheering me on, and the music rushes out of me as if some dam of creativity has broken inside me.

My phone rings. *Jackson.* I mouth out a silent curse, because innocent ears are listening. The guy has the worst timing, but chances are if I don't answer his call, he'll be waltzing through the back gate and then nothing will get done.

"Don't you ever work?" I ask in lieu of a greeting.

"I am. Right now. Listen..." he instructs, and then the distinct clickety-clack of fingers hitting keys fills my ear.

"Hear that? I just added a line of code instructing this game to block anyone named Zane Brody from access."

"I'm hurt," I say, my voice as flat as my enthusiasm to converse with Jackson. Three months and I haven't decided whether I like him or not. He's obviously in love with Faith, which puts him in the *not* column, but then he did call me. Chances are I'd still be in Minneapolis if it were up to Faith, completely unaware of being a father to these two amazing kids. So, maybe I owe him one.

Kayla shrieks, clearly not happy with the sudden loss of entertainment.

"Did you want something? My children are requesting my attention."

"We're going out tonight." He says as if there's no debate.

"We?" I make a face Zee finds hilarious, so I make another. I live for these two. Twenty-four, seven. Why the hell would I want to go out?

"You, me, and my friends Izzy and Ryan."

I've met his friends. They're... okay.

"I don't know. I'm not really the going-out type." At least I'm not anymore. Last week was my one-year anniversary being sober. Not the time to hit the bars. Not that there ever will be a time for me. And leaving Faith to take care of the twins after she's worked all day doesn't sit well.

"Fuck man, you need to get out before you start lactating. Cut loose with the guys. Have fun. Listen, man to man? Faith sounded like she needed some alone time. Feel me?"

Another thing that doesn't sit right? That he ran this past Faith before calling me.

The next second Kayla's yellow bunny—a twin to her brother's blue one—goes sailing out of the playpen. Garth gets to it first and bolts out into the yard, Sacha hot on his tail.

"Shit. Hang on," I tell Jackson, because I know the guy won't drop the subject. Then take off after the dogs with a curse. As much as Kayla likes to watch the dogs steal her toys, she'll be inconsolable if they tear Bunny apart. Which is guaranteed if they start fighting over it.

I shout a warning for Garth to drop Bunny, and another to Sacha to leave it. Jackson's laugh bursts from my phone, which is still in my hand for some reason.

I give Bunny a quick inspection, finding no rips and minimal amount of drool, then drop the thing back into Kayla's playpen with a warning shake of my finger. My daughter giggles, then tosses a sparkly unicorn her Uncle Bret got from who knows where. Someplace expensive. Before it hits the deck, I scoop it up and set it next to me. Kayla's bottom lip juts out in adorable outrage a second before Garth distracts her with a slobbery kiss.

I'm ready with a wet towel, because we've been here enough to know the drill.

"Back," I inform Jackson.

"If you're worried about us getting drunk, don't. Ryan is one of those my-body-is-a-temple health nuts. Kinda like you, come to think of it. And, back in college, Iz got blind-drunk once, vomited his guts out, and hasn't touched alcohol since. None of us have been wild men since we were undergrads."

I laugh. "You're really selling this, Jackson."

"Not saying we're not fun. We're definitely fun. Just a more mature fun, if you get me?"

Kayla's outrage spills over. Her little face collapses and next thing I know she's wailing. Which of course sets Zee off.

"Fine. I'll go. Text me the details," I say just to get him off my back, then hang up so I can deal with the twins.

AN UBER DROPS us off in front of a nondescript building with the name Sapphire Club written in cursive above the door. It's the third place on our tour of amusing LA hangouts. Previously we experienced After Dark Bowling. Black lights, neon-colored balls, and stinky shoes. After that we headed to Koreatown, where I discovered my tolerance for spicy food. Or should I say intolerance. My tongue is still smoldering.

Sapphire Club is dark, with a strong scent of spilled beer and liberally applied perfume. Black pleather booths, sticky chrome and formica tables, textured walls the color puke. Reminds me of the dive bar me and the band used to play at before we upgraded to Mill City.

The place is packed. Guys with too many muscles to have been grown naturally. Women with too much makeup and not enough clothes. It's a theme I'm finding common in Los Angeles.

A woman's singing at the front of the room, belting out some pop song like her life depends on it. My gaze shifts to a large flat screen displaying the lyrics and it hits me. We're in a fucking karaoke bar.

"Seriously, Jackson?" My voice displays the full range of my lack of enthusiasm.

A few eyes follow us as we claim the only open table, a rectangular, bar-height, six top in the back of the place. A table of women seated near us stare, whispering to each other. If there's anything I've learned tonight, it's the women of this town aren't shy about letting a guy know what they're thinking.

Izzy swaggers over to the women's table, while Jackson heads to the bar to place our drinks order. It's another theme—Jackson and his friends paying for everything. It's not sitting well.

I need a job beyond taking care of my kids while Faith is at work. But doing what? My skills are limited. Music and bartending. Pretty sure my AA sponsor would have plenty to say about the latter career option, and the former? Last time I looked classically trained musicians weren't in high demand.

Jackson passes out drinks—soda water with a twist of lime all around. Then takes off across the room. He and some guy with the clipboard greet each other like old friends, shaking hands and patting each other on the back.

The pop song ends, then a guy takes the stage, does his best with a Rolling Stone classic. After him a woman pretends she's Britney Spears. I'm no stranger to bad performers. Hell, me and the guys were one of them at one time.

Talk of Ryan's wedding distracts from the next few performers. Details about tuxes and cake and a honeymoon on some remote island in south Pacific. Maybe Tahiti? My mind wanders to where I'd take Faith if I had the money and we didn't have two babies and two dogs at home. Someplace warm. Someplace quiet. Someplace I'd get her in a bikini again. Then remove it.

"Brody," Jackson calls out, and not for the first time if I'm reading the way everyone's looking at me correctly.

"What?"

Ryan grins and points to the stage, his meaning clear.

"What? No," I growl with a firm shake of my head.

"Come on, Zane," Jackson says. "Show us what you've got."

"No way." I shake my head. "I don't do karaoke."

Izzy shouts, "Zane, Zane, Zane…"

Next thing I know the table of women join in. Soon the whole place is chanting my name. *Shit.*

"You're so fucking dead." I pin Jackson with my finger and a stare that promises retaliation.

He gives me his crazy-assed laugh. *Asshole.*

The guy at the machine, the one who Jackson was talking to earlier, calls me over. "What ya singing?"

What the fuck *am* I singing?

I STEP off the stage to enough applause to the quell the embarrassment. I've gone from headlining county fairs to karaoke. If Aaron or Dave witnessed my downfall, I'd probably crawl in a hole and never leave.

The women at the next table cheer as I walk by, and shortly after I return to the table a drink is set in front of me. A gift from one of the women, the waitress informs. *Johnnie Walker Blue.* Expensive. The amber liquid taunts, and I can almost smell the alcohol. Taste it on my tongue. Feel the burn down my throat. Jackson's eyes narrow for a second until I slide the beverage to the center of our table. Ryan grabs the whiskey and returns it to the table of women. One of them calls out an apology, which I wave off.

Moments later, a few guys walk in. They stand out in this white-collar bar. Dark jeans, leather jackets, chains. Rough looking.

The bar quiets, all eyes on the newcomers. *Bikers maybe?* Although what they're doing at a karaoke bar is a mystery.

Even the poor sucker on stage gives up singing—although that might be a blessing. Quiet murmurs break out as the men walk across the room. The tall guy with blond-tipped spiked hair does some kind of secret handshake-type thing with the manager.

"What the hell…" I start to ask, but then take in Jackson's suspicious smirk.

"Zane Brody?" Spiked Hair asks from the end of our table. Everyone looks at me and points.

I give Jackson a hard stare and then turn my attention to this stranger. "Yeah?"

"You sang earlier?"

"Yeah?" I repeat.

The guy moves closer, leaning an arm on the table next to me.

"Franklin Marks—everyone calls me Lin—lead guitar, Faithful." He holds out his hand and I take it. He points over his shoulder at the guy who might or might not have tattooed eyeliner under his eyes. "That's Nic Crosby, the band's drummer. Jones over there said you might be what we're looking for. We lost our lead singer a couple weeks back. Car accident, God rest his soul." He pauses, looking down as if offering a prayer for his bandmate. Then pulls out his wallet and hands me a card. "Call this number. Let's set up something. I want to hear you. If you don't do drugs or fuck around too much, we might be a good fit."

He leaves before I can say anything. The karaoke starts back up and the bar goes back to normal.

"Who the hell was that?" I ask the table at large.

Jackson laughs his stupid laugh. "Need to get out more, Brody. That was Lin Marks of Faithful. Their songs are on the radio all the time."

Ryan adds, "My sister knows them. Says they're going to be huge."

Ryan and Jackson exchange a grimace. Faith mentioned something once about Ryan's sister and Jackson, but I can't remember the details. Not that it's any of my business. Instead, I stare down at the card in my hand. Jack Cameron, Manager. Faithful.

CHAPTER FORTY-FOUR

ZANE

I get a job handing out shoes at the bowling alley Jackson and his friends took me to a month ago. It's not much. Minimum wage. Shitty hours. The stink of rental shoes permeating my clothes. But it's money, so I'm not complaining. Much.

I get home at three in the morning, shower, then crash for a couple of hours until I hear Faith getting ready for her day. But tonight she's still up with the twins.

Some kind of cold virus has been circulating through the school where she works for weeks. Stuffy head, sore throat, a cough that seems to only come around when you're desperate for sleep. Faith brought it home maybe ten days ago. Then I got it. Two days ago Kayla and Zee came down with it. Which sucks.

I peek my head around the nursery doorway. Faith's seated in the rocking chair, Zee in her arms. "I'm gonna take a quick shower, then I can take over."

My son lets out a pitiful cough that makes me want to scoop him out of Faith's arms and cuddle him. But there was a problem with lane six's return and our maintenance guy, Tony, was out. That left me to tinker with the damn thing while consulting an ancient manual Marco found in the back room. Don't ask me why Marco didn't work on it. Dude doesn't do anything around there, as far as I can tell. But, whatever, I'm filthy.

"Thanks," she whispers back, the exhaustion obvious in her voice as well as the glazed stare she gives me.

I'm out of the shower before the water reaches a comfortable temperature. Fucking ancient water heater. *Gotta call the plumber later.*

I towel off and throw on an old T-shirt and the pair of sweats that make Faith blush. Not because I like her blushes, but because they're the first thing I grabbed. Although I do like when she blushes. It gives me hope she's warming up to me.

When I get back to the nursery, Zee's conked out in his crib. I follow the sound of coughing out into the living room where I find Faith swaying on her feet, our daughter in her arms.

"Give her to me and get to bed. I got this," I assure her while scooping Kayla into my arms. Her chubby cheeks are all rosy from the damn fever.

I sing the silly octopus song she loves. *"I got eight hands to wave hello. Hello, Kayla. Daddy's got you."* She gives me a weak smile that just about breaks my heart.

"She had the cough medicine before bed and I just gave her ibuprofen. She should sleep soon." Instead of heading off to bed like I instructed, Faith curls up on the corner of the couch and watches me for a moment, her thumbnail between her teeth. "You think we should call the doctor again?"

I got eight arms to hold you tight. Kayla's fingers pat my cheek as I give her a gentle hug.

If only I knew what to do to make her feel better. Unlike the ball return at work, kids don't come with manuals. "I can call them later, but I think her cough is sounding better."

With this, Kayla lets out with a cough that sounds a lot like one of those harbor seals that frequent the beach. Faith winces.

"I'm calling in sick. There's no way I can concentrate at work when they're sick."

I got forty fingers to tickle your belly. Kayla's eyes drift closed, and I wisely refrain from the actual tickling that usually accompanies this verse.

I finish the song and go on to another one about five frogs jumping into a pond one by one until there's none.

"If it'll make you feel better to stay home, go ahead. But I got things covered here. Look, she's asleep."

"Give her a few more minutes before laying her down, just to be sure."

"That's the plan. But you can head off now."

The thumb is back between her teeth. "Can we talk first?"

A fist of dread hits me in the gut. "Of course."

"Jackson got a call from Lin Marks. He was wondering if you had any intention of calling Jack Cameron. You know, Faithful's manager?"

The dread recedes a bit. At least she's not asking me to leave. Which I know is unlikely, but still. "I know the guy, and no. I don't plan on calling him."

"Why?"

I let out a quiet chuckle. "Because I'm happy here."

She gives me a skeptical look. "You're happy at the bowling alley?"

"I have an interview at Hot Beans tomorrow. I'm hopefully trading the scent of bowling shoes for coffee."

"Zane..."

"Faith... I'm putting this conversation and Kayla to bed now."

Faith follows me out of the room and down the hall. "You're too talented to be wasting your time brewing coffee."

"You sound like my mother." The words come out sharper than intended. Kayla gives a little sound of disapproval but doesn't stir.

The hum of the humidifier and the scent of menthol

surrounds me the minute I step foot in the nursery. With the first sniffle, I was on the phone with my sister getting her sage advice on how to deal with a sick baby. If only she was here. I miss her so much. And to be honest, Faith and I'd feel more confident at the moment if we had Laura's assurances every few minutes.

I set Kayla down in her crib, now propped up with a book under each leg at the head to help with drainage. Also a suggestion from Laura. Then drag the light blanket up to my daughter's chin. The rosiness of her cheeks has dimmed to a more healthy pink, and the heavy cloak of worry has diminished a fraction.

"You shouldn't waste this opportunity, Zane Brody," Faith starts as soon as I close the nursery door to keep the hounds out.

There's barely an inch between us in this narrow hall. Faith smells of Vicks vapor rub, baby lotion, and her flowery shampoo. The combination shouldn't be sexy, but it is.

We've been in this position a million times in the last four months. Standing outside the nursery door, discussing whatever. It's a comforting ritual, but tonight something's different. Maybe it's the anxiety of sick kids or the frustration of work, or just living with a woman I desire more than my next breath for a third of a year without being able to touch her the way I want to.

"You're right," I say just before slipping my hand around the nape of her neck and kissing her the way I've been dreaming about every night since I moved here.

Her body goes rigid for a second, and I'm second-guessing this move. Maybe I misjudged all the time I've seen her gaze lingering on me. Maybe I misjudged her blushes. Maybe—

Before I can think of another thing, her body softens, her hands slide in my damp hair, her fingers tugging at the long strands in a familiar way I'd almost forgotten.

"Is this okay?" I ask, dragging my knuckles across the peaks of her hardened nipples.

"God, yes. Zane…"

"Shhh." I press my finger against her lips and take her hand and tow her into her bedroom.

Sacha and Garth look up from their spots on the big queen-sized bed. There's something very wrong that these two have a place in Faith's bed, but not me.

"Out," I say, pointing my finger toward the hall in case they don't understand. Both of them comply, but Sacha gives me a narrow look, letting me know she isn't pleased with the arrangement.

Too bad.

CHAPTER FORTY-FIVE

FAITH

Zane turns his attention away from the retreating dogs, and I get the full force of the desire blazing in his blue gaze. My stomach drops to my feet with an equal mixture of want and fear. I can't count how many times I've been tempted to drag him into my room over the past months, but something undefinable always stopped me.

I slip my hand under the soft fabric covering his chest as he steps closer, letting my fingers form to his hard pectoral.

"Don't think I've forgotten our conversation out there, Mr. Brody." I can't forget. Not if I'm going to convince him that he's more than a bowling alley employee or a barista.

His left hand covers mine while the right closes around the tie of my robe, giving it a firm tug. "Wouldn't dream of it."

"Wait. I have something else I need to say." I grasp the lapels with my free hand, holding the robe closed with a death grip. Underneath, is a horror show of stretch marks and doughy muscles and the damn ten pounds I can't seem to get rid of no matter how hard I try.

He slips his fingers around my wrist. "If this is too soon, if you're not ready…"

I'm not sure if I want to laugh or cry. I've been ready to have Zane in my bed for months. Needing him. But what if he's not ready for this new me? What if he looks at me with disappointment? Or worse. Pity.

And what if I'm just as stretched out on the inside as I am on the outside, and the sex is so bad he never wants to touch me again?

"No. It's just…" I hate this all-too-familiar feeling of self-consciousness. It was my constant companion back when I was married to Grayson and the number on the scale decided whether I was going to have a good day or bad.

But Zane isn't Grayson, and over the past few months he's earned my trust. Dealing with my postpartum moods, exploding diapers, Jackson's meddling, faithfully attending his AA meetings.

He sits on the edge of my bed and pulls me into his lap. His warm hand strokes up and down my back, a balm to my frazzled nerves. "Tell me what's going on in that beautiful head of yours."

"It's nothing. Stupid, really." Before he can voice the rebuttal I can see forming on his lips, I continue. "You'll probably laugh."

"If it matters to you, I won't laugh. Promise."

I let out a tired sigh. "Part of me is tempted to turn off the lights for this. This…" I wave my hand up and down my body like I'm a gameshow model presenting a shiny new car or an all-expense-paid trip to Hawaii. "Isn't sexy anymore."

His lips twitch as if he's restraining a laugh. "I beg to differ."

I do laugh. "You've yet to see all of me. I don't look like I did back in Minneapolis. I may never wear a bikini again."

He traces a finger down my cheek, his gaze so full of love I'd fall if I was standing. Who am I kidding? I've already fallen.

"Good. I'd have to beat all those men who watch you on the beach off with a stick."

I scoff at his words. "What men? No men are watching me on the beach."

"Once again, I beg to differ, but may I?" He holds the tie for my robe loose in his hand, waiting for my permission.

I nod my answer, then tell him, "Yes," because whatever doubts I have are all in my head.

He nudges my ass with his hands. "Stand up, Angel."

I smile at the nickname he gave me so long ago when we were both different people. I may be the one using a different name, but Zane has changed over the past fifteen months as well.

I stand and he follows me. Then the slipknot slowly comes undone, and my robe falls open. Zane slides his hands inside, parting the soft pink fabric until it slides off my shoulder.

Oh, hells bells. I never would have chosen my ugliest nursing bra or the stretched-out panties this morning if I'd known Zane was going to be viewing me in them.

Zane sucks in a sharp breath that might be from shock. "Damn, woman."

"I have prettier underwear. Why don't you close your eyes and forget what you're seeing while I go change," I babble on, a nervous chuckle making my voice vibrate.

He cradles my face in his hands and kisses me into welcome silence. I'd way prefer to be kissing Zane than thinking about what I'm wearing.

"I think I've died and gone to heaven," he mutters against my lips, then dives back in for another kiss that has my head spinning and my core clenching.

He touches me everywhere, skating his fingers along my soft belly, molding his hands around my hips, my breasts, pressing between my legs, making me cry out, soft and quiet so as not to disturb the twins.

His free hand skates up my back, to the clasp on my bra. *Good luck, buddy.* I swear those four little hooks on this industrial-strength bra were made by the devil himself. Zane struggles for a moment, then mumbles a curse.

"Problem?" I ask with all the innocence I can muster.

He grips my shoulders and turns me around. "Nothing I can't handle."

After a brief struggle, the cups go slack. Then the bra falls to the floor on top of my robe, and Zane reaches around to cup my breasts in his warm hands.

"Oh shit," I whisper-shout. There's a tell-tale tingle and then I'm leaking everywhere.

"Oh wow." Zane's voice is full of surprise.

"Yeah, they do that." More so since Zee and Kayla aren't keen on nursing with their stuffy nose. "Let me clean up."

"Not so fast."

I turn to leave, but Zane grabs my hand guiding me back toward the bed. He sits, pulling me into the space between his spread legs. Whatever disaster this night has become, it hasn't extinguished Zane's interest in the least.

We both stare down at his erection pulsing against the front of his sweatpants, before he grips himself in his hand. "See what you do to me, Faith Asher."

Then, before I can respond, his mouth closes over a nipple and the struggle between want and embarrassment is over. The tickle of his evening beard, the warmth of his lips, it shouldn't feel so good, but fuck it does.

"Oh God, Zane. Harder." I dig my fingers into his scalp, holding him against me. My legs tremble, and my core spasms with every pull.

I barely register his fingers hooking the sides of my underwear or the slide of the fabric down my legs.

I'm an absolute mess, but I don't care at this moment. Maybe later, but not now.

Zane releases my breast with an audible pop, just long enough to slide the waistband of his sweats just far enough to release him. *Oh hi, friend.*

"Condom?" he asks.

I shake my head. "Doctor said I can't get pregnant while nursing." At least I hope so. I'm not ready to do this again so soon.

Zane scoots back further on the bed, guiding me over him, positioning me. The hot head of his cock nudges at my entrance. He closes his hands around my hips, urging me down one inch at a time until there's no where left to go.

"Oh my God, you feel..." How he feels is beyond words. *Amazing* comes close, but not even.

"Yeah. Completely—" His voice breaks off with a groan as I rise up and make a slow descent back down his shaft.

"Glorious?" I finish for him.

"Very. Fuck, yeah. Just like that."

He lies back against the mattress, taking me down with him. My dark hair curtains the two of us in this private world as we slowly reacquaint ourselves with each other. Those beautiful eyes of his lock onto mine as he takes me over the edge, and then I watch a moment later as he comes apart beneath me.

Breathless and sticky with sweat and a whole lot of other things, I sink into the circle of Zane's strong arms. We both need a shower, and the sheets need a change, but for the moment I'm too tired to move. And too happy to end this perfect moment.

"I love you, Zane Brody," I whisper into his ear, a secret between the two of us for tonight.

"I love you, Faith Asher. Until my dying breath."

ZANE WARMS the sheets next to me. The room goes from pitch-dark to the filtered-gray that tells me the alarm is about to go off. Or it would be if I hadn't shut the thing off a few minutes ago. I've been up longer than that, though. Listening to Zane's steady breaths. Feeling his skin press against mine. Counting my blessings.

I have many. Zee and Kayla. Zane. Jackson and all the friends

I've made since moving back. Even Grayson in a strange way. If I hadn't married him I never would have ended up in Minneapolis or met Zane.

A bird composes a pretty song in the tree outside my bedroom window, just like it does every morning before the sun rises. Inside it's quiet. Not even a peep from the nursery monitor sitting on my dresser.

I send out a silent wish for peace to wherever Grayson's spirit has gone. Stupid maybe, but the one thing I learned from my time in therapy is to let go of the resentment. *Forgiveness is a gift to yourself.*

Zane's breathing changes tempo, letting me know he'll be awake soon. A smile pulls at my lips at the thought of all the little familiar things I missed over the past year. The scent of his skin on my sheets, the weight of his body pressing into the mattress, the way he reaches out for me the second he wakes as if to make sure I'm still here.

"I've been thinking..." I start, my voice quiet. A nervous flutter in my stomach begs me to wait to disturb the peace inside our little cocoon a little longer, but experience tells me the twins will be awake soon.

"I've been thinking too," Zane responds, his voice gravely from sleep. "But you first."

"Do you think fate's telling you something? My name's Faith, and this band's name is Faithful."

He chuckles. "I thought that when Aaron told me your name. Lyric, and me being a songwriter. But..."

"Hypothetically, if you were to become a member of Faithful—" Zane grumbles, but I turn and shush him with a hand over his mouth, and then continue, "Just listen. I know what you're going to say. You don't want to leave the kids—"

"Or you."

"Or me," I concede with a happy grin. "But what if we could do this together?"

"This isn't Heartattack. These guys are on the road for weeks. You'd have to quit your job."

"Not the worst thing in the world." I'm definitely not cut out for a classroom of entitled third graders. Or the snobby staff at Burkwood Academy. "You know, me and my mom used to meet my dad on tour whenever we could." Zane's quiet, so I continue. "It was a wonderful experience."

Zane hums with skepticism.

"Of course, we'd be careful. Keep them separate from anything objectionable." I sit up and stare down at Zane. "We could buy a motorhome or one of those fancy motor coaches. Customize it for the kids. A king-sized bed in the back for us."

Zane rises next to me. "Marry me."

My eyes widen. "What?"

"Marry me," he repeats, then holds up his pointer finger. "Wait here."

I frown as he bolts out of bed. Naked. Disappears out the bedroom door before I can appreciate the view of his backside.

A moment later he returns, and the view is even better. *No dad bod here, folks.*

Before I can catalogue his many assets, he pulls me out of bed. "Stand right there."

"Okay." I laugh until he drops to his knees in front of me. There's a tiny velvet box in his hand.

"Faith Ann Asher, you are my everything. You've given me direction when I was lost, value when I was worthless, hope when all around me was hopeless. I know your past gives you reason not to marry again, but if you give me a chance, I'll show you how a husband is supposed to love his wife. Yes or no, I'll plan on loving you until the end of my days, but will you do me the honor of being my wife?"

He opens the box and I gasp. The diamond ring inside is beautiful. Exquisite. A simple square stone in a white-gold setting. It had to have cost his entire savings. *Foolish, foolish man.*

"Are you asking me to be your band wife?" I paste on a big cheesy smile, 'cause I'm pushing it. For his own good, of course.

Zane chuckles. "*My* wife. The band can't have you."

"But you'll call?" *Poor Zane.* He probably imagined this proposal going a lot different. "Promise me you'll call."

"Fine. I'll call. Now back to us." He points at the ring as if reminding me.

I wiggle my ring finger in his face. "Yes, Zane Brody, I'll be your wife."

EPILOGUE

FAITH

"Come on, Zee," I shout over the chaos. "Your sister has to go."

"She always has to gooo," Zee whines, tugging on my hand. "Boys aren't supposed to go into girls' bathrooms."

"It's a family bathroom," I fib. There's no standard for backstage bathrooms. Sometimes there's separate genders, other times it's just one for all. I'm just hoping for clean. That's not a given.

Somehow we've seen them all. It's inevitable. Kayla needs to use the restroom before every show. Nerves.

"You're gonna make us miss Dad." Zee glares at Kayla. "If we miss Dad—"

Kayla sticks out her tongue at her brother. "The worm-up band is on now. We have time."

"It's *warm-up*, stupid. Not worm." Zee laughs, then sobers. "Do I have to go in?"

Not quite crowded, the dingy hall contains a few greasy looking roadies and a couple of bimbo girlfriends with more flesh on display than not. Not the kind of people you'd leave a five-year-old alone with. "Yes. And don't call your sister stupid.

The faster we get done, the faster we get back. You want to wish your dad luck, don't you?"

The first bathroom we reach has a stick figure with a skirt painted on the door. Zee gives me a stink-eye so like his father I almost laugh.

I may as well have been a vessel carrying his babies. My DNA's barely noticeable in these two. From their dark hair to their stunning blue eyes to the top-percent marks on the doctor's height charts, they're all Zane. The only thing missing is the slight dimple in Zane's squared off chin. They have my chin. After carrying them for nine months, I get chins.

I lock the door behind us. It's a six out of ten on the clean scale. Zee turns his back while I spray down the toilet with the small bottle of disinfectant that I always have in my purse.

"I can hear her peeing. Eww."

"Plug your ears, Znothead," Kayla yells.

"Kayla," I scold. Where she got that name I'll never know. A homeschool education on tour with a rock band is unconventional, to say the least.

After convincing Zane that family life on the road was possible, we negotiated hard with Jack Cameron and Faithful's recording label. They agreed to shorter tour schedules, private flights, and hotel rooms far from the rest of the band.

It didn't hurt that Lin Marks and his wife, Ann, had been expecting their first child back then, and sided with our demands.

Overnight, Faithful went from a tabloid sensation to, well, slightly less so. It's hard to take the sex and drugs out of rock and roll, but we've done our best to distance the children from most of the remaining band members' more outrageous activities. The custom tour bus, compliments of the Grayson Thorpe estate, with two master bedrooms, a communal kid's bunk room, and a comfortable, if small, lounge, is idyllic compared to the foul language, alcohol, cigarette smoke, nudity, and God knows what else goes on inside the other band members' bus.

Zane made it clear when he accepted the lead-singer spot. He was a package deal, and family came first.

What we didn't know was the trajectory of our life. Faster than his song "Rocket"—*Buckle up, baby/We're on a rocket to the stars*. Faithful had done all the hard work with Alex Barkley before his tragic death. Zane slipped in, and within a year the grieving process was over. Faithful went from opening act to headliner, to double-platinum record sales in the three years that followed.

We're back in the dressing room with plenty of time. The band's sprawled around the place, enjoying the moment of peace. Drummer Nic's scratching an enthusiastic Garth on the belly while Sacha waits her turn.

Zane's next to me in a heartbeat, his lips on mine, his fingers splayed across the backside of my leggings that are more rips and holes than fabric.

"You sure about this?" I whisper against his skin, keeping my insecurity between the two of us.

I've had a lot of those these past five years. Hiding behind this group isn't possible. I needed to find myself in this whirlwind that had become our life. First, writing children's books. Then, in the quiet hours between shows, I found myself jotting things down.

Funny things, serious things, unbelievably insane things. My life on the road. *Among the Faithful* was published last year. An instant bestseller, I found myself the focus for once. Interviews, magazine covers, TV appearances.

The woman behind the hottest guy in rock isn't the most enviable position. I learned that the hard way six years ago at a county fair. Fans can be vicious. They want their stars attainable. A wife and kids don't mesh with the fantasy most women picture when watching my husband on stage. How would they react to me, now in the spotlight with interviews on TV and radio, my face in bookstores and magazine racks?

Surprisingly, the highest-selling magazine cover, Woman's World, had Zane and I together. He stands behind me, his head down, his lips on my neck. His muscled and inked arm wrapped around my waist. But the focus is on me. Dressed in black leggings and a skin-baring top I'd never again wear in public, I stare straight into the camera. Either people were interested in what I had to say or the swarms of Faithful's female fans were using the cover as a dartboard.

"Sexy as fuck," he whispers back, his voice low enough the kids won't hear.

He'd think so. He picked out this revealing outfit, along with the four-inch heels that will probably have me falling flat on my face in a few minutes. "Too sexy. Maybe I've changed my mind."

I release a nervous laugh. "Good. So have I."

"We both have a reason to be scared." His eyes reflect his vulnerability. "But I need you."

"You have me." I give him a reassuring smile. Inside my gut, anxious butterflies are going crazy. But I promised.

After three national tours and two world tours, Faithful's fourth year skipping Minneapolis is starting to look as deliberate as it really is. The band's label said no more. They were willing to risk the possible protests that might occur from the false sexual-assault case filed against the band's lead singer almost seven years ago over shunning fans.

For me it's been like coming home. Meeting up with Grace and Aaron, and Zoe and her doctor husband, Rick.

At first the atmosphere between Zane and his once best friend was strained. But for me and Grace it had been all happy tears. After the tour we plan to get together at our Malibu home. Yes, we eventually moved into the house Grayson left me—with extensive renovations to make it family-friendly. After two years of trying to make my twelve-hundred-square-foot bungalow work, Zane and I admitted we needed more space, and the privacy and security required for a rock star.

I let out a nervous breath. The last time I was on stage I had just turned seventeen, and my father had been holding my hand. After my parents' fatal car crash and my marriage to Grayson, I'd never considered stepping on a stage again. But here I am, by Zane's request.

How could I say no when he wrote me a song. A beautiful song about love lost and found. A song about struggles and heartbreak. A song that begins with a thirty-second piano solo I'll be performing in just a few minutes. *Easy*, he said when he showed me the complicated piece of music that was anything but easy for this rusty musician.

"I love you," he says, pulling me onto the stage to the roar of the crowd. The floor shakes with the applause. And the lights… Jesus, were they always this hot?

My eyes focus on the cherry-red grand piano set center stage, and my heart thunders above the sound of forty thousand fans. Zane kisses my knuckles, his gaze steady on mine, giving me all the confidence I need.

Inhaling a slow and steadying breath, I take my seat at the flashy instrument and watch my husband head to the microphone to my left.

"Hello, Minneapolis," Zane shouts into the mic. "It's good to be home."

The fans go nuts. I look up, just enough to watch him. Dark jeans hug his ass. A dark T-shirt forms over his broad shoulders. Right now he belongs to the crowd. He fought this, but he belongs in the spotlight, connecting with his fans, the applause. He once said music must be shared, and he's right.

Before I know it he's done talking and gives me a nod. I shake out my trembling fingers and hit the first clear note. Everything else fades.

After a half minute Nic comes in on the drums and Kirk on

bass. Then Lin and Zane on guitars. These guys are professionals. A well-oiled machine. I'm thankful to be let in for a moment. To feel this magic.

Zane turns and smiles at me when the final note dies. As usual, he introduces the band. Then walks toward me, holding out his hand. "Folks, I'd like to introduce the most important person in my life. My wife, the talented Faith Brody. I want to thank her for entertaining my whim and playing tonight."

The crowd erupts in cheers and whistles, and for one brief moment I bask in the limelight, before Zane holds up a hand and the fans quiet.

"I'm so damn proud to have her next to me, and I want to share the news she gave me earlier today." He grins at me, and I nod my consent. Zane turns back to the mic and confides our secret with forty thousand fans, "I'm gonna be a father again."

The crowd goes crazy for a long minute, and when they quiet, he shouts, "Please give a round of applause to this amazing woman."

"Bow, Mrs. Brody," he commands. And I do.

Thank you for reading Secrets We Keep!

Loved it? Liked it? Hated it? You would have my undying gratitude if you took a minute to leave a short review on your preferred retailer's site.

Want to know more about my upcoming releases, including Jackson's story? I try my best to send out newsletters once a month or whenever I have something important to let my readers know about. Sign up here: darciannbaker.com

ACKNOWLEDGMENTS

Phew. What a journey, dear readers.

I started writing this book a few weeks after my family suffered an unexpected loss. Every morning I woke knowing exactly what to write. Every day. For three weeks. It was cathartic. This was the easiest story I've ever written and also the hardest.

I was damn proud of myself. In my opinion, it was the best thing I'd ever written! Only problem? Everyone hated it.

"I would call the police on this guy," one critique partner said of Zane after reading the first chapter. Ouch.

So I did what many new writers do. I wept. Then set it aside and finished Separation Game. Then started writing something else.

Two years later, I donned enough emotional armor to finally open the file on SWK. With new eyes, I could see it needed work. A lot of work.

To those who had the patience to stick with me while I whipped this story into shape, you have my endless thanks!

Dr. Mardelle Fourtier and my fellow writing students at the College of DuPage. Thank you for all your kind words of encouragement.

The awesome members of Chicago-North Romance Writers. It's impossible to express the gratitude I have for your support, resources, and friendships over the years. And for the brutally honest critique I wasn't quite ready to hear!

My fabulous editor, Lila. Thank you for loving this book as

much as I do. Once again, you made the whole editing process fun.

My husband for convincing me to accept that Zane would never do the one thing that was the key to the original dark moment in this book, even though that meant rewriting the whole second half of the book. Again. Thank you for listening to me read every chapter at least a hundred times over while assuring you that the one word I changed in that paragraph needed your opinion.

My son and daughter, for joining the school orchestra all the way back in fifth grade and sticking with it through high school and beyond. I won't admit a certain HS music teacher was my inspiration for Zane, but I won't deny it either.

And last, but not least, I want to thank my readers. Without you, none of this would be possible. Thank you for spending your time in Faith and Zane's world.

ABOUT THE AUTHOR

Darci Ann Baker spent her childhood imagining faraway lands and damsel-rescuing knights. She was always getting in trouble in school for daydreaming. Now she gets to day dream for a living, and no one is complaining.

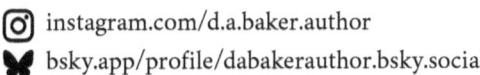 instagram.com/d.a.baker.author
bsky.app/profile/dabakerauthor.bsky.social

www.ingramcontent.com/pod-product-compliance
Lightning Source LLC
Chambersburg PA
CBHW020929020726
47495CB00002B/415